Books By Daniel J. Barrett

Conch Town Girl Series
Joe and Julie Traynor
Conch Town Girl
Can't Sing or Dance
Taking Care of Your Own
Never Say Never
Death But No Taxes
The Academy

Jack Manning and Mary Evans
You Don't Know Jack
Second Chances

SECOND CHANCES

Sequel to:
YOU DON'T KNOW JACK

BY DANIEL J. BARRETT

A Black Opal Books Publication

GENRE: Mystery,

This is a work of fiction. Names, places, characters and incidents are either the product of the author's imagination or are used fictitiously, and any resemblance to any actual persons, living or dead, businesses, organizations, events or locales is entirely coincidental. All trademarks, service marks, registered trademarks, and registered service marks are the property of their respective owners and are used herein for identification purposes only. The publisher does not have any control over or assume any responsibility for author or third-party websites or their contents.

PROLOGUE

J ack, can you read me the Powerball numbers from last night? Here's my iPad."

He went to the site and read the news. "Evidently, there's been a winner and only one winner from last night's drawing. That's weird, Mary. The winner's from Florida." He read on and said, "Evidently, the winner was from right here in Key West."

"Can you read me the numbers? Please?"

"Sure. The numbers are 5, 25, 26, 44, 66 and the Powerball number is 5. It's for a little over the announced $429.6 million dollars and there's only one winner."

Mary started to shake. "Jack? Can lightning strike twice?"

"What do you mean?" he said.

"Here," she said and handed him the ticket.

"Oh my God," was all he could say. Then he said, "Are you sure? I'm going to have a heart attack if you're right."

She read back the numbers again and they stared at each other. They now knew what was happening unlike the first time when he knocked on her door at her apartment in Lansingburgh not that long ago. Then, they had no idea what to do. If it weren't for Mary's friend, the attorney, they would have been lost. Now, they just shook their heads and took deep breaths. They had a lot to do. They might not be leaving for home in the next few days. They had calls to make.

Buying the lottery tickets the night before had been a spur of the moment thing. They wanted dinner and to fill up the SUV before leaving Key West. They had hopped into Mary's SUV. They had headed to Duval Street for dinner so they stopped at Dion's Quik Mart, right near Duval Street and Truman Avenue. Jack filled her tank and Mary went in and bought her tickets. Jack finished filling up the SUV and went in and paid for the gas and bought his old ticket numbers and a few quick picks. He had hopped back into the SUV and remembered saying, "Hey, this is your vehicle. Do I have to pay for the gas, too?" He had smiled at her. He laughed and then said, "Good luck on your numbers."

Mary said, "Thanks for filling up my tank. You've got more money than me anyway."

"Yes, but I'm down to my last sixty million dollars or so. We'd better start cutting back or we won't make it."

"Please," she had said not knowing that life would change again. They had gotten back late, after midnight, knowing that this was their last dinner out in Key West. They were headed home in two days so they had to pack and make sure everything was set and the Key West bills were caught up until the next trip. The neighbor's daughter, Jamie, would come over before they left for her next 'To Do List". She was thrilled to still be working for them since they'd been coming down more and more. She also loved driving around in the new Highlander.

It was the next morning. They had slept in and had breakfast on the deck. They went out one last time for a moonlight boat ride with the Lennons that night as a farewell gesture from them.

Mary had her iPad in her hand and went to the Powerball site. They had gone to bed last night as soon as they got home and had already missed the 10:59 p.m. broadcast. Ever since they'd moved into the house on Old Plank Road, Jack and Mary watched the Wednesday and Saturday drawing, at the beginning of the late news, for the Powerball numbers. It was tradition but they had missed last night's drawing. When the numbers popped up on the iPad, Jack and Mary were in shock. Here we go again they thought, smiling from ear to ear.

CHAPTER 1

Miller, Reynolds, Coleman and Straus. May I help you," asked the receptionist.

"Hi Melody, it's Jack Manning and Mary Evans for Kristen Sanderson," Mary said.

"Hi Mr. and Mrs. Manning, I'll page her right away," she answered.

"Melody, it's Jack and Mary, please," she said.

Mary hadn't had time to change her name to Manning so as of now she was still Mary Evans. Her driver's license, credit cards, address information and insurance all had to be changed when she got back home.

"Jack, will this complicate things since I'm still Mary Evans?" she asked.

"Actually, it might even be better when you hand in your ticket, not as a Manning but as yourself, so no one will add two and two and get that you're the wife of a national lottery winner," Jack said.

"I guess that will be one of our first questions to Kristen," Mary said.

"I guess so," said Jack.

Kristen Sanderson, now a senior partner, was one of Mary's best friends and like Mary, ex-Sisters of St. Joseph from the Roman Catholic Diocese of Albany. Both left the convent many years ago and moved on with their lives.

Kristen was a very successful partner, married with three young children, ranked at the lowest end, but still considered a very competent attorney. With Jack and Mary moving their vast fortune to the law firm for every financial and legal aspect, Kristen became a well-respected senior partner. This call from Jack and Mary would probably increase that status as well.

Jack was standing by Mary's side in their living room in Key West. The day, as usual, was beautiful. It was 85 degrees, slight wind at five miles per hour, as they stared at the ocean right in front of their door. Neither wanted to leave for home at this point but they already had tons of obligations up north, now complicated by what they had to tell Kristen about Mary's new found lottery winnings.

"Mary and Jack, how are you doing?" said Kristen. "How's married life?"

"Great, Kristen. I have some news for you so you'd better sit down," she said.

"Is everything all right? I certainly hope so. Are you coming back soon? We miss you."

"Everything's fine and we hope to be back soon but life just got a little more complicated, Kristen," said Mary.

"How so?" said Kristen.

"Are you sitting down, Kristen?"

"Yes, I'm ready. What's happening?" said Kristen.

Mary said, "Kristen, did you happen to see the lottery winning ticket numbers yesterday?"

"No, why?" said Kristen.

"Well, it looks like I hit the big and only prize last night for $429.6 million dollars. There was only one winning ticket and it came from a gas station in Key West. I bought the ticket and I have it in my hand right now," said Mary.

"No way," said Kristen. "Are you kidding me?"

Mary said, "Not kidding, not even close, Kristen. I have the winning ticket in my hand right here and I'm starting to get nervous again, just like before. Jack has been shaking his head all morning."

"Can you hold on a minute and let me catch my breath," said Kristen. "Let me get the team in here right now. Don't go anywhere. We need to get that ticket into the hands of the Florida Lottery Commission as soon as possible. However, having it in the hands of a local attorney down there, that we trust, should be the first step just like we did for you when Jack hit the lottery up here."

Kristen ran down the hall, knocking on doors of everyone assigned to Jack and Mary in all their dealings. There was a fully assembled team that was formed when Jack hit the lottery before. Everyone was in place. She needed Andy Miller, the managing director, and Frank Smith, the chief accountant and CPA for the firm. Both came running after she waved them to immediately respond.

"Kristen said, "I have Mary and Jack on the phone from Key West with unbelievable news."

She put the phone on speaker and said, "Mary can you repeat to Andy and Frank what you just told me?"

She said, "Sure. Hi Andy. Hi Frank. I just hit the lottery down here in Key West and I'm the only winner. I have the ticket in my hand. Can you believe this?"

"Really?" both said at the same time. "That's unbelievable. How much? Sorry that was my first response," said Andy.

"As of today, and you know it could change, it's $429.6 million give or take. I'll bet it's more when finalized," she said.

Kristen jumped in and said, "When do you need us? I can be there by tomorrow, wherever you need to be. I wish we had an office in Florida but we don't. We can make a few calls but I don't want to guess at this point as to whom is the best to handle it down there."

Mary said, "Our best bet is to call Joe and Julie Traynor.

I know they have an attorney, a good one I'll bet since Julie is a nationally published author and Joe must know a lot of people in his position. I'll call them and then call you back. We need you, obviously."

"I'll wait to hear from you but don't wait long. Keep the ticket safe. Make a copy on your desktop copier and then make a PDF and email it or just take a picture front and back and text it on your phone. Keep it on your phone," said Kristen.

"Good advise. I'll call you back as soon as I can," said Mary. "Jack says thanks as well."

CHAPTER 2

"Jack, do you have Joe's cell phone number handy?"

"I believe it's on my phone. Let me check. Here it is. Do you want to call the home or at his office at the community college?" Jack asked.

"Call him at the college. It's the middle of the day. I'll bet he's there all day. He said he doesn't leave for home before 5:00 p.m. It then takes him an hour to get up to Tavernier, close to Key Largo, if the traffic is light."

Jack called Joe's cell phone at the college and he immediately picked up. "Joe, it's Jack Manning and Mary. Is this an okay time to call you? I have a very important question to ask you if you have time," he said.

"Hey guys, great to hear from you. Didn't we just attend your Key West wedding reception a short while ago? How are you?"

Joe Traynor was a lieutenant in the Coast Guard, on the fast track, currently stationed as vice president of the military wing of the Florida Keys Community College. He was getting his doctorate and eventually planned on moving to the Coast Guard Academy up in New London, Connecticut. They were grooming him to become the Assistant Superintendent of the U. S. Coast Guard Academy, and after a period of adjustment, the

Superintendent. He would be the youngest Superintendent in history.

Joe and Julie met Jack and Mary at Sloppy Joe's on Duval Street in Key West when they were sent on an immediate vacation by Kristen Sanderson after Jack hit the lottery in Troy, New York, a while ago. It was a chance meeting as Joe and Julie sat at a table in the crowded bar. Joe and Julie took a short weekend vacation after everything had happened to them. They hadn't had a day off since their wedding and the adoption of their daughter.

There were two empty chairs at their hi-top table and they invited Mary and Jack to sit down. Little did they know that Joe Traynor grew up a few blocks from Jack and Mary in the Lansingburgh section of Troy, New York. Joe actually attended Catholic High at about the same time Mary was a teacher there. He attended St. Augustine's grammar school as well where Mary also served after leaving the convent. Joe was beside himself that this was more than chance. After becoming fast friends, that also included the Lennons, they stayed in touch. As a matter of fact, Joe's father and brother built Jack's new Career Center, serving as the main contractor as Traynor Electric Inc. Jack and Mary bought the house right next door to the Lennons on 10 Allamanda Terrace in Key West and the Lennon's daughter, Jamie, took care of the place when they were away.

"We're fine, Joe. Hope you, Julie and Bella and Tillie are doing well," Jack said. "Mary has something to tell you and then needs to ask for your advice."

"Hi, Joe. It's Mary," she said.

"Hi, Mary, how are you and what's up? We need to get together before you head home," Joe said. "Julie asked me to set up something as well."

"We love Julie and we'll love to. But, this news may overshadow that request for a little while," she said. "Joe, I just hit the lottery with a ticket from Key West, the only ticket for the numbers, this week. It's at $429.6 million dollars and climbing. That's a lot more than Jack hit on his."

"Are you serious?" he said.

"That's the second time someone asked me that. Yes, Joe, I hit the lottery for $429.6 million dollars all alone. We need an attorney down here as soon as possible. Our attorney, and my close friend, Kristen Sanderson, is flying down as we speak to help us out. I have the ticket in my hand. Do you know of any good attorneys?" she asked.

"As a matter of fact, not me but Julie has the best law firm in Miami who helped her with her publishing, her grandmother's power of attorney and our home in Tavernier," he said.

"What's her name and her phone number and the firm's name and location? I'll have Kristen fly into Miami instead of Key West, saving time. I don't like having this ticket worth millions still on me," Mary said.

"Here's the information. Call your attorney and give it to her. Are you ready?" he said.

"Ready," she said.

"Her name is Jane Swanson. Her specialty is estate planning but she does it all and is very smart, trustworthy and a very good friend to both of us. The firm is Clyne, Roberts, and Lynch, located at 1395 Brickell Avenue, Miami Florida. Sidney Clyne is the boss and very close to Jane. They did everything for Julie and she couldn't have done it without them," he said.

Joe gave her the phone number for Jane and said he would call her right away. He mentioned that he would bring them up to Miami tonight from Key West as soon as he gets all his meetings completed. He said to call Skip Lennon, next door, and have him ready and armed to go with them to Miami. He said you never know what can happen at any time down here. The trip is 161 miles and three hours from their house so to pack an overnight bag and tell Skip the same. We'll make a quick stop in Tavernier to pick up a few things. He said they would be fine since he would be driving a Coast Guard official car. He said his Coast Guard Division 7 was around the corner from the law firm, a half mile away. He could park there overnight and the hotel was right next-door.

"Joe, thank you, thank you, thank you. This means so much you don't know. We will be waiting here for you. How long do you think?" she asked.

"About an hour. I'm only ten minutes away from your house from my office at the college. See you then," he said.

CHAPTER 3

Joe called Jane Swanson in Miami and explained what was happening. He told her Mary needed a secure place to hold the lottery ticket before handing it over to the Florida Lottery Commission. He said he was sure that they'd be getting a big chunk of the business since Jack had already won the lottery in upstate New York and was in the middle of most of his plans to reconstruct and improve the City of Troy's housing and education. He said, knowing Mary, he was sure she'd be doing the same thing. He gave Jane the phone number for Kristen Sanderson to call directly and then have her picked up at the Fort Lauderdale Airport, which was much more convenient than flying into Miami International on the west side of Miami and with tons of international travelers holding up arrivals.

Mary called Kristen and gave her the information and to expect a call from Jane Swanson, almost immediately. She gave her flight instructions and that she would be picked up at the Fort Lauderdale Airport and brought directly to the law firm. Mary told her they were leaving for Miami within the hour and they'd be in Miami after 6:00 p.m. She said she'd call when they got there. They would be booking a suite for Jack and Mary and Kristen and Joe and Skip would get a separate smaller suite. They would be staying at the

SLS Brickell Hotel & Residence at 1300 South Miami Avenue, right in the Brickell Plaza, near both the Coast Guard 7th Division headquarters and the law firm. The lottery office for Miami was a little to the west in Miami Lakes region, Hialeah. They would book an appointment at the lottery office as soon as all the legal ramifications were settled and the ticket fully secured in the safe at the law firm.

Joe arrived at Jack and Mary's house at Allamanda Terrace in Key West. He pulled up in his obvious Coast Guard vehicle with U.S. Coast Guard license plates. He could make the trip to Miami with his eyes closed after all these trips back and forth. Skip had his bag and his "official" Coast Guard clothing. He was very happy that the outfit still fit after all these years. He was also armed with several weapons that would be concealed under the front seat. Joe had a suit on but would be stopping at home to change clothes, and say hello to Julie, Bella, and Tillie, who was visiting from Key Largo for the day. It was only a few miles out of the way. After hearing what was going on, Julie said everything he needed would be ready and a few sandwiches and drinks in a cooler for their long drive.

"Joe, we can't thank you and Skip enough for what you're doing. You dropped everything for us today and it's very much appreciated. We don't know anyone down here especially anyone we can trust other than you and your two families. Thank you."

"Glad to do it," Skip piped in. "I just can't believe that you, Mary, hit the lottery after Jack already did. That must be exciting," he said.

"Skip, I won't lie. It's exciting but also dangerous and fraught with tons of immediate decisions. Thank the Lord we already went through this once before. Not me as much as Jack. But, you know what I mean," she said.

Joe said, "I know what you mean Mary and you're in good hands. He added, "Nothing is going to happen especially since no one in Key West has the foggiest idea who won or where they're from."

"That's a good perspective but maybe you remember once the cat is out of the bag, all hell breaks loose. Everyone wants a piece of you and your money and your plans, and your life. I could go on and on," Mary said.

Tavernier is a straight shot up the only main highway heading in and out of Key West-the Overseas Highway, U.S. 1. At fifty miles an hour, they would arrive in seventy-five miles in an hour and a half. The rest of the trip to downtown Miami would be about eighty-six miles and an hour and three quarters, arriving a little after 6:00 p.m. They would go directly to the law firm of Clyne, Roberts, and Lynch and meet Sidney Clyne and Jane Swanson at the front door after calling when they got near. The firm closed to the public at 5:00 p.m.

Joe stopped at his house and was handed his overnight bag and cooler by Julie as soon as they got there. They all got out to stretch their legs. Joe went into the house to change, get his weapons and give Bella and Tillie a kiss. He told Julie he would stay with Jack, Mary and Skip for as long as he could and then he needed to meet his Rear Admiral about his plans for the college for the coming year. He wanted to kill two birds with one stone as he said.

Julie spoke to Skip, Mary and Jack for a few minutes but they were obviously in a hurry and a little shaky so she smiled and said goodbye. Mary asked her something privately and said she'd give her a call the next day to elaborate on what she wanted to do. Julie was surprised and obviously delighted with the short conversation. Joe looked puzzled but didn't say anything. They hopped back in the car and headed out. At fifty miles an hour, you could practically pass out and still arrive on time.

Mary asked Joe, "Joe, just curious. How did you ever get the law firm that we're going to see tonight? They must be very pleased with you and Julie to say the least."

"It's mostly Julie," Joe said. "A little background. Before I came back and rejoined the Coast Guard, I'd just completed a decade as a noncommissioned officer. I was tired of the Coast Guard and wanted something different. I'd finished my bachelor's degree at The Coast Guard Academy after bouncing all over the place and went to Rensselaer Polytechnic Institute in Troy to get my MBA. I did that and joined a small nonprofit, the Albany Coalition for Families, in Albany. As I mentioned previously, there was a lot of trouble with the organization. The Executive Director, Ted Simmons, was killed in a supposed car accident that later turned into murder by the Mexican Mafia. We got to the bottom of it with Ted's son, Dan Simmons, who was already a very close friend of mine. After everything happened, Dan took over the organization and it's now thriving. To make a long story longer," he laughed.

"Jane Swanson is a very close friend of Dan's. They both went to Albany Law School together. Jane's husband, Nick Snyder, also from Albany, graduated as a neurosurgeon from Albany Medical Center. He is doing his residency at Jackson Memorial Hospital, right around the corner in Miami. When Julie's grandmother was in a coma, before I rejoined the Coast Guard to help her out in Key Largo, I called Dan Simmons, who highly recommended Jane. She's been nothing short of brilliant in handling all our legal and financial matters. She's also an expert in estate planning and good at everything else. Her boss, Sidney Clyne, has been wonderful as well. Not just because of Jane, but he's a very good guy and looks out above and beyond for Julie. He's treated her like a daughter. Need I say more?"

"No that covers it," she smiled and laughed.

As they passed through Key Largo and made their way off the Keys, heading to Miami, they all dug into their sandwiches and drinks. Joe was constantly alert for any issues and Skip saw him and responded in kind. You can't teach that kind of responsibility and awareness. Jack and Mary not only hit the financial jackpot but the friendship jackpot as well. Joe remembers very well two incidents that informed his thinking about danger right around the corner. When Luis pulled the gun on him in the offices at the Albany Coalition for Families, Luis was unaware that Joe was left-handed and already had a gun in his hand and shot him and Luis's three gangbangers barging in the door. The other incident was when he was driving up I95 to Fort Lauderdale and two cars filled with cartel members pulled in front and in back of him on the road. As soon as he became aware, he rolled down his window and started shooting at them, pulling them off the road in complete surprise. When his Rear Admiral asked him why he started shooting first he simply replied because it was easier to tell him what happened exactly since he was still alive. Those were both lessons learned. Jack and Mary couldn't ask for better protectors on the way up to Miami.

CHAPTER 4

It was 6:10 p.m. when they pulled up to the law firm. Jane and Sidney were waiting for them at the front door. Joe had called her fifteen minutes before telling them to wait by the door and they would be there momentarily. Skip opened their door and Mary and Jack got out of the vehicle. They were nervous, obviously, but moved quickly to the front door. Joe had opened his driver side door and looked around carefully to see if they were followed or had any sense of danger. There was none. Jane opened the door, introduced herself and Sidney and they went up to the 5th floor. Joe said he would head to the hotel around the corner and park his car and check in to the two suites they'd booked that afternoon. He would unload the car at the door and then go to the suites and make sure the rooms were clear. He and Julie had stayed there before and he was registered as an officer at the Coast Guard District 7 headquarters if there were any issues. He would move his vehicle to the Coast Guard parking lot in the morning. He still had a reserved space since he reported directly to the Rear Admiral for District 7.

Everyone got off the elevator and entered the law offices of Clyne, Roberts and Lynch. They entered the conference room and were surprised to see several other individuals in attendance. Jane made introductions and then said, "I'm sure you're tired, nervous, overwhelmed, and anxious. Does that cover it?" she asked Mary. "We thought it might be wise to have a few extra witnesses here just in case. May we see your winning ticket?" she asked

"Of course," Mary said as she handed the ticket to Jane who immediately took a photo of it on her iPhone, front and back and then went over to the copy machine and made copies for everyone to sign as a witness.

"That's a good idea. We didn't do that the first time," Mary said.

Sidney said, "We understand this isn't your first rodeo." He smiled.

"No it's not," Mary and Jack both said. They then took turns going over Jack's three hundred and thirty million dollar lottery winning and what he did with it. How he set up the Evangeline Trust Fund and realty companies and what they both learned over the last few years on how to keep, maintain and grow your winnings while helping out those less fortunate.

Joe called an hour later and showed up at the front door. He gave Jane a hug and she took him up to the group meeting.

"Everything is set on my end," he said. "Here are your keys to your suite. When Kristen comes she'll be in your suite and Skip and I'll be down the hall."

When Joe arrived they all got on the speakerphone and called Kristen who was still at the office with her two partners. They were relieved that everything went well so far. They did video conferencing on Zoom so everyone knew what everyone looked like. Mary held up the winning lottery ticket, numbers 5, 25, 26, 44, 66 and the Powerball number 5. It's for a little over the announced $429.6 million dollars and there's only one winner, ME," she said smiling.

Sidney had gone online and found the page with the

winning numbers and put it on the overhead screen, matching the ticket that Mary had just produced. "By the way," Sydney said, "The official new number is $465,982,412. It went up over thirty-six million dollars overnight when the final results were tallied. They still don't have a clue who the winner is, but they're certain there's only one winning ticket.

"Can I get a receipt from you for my winning ticket and can you place it in your safe and have it guarded twenty-four-seven until we hand it in to the Florida Lottery Commission," Mary asked. She'd never been so direct but it seemed to be coming rather easily now, just as it had for Jack after a while.

"We will immediately put it in our safe. As soon as Kristen gets here, we can figure out how to present the winning ticket to the lottery commission and when. I'd rather have it done right than done too quickly. Do you agree, Mary? You're the only one who counts," he said.

"Well I'm not the only one who counts, certainly but I'll tell you a few things right now. When Jack gave me $15.0 million to do as I wanted, I immediately took some to secure my future, that of my dear ex-nun friends and my mother. I then opened the Teresa Trust Fund, in honor Mother Teresa. Most of the winnings will be deposited into that fund with a large chunk paid directly to me and I'll pay taxes. However, to inform you, I'm still Mary Evans because we haven't had time to change to my married name of Manning. It might be better anyway so there will be no direct tie to another large lottery winner. That publicity alone could ruin our lives. We also live in New York, which has an 8.8% state tax rate and Florida has no state tax and a very promising homestead act where no one can take your home regardless of liability. Is that right?" she asked.

"Yes it is," said Jane. "We need to be very careful with this. My expertise is Estate Planning but whatever you decide to do with Kristin, we're fine with it. We're just glad to help."

"By the way, I'm not sure you know, but I'm an ex-nun and when I left the convent, I worked at the Troy Community Council for twelve years with Jack before they let us go. We need to discuss that tomorrow as well. And, by the way, Kristen Sanderson is formerly Sister Evangeline, for whom Jack's trust fund is named," she said.

Everyone in the room smiled. Joe said, "Jane you and Sidney better hang on a for a very interesting ride over the next few years. I'll bet you'll enjoy the hell out of it. Just ask my father and brother. They built Jack's new Career Center, under budget, on time and completed, thanks to Jack and Mary."

Sidney said, "Jane, this is all yours. They're your friends and now our friends as well. I'm sure Julie will be involved in this somehow," he smiled.

Joe said, "In case you think I missed it, Mary, I saw you talking to Julie on the way up here. She had a big smile on her face and gave you a big hug. Care to share," he asked.

Mary smiled. Joe smiled. Jack smiled and Mary said, "Let's discuss this further tomorrow. Is that all right everyone? I'm mentally exhausted," she said, "Pack up the ticket, guard it with your life, bill me whatever is needed, and I'm out of here."

"Mary, Skip and I will stay the night at the hotel and make sure you're safe. The hotel staff knows who I am and they understand security being next to the Coast Guard District 7 headquarters. Tons of staff come through this hotel on a daily basis. I'll meet Kristen with you guys tomorrow band then Skip and I need to head home but I have to stop at my office first thing tomorrow. I have a meeting with the Rear Admiral about our new college curriculum for the military side of things."

Joe added, "I think you need some protection down here

while they're processing your winning ticket and while you're at the attorney's office. I have some Coast Guard friends at headquarters that could hang around for a while, take our hotel room until you're done, and then see you get back on an airplane safely back to home. I'm not trying to get rid of you. It just makes sense. This is south Florida and we do have our criminal issues. When you land at the Florida Lottery Office with your ticket, and then they give out your name, you already understand the ramifications from before."

"We certainly do," said Jack. "We both understand. That's why you got us the two retired FBI agents following us around in New York until everyone seemed to forget us. If you could scrounge up a few of your friends, we will be more than happy to pay them for their overtime while watching over us."

Skip piped in, "I can certainly vouch for their generosity to everyone in my family."

"No need," said Joe. "We already know the kind of people Mary and Jack are. I'll make calls as soon as we get to the hotel and see that you're shadowed as soon as we leave. They'll follow you everywhere until you get on the plane," said Joe.

"Thank you. That's great," said Mary. "Let's head out. I'm hungry but exhausted. Maybe we can order room service when we get to the hotel, for all of us."

Jane and Sidney shook hands and said they would be available anytime the next morning that Mary wanted. Kristen would get there around 3:00 p.m. but she'd already forwarded Mary's paperwork from Jack's winning lottery. The Teresa Trust Fund was already set up and would be the main vehicle to be used to receive the transfer from the Florida Lottery staff. They would invite the lottery administration to meet them at their offices at the law firm or, with armed guards from the Coast Guard, meet at the local lottery office in Miami Lakes.

CHAPTER 5

Back at the hotel, they ordered dinner and drinks. Jack and Skip went to their suite and changed into more comfortable clothes. Mary and Jack barely had any time at all back in Key West before Joe arrived to bring them to Miami. They threw their stuff in an overnight bag and then Skip knocked on the door and ten minutes later, Joe had arrived in his obvious official federal government vehicle with Coast Guard plates. Mary was tired, hot, and wanted a shower badly. The food was delivered to Jack and Mary's suite as Joe and Skip arrived. All were famished and ate quietly. They all took a deep breath.

"What a day," said Mary. "We can't thank you enough for helping us out."

"No problem," said Skip with Joe nodding while finishing his beer.

Joe asked both Jack and Mary, "What're your plans tomorrow? As you know I'm getting you coverage by some of our off-duty friends down the street and I have to meet my boss early tomorrow morning before heading back. I have a 3:00 p.m. meeting at the college with the president to review our plans for the year. We're strapped like every other college in America. There will be some belt-tightening."

"Really, that's a shame, Joe," said Mary. "If I may be so bold to ask. How much is your deficit for next year?"

"My military side is okay because it's fully supported by the Coast Guard and the other branches, depending on how many service men and women are placed at the college. The big problem is supporting the husbands, wives and children, who are also attending the college on the public side. We can't fund them and on a service salary for a family, they can't either. It's a big problem."

"Not to belabor the point, Joe, but do you have a real estimate as to your shortfall?" asked Mary.

"For this upcoming semester, the public side will have a shortfall of one million two hundred thousand dollars that can't be made up at this late date, and the state of Florida, isn't funding the deficit, so we might need to lay off twenty-four professors and staff at an average salary and benefits of $50,000.00 per person. That's not a lot to live on in Key West as you know. That's almost 20% of our staff," Joe said.

"Joe, not to be facetious but, Jack and I have already had discussions on what we might do with his money and now with mine as well, both at home and down here. As you know we're planning on living here a great amount of time after we resolve all our issues at home with construction, the Center, and what we planned moving forward," said Mary. "Would you mind if we write you a check for one million two hundred thousand dollars right now to bring down to your college president?" asked Mary.

"That's very generous of you two, but I don't want you to think I'm helping you for a handout. We will get over the deficit and we have plans on how to do this by building up our programs and student base by maintaining a solvent tuition base. My boss will be dumbfounded if this happens. I really can't turn down an offer like this but I just want you to know you don't have to do a thing. Julie and I and Skip and Linda and their children truly value your friendship," he said.

"Jack, do you have your checkbook with you?" asked Mary. Obviously, I don't have my checks with me and I better not until Kristen arrives and we're assured that this goes through but can you write Joe a check to the Florida Keys Community College for $1.2 million dollars and call Kristen to make sure it clears. Thanks," said Mary.

Joe just shook his head as he took the personal check from Jack.

"I'm now more afraid to head out than I was coming here. Can you imagine if I lose this check before I get to the college," he said.

"Don't worry, it's too big to cash if lost and we can stop payment if it was lost at anytime," said Jack.

"Is thank you enough?" Joe asked. "Wait until I tell Julie," he said.

"Don't tell her yet," said Mary. "I have a few things to discuss with her tomorrow after my meeting with Kristen," she said.

"Okay, I won't say a word until after I present it to my boss, Morgan L. Hennessy, Ph.D. His name says "stuffy" but he's far from that. Both Julie and Morgan are Brown University graduates. As soon as they met before I got the job, they hit it off immediately and I did too," said Joe. "At forty-two, he's not that much older than me, and I could be Assistant Superintendent of the U.S. Coast Guard Academy by that age as well, after getting my Ph.D."

Mary had called Kristen at home. She'd just arrived. Instead of arriving at 3:00 p.m. tomorrow at Fort Lauderdale, she got a canceled seat on Southwest Airlines, flying from Albany International at 8:45 a.m., flight 1278, arriving at Fort Lauderdale International at 11:25 a.m. with a quick change of planes in Baltimore. She could fly back anytime, so she left it open-ended to make sure everything was set with Mary and Jack. After all, they were the firm's biggest clients by far before and now even more so. Kristen already called Jane and someone would pick her up at Fort Lauderdale and they should be in Miami by noon. Jack picked up the phone and told Kristen to have the bank honor the check he just wrote to the Florida Keys Community College or The College of the Florida Keys, for $1.2 million dollars. He said Mary would reimburse him when the money got turned over by the Florida Lottery Commission. Jane also said, they were starting to meet tomorrow at 9:00 a.m. to outline their plans for meeting the Lottery Commission and it was set for 2:30 p.m.

Joe couldn't believe his good fortune and on the way back to their room, he said to Skip, "Do you believe what just happened? How could I turn that down? I certainly didn't want to look desperate. I hope I didn't. Did I, Skip?"

"Not at all," said Skip. "You'd have been crazy to turn that down."

As they walked through the door, Joe pulled the check out of his wallet and looked at it. "Holy shit," he said. "Can you believe this? I can't. I'm now officially scared to death. I've never held a million-dollar check before. Hell we confiscated millions in the last drug bust but this is real. This is very real," he said.

"I'll take the check if you don't want it," said Skip, smiling.

"Thanks for the offer but I'll pass," said Joe, "Do you think this is real?"

"Very," said Skip.

"Shit," said Joe.

The following morning, Joe and Skip went down for breakfast to meet Jack and Mary. Joe's friends from the Coast Guard, off-duty, were already there sitting with them having breakfast.

"Thanks for the cake job, Joe. We never knew you were

this nice a guy," said Sam Marconi, one of Joe's close friends. The other, Pete Williams, a good old boy from Alabama, was unusually quiet but said hi.

"Pete, you're very quiet. Are you okay," asked Joe.

"Yes, but nervous. I never did this before. I hope everything turns out all right. I'm prepared but hesitant. I won't lie. Joe, I know you've been through a ton of these events but I have not," said Pete. "We're both off for two weeks before our next assignment. I hope that's enough time to get done what Mary and Jack have to do, but after that you'll have to get someone else. By the way, they already paid us, very nicely, for the next two weeks plus all our expenses. We're fully ready, Joe. If that helps."

"It does, Pete," said Joe. "So, you're both ready?"

"We are," said Sam.

Mary said, "We already met your friends, Joe. No hassle. We already paid them and after breakfast, you can go to visit your boss and then you and Skip can head out. Is that, okay," she asked.

Joe nodded and went up to the breakfast buffet. He didn't eat much last night and after getting the check, he had a knot in his stomach but was ready for breakfast, his favorite meal of the day. Sam and Pete had their own personal vehicles in the lot and would use both as backup in case of any problems. They were Coast Guard lifers and had seen many a situation, not as many as Joe, but they would be able to protect Mary and Jack or die trying for sure.

Mary gave Joe a kiss on the cheek as they walked out the front door. She said she'd be calling Julie on her break at school around 10:30 a.m. They headed to the attorney's office around the corner, with Sam and Pete walking in front and behind as they approached the building. At 9:00 a.m. exactly, Jane met them at the front door and unlocked the offices for the day. They took up several floors but the floor that they were heading to was secured, locked and guarded

until the lottery people showed up and verified the winning
ticket.

Chapter 6

Mary and Jack, with Sam and Pete, made it to the main boardroom where Sidney Clyne's staff was now waiting for them. Their chief financial officer, real estate expert, foundation expert and tax accountants were all introduced and sat around the table. Mary introduced Jack Manning, her husband and the two Coast Guard staff who'd be with them until they departed to New York. Both Sam and Pete excused themselves and said they would be right outside the locked conference room door. If a problem arose, it would be seconds before they went through the door. They politely let that be known. The staff looked at each other and the meeting began.

Mary started the meeting like she was in charge of this operation. It was a far cry from that little old ex-nun toiling in Troy, New York, for a non-profit that didn't value its employees. Over the last few years that had changed immensely and Mary changed as well. The changes that Jack made, made Mary understand that they had a new opportunity at life to make things better but it was up to them to do it and not rely on others who'd disappointed them. They now only worked with the caliber of people who understood change and value.

Mary addressed everyone. "Our personal attorney,

Kristen Sanderson will be here by 12:30 p.m. today, flying in from Albany to ensure a smooth transition. Let me give you our history and background, so you'll understand where we're coming from. This isn't our first rodeo as they say. A few years ago, Jack was one of three individuals who split nine hundred and ninety million dollars, three ways. On Wednesday of this week, I just hit the lottery by myself, the only winner, for $429.6 million dollars and I think it will be higher when all is set and done."

Mary then went on for the last half hour explaining how they both worked together, split up the winnings, and went on and built the largest nonprofit in the capital region of New York State. She also explained that Jack had given her fifteen million dollars to do with what she wanted. She hadn't done anything to date other than making inquiries on how to benefit the community through a faith-based nonprofit that she set up, named the Teresa Trust Fund, after Mother Teresa and attempting to set up a new charter school in Troy.

"By the way," she said, "I'm an ex-nun, in the Order of the Sisters of St. Joseph. The only job I ever had, outside the convent, were twelve wonderful years, working at a non-profit in Troy, New York. They fired us to their detriment trying to keep up a facade of success but failed. After hitting the lottery, Jack set up his own non-profit, The Evangeline Trust Fund, named after one of my best friends, Sister Evangeline. We built a Career Center right next door to the non-profit that fired us. We're Irish, Jack says and that proved it, "You'll get to meet Sister Evangeline shortly. She is now Kristen Sanderson, mother of three, happily married, and a senior partner at the best law firm in Albany. If you want brains, beauty and honesty, you can't beat Sister Evangeline. You can call her Kristen though," and smiled.

"Also, we want Jane Swanson to be in charge of our account with your law firm, Clyne, Roberts, and Lynch. Is that all right with you Sidney? We always pre-pay or pay our bills on time," said Mary. She was on a roll.

Sidney smiled. "Does this have anything to do with Jane's relationship with Joe and Julie?" He laughed.

"Everything and nothing," she said. "We want the best people and Jane, to us as well as you Sidney, are the best. Also, keep your pencils sharpened, I'm keeping half my money here and the other half with Kristen. Is that okay?"

Jane was speechless. "Don't you need to do more investigation of us before that commitment, Mary? I mean that's a lot of money," she said.

"If Joe and Julie trust you, then we do as well. Can I take a break? It's closing in on 10:30 a.m. I have to call Julie during her break at school. I might take a half hour. Kristen will be here by 12:30 p.m. and I want documents ready to go so we know exactly what we need to do to meet with the Florida Lottery Commission today. Thank you," said Mary.

Jack just shook his head as to say, "What the hell am I doing here? I guess to write a personal check for a million dollars. Maybe that's all I need to do. Great feeling though. He broke out into a large smile. Mary looked at him and shook her head as if to say, *"What's up with you?"*

The phone rang and Julie picked up. She obviously had call waiting and knew it was Mary on the line. "Mary, how are you? Wonderful news. Congratulations. Are you in Miami right now?" she asked.

"Hi Julie. Yes Jack and I are with Jane and Sidney at the law firm. Joe went to his meeting with his boss. Skip is waiting for him and then they'll head back home. I'm sure he'll call you on the way," she said.

"Already did but he seemed weird. Do you know?" she asked.

"I believe it might be because he's walking around with a check for $1.2 million dollars payable to the Florida Keys Community College to cover an unforeseen deficit this year.

Please make sure he hands the check in and gets it deposited. I wouldn't want Jack's checkbook unbalanced to the tune of a million two, you know," she said and laughed.

"Seriously, is this real? Did you really give him a check? He must be beside himself by now. He's antsy most of the time. This might put him over the edge," said Julie.

"Well Skip is with him, so I hope he watches over him until then," said Mary.

"Thank you, Mary. You know Joe doesn't think that way. You need to earn every dime you get. His father pounded that into him. He still has his work boots that he still wears since he was sixteen years old, working for his father doing construction. He replaced the soles on those boots three times so far."

Mary laughed and told her it sounded just like Joe's father, John, and his brother, Peter. It was like they were all family. Joe's father and brother were the contractors that constructed his new Career Center and helped rehab most of the homes in the north central part of Troy, the worst section in the city.

"I didn't call to get Joe in trouble," Mary said. "I want to ask you something important and I want to sit down with you at length to discuss plans that I'd like to propose but I don't have time. The Florida Lottery Commission is coming to the office here this afternoon and I am to turn over my winning ticket. By the way, it's up to $480.0 million, not $465.0 million from $429.6, two days ago."

"Go ahead and ask," said Julie.

First, I want to set up a separate foundation to donate money to good causes in south Florida, specifically the Florida Keys and Key West. There are more poor people in the Keys by a factor of five more than the rich. I have set up a foundation and called the Teresa Trust Fund, in honor of Mother Teresa. After I take out funds for my future from these lottery winnings, I want to split the proceeds evenly about $77.5 million dollars for the Teresa Trust Fund and $77.5 million dollars for Teresa Trust Fund South for south Florida and the Florida Keys. I want you to be Co-Chair of the Board with me and then make decisions on giving all this money away. What do you think?" said Mary.

"I'm honored and flabbergasted. I don't have a finance degree. I do know about the poor here, growing up that way, raised by my poor grandmother, Tillie Carpenter, after both my parents died by the time I was eight. I still want and need to do my job at the school and continue as a nationally published author. Can we work around those things as well as Bella and Joe and of course my grandmother Tillie?" she asked.

"Whatever you want or need is fine by me. I also want your opinion about asking Linda Lennon, and even Jamie, who's like a daughter to us but we can wait on that, to be part of a team. Maybe not a voting member but someone whose input we trust."

"I accept with great hesitation but I accept," she said. "Kind of makes Joe's check seem like peanuts you know?" Julie laughed.

"You know I never thought a million dollars would be peanuts but between what Jack and I won, almost eight hundred million dollars, it does seem kind of puny doesn't it?" Mary laughed. "Of course it's less with the payout and taxes. It's still a lot though," she said.

"Don't ever say that in front of Joe or he'll freak," said Julie.

"By the way, this is one other caveat that I am imposing. We're setting up the Joe and Julie Traynor Trust Fund, funded with one million dollars, taxes paid, for your family's benefit and your children's education. Please say yes. After all, it's only a million dollars. Peanuts," she said. You could see her smile through the phone.

"That I accept since it only a farthing anyway," said Julie

in jest. "Mary, I don't know what to say. Joe and I have a lot to discuss when he gets hone." She went on, now flustered, "Mary, you know Joe and I are doing very well. My books have sold nationally and we've been rewarded quite nicely. Joe makes a very good living and he could be a Rear Admiral by the time he hits his forties. So, we're well taken care of. However, you just don't turn down a million dollar gift. Tillie is getting up in age and if she needs a nursing home, we want to give her the best we can. It costs almost seventy-five thousand dollars a year for full care down here. Could we use it to cover Tillie's bill? That would be a great relief for us," she added.

"You can use the money for anything you want and if Tillie's expenses become a burden then certainly this could provide financial relief for you. Also, Bella and any other children will need funds for college. Who knows what that will cost in ten or fifteen years," Mary said.

Julie said, "That would be great. It's a relief knowing that we will have enough to cover any expenses for Tillie. After selling her house and moving into an apartment in Key Largo, she's living off a small social security pension and her savings. I cover her for medical as part of my school policy along with Medicare. It's never enough."

Mary said, "Julie, if it's a burden and not a joy let me know and we will fix it. I just needed your reaction to my request before handing over the ticket. I haven't even told Jack my thoughts yet, at least not in total. By the way, we'll fund the Lennon family the same as you. So, don't feel guilty. As a matter of fact, if it becomes a burden co-running a $77.5 million dollar foundation, I think we have enough in the coffers to compensate you or anyone else you want involved. I'll leave it at that. I have to go. Thanks, Julie. You're the best."

"No, thank you, Mary," said Julie and hung up.

Mary went back into the boardroom and started

discussing strategy on how they would handle the Florida Lottery Commission staff as they arrived in the afternoon. Back when Jack won, they were in and out of the New York State Lottery Commission headquarters in Albany, New York. Kristen Sanderson and two retired FBI agents went with Jack Manning for the presentation. Jack was polite and smiled for the press and got out as soon as he possibly could. They headed out the back with the FBI car already running and waiting for Jack and Kristen. At least here, they would be on their own turf so to say. Kristen held the first lottery meeting when they arrived at her offices in Albany to hand them the winning ticket. She had put Jack and Mary, then single and friends, on a plane to head to Key West. Jack didn't have a dime to his name. He didn't have a car and borrowed Mary's when needed. His ex-wife took him for everything he owned and his children went with their mother who moved her lover into his house as soon as Jack left home. Things really changed for Jack after winning the lottery, most for the good and the best was marrying Mary. He never believed that would happen. His children have come around and his ex-wife and her live-in boyfriend didn't seem to be living a very happy or productive life. Losing out on $330.0 million dollars probably could do that to someone over time. Now, Jack and Mary had a second chance to help those most in need. They wanted no publicity at all. It was simply engrained in their psyche to help others in need. Could they do this all over again? Looks like it.

CHAPTER 7

Kristen arrived on time at Fort Lauderdale International Airport and was met by the driver for the law firm. He held up a sign as she was coming down the stairs for the front door. An older gentleman was holding a sign reading, "MRS. SANDERSON".

Kristen went over and introduced herself. The gentleman told her his name was Jeff Sheldon and showed his driver's license and a letter from Jane Swanson explaining who he was and exactly what route he was to follow.

He said, "A woman alone getting off a plane can never be too careful so I'm not offended quite frankly. I believe you need to be assured that you're safe in today's world. Mrs. Sanderson, I'm parked right out front with another gentleman holding the door. He's a friend of mine and works for the airport, getting guests in and out. Please follow me."

Kristen settled into the limousine and placed her carry-on bag and her computer bag next to her in the back seat. She'd never been to south Florida and was looking forward to the sights and sounds, even if it were for only a day. Maybe she'd stretch it out for a few days, not to charge Mary and Jack, but to check out Miami and this law firm. Hey, you never know what the future holds when the kids were grown and gone after college. Might be nice to make friends early than too late.

Jeff said, "Mrs. Sanderson, there's bottled water, soda and other drinks and snacks in the small refrigerator by your feet. Please feel free to relax. It takes about a half hour on good days and much longer other days. We shall see. It's noon traffic, but we're moving okay. I think we'll pull up right around 12:15 p.m. Just in time for lunch." He smiled in the rearview mirror.

They arrived and pulled up to the front door. Jeff got out of the limousine and opened the door for Kristen. She thanked him for his kindness and hospitality and offered a tip but he smiled and reassured her everything was fine. She thanked him again.

Mary was looking out the window as Kristen arrived so she hurried down while saying, "Kristen just arrived. I'll meet her downstairs." She headed down, opened the front door and waved to Kristen as she was walking up the stairs. "Kristen, how was your trip?" Mary asked as she held the door for her.

"Great, Mary. Congratulations. It's just sinking in. I can't believe it. I'll bet you can't either. How is it here? Are they nice? I have a million questions," she said.

"I can see that," she said. "Slow down. Let's take a few minutes alone and I'll bring you up to speed. Everything here is fine. I'm going to do some work down here and I want to explain my thought process to you. It looks like our work back home might even double and we have a big chunk of funds to see if we can help down here. We have very good friends here in the Traynors and the Lennon family and they've been exceptional in helping us out. Like you, we could never get through this without you or them," Mary said. "Let's get lunch and sit by ourselves right after I introduce you to everyone. And I mean everyone. God, they have a team just like yours," she said and laughed.

As soon as Kristen entered the conference room, Mary introduced her to Jane, Sidney and the law firm staff prepared to meet with her before the Florida Lottery Commission arrived mid-afternoon. Mary told the assembled group that they would take their lunches to a separate room so that Mary and Jack could update her on what's currently happening and what Mary's expectations for the day would be. In passing, Kristen mentioned that she had called the bank about the check they handed to Jack and there would be no problem with it. Kristen did ask if it was a spur of the moment decision and Mary smiled.

"Of course it was a spur of the moment decision," Mary said. "Didn't you ever have one of those moments?" she asked.

"Yes, but not for $1.2 million dollars I haven't," Kristen said. "Is it burning a hole in your pocket? Are you spending it before you get it? Just asking?"

"Now Kristen," said Mary, "I know what it looks like but if you could have seen the look on Joe's face, it was worth it. When I called Julie she asked if Joe went nuts on the spot or words to that effect and I think he did. In a good way though," she said.

"Well at least you got that out of your system," said Kristen. "I'm sure you've thought of nothing but this for the forty-eight hours. So what do you want to do?" Kristen asked.

"For starters, it looks like I'll be getting $480.0 million dollars, way above the originally announced $429.6, when the numbers were called. Jack and I have discussed this and at the end I want to have exactly what Jack has in his name in the bank, after taxes. I know I got a lot more than he did, $330.0 million for Jack versus my $480.0 million dollars, so my trust fund will be higher. I want to keep, after taxes $68,362,000.00, the exact same that Jack wound up with. Now that we're married, we're equal partners in everything.

So, I did the math and the $480.0 million paid up front, as opposed to annually over twenty years, will be calculated at 60% of the final $480.0 figure. That gives us $288.0 million. I need to net $133.0 million so that both the Federal Taxes at 39.6% and New York State at 9.0% will come to $64,638,000.00 for both, leaving me $68,362,000.00. The difference between the $288.0 million and the taxable $133.0 million, leaves $155.0 million to be placed into two trust funds set up for us to give away to worthy causes. The $155.0 million will be split two ways at $77.5 million going to the Teresa Trust Fund already set up for our ventures up north and I need a separate trust called the Teresa Trust Fund South set up for projects in south Florida and the Florida Keys. I already spent $1.2 million in the check for the college and that has to be returned to Jack. Is all this okay?" Mary asked. "There will be no quibble in paying the 9% New York State tax. We have more than enough money."

"When I asked what you thought you might do with the money, I didn't think you had it all thought out like this. That's great. I wouldn't have the foggiest idea what to do with the funds but you and Jack have already gone through this before. That must help," Kristen said. She then laughed, got up and hugged Mary knowing that Mary knew exactly what she wanted to do.

"By the way Kristen, when we go back into the boardroom, I want them to know that you're handling half of the money for a fee and they're handling the other half. That's for both the trust fund and for my own personal money that I'm keeping after taxes. You should wind up with another million dollars in fees to help with your overhead and that should move you to the top of the food chain at Miller, Reynolds, Coleman and Straus, Attorney at Law LLC. And, we expect them to add Sanderson to that firm's name. I'll call them personally to confirm that," said

Mary.

Kirsten was overwhelmed. "I don't know what to say Mary. Here we were twenty years ago as Sisters of St. Joseph, teaching at St. Augustine's and at Catholic Central High School and boy have our lives changed dramatically." She added, "Thank you for your friendship, trust, and kindness. This was never expected but thank you again."

"Let's go back to the meeting. I'm sure they're on pins and needles waiting to see what was being planned without their input. Let's see the surprised look on their faces. Jack are you all right with this? I know I haven't consulted you about this but I figured you had your own set of problems to deal with without this being added to those issues," Mary said.

Jack simply nodded and shook his shoulders as if to say, *"Do what you want."* You let me do what I wanted. This is your time. Let's make some friends and hopefully no enemies, if that's ever possible with this kind of money floating around."

They walked back together as everyone turned around to see what was coming next. Mary smiled at Jane and Sidney and took her seat.

Mary said, "I believe we have a very good working arrangement that will fully involve this law firm for our south Florida and Florida Keys operation and our Albany-based law firm with Kristen, who's already up and running and doing a remarkable job with Jack's vision and now mine." She went on, "I think of this as a partnership with Jack and I running two trust funds and two law firms backing us up every step of the way so we're in full compliance with every legal requirement that comes along. On top of that, we want our personal funds to grow that down the road we can add even more to both foundations. Let's talk about what I'm prepared to do and what we need to say and do as soon as the Florida Lottery Commission people arrive. I guess we have about an hour."

Everyone at the table shook their heads and smiled. Jane Swanson seemed very relieved. This was a very big deal for her just like it was for Kristen a while ago. Kristen grew into her role. Jack and Mary grew into their roles and Jane would grow into her role, in time.

CHAPTER 8

Jane took over the meeting asking a series of questions that her staff wanted answered. They were unaware that Mary Evans never got a chance to change her name to Manning at this point. That was a blessing so that when the winner was announced it wouldn't immediately tie back to Jack Manning, previous large lottery winner in New York State. Her address was still in the Town of Brunswick, just outside the City of Troy, New York and that's why she'd pay a 9% New York State personal income tax rate on $133.0 million. That's almost $12.0 million dollars that would go to the State of New York who had nothing to do with this winning ticket. Mary said she certainly had no complaints and would make that up in earnings in municipal bonds over the next several years. Also, Jack and Mary's house at 10 Allamanda Terrace in Key West was owned by Evangeline Realty, Inc. The corporation was started by Jack so he could maintain ownership of the Evangeline Career Center and the Troy Community Council buildings. Jack was well aware from his days at the Troy Community Council what happens to buildings owned by nonprofits with terrible management. They usually refinanced the property to pay operating costs or sold buildings for the same purpose making the organizations insolvent over time.

Jack vowed that wouldn't happen again.

Jack mentioned the above real estate ventures to let the staff know that the lottery people couldn't trace Mary back to the house in Florida since she doesn't own it nor does she have a permanent Florida address or driver's license. Now, with personal questions behind them, Jane asked Mary how she wanted to handle the funds that will be sent to her very shortly.

Mary said, "Jane, it's not that complicated. We've been through this before. Can I use a blackboard? I'm a teacher after all. And I taught 5th grade mathematics which is all this is, really. It isn't two trains left Chicago at 5:00 p.m. going sixty miles an hour and how far apart will they be in ninety minutes," she chuckled to herself. Everyone laughed and it lightened up the room.

Mary put the names Jack at the top left and Mary at the top right, and drew a line down the middle. She started with the label "winnings" and put $330.0 million on Jack's and $480.0 million on Mary's side. She then put the 60% percentage, meaning that this is the normal cash payout expected if taken in a lump sum versus over time and put $198.0 million under Jack and then $288.0 million under Mary.

"As you can see," she said, "I received $90.0 million more than Jack and that's going into a trust account to be given away."

Next, Mary skipped a spot labeled Trust Funds and went to Net Funds, the amount they both received for themselves in order to pay full taxes and have a final tax-free amount at the end to keep or do what they wanted to do in the future. Jacks gross number was $133.0 million, the same for Mary. Both paid taxes on that amount at a rate of 39.6% Federal and 9% New York State, leaving the exact same bottom line of $68,362,000.00 each.

"As you can see," said Mary, "We're equal partners and

want exact same bottom line So the difference in our amounts are that Jack put $50.0 million into the Evangeline Trust and gave me $15.0 million for my charitable events. With the $15.0 million I started the Teresa Trust Fund and I'll be using this fund for part of my nontaxable trust ventures. I'll have $155 million dollars to put into trust. I'll put $77.5 million into this trust and start a Teresa Trust Fund South with the other $77.5 million dollars. I need this set up immediately so I can get money from the lottery deposited."

Jane looked at Mary and said, "That's fifth grade math?"

"Yup," she said. "At least in Catholic school," she laughed. But there's more folks."

Jack just shook his head. He was thoroughly enjoying himself. Mary was on a roll and Kristen was having a ball.

"Jane, I want you as attorney in charge of my personal and trust fund accounts for south Florida. That means, you'll be in charge of $77.5 million for the Teresa Trust Fund South and half of my personal funds after taxes paid $68,362,000. At 1% fee, the same that Kristen is charging us, it will be a fee around $1,891.810 for year one as per my $10.00 old RadioShack large key calculator," as she turned around and showed them the figure on the calculator. "I can't leave home without this," she laughed.

"By the way, I called Julie Traynor this morning and asked her to be Co-Chair of the trust fund and she agreed. In addition, Jane I want you on the board and I may ask Joe and Linda Lennon and her daughter Jamie. I want all ages on the board, but I want people I know and trust. I asked Julie to ask her grandmother if she was busy and if she could represent seniors and their needs in south Florida. I imagine the needs are great. What I really want to do is open the first Catholic Elementary School, grades K-8 in Havana, Cuba, but I know that will be a long time coming. Remember I am still an ex-nun. It's "ex" but not forgotten."

Mary said, "Jane, I almost forgot. I offered a million-dollar family trust to Joe and Julie and I think I might do the same for the Lennon family. Can we at least get the paperwork started as soon as the funds arrive? That's the only addition for now besides the gift to the college. I'm now ready to talk to the lottery people. I guess we have enough time to go to the bathroom."

CHAPTER 9

Jack was just sitting in the boardroom and playing with his iPhone and said to everyone still at the table, "I just did a quick research for lottery winners. Did anyone here know that the largest lottery winning ticket was for $1.5 billion dollars and it was split three ways? I was part of the next largest at $900.0 million, split three ways and then there were several in the $500.0 million range split among a bunch of people. However, if you combine my winnings and Mary's, then we'd be the third largest ever. Also, we're the only duel winners from the same family, winning two separate times in two different lotteries. There have also been several winners that have multiple wins with one woman winning four times for a total of $5.0 million. I just thought that was interesting," Jack said.

"Bored, huh?" said Mary and laughed.

"Yes," said Jack. Everyone laughed.

Jane said, "I just got a call from the lottery administrators. They said they would be here in ten minutes. I'll meet them at the door and bring them up to the boardroom. Evidently, the Secretary of the Florida Lottery, John F. Davis, is coming with the local Miami District office manager, Sandra Alvarez. The security staff will also be here with them. Evidently, we were lucky that there are meetings here in Miami this week instead of Tallahassee. They switch sites quarterly to meet everyone at all the offices across the state. I think we may still have to head to the Florida Lottery headquarters up in Tallahassee where their media studio is located. We'll find out shortly."

Sam Marcuso and Pete Williams came in and asked how everything was going. Mary told them they might have to head to Tallahassee within the next day or so to face an audience at a press conference, announcing Mary's winning ticket. They nodded their head and said their cars were filled and ready to go. They also said they had U.S. Coast Guard offices up and down both Florida coasts and an office in Tallahassee where they could draw on others to help if necessary. They let Jack and Mary know that Joe Traynor had that kind of pull. They sort of understood that after meeting them for the first time but now it seemed to be more real in the moment. Sam said they were there for at least two weeks and could certainly get others to cover if their duties moved them out of town.

It was 2:30 p.m. on the dot when the lottery people arrived. Secretary Davis walked in with Ms. Alvarez and the security team led by Steve Harriett. Jane made introductions to everyone in the room and pointed to Mary Evans, the lottery winner. She didn't introduce Jack as her husband at this point, keeping Jack out of the picture and the focus on Mary only.

Mary got up from her chair and went over to the lottery staff and said, "Hi, I'm Mary Evans. It's nice to meet you. I'm very nervous so I'd appreciate it if you'd validate my ticket and take passion of it. That would greatly ease my mind."

Secretary Davis said, "That's why we're here, Ms. Evans. May I see the ticket?"

"Of course," said Jane as she handed him the winning lottery ticket.

"The numbers are 5, 25, 26, 44, 66 and the Powerball number is 5. I believe it's well over the original announced $429.6 million dollars and there's only one winner," Mary said.

Both Mr. Davis and Ms. Alvarez verified the winning numbers, the date and the back of the ticket, signed by Mary. He said, "These are the winning numbers. We have verified the ticket and you Ms. Evans are the only winner. It is, at last count, for $480.0 million dollars.

Jane stepped in and asked for the procedure and paperwork involved. Kristen moved a little closer to Mary and Jane and she winked at Jane and said, "I've reviewed all the paperwork and receipts required. I guess our only question now is will Mary have to show up for a "meet and greet" and when and where? You're now aware that Ms. Evans resides in upstate New York in the Town of Brunswick, just outside the City of Troy. It would be a hardship to travel to Tallahassee for the announcement. Can you do this down here at your Miami Lakes office? It would be more convenient," said Kristen.

Secretary Davis said, "I think that could be arranged but we'd need a few days. Mary, are you staying in town or are you planning on coming back?"

"I'll stay here for a while, hopefully no more than a week, and then I have to head back home," she said.

"How about next Monday? We can meet at our Miami District Office at 14621 Oak Lane, Miami Lakes at 11:00 a.m., he said. "It's only a few miles from here and if the traffic cooperates, maybe a twenty minute drive."

That sounds great," said Mary as she nodded to both Kristen and Jane. "By the way, I'm taking the lump sum award. My attorneys know exactly how the funds should be distributed but it all goes directly to me and then will be put into appropriate accounts that will be set up to receive the funds." She went on, "I believe that the $480.0 million will have a lump sum payout of 60% or $288.0 million."

Ms. Alvarez nodded her head and said, "That's correct Ms. Evans. We believe the lump sum will be a minimum of $288.0 million if the final numbers match what we're predicting."

At that point, with ticket in hand and all receipts and paperwork completed, they said goodbye and left the room. They said they would see them next Monday.

"Well that went fine," said Jack who was completely invisible in the room. He smiled at Mary and said, "Great job."

Mary said, "Everyone, thank you for everything you did and especially thank you Kristen for flying down here and taking care of the check for Joe Traynor. I'm mentally exhausted but I'd like to treat everyone here to a nice dinner if you're up to it." She looked around as everyone nodded his or her heads. It was hard to turn down a dinner offer from a multi-millionaire and now biggest customer at Jane's law firm.

Mary said, "Jane, don't forget to invite your husband. It feels like we already know him after talking to Joe. We'll head back to the hotel and get ready. We still have Sam and Pete here to watch over us for another week. You guys are family too now, as Joe said."

Walking out of the office, Jack asked Mary how she felt. She said fine but she was kind of upset that he couldn't participate in this event the same as she did at his winning event. He told her it was best. Eventually, someone would point out that she was married to another large lottery winner and then all hell would break out. Hopefully by then, all the trusts would be fully set up and money would start to be distributed so that there was no question of any funny business going on. He knew what he went through the last year with family with business and with publicity that it would be difficult but this would be twice as difficult, winning a second time.

CHAPTER 10

Joe and Skip made it to Joe's home in Tavernier and Skip had called his wife, Linda, to see if she could pick him up at Joe and Julie's house. He had ridden up to Miami with Joe, Mary and Jack and he would have to stay over and get a ride back to Key West when Joe went to the college in the morning. Joe was driving his Coast Guard vehicle and Skip was retired so he wasn't able to take's Joe's vehicle home.

Linda called Julie as soon as Skip called her and asked her if she'd mind if she could bring dinner to Julie's for a cookout at 6:00 p.m. that night and Julie said that would be great. After dinner, Linda and Skip would head home. Little did Skip know that Mary had called her right after talking to Julie and invited her to sit on her newly to be formed foundation trust fund board. She was thrilled. She was beside herself when Mary told her, like Joe and Julie, she was setting up a million-dollar trust fund for the Lennon family to include Skip, Linda and her children. She also mentioned that she wanted input from Jamie as well because she was young, energetic, and very bright and caring. Both Linda and Julie had this secret and neither Joe nor Skip was aware. All Joe knew was that he had a $1.2 million dollar check burning a hole in his pocket and couldn't wait to get to the college to hand the check to the president to deposit into the college's general fund.

As Joe and Skip pulled in, the coals were already lit and the steaks and Key lime butter grilled grouper were ready to go. Corn on the cob was boiling, the cornbread was warm, and the beers and wine were on ice.

Joe got out of the car and as soon as Julie saw him she said, "Let's see it."

He smiled and pulled the check out of his wallet and showed it to Julie. Skip shook his head again and Linda came over and asked to see it as well.

"Wow," said Julie.

"Wow, is right," said Linda.

"I'm scared to death. I won't sleep a wink tonight with this check in my wallet," Joe said.

"I thought you weren't afraid of anything?" said Skip.

"Certainly not of you, pal. However, this is a big deal and I can't help think that it will blow away in the wind to never be seen again. Can you imagine if I had to call Mary and tell her I lost the check? Can you imagine? Can you stop payment on a check for $1.2 million dollars? I'll bet it's more than the $25.00 fee for a regular check," Joe said.

"That's what you're worried about, the $25.00 stop payment fee for a lost check? Have a beer, Joe. You're nuts and this proves it," said Skip.

Joe said, "You're right. I'll put the check in my gun safe until morning and then I'll lock it in a box and put it right next to me on the way down."

"Let's eat, the coals are ready, said Julie. "It won't take any time."

Bella came flying out the door to give Joe a big hug. She had grown so big in the last year. Her English was getting better but they always conversed in Spanish. Julie was becoming more fluent as well. She was now in second grade, adopted two years ago, after her mother died of cancer and she had no one else other than foster care. Julie was a friend of Bella's mother, both working at the elementary school. Both Joe and Julie fought like hell to become her foster parents and then adopted her as soon as they could. Their lives had changed becoming immediate parents right after they were married. They wouldn't change a thing.

During dinner, Julie asked Linda to help her in the kitchen. Julie knew that Mary was going to call Linda right after she spoke to her. Julie asked her if she was going to be on the board and she said yes. Then she said Jamie would be a junior member and work herself into a full board member with experience and time. Both those ingredients can't be taught but can be acquired with patience over time. Julie was reluctant to ask Linda if there was anything else and Linda said yes, Mary was setting up a trust fund for the family. Julie was relieved and said Mary was doing the same for them. They both looked at each other and hugged and said how wonderful this was. It gave their children a leg up. The leg up they never got as kids. They then said they would both announce it to Joe and Skip right after dinner.

"Joe and Skip, Linda and I have something to tell both of you," said Julie.

"What is it? It can't be better than the check I just got," he said.

"It depends on how you look at it, Joe. The check you got is for someone else. Yes, it's a wonderful thing but Mary pulled another fast one. She's in the process of setting up her trust funds and wants both Linda and I to be board members for the Teresa Trust Fund South, covering south Florida and the Florida Keys. That check, you just got, is just a small portion of what's to come. She's putting $77.5 million into the fund that your check will come from. The board will consist of Mary, Jack, me, Linda and Jamie, as a junior member, along with Jane, who will be the attorney in charge, and also Tillie and Joe. That should put quite a feather in Jane's cap at her firm. In addition, Linda go ahead," Julie said.

"In addition," Linda continued. "Mary is setting up a trust fund for one million dollars for the Lennon family including Skip, me and the kids and a one million-dollar trust fund for the Traynors including Joe, Julie and Bella at this point."

"Are you shitting me?" asked Joe.

"I shit you not," said Julie and laughed. "Isn't that the line you used when we met Jack and Mary at Sloppy Joe's, when they said they were from Troy, New York, lived in Lansingburgh and Mary taught at Catholic High?" I believe that was, "Are you shitting me?" said Julie all smiles.

"Why?" asked Joe. Skip was just sitting there dumbstruck. Linda asked, "Are you okay, Skip?"

"I don't know," said Skip. "Ask me later on the way home."

"Mary and Jack are very generous people. We all know their story. He was dumped by his wife and kids. Mary was an ex-nun making her way, living with two other ex-nuns next to her high school. Living hand to mouth and now they're two of the richest people on the planet. It couldn't happen to two nicer people and I guess we're around for the ride. Let's see where it takes us. The only problem is that much money creates a frenzy, enemies and rip-off artists, so we have to do our part and be very vigilant down here to protect them. They're giving a majority of the money to good causes and I believe we can help," said Julie.

Dinner was done. They cleaned up and Skip and Linda said goodbye and headed back home to Key West. Joe sat on the patio drinking another beer and simply smiling to himself. He decided to call Jack and Mary and see how their day went and to thank Mary for the very generous gift.

"Mary, Hi. It's Joe," he said.

"Hi, Joe. How are you doing? Jack is here and our two bodyguards and Kristen. Say Hi everyone. It's Joe," she said.

"Hi, Joe," said everyone.

"We made it back safely even though I was scared to death with the check in my pocket. I put it in the gun safe until morning and I'll be heading out as soon as I can to turn it over to Morgan, He's the president of the college you know?"

"Yes, you told us. We're meeting the lottery officials on Monday for the meet and greet. We decided that Jack shouldn't be involved just in case someone picks up that we're now two-time winners," said Mary.

"Good idea," piped in Julie. "Hi, Mary," she shouted out. "Joe has something to say to you," she said.

"Thanks for taking my thunder," Joe said as he smiled with nods from Linda and Skip.

"We're sitting here with Linda and Skip and we really don't know what to say about your generosity toward us," Joe said. "It's like you fell from the sky and showered us with gifts that were beyond our wildest dreams. As Julie said, we can use it for Bella's education and our future kids, if we're so lucky to have them. Two or three more would be great."

Julie said, "Hold on fella. Aren't you getting a little ahead of yourself here?" She shook her head.

"Just dreamin' babe," he said. Now we can really plan without worrying about the future. Besides, this covers Tillie as well. Isn't that a great relief?"

"Hey guys. You called us remember?" said Mary as she was talking over the speakerphone.

"Sorry," said Joe. "I got a little carried away. So everything went well at the attorney's office with the lottery people?" Joe asked.

"Yes it did. Thank God that Kristen was standing right

there and kind of took over a little. Jane and Sidney, as good as they are, never had lottery winner clients before. Within minutes, Kristen had all the paperwork signed and in the hands of Secretary Davis, head of the Florida lottery. Again, we're meeting them at their Miami office on Monday. It should be quite a show but we will make it as short as possible. We'll go in two cars as backup with Sam and Pete and when we leave, we'll head for a charter plane out of Fort Lauderdale to Albany International. Jamie is packing our luggage and delivering it to our hotel here so we don't have to go back. If it leaks no one will be around. She'll stay with us until Monday and then head back. Linda and Skip should take advantage as well so they don't encounter any media attention. Remember, our house in Key West is owned by the Evangeline Realty Trust. So, it won't come back on us. To everyone's knowledge, we're from upstate New York and it will stay that for as long as we can and get all our ducks in a row, as they say," she said.

Mary continued, "Linda and Julie, I'll be back without Jack in a few weeks and I want to set up a series of meetings with you two, Jamie and Julie can you ask Tillie to attend as well?"

"I'll do that as soon as I can," she said. "I'm still at school so I have to work around my schedule as you know. I'm still the coach of the cross-country girls team and I'm fully involved with my job as career development specialist and college advisor. So, let's make it work," she said.

"Linda, here," she said. "Mary, I want to thank you as well. My life isn't nearly as hectic as Julie's. So, call me anytime. When you get back, call us and Jamie or I'll pick you up. It should have calmed down by then. If not, we'll let you know before you arrive and we can make other plans."

Thanks everyone, for everything. It's appreciated," said Jack. "I'm just here for the ride," he said kiddingly.

Chapter 11

Joe left for the college at 7:15 a.m. It was about seventy-five miles, going over back roads once off the main road but could take forever depending on the crowds going to Key West on the only highway, Route 2, the Overseas Highway. They live at the south end of Tavernier and he's heading to the north end of Key West at 5901 College Road, on Stock Island. The college was just renamed The College of the Florida Keys, on June 7, 2019 by the Florida legislature.

The College of the Florida Keys, formerly Florida Keys Community College, is part of the Florida higher education system. Its main campus is on Stock Island, adjacent to what it purports to be the only living coral reef in North America. It also operates two additional locations in the Florida Keys. one in Marathon and another in Key Largo. With its Key West location, it's the southernmost post-secondary school of any type within the contiguous United States.

The college still offers two-year associate degrees in various programs and associate degrees for students planning to transfer to four-year institutions. It also offers an array of bachelor's and associate's degrees, certificates, and career training programs to suit a variety of academic and professional goals.. It had graduated over 1,000 nurses. Among the college's unique degree programs (based on the needs of the Key West area) are Marine Technology, Marine Environmental Technology, and Diving Business & Technology. The college also offers Licensing programs for professional mariners. All of this in addition to the side managed by Joe for all the service men and women sent there to further their education and training for specific service careers.

Joe arrived in a little over an hour and a half, pretty good time for this time of year he thought. It was a little past 9:00 a.m. when he knocked on Morgan Hennessy's administrative assistant's door. He was still very nervous and would be until he handed the check to Morgan.

"Hi, Louise," said Joe. "Is he in?"

"He is, Joe, but he has a board meeting in about fifteen minutes," Louise Butler said.

"This is really important and he might want to mention it at the board meeting," said Joe.

"Let me go ask him, Joe. I'm sure he'll see you for a few minutes," she said.

Louise came back out of Morgan's office and told Joe to go in but he had to be quick because Morgan had a big presentation to make concerning the $1.2 million dollar deficit and he was not in so great mood.

"In about two minutes you'll hear screaming with delight if I'm not mistaken. Don't let anyone in other than you to see what happened," said Joe.

"Hi, Morgan. This won't take but a minute. Do you believe in miracles," he said as he handed him the check from Mary Evans for $1.2 million dollars. "We need to get this deposited today. I was a nervous wreck driving down here with the check in my wallet. Let me quickly explain how all this happened," he said.

Morgan looked at the check with confusion on his face and then he looked at all the zeros and the decimal point at the end. "Is this really for one million two hundred thousand dollars payable to the college's general fund?"

"Yes it is," said Joe. "Not bad, huh?" He then went on to explain how his friends Jack Manning and Mary Evans, Jack's wife, both hit the lottery on separate occasions. Jack hit for $330.0 million dollars and Mary hit for $480.0 million dollars. They obviously netted a lot less when they took the one time payment and then paid taxes on a large portion of it. They also still have left a major portion set up in separate trust funds to give to worthy causes. Joe explained that a trust fund for south Florida and the Florida Keys was being set up with $77.5 million of which this check would eventually be deducted. He told Morgan that Julie was asked to be a board member for the Teresa Trust Fund South and would be part of the decision making team for distribution of funds. He also told him that their personal attorney Jane Swanson would be the trust fund attorney, giving more credibility, honesty and integrity from the starting gate.

"Joe, I have to go to the board meeting but can you join me and quickly explain this miracle that just happened. I was prepared to lay off over twenty professors and staff members because of the deficit. This will give us the time we need to do marketing to increase our student base and secure more funding. Can we meet Mary Evans and Jack Manning to thank them?" asked Morgan.

"Eventually, but they want to keep a low profile. No one down here knows that Jack and Mary are married and both hit large lottery payouts, except for a few of us and we pledged to keep it that way. Please don't divulge her name to anyone at this point. I don't want to jeopardize any future gifts from either Mary or Jack."

"Good point. I hear you loud and clear." Morgan let out a loud, "YES!!!"

Louise came running in and said, "What happened, Joe? You were right. What happened?"

Morgan turned to Louise and put his finger up to his mouth to say shush and handed her the check. "Can you get me a deposit ticket immediately. We need to get this to our bank ASAP," he said.

Louise looked at both of them and said, "YES, IS RIGHT!!! HOLY MOLY!!! Is this real?"

"Told you," said Joe and smiled from ear to ear. Morgan was beaming.

He and Morgan, as Morgan took the check back with a deposit ticket, left for the board meeting. Morgan said, "Joe, you never stop surprising me with what you do and have done for us since you've been here, but this is beyond belief. I can't wait to see the expression on the board members' faces."

They walked into the boardroom and Joe took a seat against the back wall, away from the board table. He smiled at everyone as Morgan took his seat and the head of the table. After sitting down, Morgan said, "I was prepared to give you some very bad news with a list of names for a layoff of twenty employees to balance this and next year's annual budget. However, there's been a miracle of sorts that's just taken place. I'd like to yield the floor to Joe to explain what happened and then we will excuse ourselves to make a very important, the most important deposit in the history of the college. Joe, go ahead."

As Joe rose from his seat and walked toward the front of the board table, Morgan handed him the check. Joe was nervous but this was a good nervous because he knew that this meant that the college was now on sound footing and they could move ahead with the plans that they developed for major improvements and increasing student achievement, graduation and increase in the student base. The military wing that Joe ran was always safe but only as safe as the regular college. If the college failed, it would definitely impact the costs on the military side and considerations for moving the military wing could happen.

Joe showed everyone individually the check that they'd be immediately depositing. It was from the Evangeline Trust from Jack Manning that would eventually be paid back by Mary through her new Teresa Trust Fund South funding. Joe said that the names involved were to be kept secret at this point and eventually they might let themselves be known once the trust fund has been established. Joe mentioned that at this point, no one knew who the winner of the lottery was, other than there was only one winner and that ticket was sold in Key West. Everyone clapped and thanked Joe and Morgan and were thrilled that they escaped a very tough road ahead. Joe said they needed to leave immediately and would take two of their security staff from the military side to drive them to their bank to deposit the check.

On the way to the bank, Joe called Julie and told her mission accomplished. She could tell how relieved he really was after all this. He said he would be more relieved once the check cleared. They'd called the bank manager and they were ready for Joe and Morgan when they entered. Joe called Mary and Kristen to ask them to see if they could clear the check quickly. Instead, Kristen said that she could get the funds transferred electronically today rather than wait for the check. Morgan could put the check in the vault and write void over it and the funds would be there in less than two hours. Joe and Morgan thanked Kristen and Mary profusely. Mary said she didn't do anything for the logistics. All she did through Jack was supply the money. Joe said that was no small task. He said if they need any of them at any time to call and mentioned that when she got back to Key West that he would introduce her and Jack to Morgan. The funds arrived in the college general fund account by the time they got back to Morgan's office. *What a relief.*

As Joe and Morgan arrived back at the college, Morgan

said, "I just can't believe this, Joe. I'm dumbfounded on how this all transpired. I think someone is watching out for us and I'm not kidding."

As soon as they walked into the president's office area, Morgan's assistant said she just received a call from their bank and the wire transfer had just arrived. She was beside herself. Only she, Morgan, Joe and the board knew what would have happened if they didn't get this windfall. Joe had mentioned to Morgan that he didn't believe this was the only funding they'd get from the trust fund set up by Mary Evans to serve south Florida and the Florida Keys. He said to Morgan that they needed to immediately update their five-year strategic plan for both the academic student side as well as the military side of the college and to start looking at new programs that would bring economic opportunity to those in the region who'd have never been able to fund any future for themselves and their families.

It was time for the college to step up to the plate and make it known that it was planning on being on the cutting edge of job creation using technology as a base for future high-tech jobs to come. Morgan was totally energized by Joe and told him so. He wished that Joe would never have to leave The College of the Florida Keys but he knew that Joe was on the fast track to be in a major leadership position at the Coast Guard Academy as soon as he received his doctorate.

Joe would be headed to the Coast Guard Academy as soon as he received a Doctor of Philosophy in Leadership and Education Specialization in Higher Education Administration from Barry University in Miami Shores. This was the degree he'd need if he were selected as the next Assistant Superintendent of the Coast Guard Academy. This would eventually lead to the Superintendent position, which was the intent of Joe's Rear Admiral mentoring his career.

Joe was thinking about leaving the Coast Guard when his enlistment time was up for many reasons but then he was offered a position he didn't think he could turn down. They told him they'd groom him for a career that met his ambition and this Barry University doctoral program is centered on the student and not the faculty, exactly what he was interested in pursuing, inside or outside the Coast Guard.

Joe has researched and read from his material that this Ph.D. in Leadership and Education was a specialization in Higher Education Administration, diversified in scope and would prepare him for teaching and administrative positions in higher education, a career path in high-tech industry or he could continue his climb through the ranks of the Coast Guard.

This doctoral program would prepare Joe to positively contribute to areas such as research, policy development, law, history of education, and the teaching and learning process. Joe would be exposed to leadership theories, dynamics of change, and the integration of a cybernetics framework and prepare him to work toward a research platform and teaching agenda that complement the higher education context. Joe had read that in the brochure and wanted to better understand what that meant from Dr. Hennessy's perspective. He had to accumulate 54 credits, produce a thesis, which he'd already planned. He was already using his newly acquired knowledge at the College of the Florida Keys, and it was working. Students were learning entrepreneurial skills they never knew they had. It was a shame that the current deficit budget would have curtailed their ambitious goals. Now, they were back on target and would add new programs to move them to the next step as a major institution.

<h1 style="text-align:center">CHAPTER 12</h1>

Mary has been on edge all week, ever since she received the news that she was the latest lottery winner of a substantial amount of money. She was not only nervous about the presentation of the award on Monday at the lottery office in Miami, but she wasn't there when Jack received his check and national attention back in Schenectady, when he hit the lottery for $330.0 million dollars. She wasn't sure how to handle this. She watched Jack's video acceptance as it flashed across the national news. He was told by Kristen not to say too much and he followed her advice. It worked out fine so she decided to copy, not word for word, but enough of Jack's short speech that it would curtail a lot of the questions she knew would be coming. "How does it feel to be a multimillionaire? Are you married? Why are you down here in Florida? How did you pick your numbers? What're you going to do with the money? Are you moving here? Where do you actually live?" She didn't want to answer any of these questions.

She would be with Kristen, backed up by Pete and Sam. She was going to bring Jane Swanson but then everyone would be wondering and then asking how she was able to get this prestigious law firm to help her with such short notice. Jack would ride with her to the lottery office but then stay in the car, acting as the driver while Sam and Pete walked her into the event. She knew that eventually everyone would know that she was the wife of Jack Manning, another major lottery winner from Troy, New York. She wanted to avoid that today and then have a plan to announce on how she'd be developing a major trust to help those in need in south Florida and the Florida Keys. She needed to buy time. It's been a week since all this happened and her head was spinning. She found it amazing how Jack wound up handling everything when he had only his instincts to work with and the help of Kristen and her law firm back in Albany. She thought Jack could actually have his own Ph.D. now in how to develop strategies to give money away for millionaires. His plan was working, not without some major flaws, but it was working and he was avoiding the media like the plague while doing good things for the people in Troy, New York. Hopefully she could follow Jack's path and wind up with positive results as well. She just knew in the back of her mind that when the world found out she was married to another major lottery winner, the hounding wouldn't stop. They needed to prepare for the worse, hoping for the best. This was what was making her nervous. She finally figured it out.

The presentation was to be at the Miami Lottery Office at 14621 Oak Lane, Miami Lakes, Florida, which was actually considered Hialeah. The trip on a good day would take about three-quarters of an hour to go 21.3 miles, door to door from the SLS Brickell Hotel and Residence on South Miami Avenue. The hotel was only a few blocks from her attorney's office, in the Brickell Plaza. Mary got in Sam's car with Kristen. She sat in the front passenger seat while Kristen sat in the back and Jack went with Pete in his car. They'd follow bumper to bumper until they got there. They were told that they could park right in front of the building, making it easy to arrive among all the expected media.

As they left the lot, they meandered along the surface streets for about two miles and then at SW Third Avenue, both cars merged onto I-95N. They traveled about eleven miles, merging onto Palmetto Expressway for about eight miles. They took the NW 154th Street/Miami Lakes exit and about a mile down the road, they turned left onto Oak Lane. They arrived.

Mary was now very nervous and said to Sam, "Are you sure we're safe pulling up here?"

"As safe as can be," he said. He added, "they said they'd meet us at the door and walk us to the presentation room. I'm sure they'll have plenty of security. Remember this is as big a deal to them as it is to you. They get to be on national television, which is a politician's dream."

"I guess you're right," she said.

Kristen said, "Mary, I did this with Jack in Schenectady. He was very nervous as well. He got though it. Any questions defer to me and as your attorney, I'll give them a nothing answer in return." She laughed.

"That doesn't sound like you, Kristen, but what the hell," Mary said.

Sam got out of the car and went to the passenger side and opened the door for Mary and then Kristen. Jack got out of Pete's car and went to Sam's, took the keys and pressed Mary's hand for good luck and said, "Don't think about it. It will be no more than a half hour at the most. The minute you get antsy, just leave. I'll have the car running. I love you. I wish I could go with you but it would be too much all at once." He smiled and said, "Kristen is with you. That's all you need. And of course Sam and Pete to beat the hell out of anyone who comes near you." He blew her a kiss and laughed. Kristen shook her head.

Pete locked the doors on his car and stood on the left of Mary and Kristen while Sam was on their right side. Sam said, "You ready, Mary? Piece of cake." He laughed and Pete smiled.

"Our first time too," said Pete. "Let's do it." And they did.

Meeting Mary, Kristen, Sam and Pete at the front door was John F. Davis, Secretary of the Florida Lottery and Sandra Alvarez, the Miami District Office manager. Mary smiled because they were familiar faces since meeting them at the law office a few days ago. They both shook hands with Mary, Kristen, Sam and Pete. She told them Sam and Pete is her security team for the duration. They knew that Kristen was her attorney from Albany since she ran the show at the law offices over in downtown Miami. Both lottery officials had a team of security as well, led by Steve Harriett and waved them into the building.

As they walked into the presentation room, there was a bank of cameras and a flock of news people, in the hallway, including local and national television, along with reporters from the Miami Herald, Fort Lauderdale Sun-Sentinel, Key West Citizen, Miami Today, the Orlando Sentinel and Tampa Tribune. Cameras from MSNBC, CNN, FOX and local television stations were set up and started filming the proceedings.

Kristen took the lead as Mary's attorney and quietly spoke to the commissioner and his staff and then introduced Mary to everyone else. Sam and Pete stood quietly by Mary's side. Kristen told the officials that the ceremony shouldn't be dragged out and that Mary was there to fulfill her obligations as a lottery winner and to be officially introduced to the public.

A podium was set up for the occasion and the Secretary moved all the media near where they were standing. He spoke on behalf of the Florida Lottery Commission and as a faithfully appointed official by the current administration. He glowingly told the public that Florida was honored to have the lottery winner buy a ticket in Key West. He didn't mention that she was from New York State.

Secretary Davis brought out the signed ticket and showed everyone the numbers on the front and the signature on the back. He told the crowd that it was the official winner of the lottery drawing and the dollar amount was finalized at $480.0 million dollars. It hadn't changed since they mentioned the amount a week ago. He then handed Mary the large blown up check for the presentation. She could hardly hold it up. It was about two feet high and four feet wide with the $480.0 million dollars showing in the box and written in cursive as Four Hundred and Eighty Million Dollars and 00/100 Dollars. It had the Pay to the Order of "Mary Evans".

The Secretary asked Mary to speak and she simply said, "I'm very pleased to be the only winner for this lottery drawing. I'm in the process of developing a plan for the money, so at this time, I'm unable to tell you what I'll be doing with the proceeds, obviously after taxes are taken out. However, I'll be taking the lump sum cash plan as opposed to the thirty-year payout. Thank you for coming today but that's all I have to say for the present time." She said the exact same thing that Jack was told to say by Kristen, back in Schenectady when he won.

As Mary was speaking, the flashes from the cameras were blinding her as she spoke. Reporters were shouting out questions. "Where do you live? What do you have planned for the money? Do you have any family here? Can we talk to you afterward? What do you do for a living? How old are you? Are you married? Who's the woman with you?

As soon as the questions arose and became a little overwhelming, Kristen took the mike from Mary and told the crowd that Mary wouldn't be speaking any more today. She said as time went on, she'd contact the press and news outlets if she had anything further to say. She thanked them for coming and took Mary by the elbow and turned and both shook the Secretary's hand as well as the office manager and the staff assembled for the meeting. They both followed Sam and Pete out the office door and toward the front door.

"Well that went well. Don't you think? What was it about a half hour in total? Jack was right on the money, literally." She smiled at Kristen from ear to ear.

Kristen smiled at Mary and said, "You did good. You remembered exactly what Jack said and then you said it. Great job."

Mary and Kristen got in Sam's car and Jack immediately put the car in drive and left the front of the building. Sam got in with Pete and caught up with them. Pete flashed his lights a few blocks away and they pulled off the side of the road. Jack got in the back after handing the keys to Sam as he got in the driver's side. "Where to madam?" he said jokingly.

"Let's head back to see Jane and Sidney and all the law partners. I think they have something set up for us there. I don't want to get off on the wrong foot and disappoint them," said Mary.

So they headed back. It was around lunchtime and traffic was heavy. Mary said, "I can't believe I thought downtown Albany traffic was bad. This is unbelievable. How do they do it day in and day out? I'd go crazy."

Jack said, "Well you could simply hire a helicopter for your daily commute since you're now rich, Mary Evans."

"And don't forget it," she said and laughed. Talk about being in a good mood she thought. She hoped that this would always be the case but with this much money involved she knew there would be a lot of problems down the pike as they say. She just hoped that with the team she chose, it would lighten the load. She had a lot of plans, many she discussed with Jack but many she kept to herself. Being an ex-nun didn't mean she didn't have the same thoughts just transferred to a different life. She hoped that she could change lives for the better with this much money but she knew some plans, just like Jack's would blow up in her face. She was once told she couldn't save all the whales so just pick one and name it and stay with it. Some religions believed that if you save one person's life you saved the world because that person could have been Dr. Salk who cured polio. She hoped that would be the case.

They arrived at the law offices and were met at the door. They went to the boardroom and there were balloons and cake and lunch and bottles of champagne, compliments of Jane and Sidney and the rest of the partners and staff. Mary smiled but was now becoming overwhelmed. She just wanted to hop on a plane and head to their home on Old Plank Road in the Town of Brunswick. Once there, she could begin the rest of her life, if that was possible. The challenges were getting to her. She needed rest, relaxation and perhaps a new improved brain. Maybe she could buy one she thought and smiled. *"That would help,"* she thought.

CHAPTER 13

They made it back to the hotel, a little light headed and took a nap before meeting Jane and her husband for dinner with Kristen and Jack and their security, Sam and Pete. They'd be chartering a private plane out of Fort Lauderdale. Jet One Aviation charters premium jets out of Fort Lauderdale International Airport. Sidney Clyne ordered the service after Mary told them at the party that they'd be leaving for home now that all the paperwork was done. She said she was exhausted and wanted to treat Kristen to a private jet as well for all her work. Sidney took care of it with a champagne lunch. They'd leave by 10:00 a.m. from the hotel and arrive at 100 Terminal Drive at the airport within a half hour. It was twenty-seven miles door-to-door. The flight was scheduled for 11:00 a.m. and would take about five hours to land at the Albany International Airport. Sidney arranged for his driver, Jeff Sheldon, and his limousine to pick them up as well. Jeff was the driver who met Kristen when she got to Fort Lauderdale. He was a wonderful older man and enjoyed the ride into Miami.

As Sidney laughed, he told her, "We're a full-service law firm by the way."

"Thank you Sidney," said Mary. However, we'd still feel safer with Sam and Pete tagging along with us until we got to the plane. We'll be met by our security when we land in Albany but until then, let's be safe. You never know. I know no one knows who I am or anything else because we left it that way but it won't last."

"No problem," said Sidney. "Whatever you need, you got," he said.

Mary nodded her head. She didn't tell Sidney or Jane that as soon as they left the lottery office, they stopped at the side of the road so Sam could gather himself because tons of media were following their cars. They were snapping pictures of everyone in both cars and would certainly try to identify anyone that they didn't know. Sam knew the area inside and out and took off, rounding side streets until they weren't followed anymore. Pete slowed and blocked cars trying to get around him filled with media personnel. Sam called Pete and let him know that they'd backtrack several times before heading to the law firm so Pete was to do the best he could and then take off as well, meeting them later on. It was a very good thing that they drove separate cars. If Pete couldn't shake the cars following him then he was to lead them on a wild goose chase throughout Miami until he lost them.

Jeff pulled up in the limousine a little before 10:00 a.m. to make sure he could get all their luggage packed into the vehicle, get them settled, and leave plenty of time to board the private jet by 11:00 a.m. The last thing they wanted to do was wait around for the flight to leave giving anyone in the media the opportunity to take pictures or attempt interviews. They were very good at getting information and finding out about their schedule and would show up out of the blue. Television stations, national media outlets and major newspapers had plenty of people willing to drop a dime on Mary and Jack if spotted.

Mary, Jack, Kristen, Sam and Pete skipped breakfast and went right from their rooms to the back of the hotel, where

Sam and Pete had parked their cars overnight. Jeff was notified to pull to the back, where their luggage was waiting as they got in the limousine. Jeff gave coffee and breakfast sandwiches to Sam and Pete as they went back to their cars. Sam would lead the parade as usual with Pete tailing them right behind.

Jeff said, "Mrs. Sanderson, good to see you again." To Jack and Mary, he said, "Mr. and Mrs. Manning, it's nice to meet you for this short ride. It's about a half hour to forty-five minutes up to Fort Lauderdale International Airport. To be specific, we're heading to 2545 Northwest 55th Court Hanger 26 in Fort Lauderdale. I just called Sam and Pete to put the address in their GPS system in case we have to split up or traffic gets heavy. The plane will wait for us if they have to but it's always better to get there a little early to make sure all your luggage and personal items wind up on the plane." He added, "I have breakfast sandwiches and coffee, juice and donuts for you. Please enjoy."

Kristen said, "Thank you Jeff. It's great seeing you again. We appreciate your hospitality and kindness. Please thank Sidney as well. It's greatly appreciated."

Mary and Jack piped in, "Thanks, Jeff."

They headed out from the hotel with Sam pulling into the lead, followed by Jeff in the limousine, followed in the rear by Pete. They once again meandered over a few blocks and then hit I-95N where they'd travel for about twenty-five miles and got off at Exit 27. The private hanger was only down a few miles off Andrews Avenue.

About halfway up I-95, Pete called Sam and told him that he thought they had someone following them but wasn't sure. He said he would slow up a little and see what the driver would do. He told Sam to keep moving and speed up a little as well. Sam would know enough that when he got off the Exit ramp that he would go a different way to lose anyone following. They had plenty of time and the plane would be waiting until they arrived. The state of Florida only requires a license plate on the back of the car. So, Pete slowed down a lot forcing the other car to pass him and then he pulled behind them. There were two people in the car with a man driving and a woman in the passenger seat. He wrote down the license number on the Florida plate but when they passed him, he noticed that the front had a vanity plate where a license plate would be placed. He smiled and called Sam and said, "We don't need the license plate even though I got it. The front vanity plate read "WLTV", the largest television station in Miami. It's Univision so they're tailing Mary to see where she's heading. Try to lose them and I'll pass again and slow them down when you get to the exit."

"Got it. Will do," he said. Sam sped up allowing Pete to move in behind the limousine and then slowing down the WLTV car. Jeff had been listening in so he knew what was going on. As soon as they got to the exit, Sam went left instead of right and the limousine followed. They pulled into a gas station and Pete went the other way. Little did Pete know but there was another car following the limousine, sitting back a few cars. Sam picked up the other car and made a note of it. It was a late model Ford Focus with two men in the front seats and one guy in the back. He couldn't get the license plate but he had a good description of the car and he could identify the men in the car as probably in their 40s and white. The front two had shaved heads. He wondered if they were cops or military. He phoned Pete back and told him to keep an eye out for them and if he saw them to get the license. Sam thought to himself, "*This is never easy no matter what you might think. These people are worth a lot of money and someone somewhere can do them harm.*"

The limousine arrived at the Jet One hanger and they proceeded to get the limousine unloaded and everything put into the plane, which was now running and ready to go.

Jack turned to Sam and said, "I know we paid you up front before you started but this is little extra to thank you for staying with us through the entire time." He handed two checks to Sam for $1,500.00 each, payable to Sam and Pete.

"Thank you Mr. Manning but that's not necessary. Joe said you were very generous people and I've noticed that myself. This isn't necessary but we're grateful. Pete will be here in a minute. Not to scare you but WLTV in Miami was following us, which is fine but there was another car, a Ford Focus with three guys in it and they didn't look like news reporters. Please tell your security in Albany to keep their eyes open. These are tough times and people may be upset with Mary's winnings."

"Thank you, Sam for the advice but we never told you that I hit the lottery for $330.0 million in upstate New York only a few years ago. So, together, we're very lucky," said Jack.

"Wow, didn't know that. Thanks for telling us. When you come back, please call Joe and us and we will see if we can provide security again. If not, we can pull from the Coast Guard ranks. As you know, we aren't getting rich in the service and this has been a Godsend to us. Thanks again," said Sam.

With that, everyone hopped on the plane. With a good headwind, this plane could be home in four to five hours with a straight flight to Albany. As they were taxing out to the runway, Pete pulled up in his car. Sam handed him the bonus check and he looked startled. "Really?" Pete said.

"Really," said Sam.

Pete said, "Nice of them. That's great. By the way, I got a partial plate number on the Ford Focus as it blew by me. Let's call Joe and see what he can do with it. I'm sure he'll get something. I wouldn't worry about the television station car. They were just hoping to get lucky with a story. Let's head back. I have to report in by 4:00 p.m."

Before heading back, Sam called Jack before they left. He told them about the television station car following them, which he said was fine because they lost them. However, he told them there was someone following the television station car and they'd be checking it out. He said there were three guys in a Ford Focus and they were white, appeared to be in their 40s and had shaved heads, at least the two men in the front seats of the Focus. Sam said he would call Joe who'd then probably follow it up and get back to both Sam and Pete and then Jack if there was anything suspicious. Sam also told him that a lot of shady characters followed reporters to see where they would lead and see if they could make any money on it. Those investigative reporters tended to follow leads down very dark holes and might give these guys some information that they could use to extract money. It was just the way it was in south Florida.

Jack told them to get back to him anyway regardless of what they found and asked them to have Joe call him as well. He wouldn't tell Mary or Kristen at this point but may have to if it amounted to anything. At least he thought they'd be safe with John and Fred, who were only a phone call away from Tom Matthews, head of the Albany FBI office.

Pete said, "I'm not due back until tomorrow. I'm heading to the bank. I can now buy the new tires that I've been putting off. Nice people though. I hope we can do this again and soon."

With that they headed back to Miami and home. The plane took off smoothly and was headed home to Troy, New York. It had been a merry-go-round week and they couldn't wait to get back. Kristen was just happy to be on a private jet after coming down on Southwest Airlines. Overall, everything went as smoothly as could be expected. Now the fun begins.

They were about halfway into their flight, around 1:00 p.m. when the flight attendant gave them their menus for lunch. Kristen, Mary and Jack all ordered lobster salad sandwiches with splits of champagne. Jack had said previously that the flight down to Key West cost around thirty thousand dollars with lunch and this was about the same. He said, "So ladies, please enjoy lunch and some bubbly."

Kristen said she could get used to this luxury. Mary was still exhausted and barely ate her lunch and had one small glass of champagne. She said the luxury part was not standing in line and going through security. All they had to do was pass through the private check-in area, go through a hand-held wand, and then step up the stairs into the plane. When they'd land, John Jefferson and Fred Tucker would meet the driver for Kristen's law firm and once again follow the limousine provided. The driver would drop Kristen off at the law firm in downtown Albany. They'd then head to their Brunswick home on Old Plank Road, just over the Troy city line.

John and Fred had already stopped at the house before arriving at the airport to make sure everything was okay. They met Jack's daughter, Debbie, who was staying there as she attended the University at Albany for her master's degree. She'd used Jack's credit card and had stocked up on groceries and necessities and she was ready for their arrival. It was a lot different this time than it was when she had believed her mother that her father and mother's divorce was all Jack's fault. She now knew better, especially with her mother living with the guy she was seeing while married to Jack. That's the main reason she came around and settled in with Jack at their home on the hill.

Before Mary nodded off on the plane, Jack asked her if everything was okay. She said yes but she was a little nervous. "Did you see those cars behind Pete? I think they were following us, Jack." She continued, we'd better be on our toes from now on. Once the news breaks that we as husband and wife are now double lottery winners our lives may never be the same. It was bad enough with your winning the lottery, but now, we're wide open to criticism, jealousy and no matter what we give away it will never be enough."

"I didn't notice them so good catch. But, both Sam and Pete noticed both cars. One was a bunch of reporters with cameras from the local Miami television station. They just want a story. Sam and Pete are worried about the car behind and they're calling now with a description of the passengers, a partial plate number and the make of the car. It was a newer Ford Focus, maybe 2016 or 2017. There are a lot of those cars around," he said. "They'll call me no matter what they find out and I'll let you know as well. Sorry, I didn't want to bother you with this on the way home."

"Thanks, Jack. But, I was well aware of the situation and just didn't let on. I didn't want Kristen to be upset either so I said nothing. We can let her know if and when we hear anything," said Mary. "By the way, when am I going to be Mrs. Mary Manning and not the old maid, Mary Evans?" She laughed.

Kristen laughed and said, "Just like me. But, I was a little younger and wiser and got out earlier so I could claim the Sanderson name for all its fame and fortune."

"How did that work out?" said Mary laughing.

"About as well as could be expected with a husband, three kids later, a very large mortgage and a career that eats into my soul," said Kristen.

"Excuse me Sister Evangeline but we're the same age," said Mary with a smile.

"Touché," said Kristen.

Mary fell asleep and finally woke up fifteen minutes before landing. It was amazing to her as they flew over Bald Mountain in the Town of Brunswick. They looked out the window and could see their house from the air. It always amazed Mary. Ten minutes later, they were opening the doors and were debarking into a limousine with John Jefferson and Fred Tucker holding the doors open. Flanking the car was Tom Matthews with a surprise visit. Joe had called him when he knew they'd be landing and Tom said he wanted to greet them as well. He laughed and told Joe that all he wanted to do was make as much as John and Fred did, which was substantially more than he was making as FBI Director for the Albany office. Joe had laughed and told him, "Welcome to my world. I just got a check for over a million dollars from Mary and handed it to the president of The College of the Florida Keys to cover this year's deficit."

"I guess I don't feel so bad now," said Tom. He added, "I wonder what it's like knowing you never have to worry about money for the rest of your life. Or the life of your children or your children's children and I could go on," he said.

"Are you done, Tom?" said Joe. I got a call coming in. Maybe it's another million-dollar donation I have to worry about. Thanks for showing up to say hi."

"Will do," said Tom.

"Joe, it's Sam calling. Do you have a minute?" he asked.

"Sure, what's up? I'm just heading up home to Tavernier. Bella has soccer tonight at 6:00 p.m. I can't believe I'm saying that," said Joe.

Sam told him it was short and sweet. Mary, Jack and Kristen flew out of Fort Lauderdale around 11:00 a.m. and would be landing in Albany around 4:00 p.m. He then went on to tell Joe about the television station car following the limousine, which he said was no big deal but he was concerned about the car following the reporter's vehicle. He gave Joe the partial plate number, Florida of course, and the description of the car and the two people in the front. He said there were three guys about forty years old who had shaved heads and looked suspicious to both Sam and Pete. He said, "Joe, you know when you get a feeling but can't explain it but it's in the pit of your stomach that something just isn't right? Well that's the feeling I got and so did Pete. Can you check it out?"

"Thanks for the update, Sam. Of course I will. I'll call you as soon as I hear anything. I'm calling Paul Philips, FBI Director for Miami, a good friend, and my friend and yours, Mark Silva. You haven't met Jack Forest up in Virginia in charge of intelligence for the Coast Guard. We were together in boot camp and have each other's backs for many years. It's impossible to find out anything without your friends' help," Joe said.

"I hear you. Just call Jack and Mary. This is a good gig for us and they're really nice people. I don't want them to get hurt when they come back," Sam said.

CHAPTER 14

On the way home, Jack asked Mary how they'd handle going into the Evangeline Career Center within a few days. He said that the only ones who knew about her good fortune were her attorneys in Albany including Kristen, her partners and her staff. Kristen knew not to say anything. Jack's own children didn't know a thing and neither did John and Fred, their two retired FBI agents serving as security in the Capital Region. They didn't go with them on their honeymoon to Florida even though they thought they should to protect them away from home but Jack insisted no. So, they were being paid as usual and had just waited around until they heard from them as to what they needed. Jack and Mary wanted to tell John and Fred exactly what was going on in case they felt that they needed more support over the next month or two. John and Fred were more than protection. They became friends as well. Whenever Jack and Mary felt the need for protection, both John and Fred stayed in their Old Plank Road home or were only minutes away across the river in Waterford and Menands.

The only worry Jack and Mary could anticipate was when all the news media gave national coverage to Mary's winning the lottery. There would certainly be news in

Florida but they checked already and there was nothing significant in upstate New York other than there was one winner in Florida. No one in the Capital Region would pay much attention to that. However, they were very aware of the fact that sooner than later, someone would show up at their door on Old Plank Road and start filming. The news of Mary's winning was significant but the two of them winning was national news. When the media put two and two together Mary and Jack would hopefully have a plan in place that would let everyone know that they'd be giving away a substantial amount of money within the Capital Region and in south Florida and the Florida Keys. They hoped that would put a damper on everyone invading their privacy every waking moment.

They arrived at the house a little after 6:00 p.m. Debbie waved to them as they came down the long driveway in the limousine with John and Fred pulling up alongside the limousine. Jack could smell the grill and started to get hungry. As they got out, Debbie greeted them and hugged both. "How was your trip?" she said. "Did you have a great honeymoon?"

Mary said, "Hi Debbie. I see you got the grill going. Your father is starved, especially when he smells steak grilling."

"I do," she said. "I also have baked potatoes and grilled mushrooms and salad. Hope that's enough," she added.

"More than enough," said Jack. "How are you, Debbie? You look great. We had a wonderful time but we're glad to be home. Is everything all right here? After dinner we have something to tell you."

"Something to tell me? What?" she asked. "Dinner will be ready in a half hour. There are some snacks on the deck. I know you, dad. You can't wait," she said and laughed. Take some cheese and crackers and I'll help the guys unload the limousine."

Jack grabbed a beer out of the cooler on the deck and handed one to Mary as well. He looked around and saw that the view hadn't changed. On the top of Old Plank Road, at the foot of Bald Mountain, you could see in three directions for close to thirty miles, all the way up to Saratoga Springs and down to the Helderberg Mountains, south of Albany. He loved Key West but still loved the greater Troy, New York area. It had four seasons, and the beauty of the region could not be surpassed. It was at the foot of the Adirondack Mountains and only twenty-five miles to Vermont. He asked Mary, "Glad to be home?"

"I am," she said. "I'm going in and take a quick shower. Thanks for the beer. See you in a half an hour."

Jack simply went to their room, grabbed a clean outfit and put his clothes in the hamper. It had been a very long day and he was looking forward to a nice dinner on the deck overlooking the thirty-mile view. He wondered how Debbie would handle the news about Mary winning $480.0 million dollars after he already won $330.0 million. He could tell her it wasn't that much after taking a one-time payment reduced by forty percent and then New York State and Federal Taxes taking almost half of whatever they didn't put into foundation trust fund. He laughed to himself. Who was he kidding? Together they had a fortune for themselves and a fortune to give away. Anyone in the world would trade places with Jack. Nonetheless, no one knew what he had to go through to toughen up and change the way he was in order to do the things he wanted to help everyone that he could.

On the other hand, Jack always felt that Mary was smarter, more compassionate, more caring and better suited to handle all the problems that come with being rich. She called her fund, the Teresa Trust Fund, after Mother Teresa but it didn't end there. As an ex-nun, originally taking vows of chastity, poverty and obedience, Jack knew she was better suited to handle any upcoming crisis. She could walk away and not be affected by any of it. At the same time, he also knew that Mary handled challenges very well.

The way Mary had turned his daughter into a close friend, after his emotional battle with his ex-wife, was a remarkable achievement. She never raised her voice. She always listened intently at everyone who had something to say and then gave her weighted response in a way that offended no one but made her point well known. Jack was truly the luckiest guy in the world. The money helped to change him but without Mary, his days would have been meaningless and unrewarding.

As soon as dinner ended, Debbie asked her father, "So, tell me, what's the big secret?"

"I'll let Mary handle this one," he said. "Mary?"

"Debbie, thank you for everything including dinner and keeping our place up while we were away on our honeymoon. Especially thank you for your friendship. I know it was tough on you. Especially tough in dealing with your mother and I appreciate the fact that you and I are now very good friends. I'll never take the place of your mother and I'll promise you that I'll never try to do so," said Mary. "On the other hand, I've some news that I'd like to share with you," she said. While we were in Key West, I bought a lottery ticket, the same as I do every week up here. Your father uses his numbers that he won big on and I use a formula that I've used every time I play. It doesn't really matter because winning the lottery is out of your hands. You know the New York State Lottery ad stating "A dollar and a dream?"

"Mary, what?" said Debbie. "What're you trying to tell me?"

"I hit the lottery a week ago for $480.0 million dollars. I had the only winning ticket nationally. I was presented with an oversized check by the Secretary of the Florida Lottery in their Miami office yesterday. We left the office without saying much and flew out this morning on a private plane out of Fort Lauderdale. I don't know who knows what but you're the first outside of Kristen and her team up here."

"My God," she said. "Really, no shit?" asked Debbie.

"Yes, as the famous Joe Traynor stated so well, no shit." She said and Jack laughed.

"No shit? Wow," Debbie said again. "So what're you going to do now that you two are some of the richest people in the world?"

Mary told Debbie that she was taking the same amount for herself so they'd be equal partners in the marriage and giving the rest away through her Teresa Trust Fund already established and a new trust fund being set up for south Florida and the Florida Keys. They'd each have $77.5 million dollars for worthy projects. She then asked Debbie if she'd like to contribute her time to work on worthy projects within the Capital Region of New York State. She'd get a small stipend and would be groomed for a board seat down the road, if her contribution of time and talent were also worthy. She could work on projects that reflect youth and present new ideas from those her own age. Mary was very firm on having representation from all walks of life and all ages. That's why she really wanted Julie's grandmother, Tillie, on her board in Florida. She knew more about growing up poor and being a senior that was poor than most everyone and she succeeded in raising Julie. That's the support she wanted. She didn't want classic MBA candidates and attorneys but people who really cared about others and wanted to make a difference in their own communities, north or south, Democrat or Republican, Catholic or non-Catholic or whatever religion they chose, Mary didn't care. She simply wanted results that were quantifiable with a complete external program evaluation. She had someone in mind for that role as well.

"Mary, I'd be honored to be any part of this. I've already seen the good that my father has done with his projects and this could only be as good if not better with you in charge of it," Debbie said.

"Hey, wait a minute. What do you mean better? I think we've done a pretty good job so far?"

"Sure, dad. Whatever you say," Debbie said and started to laugh her ass off. Mary laughed.

Jack said to Mary, "I think we need to tell John and Fred exactly what's happening here in case there are some problems."

"I'll go tell them everything right now," Mary said. She went outside and waved to them both. "Hey guys, as soon as you eat, can I see you for a minute? I've something to tell you."

"Mary, I think we know. It was just announced on Channel 13 that a local person hit the lottery in Florida. Is that you?" John asked.

"Boy that was quick," she said. We haven't been home for a whole day and I only had the presentation yesterday down in Miami," she said. "Let me tell you the whole story." She did.

"I think we'd better be a little more careful," said Fred. It's one thing to hit it once but another to hit it twice when they put it together and they probably will."

"We thought about that and you're right. Do we need more protection at this point?" said Mary.

"We won't know until they show up here at the house. I need to call Tom Matthews and see if we can get any more of our retired buddies just in case. You never know," said John.

"Since it's now out there, I'd better call our friends down at the Career Center. We were going to wait and spring it on them in a few days after we got settled but I think we better call them now," said Mary. She walked back into the house and told Jack that the local news picked up the story so they needed to call Karen Steele and Sam Ryan immediately. They could show tomorrow at the Center and be swamped by news trucks.

"Hi, Karen," said Jack. "We're back and we have some news for you if you haven't seen the news tonight already."

"Hi, Jack. Glad you're home. No I just left the office and I'm on my way home. Sam and I are walking out together. We just finished the year-to-date report and everything is running as planned. Don't you love it when a plan comes together?" She laughed. "Sam says hi."

"Here's Mary," said Jack.

"Hi, Karen. Can you put it on speaker phone for Sam?" asked Mary.

"She just did. What's up?" said Sam

"Last week, I hit the national lottery in Key West for $480.0 million dollars, netting a lot less of course but as exciting as that is, it creates a very large problem for us. We need to talk to you tomorrow. Can you come up here where it's quiet with no one around to hear anything?" asked Mary.

"Wow. That's great news," they both said at the same time. "We'd like to have that problem Mary," as they both smiled.

"I know. But, it might be an overwhelming problem when the media picks up the fact that we both won the lottery for substantial amounts. We need a game plan up here for our programs and I need to set up a foundation down in Key West, which I'm doing right now," said Mary.

"Sounds good. We'll see you around 9:30 a.m. tomorrow morning. I have to hand in paperwork for the accountants and the attorneys for our year-to-date results. We'll come to your house together for less confusion," said Karen.

"See you then. The coffee will be on," said Mary.

Mary shook her head and headed for bed. She was

mentally exhausted. Perhaps tomorrow may be more enlightening but she doubted it.

CHAPTER 15

Joe was a little worried after the call from Sam Marconi. He knew that sooner or later something like this might happen. But, he was surprised that it happened so soon. There were more leaks in the media and in government than he cared to think about. Mary and Jack, in a limousine, with two well-trained Coast Guardsmen as security, were still followed by the media and then three suspicious guys followed them in a Ford Focus. They could have been following the media car but he wouldn't take any chances.

Joe also knew whom he could call and knew that he could get information ASAP. The information could be in English, Spanish or even Russian. He spoke both Spanish and Russian fluently. If it were south Florida, gangs connected to Mexican cartels or even the ever-growing Russian underworld, now firmly established in the greater Miami area, he would have the information at his fingertips and didn't need any translation. He wasn't up to speed on white supremacy groups. He'd been chasing international terrorists for years so these internal groups weren't a surprise to him but the growth of these organizations were frightening and a big surprise to Joe Traynor.

Joe did a quick search on the internet and to his surprise, Florida was a hotbed of white supremacy groups. A recent study showed that the state of Florida has the second highest number of hate groups in the country. Joe worked with the Southern Poverty Law Center on previous occasions that involved drug-related crimes. He was surprised that the Center had identified sixty-eight known hate groups residing in the state of Florida. Forty-seven of those hate groups are white supremacy in nature. The others were black and Latino groups with their own ideology. They all needed money to continue their operations and what better way to get funded than to identify one or two people who were rich.

In this case Joe thought that combined, Jack and Mary, would have a big target on their backs. He didn't want to bring this up but he knew that he would have to if they headed back to Florida and the Keys to start funding projects. Hopefully, they'd be safe up north but you never knew, until you did. If and when, Mary and Jack came back to set up Mary's new foundation, they'd probably need even more security since the world would know that they were dual winners of the lottery and were worth a fortune. These hate groups didn't care that the fortune was going to be spent to help others, they wanted the money to build their own status and war chest.

On the way home, Joe called Paul Philips right before Paul was heading out the door from work. He told him the story and Paul was simply amazed by Joe's friends' good fortune. He too was a little worried when he heard about the second car following the media car. When he got the profiles of those in the Ford Focus after Joe emailed him and texted, he became more concerned. Paul pulled over and took down the information. The email included a partial Florida license plate that Joe thought was from Dade County, right in the heart of Miami. The partial plate number was "ZGR, ida, and de". Joe said this was the right side of the plate, from the rear end of the car, spotted by

Pete. Pete took down the info as they were driving past him and he only had a split second to see the plate but his training kicked in and he got what he could. The front didn't have any plate. Florida didn't require front plates and they were lucky that the media car had a vanity plate on the front bumper with the call letters for the television station, WLTV or he wouldn't have gotten the rear plate under the conditions looking back.

Paul said he would see what he could do in the morning. He also said he would call a friend of his who worked for the television station and find out who was shadowing the limousine when they were heading to the airport. Specifically, he wanted to know if the Ford Focus was following the media car or the limousine or if they didn't have a clue. Paul told Joe that they probably didn't have a clue.

Joe made a few more phone calls just to keep his friends informed in case something happened down the road. When Joe was in Albany and out of the service, his friends still came through and they were able to take down the Mexican Mafia that had infiltrated his local nonprofit. He called Mark Silva first, his best friend ever. They started together in the Coast Guard and both wound up together as Lieutenants, achieving the same rank after another successful intervention. He also put Jack Forest on the same call. Jack also started his service in boot camp with both Mark and Joe. He was now up in Virginia and Director of a well-classified intelligence wing of the Coast Guard and was considered a computer genius by everyone he encountered.

"Hey Mark. Hey Jack. How are you guys," he asked.

"What do you want?" said Mark.

"Yeah, Hi Mark. Joe, what do you want? You only call when you need something," Jack said.

"That's not true," said Joe. "It's mostly not true,

anyway," he said. You could see the smirk through the cell phone. "You guys got a minute?" Joe asked.

"Yes, sir. I do," said Mark.

"Me too," said Jack.

Joe went through Jack and Mary's great adventure, as he called it, from beginning to end, ending with Mary's newest lottery winnings. He went on as to how they were giving most of it away to needy organizations and projects. He then brought up the fact that he thought that the media car, on the way to the Fort Lauderdale International Airport, was being followed by someone or some people with not so good intentions. He told Mark and Jack that he called Paul first to get the FBI rolling.

They knew that Joe has great influence over a lot of areas and that he carried multiple IDs for the Coast Guard, the FBI and Homeland Security. Both the Coast Guard and the FBI were under the Office of Homeland Security. Other operational and support components of Homeland Security also included U.S. Citizenship and Immigration, United States Customs and Border Patrol, Cyber Security and Infrastructure Security, FEMA, U.S. Secret Service, TSA and other notable sub-agencies. Joe has dealt with most of these offices during his Coast Guard tenure. Just because he was now on the fast track to the Coast Guard Academy didn't mean that he wasn't called on every now and then for his expertise and knowledge especially in the areas concerning the Hispanic and Russian communities throughout the region and up to headquarters in Washington D.C. where he was reporting on a secondary basis, right after reporting to his Rear Admiral in Miami.

Mark and Jack also knew that whatever they needed Joe was always there for them. They wrote down the information and told Joe they'd start on it immediately. Joe hung up, grateful for good friends. He walked into the door of his home in Tavernier and was greeted by Bella first with a big hug, by Julie, and then by Tillie who'd stopped by for a visit. His head was spinning and need a quick time out. He grabbed a beer from the refrigerator and walked to the bedroom where he would take a shower and change. He would have a long discussion with both Julie and Tillie since both were being asked to be on Mary's new south Florida and Florida Keys Board of Directors under the Teresa Trust Fund South. He didn't want to unnecessarily alarm them as to what they discovered but he also wanted them to be aware of their circumstances at all times.

As soon as Joe walked to the dinner table, Pete Williams called him. "Joe? Hi. It's Pete Williams. Do you have a minute?"

"Hi Pete, my good old boy from Alabama. What's up?" Joe asked.

"Don't start with that Alabama crap," Pete said. "It was hard enough in the Coast Guard coming from Alabama. Nobody knows we're actually on the Gulf of Mexico for about twenty miles. It's known as the Redneck Riviera, Joe."

"I know. I've heard this before," said Joe.

"I completely forgot that when I was giving my description of the car, the Ford Focus, trying to remember the partial license plate, I forgot that on the way toward me, I had my phone camera taking a bunch of shots just in case. I just checked and I have a picture of the front of the car and a clear picture of the two guys in the front. It's from thirty or forty feet but maybe you can do something with it. I forgot all about it trying to get the license plate number. Do you want me to send it to you?"

"That's great, Pete. Of course send it. Maybe we can do some facial recognition from it. You know Jack Forest. You met him when he was down here and we went out for beers. He can do almost anything with a computer. If he can match the faces in the car to something we have in the system, we're much better off. Just having a car doesn't mean much. They can say whatever they want but with a picture, we might get more information. Send it, Pete. Thanks," said Joe.

Pete sent the video immediately and Joe forwarded it to Paul, Mark and Jack as a follow up. He then sat down to eat and talk to Julie and Tillie.

Around 9:00 p.m., Jack Forest called Joe. "Joe, I might have something. I stayed late when no one else was around. I am the Director but I don't want anyone else looking over my shoulder," he said.

"What did you find, Jack?" Joe said.

"There were a ton of Ford Focuses but Pete thought it was a 2017 because they changed the back taillights and grill slightly in the front."

Joe remembered originally that Pete said that he used to own a Focus like the rest of the world and was well aware of the design.

Jack Forest then said, "I used Pete's video and compared it online to Kelly Blue Book Ford Focus and the car is definitely a 2017 at least. I don't know if they changed it for 2018 until now. However, they stopped making them during that time in May of 2018 to be precise. So, I looked for 2017 and 2018 license plates for a Ford Focus using that partial plate number. The "ZGR, ida, and de" is actually 982 ZGR, FLORIDA, at the top of the plate and DADE at the bottom, middle of the plate. It is very clear that this was the only match for a 2017 Ford Focus in Florida," he said.

"Joe, it's registered to a Kevin Strom. He lives at 6700 S.W. 7th Street, Apartment. 4, Miami, Florida. I then went to the Florida Department of Highway Safety and Motor Vehicles and got a picture of his license. By the way, he has two DWI convictions in the last three years, so that might tell you something. He's born in 1979, making him forty-two years old. Then, I took his driver's license picture and placed it next to Pete's picture of the driver and passenger in the car and ran it through my facial recognition software. I had to refocus the video and get a still picture for the comparison. Guess what, Joe. They matched at an 88% probability rate. If I played with the pictures, I could get it higher but why bother. This is our guy," said Jack.

"Jack, that's unbelievable," said Joe. "Thank you. Thank you. I'm passing it on to everyone at this point. I'm not sure what to do with the information as of yet," he said.

Joe immediately texted Paul and told him that he was sending him confirmation from Jack Forest as to the Ford Focus and identity of the driver. He asked Paul to check his various FBI sites to see if he was affiliated with any hate groups. He said that Jack would also see if he could identify the other guy in the passenger seat. There was no way he could identify the man in the back seat, other than all three had shaven heads. Paul said he would still contact his friend at the television station to see if they thought they were being followed. He would call in the morning. Joe sent the same text to Mark Silva and would wait before contacting Mary Evans and Jack Manning. Joe wanted to be certain as to who was tailing whom.

Joe was on his way back to the college when Paul Philips called. Paul told him that he talked to his friend at the television station and he knew right away who the investigative reporters were, since he'd assigned them the task of developing a story for the new lottery winner. He asked them if they thought they were being followed. They said they never suspected a thing and that made them nervous. He knew that on several occasions reporters were followed by people with ill will. That happened to them before. Paul gave them the information about the Ford Focus and told them to keep an eye out for the car. He also told the other reporters to keep their eyes out as well. He owed Paul for a few heads up over the years and wanted to reciprocate, not to jeopardize a story. That would never happen. But, Paul gave him a heads up and he would do the same. Joe thanked him and said he would be in touch. Paul said he would see if Kevin Strom's name came up anywhere in the system. He would let Joe know.

Joe called Mary and Jack and let them both know what the situation was when they were heading to the airport. Joe said there was no definitive answer as of yet but he would stay on top of it. He wished them a Happy Thanksgiving. Joe would be at the college today but headed home tonight for a long Thanksgiving weekend. He loved Thanksgiving with all the trimmings. It was his favorite holiday back in Troy. The weather was getting colder with maybe a hint of snow in the air. Football was on the television, two games back-to-back, watching with his father and brother. Just pigging out for the day. No expectations of presents. When he had his fill, he could head home to downtown Troy and sleep.

It was much different now with Julie and Bella, and Tillie. Many in south Florida and in the Keys, were of Cuban heritage and would have a pig roast with all ethnic specialties. Joe was going to see what he could do for his and Julie's adopted 100% Cuban daughter so she would know tradition. Mark Silva was no help even though he was Mexican and his wife was Irish. They'd be coming. One of his neighbors, a longtime resident of Tavernier, told him he would help him with the basics and he would supply the pig roast. Life was just getting better and better he thought. Hopefully this little problem with Mary and Jack wouldn't get out of hand.

Chapter 16

Karen Steele and Sam Ryan were right on time Tuesday morning. Jack and Mary were up by 8:00 a.m. and were well rested. They arrived at 9:30 a.m. as expected. Mary had breakfast ready for Karen and Sam and the coffee was hot.

"Hi Karen. Hi Sam. How are you? It seems like forever since we saw you last. It's been only a month we've been away but seems like forever," said Mary.

"Hi Jack. Hi Mary, same here," said Karen. "I'll bet the honeymoon was fun but now you're back and you have a little more funding we understand," Karen laughed.

"A little more," she said. "You know millions can only last a little while and then you start counting your pennies," said Jack. He smiled.

"Sure, Jack," said Sam Ryan. "You'll probably be unable to feed your polo ponies as Ralph Kramden once said in the *Honeymooners.*" Then added, "You were honeymooners, right?"

"You're on a roll, Sam," said Jack. Sam smiled and sat down to eat. "Looks good, Mary. Another fine domestic quality has arisen since you married Jack," he added.

Karen said, "Sam, don't put your foot in your mouth any further. You won't be able to eat."

"Got it," Sam said and continued eating.

Mary then got serious. "All kidding aside, we have great news but it's opened up a big can of worms. We're now on the radar screen for those who want to take advantage or harm us for money. Joe Traynor, John's son and Pete's brother, as you know is a bigwig down with the Coast Guard in Florida, stationed at The College of the Florida Keys. He and his friends have identified someone who may have bad intentions following us to the airport. His Coast Guard friends and the local FBI Director are now investigating if they were after us or after the television station car that was following us. Joe said he'd get back to us when he heard anything of value. In the meantime, we believe we're safe here with John and Fred staying with us but when the news hits locally, it may get bad."

"Wow. We never thought of that," said Karen. "What can we do?"

"Nothing yet, especially until we hear from Joe," Mary said. "However, we need to update our goals and objectives for the Center and see if we can add anything from Jack or my various trust funds and start expanding as soon as we can. I'd like to give away my $155.0 million split between here and Florida within the next five years. I really don't think I have Jack's stamina or patience to spread everything out over ten years. I know he's already allocated at least half of his $50.0 million Evangeline Trust Fund to the Evangeline Career Center so that's yours to use. He has a lot left over for graduates to start businesses as seed money, but that will take time. Jack originally gave me $15.0 million to use as I wanted but I'll give that back to the Evangeline Trust Fund because I have more than enough. No matter, it's tax free regardless of which trust fund it is."

"That's extremely generous," said Sam. "I can't believe how fortunate we are to have you here, right Karen?"

"Yes, I totally agree. Let's figure out how we can move

up projects so that you too can actually have a life together. You've been married for a month for God's sake," Karen said. "By the way, we're set up for our Thanksgiving dinner event. You're coming right? We need a turkey slicer, Jack. We hear you're the best at it."

Since it opened, the Evangeline Career Center and the Troy Community Council, fully supported and funded by Jack Manning, has sponsored a large Thanksgiving dinner event at the Center for former graduates, their families and current graduates and their families. Everyone looked forward to it. Several hundred people have shown up both years that the event was held. It was a great time, a time for bonding for students and families and all the employees. Everyone helped out cooking, doing the dishes, setting up, preparing the turkeys and baking all kinds of desserts. This event was not catered and everyone appreciated the fact that it brought everyone together. Jack's son, Mark and his girlfriend, Cara Brooks, his daughter, Debbie, Louis and Addie Freeman, their eighty-year-old friends and benefactors and best man for the wedding, and all those who attended their wedding only a short time ago, would be there. Thank God for Karen and the crew. She pitched in just like everyone else and paid for everything out of the budget that was planned. She was the one who suggested it the day they met and Jack begged her to take over. He was grateful that she accepted.

It was around noon when Karen and Sam left. It was a good meeting. There wasn't much they could do until after Thanksgiving weekend. Kristen and her team were busy with paperwork and taking charge of millions of dollars and planning on investments that were prudent based on the future plans. Jane Swanson and Sidney Clyne and his team of lawyers down in Miami were doing the same. Mary wasn't aware of the situation with Jane until Kristen let it slip after talking with her about their mutual work on behalf of Mary, that Jane's husband, Nick Snyder, owed almost a half million dollars in education loans to become a neurosurgeon. It took its toll on both of them, especially after buying a home in Miami.

Christmas was coming up and what better way to celebrate than to reward those who've been working the hardest on their behalf. Mary was generous to a fault. She could care less about the money she now possessed. If she couldn't help those who've bent over backward for her, what good was it? She remembered that the New Testament quotes "It is easier for a camel to go through the eye of a needle than for a rich man to enter the kingdom of God".

Jack said they should pay off Nick's loans and set up a trust fund for Kristen's kids college fund. It was about a half a million dollars for Nick and the same for the education fund for Kristen's kids. Jack immediately wrote her a check from his own money, not the trust fund, and Mary would do the same. They'd get two bank checks made out to Kristen and Jane for five hundred thousand dollars each, to specifically take care of the education needs for Kristen's kids and to pay off Nick's student loans. They'd write a joint letter and place each check with the letter into the Christmas card. They'd FEDEX both cards, next day delivery, to make sure the envelopes would remain unopened when the cards arrived by Christmas.

Jack and Mary had a glow about them. If they couldn't help their friends whom could they help? They already took care of Joe and Skip's families so this was as appropriate. They also thought about Karen Steele and Sam Ryan. Sam did his job but Karen went out of her way to make the Center a success. Jack would update her long-term contract and add thirty thousand dollars a year to her paycheck. That would help her when she retired. She was fifty-five years old when she started at the Center and not that far away from retirement. Sam was a very competent accountant and Jack would reward him with a ten thousand dollar increase in pay as well.

He also thought about the one hundred plus students at the Center. They were working their tails off and should be rewarded. He would ask Karen to cut checks for $500.00 each for every student in good standing. That meant those that were always on time, no days off, and on the path to getting their training and degrees. Slackers wouldn't be tolerated. There were always a few of those. It was what life offered. When the students started, Karen set up a savings account for each student at Key Bank, around the corner. There were no banks, stores, grocery stores or gas stations in the North Central part of Troy. It was the gut. Through Jack's intervention and sheer will and no rent payment for two years, he made deals that no one could refuse. He subsidized this entire economic plan to bring back business to this underserved area. As soon as Key Bank opened their office a block away, Jack transferred several million dollars to their office and set up over one hundred savings accounts. Giving a student a check when that student has no bank accounts is worthless at best. No one could cash a check without an account and identification. Every week, a student would have one hundred dollars deposited to their savings by the Evangeline Career Center from Jack's Evangeline Trust Fund. They worked for it and received a stipend for training not for working to keep their employee books clear. This stipend agreement with each student was suggested by Kristen, the tax attorney, and Sam Ryan, who was a master at finance.

CHAPTER 17

It was the day before Thanksgiving and Joe Traynor got a call from Paul Philips who was sitting at his desk with a few of his FBI subordinates. "Hi, Joe. Got a minute?" He asked.

"Sure do. Happy Thanksgiving," he said.

"I'm sitting here with a few of my staff that you know. I have some news. Not bad, not good, but something you need to keep an eye on," said Paul.

"Go ahead. I'm all ears, like Ross Perot." He added, "A little before my time but what the hell."

"Ross Perot? He had big ears, right?" said Paul.

"Yes, Paul. Hence the joke." Joe laughed.

"Okay. Enough frivolity. Here's the scoop. We checked up on our friend, Kevin Strom. No one at the station knew they were being followed but they had been followed a lot and now they're nervous. My friend, the station manager, as a news scoop, sent them to follow Mary to the airport, even though they got lost and didn't figure out where they went. So much for investigative reporters doing any meaningful investigations. Our friend, Kevin Strom, is forty-two years old, born in 1979 and lives at the address you provided. He's also a member of a Mississippi hate group called the Nationalist Alliance. The group is now headquartered in the Hialeah area of Miami, right around where Mary had her announced winning ticket. Thanks to Jack Forest, we got the other picture as well and identified him as Luther Pierce, same organization. We now speculate because they're in our system, and there are three of them, the other being a guy named Richard Butler. All three are card-carrying members of the Nationalist Alliance. We will now put some tracking on these guys. They've broken no laws following your friends. They didn't do anything but follow them. All three have minor records associated with rallies and fighting. Nothing jumps out and none have a record more than a misdemeanor. However, one more DUI and Kevin Strom will be going to jail on a felony, if it's within the next three years. Sorry I can't tell you more," he said.

"I'd rather know the devil I'm dealing with than not know," said Jack. "Thanks and if you gather any more information on the three, please let me know. We'll make sure that Mary and Jack are well protected when down here. I don't think much will happen to them over the winter in Troy, New York. From what I'm gathering, they've a lot to do over the winter to set up all their trust funds and get ready to come back to Key West. Mary was thinking about late January and Jack would come in February. Thanks everyone," said Joe and with that he hung up.

Joe let the Lennons know what was going on. He called his boss, Morgan, at the college and Julie and then called Jack and Mary and let them know the status of what he learned. He called Sam and Pete and told them to start recruiting more security team members along with themselves for late January and February for when they might be back. He'd let them know.

Jack said that Mary had planned to come back to Key West in late January after all her trust funds were set up and had the boards of directors and advisors formalized. Jack had to stay back home to recruit a new one hundred students for the upcoming class at the Evangeline Career Center. It wasn't like recruiting for Hudson Valley Community College where every freshman was eighteen years old and starting college for the first time. His recruits were mostly considered failures by standard education norms. They've been out of school for a year or two, dropouts mostly. They had to be acclimated to an everyday schedule and a hundred dollars a week stipend was not a great incentive. What was the incentive was that it led to a job with National Grid, Spectrum, AT&T, Verizon, local police and fire departments that have EMT units, and building contractors who need journeymen construction workers and new cutting edge technology based energy saving installers. These jobs paid in excess of fifty thousand dollars a year with the new GED/TASC based diplomas with certification by the state of New York. Troy was also the home of Rensselaer Polytechnic Institute which did training for computer coding, with over 2,500 jobs unfilled within the region. The Capital Region of New York State was known as Tech Valley but didn't have enough essential tech workers for the jobs needed. After six months training, students could start at $20.00 an hour and more depending on certifications and competency. Jack had a big recruiting job to do. That's why he was offering young men and women, who completed the training, a huge discount on all the homes they had been remodeling within the North Central section of Troy. Right now, he had a waiting list but that could end if anything happened to put a damper in his plans or in the funds he allocated for the projects under way. Only time would tell, he thought.

During the Thanksgiving dinner at the Center, Jack went from table to table to make sure everyone ate well and had enough food to take home with them for later. The party went great but was exhausting. All the mental gymnastics caught up with both Mary and Jack. Mary had a road map for what she wanted to do. Jack had to do it from the seat of his pants. As he knew though, Mary was so much quicker on the uptake than he was and she'd be on top of things from the start since she was a teacher and a planner. She knew what she wanted and was pretty sure how to accomplish her goals. It wasn't the money. She relied on everyone and let each do their own part so they too could feel successful. That's what teaching was all about she explained.

Mary reminded Jack that they should make sure that the bonuses and gifts they planned on giving were sent out with a handwritten note by both of them not only to Kristen, Jane, Karen and Sam but to the hundred students that would be receiving $500.00 Christmas gifts. Mary and Jack planned to give the gifts to the students at lunch at the Center about two weeks before Christmas. That would give the students time to buy unexpected presents for their families. Mary bought the cards and Jack wrote out the checks. They'd both place a note in each card. Originally, Jack was just going to simply add the gifts to the students' savings but they both thought that a gift given by them in person would be more meaningful. Mary wrote a note to each student and mentioned each family member. Jack did the same. That's how close the students were to them.

They had a luncheon ready on a Wednesday at noon and the students were delighted to have a nice lunch but their minds weren't on training at this time. Their minds were on the holidays. No matter what anyone had, good or bad, the holidays were always the highlight of the year. At the last moment, Mary mentioned that they forgot the teachers and maintenance staff and the office staff so they cut more checks and Mary got more cards ready.

Jack was thinking of being Santa but Mary told him that was the last thing they needed. Right at the end of the luncheon, Mary made a short speech thanking everyone for all they've done to make the Center a success and Jack only said thank you. Jack went to each table and handed a personalized card to each student, to each teacher and each staff member. They were all in shock. The students and staff thanked Mary and Jack profusely and it made them blush. Jack asked Karen to see them at the end of the luncheon and asked Sam to stay around. After everyone cleaned up and got back to class and their offices, Mary and Jack went to Karen's office first.

"Mary and Jack, I didn't see that coming," she said. That was a wonderful gesture on your part. You know they still don't know about your winning lottery ticket, Mary," Karen said.

"That's great," she said. "Let's keep it that way. By the way, Jack and I have something to share with you. Jack do you want to do the honors?" she asked.

"Sure," said Jack. Karen, on behalf of both of us, we're immediately adding thirty thousand dollars a year to your salary. We want you to be comfortable here and view us as partners not as bosses or anything else. You need to save for your retirement so we're adding that clause to your ten-year contract. Hopefully, that will make a difference," said Jack.

Mary said, "Karen, we both agree. This place wouldn't function without you. So that's a token of our appreciation."

"I don't know what to say," said Karen. "Thank you. You made my Christmas and my retirement. You people are the best," as she gave Jack and Mary a hug. She wiped away a tiny tear in her eye. Karen never cried, never.

Jack went alone to see Sam Ryan. He told him the same thing and added ten thousand dollars to his pay. He wanted it to be permanent and not a bonus, which could be taken away from year to year. Sam was flustered. He said no one has ever showed him the kindness that Mary and Jack and Karen have shown him since he's been here. He didn't know what to say either.

It was about ten days before Christmas when Mary and Jack sent the FEDEX checks to Kristen at her office in Albany and to Jane, down in Miami. Obviously, Kristen got hers immediately. It would take a full day for Jane's package to arrive.

"Mary, Hi. It's Kristen," she said. "I don't know what to say. A package arrived today at my office. It was from you two. I opened the card and started to cry," she said. "I don't know what to say. I called my husband and told him what you did for our three children and he was beside himself. He said that you two must be very, very good friends." She started to choke up.

"Kristen, without you and your law firm, we'd have been in a very different place. Of course with Jack's three hundred million dollar winning ticket, we could have figured it out but you did that for us. This isn't about that. You have been my friend for twenty-five years, at least, as we were in the convent together. You made a new life. I made a new life. I want you to be as happy as I am. I hope this helps. Jack, it's Kristen. Say Hi," Mary said.

"Hi, Kristen. We sent it early so you could get everything set up before the holidays. You need to sign a bunch of paperwork. Your staff pulled this off without your knowledge," he said. "Have a great Christmas."

With that Kristen said goodbye and went looking for her staff who pulled off making a trust fund for a half million dollars for her children. On top of that, from a pure business transaction, Jack and Mary were adding almost two million dollars a year to her firm's fees, establishing her as the firm's rainmaker.

It was the following day and the phone rang at Old Plank Road. Mary didn't recognize the number but knew it was from a Florida area code. "Hello," she said.

"Mary? Hi," said Jane Swanson. "I was trying my very best to get through this phone call and it was all I could do to call you. Why in God's name did you and Jack do what you did for me and my husband, Nick? I know you won the lottery both of you, but why do this for us? What've we done to deserve this? Nick and I are flabbergasted," she said.

Mary said, "Jane, let's start with what the hell did Jack and I do to deserve to win two lotteries for over eight hundred million dollars combined? Nothing. That's what we did. A little bird told us of your situation with Nick and his huge student loans to be a doctor. Why should you be burdened while we have plenty? You're to use the money to pay off his student loan and if there's any left over, pay down on your mortgage. We want you around for a long time," she said.

"I can't believe this. Nick just shook his head like we won the lottery. We now know how you feel. Trust us that when Nick starts to make money in a few years, we will pay it forward just like you did. Thank you Mary and please thank Jack," Jane said.

"Jack's not here right now but I'm sure he's very happy that you are pleased. I'll be down in late January if everything goes well up here and Jack will come in February. By the way I also need to tell you about what happened to us on the last day we were down there in your limousine heading to the airport. Your friend, Joe Traynor, is helping us out with it. Let me tell you what's going on."

She did. After explaining the problems, they said Merry Christmas and hung up. Mary told her not to tell anyone at her law office except for Sidney Clyne, her boss and good friend. She did ask her to check with her limousine driver, Jeff Sheldon, to see if he heard anything more about the last trip or if he had been followed lately. Jeff seemed to be very much on top of things. Not only had Kristen mentioned that but both Jack and Mary noticed it as well. They were sure that if anything popped up, he would definitely let them know. He did say that he'd noticed the media car following them but never noticed the Ford Focus. He said he would definitely keep his eye out for anything that looked out of place. The next time Mary and Jack flew in to Miami, he could use his own car to pick them up so it wouldn't look so conspicuous. The first time Kristen flew in, she didn't know him nor did Jack and Mary. Now they did and would recognize him immediately without him holding up a card at the baggage handling area.

CHAPTER 18

Jack told Mary that he's meeting his son for lunch in Albany and wanted to know if she wanted to go. She said it would be best if Jack went alone and to tell Mark about her lottery winnings. Debbie had promised not to say a word and she didn't. She was getting much better at keeping her word to her father after a year or so of being on the outs with him. From the beginning, Mark knew that it wasn't his father's fault for the divorce but in fact it was his mother's infidelity that caused the breakup. He knew that Jack was partially responsible because he spent so much time with his work but that was no excuse. Mark actually told his father that if his ex-wife, Maureen, didn't toss him out that he wouldn't be a millionaire now. He said she did him a favor and it cost him nothing. Jack quietly advised him that it almost cost him his life because he was so down and out before hitting the lottery. He said if it wasn't for Mary, he probably wouldn't be around anymore. Mark knew that as well. He has nothing but respect for Mary he told his father the last time they saw each other at the wedding.

Mark also mentioned that he was going to propose to his girlfriend, Cara Brooks, in a few weeks. She kind of knew but was waiting for Mark to pop the question. They had been living together since he graduated from the University at Albany last spring. Cara was a knockout and appeared to be nobody's fool. She'd just graduated from the University at Albany with an MBA at the same time that Mark was getting his BS in Accounting. She was two years older than Mark but Jack thought that's what Mark probably needed.

Lunch went well. They went to Jack's Oyster House in downtown Albany, at the foot of State Street. They talked and Jack let him know that Mary also hit the lottery for four hundred and eighty million dollars in Key West about a month ago. He told him that he wanted to wait to tell him in person and Mary wanted Jack to tell him first and then she'd follow up. Mary seemed closer now to Debbie and was just getting to know Mark. She watched him grow up while employed by the Council in Troy along with Jack for ten years. It wasn't the same though that he was now a grown man, a college graduate, with a good job, and about to be married. Jack told him that upon his marriage, he would receive enough for a down payment on a house and fifty thousand dollars a year that would be coming out of a two million dollar bequest when he turned thirty-five. Jack quite clearly told him that he wanted him to be his own man but everyone needs a boost every now and then. Mark was very pleased with the bequest and told him so. He asked his father if he should say anything to his mother and Jack said that Debbie would be speaking to her this week on their behalf. Mark said that it was okay with him. He really didn't know how to act around his mother anymore. He loved her as his mother but had very little respect for the position she had put herself and her family in with her live-in boyfriend. He said she was responsible for her own mistakes and he wouldn't intercede.

Later in the week, Debbie stopped by her mother's bank where she was the branch manager in Lansingburgh to say hello and let her know about Mary's good fortune. Maureen seemed to have aged substantially over the last few years, especially still living with her boyfriend, Chuck Falcone. Debbie entered her office as she was hanging up the phone to what appeared to be a call from Chuck.

"Hi, mom," Debbie said.

"To what do I owe this honor?" she asked not so pleasantly. She added, "How are things at your father's place?"

Debbie told her everything was fine. She was getting her masters and had support from her father until she finished and then she'd be on her own. She didn't mention that he also gave her fifty thousand dollars along with her brother a while ago and bought her a car. It took her a very long time to see the good that her father and Mary were doing with Jack's winnings but it didn't take her long to see how her mother was doing. All she did was fight with Chuck. The jealousy about Jack's hitting the lottery and Maureen getting nothing wasn't a happy event for Maureen, especially with Chuck demanding that she get millions from Jack. He had said that after all, they were married for twenty-five years and had two children. The least he could do was give her a check for a few million dollars. At least Maureen mentioned to Chuck that the reason she wasn't getting anything was because she was cheating on Jack with Chuck for quite some time. It came out later and Jack was none too happy. Chuck tried to take it upon himself to do something about it and wound up in jail. Maureen refused to bail him out but eventually he served his short sentence and he was back with her. She had nothing else going for her.

Debbie said to her mother, "Eventually it will come out. Mary hit the national lottery while they were down in Key West on their honeymoon. She won four hundred and eighty million dollars and would wind up with a lot more than my father did."

"What? When? How?" Maureen was bent out of shape. "How much?" she asked.

"A lot," said Debbie. "Does it really matter how much, Mom?" She just wanted to see her reaction.

"So together, they won maybe eight hundred million dollars?" Maureen asked.

"Sounds about right but my father has already pledged most of it to the Evangeline Trust Fund for the Career Center in Troy and rehabilitation in the city itself. He's also allocated money directly to student graduates to start businesses. I was also part of group of ordinary people who funded a few million dollars to individuals who were destitute or needed medical assistance. He still had a shitload left but it's all in municipal bonds," Debbie said.

"Why did you stop by? To gloat?" asked Maureen.

"No mother. Believe it or not, you're still my mother and I love you for being my mother. I don't love the rest of the package as you might surmise," she said.

"Well thanks for letting me know. Who else knows? Anybody? I haven't heard a thing," she said.

"I'm not sure. They've a ton of lawyers, accountants and staff who needed to be updated. Other than that, I'm not certain." With that, she got up and said goodbye to her mother. She didn't know what else to say. She could only imagine that if her mother was unhappy what she would do, especially after talking to Chuck.

That night, after talking to Chuck, they were both beyond jealous. They were really bent out of shape. Not only did she wind up with nothing, Chuck went to jail for several months for assault and battery on Jack after demanding he give his ex-wife a ton of money. If she couldn't get anything, she bet her children probably would. Would they support her? She really didn't know. She knew neither Mark nor Debbie were on her side. Why did this have to happen? It was late, around 11:00 p.m. Chuck was out drinking with his buddies. At least that's what he told Maureen. She called the *Times Union* to ask if anyone knew anything about the recent lottery winner, Mary Evans. The night crew said they'd leave a message for the regular staff in the morning. I'll leave a message. "Does anyone know that Jack Manning, lottery winner two years ago and Mary Evans, most recent lottery winner in Florida, are a married couple, now sharing eight hundred million dollars in winnings. Do you think this might produce some headlines?" She thought, *"Let's see how this plays out. I'll just make life hell for them."*

CHAPTER 19

Debbie told her father and Mary that she had stopped by the bank to visit her mother to tell her about Mary's good fortune. She thought her mother didn't handle the news very well. She said she was kind of belligerent toward her. Debbie said she'd only stayed a few minutes after telling Maureen the news because it was quite clear her mother was not happy. She told her father to expect a call from her mother after she spoke to Chuck, her live-in boyfriend. Originally, Maureen was to get a large amount of money from Jack's lottery winnings upon her retirement, because as he said, she's the mother of his two children and they were married for twenty-five years. If Chuck Falcone hadn't demanded a large settlement for Maureen from Jack, she'd have been sitting pretty in only a few short years. Maureen listened to Chuck and lost it all. Jack was still thinking of giving her something when she retired but not to the amount he was originally contemplating.

Jack would never have even considered getting an annulment from Maureen if it weren't for Mary. It was so he could remarry in the eyes of the church but it didn't really wipe away all the time he spent together with Maureen. She did hurt him deeply but if it didn't happen, he would never have been living in Lansingburgh, working for Stewarts on the late shift. He never would have used his meager earnings to buy a lottery ticket and split nine hundred and ninety million dollars with two other winners. He really couldn't credit Maureen for his success. Maybe his success and Mary's success was a gift from heaven after what happened to both of them losing the jobs that they loved and he being cast away after twenty-five years. He never saw it coming. Mary suspected that Jack's private life was falling apart and she never said anything to him about it. She never wanted to compromise their longtime friendship. However, there was no mistaking the fact that she liked Jack from the day he hired her, right from the convent. She knew he was a good man and that's all that really mattered. She was totally surprised by his complete and utter downfall but watched him pick himself up and try, try again and again. She never thought his hitting the lottery was just a stroke of luck. She always believed that good things happen to good people. She hoped that her winning the lottery was also a sign of good things happening to good people as well.

Debbie called Jack the next day and told him that the *Times Union* ran a huge article on both him and Mary and how they hit the lottery two separate times for the third largest amount in history, when combined. Debbie told her father the timing with telling her mother was very suspect. She wondered if she told anyone about Mary and Jack both hitting the lottery out of spite. It would be hard to prove unless Maureen said something down the line.

As soon as Jack got up, he shook Mary awake and told her the news. They got up and made coffee. John and Fred had already walked the property from 7:00 a.m. and on. When they came in for breakfast, John informed them that there were several trucks and cars parked near the entrance to their property.

Old Plank Road was very narrow and had no paved sides for parking so they were simply parked in the road near their entrance. Because they were on the mountain, about halfway up, both sides of the road had steep gullies so that mountain top rainwater could make it to the bottom of the road where the City of Troy began. Drains opened up to catch basins where Route 142 met Old Plank Road. John mentioned that he called the state troopers earlier at the Brunswick station and asked them to drive by and ask the people to not block the road.

As a retired FBI agent, John Jefferson got an immediate response. Through the kitchen window, Jack and Mary could see the trooper car arriving with the thump, thump, thump sound and the flashing lights. They could hear a loud announcement coming from the police car to please move the vehicles from the roadway. There was no parking allowed on Old Plank Road. Once the cars were moved, Jack and Mary knew that both John and Fred could bring them down to the Center where they had scheduled a strategy meeting for the next campaign steps. They quickly showered and dressed, ate a muffin each, and headed to the cars parked by the side door. As soon as the vehicles were moved, John waived to the trooper and headed out the driveway with Fred following. There was no sense for Mary or Jack to be driving. It would only add to the confusion and lessen the security if there was a problem. They both felt like captives being moved from one location to another. It got old quickly and they both knew that this would be a way of life for some time.

As soon as Jack and Mary arrived at the Career Center, it was obvious that the news of Mary's winning the lottery spread like wildfire. A bunch of the students waved to Mary and gave the thumbs up with the obvious meaning. Mary waved and mouthed "hello" to everyone as they walked through the front door of the Center. Karen was standing there holding the door open and said to Mary, "How are you holding up, Mary?"

"I'm fine. Jack's a little shook but we knew this was coming. We think a little bird told the *Times Union* about our fate, but we'll have to come up with a response before the whole world is at our door up on Old Plank Road and even here at the Center," she said.

They headed up the stairs toward the boardroom where they'd meet with Karen and Sam Ryan and some of the key staff to hammer out a strategy for the long term and how to handle the potential explosion of news that was right in front of them. They'd spent the rest of the morning, had lunch, and finished up around 5:00 p.m. before heading home.

Debbie had purchased enough food and supplies to last for the next two weeks so they wouldn't have to go out in public other than to attend Christmas Mass at St. Augustine's Church in Lansingburgh. The midnight Mass was a little late for them to drive up the old country road, especially with snow starting to fall. They'd attend the 10:30 Mass on Christmas Day and put the twenty-four pound turkey in the oven to reheat for a 4:00 p.m. dinner. Mary would start the cooking on Christmas Eve just to make sure everything came out hot at the same time. Heating up was a lot better than starting from scratch.

Jack and Mary invited Mark and his girlfriend, Cara, Debbie and a date, the Freemans, and Mary's two ex-nun roommates who still lived next to Catholic High. Karen and Sam from the Center and Kristen and her family were invited with their families but they already had other family obligations. This was Jack and Mary's first official Christmas as newlyweds. Debbie surprised Jack with the news that she was bringing someone, a date, to the dinner. Debbie's previous dating consisted of two guys for about a month long in both cases as he recalled. She never brought a date home so this might be something special, thought Jack.

The meeting ended right at 5:00 p.m. They came together with a plan. Mary and Kristen would address the *Times Union* and then afterward, other media outlets after Christmas. Kristen was charged with setting up the announcement at the attorney's office in Albany to take away crowds at the Center and at their home. Kristen called the *Times Union* and got the Editor and set up the meeting. They had the exclusive at first and then soon afterward, after they published the meeting, Mary and Jack would release the announcement to the rest of the media. They'd be a little specific based on what was already done but not so specific as to tie their hands for future projects.

During the meeting, Jack discussed how the Evangeline Career Center and its projects were going. Everything was right on plan. The fifty million dollar trust fund created to fund the Center over the next ten years included training, rehabbing houses in the vicinity, and funding new businesses that would be created by graduates of the program. In addition, with the Freeman's additional funding, they were on target to open a new school, North Central Village Charter School, for neighborhood kids and have enough left over to fund college tuition for those students as they moved through the newly created education process. The process included Pre-K through Grade 12, two years at Hudson Valley Community College and then on to New York State four-year colleges and universities and graduate school. The funding would supplement all the New York State programs offered for free tuition for students, especially students of color. All this, coupled with partnerships with Rensselaer Polytechnic Institute, Siena College, HVCC, and the University at Albany, has been eye-opening for local government officials.

These politicians never believed that private funding existed, let alone be placed in the heart of Troy, for the benefit of its residents. Jack also paid full property taxes on both Centers, never heard of before for a nonprofit organization that was run like a for-profit business. That's why Jack put the buildings in a special for-profit, separate corporation that would pay its fair share of taxes. It was a point that Jack was making to the residents of Troy. Rensselaer Polytechnic Institute, as fine an institution as it is, paid minimum taxes for water, sewer and garbage collection only on the millions of dollars invested in property in the city of Troy. In fact due to the non-profit organizations in the city, its colleges and universities and churches, 100% of the taxes to run the city were paid by only 40% of the residents Jack wanted to change that and was making progress with the others through meetings and gestures to help raise funds within the city of Troy. The burden on those left to pay the bills was overwhelming, leaving properties vacant, especially in the areas where they were rehabbing. Bringing those buildings back on the tax rolls was a main objective to increase property values, lower tax rates and make the city a destination for new young families to grow and thrive.

When Jack gave Mary the fifteen million dollars from his lottery winnings, she decided to wait until Jack had all his plans in place. She obviously wanted to take care of her mother and her two roommates and she wanted to develop a new charter school in the north end of the city, Lansingburgh, since St. Augustine's School was closed and sitting vacant along with their gymnasium. On top of that, she wanted to help out the Lansingburgh Boys and Girls Club, only a block from the school. The club has been home to thousands of students over the years and has suffered hard times due to lack of funding and a growing poverty rate in this section of the city. The club used to be the sole after-school babysitter for hundreds of students on a daily basis. The club had been fully supported and received money to serve thousands of lunches and dinners to these students.

Now, the local school district started to serve these students with grants secured through the New York State Education Department. Those funds were never intended to have the district compete with the club but that's exactly what happened. Now, the club is a shell of its former self and the school district's programs never met the needs of the children they intended to help. Mary met with the church to lease the school property, and she filed an application with New York State to develop a charter school at the site of the former St. Augustine's School. Across the street was the original Lansingburgh Academy, full of history, was established in 1796 and signed into law by John Jay. Chester A. Arthur, president of the United States and Herman Melville, well-known author, were both teachers at the academy. The former president of Rensselaer Polytechnic Institute, the Reverend Chauncey Lee, was the principal of the school that offered the equivalent of a two-year college degree to students at the secondary level. He was a noted author and educator and invented the dollar sign.

Mary wanted the new charter school to be named the Lansingburgh Academy Charter School in its honor and she was using her own funds to supplement all the initial stages of development. She received word from the state that it was expected that the charter school would be approved along with Jack's charter school in the north central area.

At this point, Mary offered the fact that she'd place $77.5 million dollars into a separate trust fund, the Teresa Trust Fund, and anyone on the committee or at the Center could offer suggestions on how to use the funding. The stipulation was that Mary wanted these funds depleted within five years from today. That opened a bunch of eyes and Karen just shook her head and told Mary she needed time to reconcile all that's happened so far. Karen mention that she has had more surprises in the last two years than she did in her entire career at the New York State Labor Department as Assistant

Director and department attorney. Mary smiled and told her to simply do her best. However, she did mention, that Mary, through her Trust, would step up security at the Center, knowing that things may get a little unsettling in the near future.

Christmas day came and went. Mary and Jack and Debbie went to the 10:30 a.m. Mass at St. Augustine's Church in Lansingburgh. There they were greeted by a slew of old friends who congratulated them on their good fortune. They felt like they were running for office but eventually got to their car and stopped for the *Times Union* and milk at Stewart's at the top of the hill before heading home. As they got there, there were several cars parked on the road but they were able to pass through to their driveway as they were met by John Jefferson. Fred had followed them to church in his car so they'd be safe either way. It became hectic as Mary and Debbie started dinner. Thank God the turkey was done and only needed to be reheated. Guests arrived including a young man named Patrick Valente. Debbie met Patrick at the door and she made introductions to everyone. He went to school at Rensselaer Polytechnic Institute and was near completion of his MBA. He was the same age as Debbie. Evidently she knew him previously in high school. He had gone to Troy High and they met at a football game. Evidently, they stumbled upon each other Christmas shopping around Thanksgiving in downtown Troy at the Victorian Stroll. He invited her to lunch and had no idea who her father and stepmother were. They hit it off and had a few dates over the last few weeks and she invited him to Christmas dinner. Jack thought she might be a little sweet on the guy. Jack started a conversation with him and he seemed like a very nice guy, with good manners and was certainly familiar with the area growing up here.

Dinner went well. Patrick asked why all the cars were out on the road and why they had men walking around the premises. He kiddingly asked Debbie if he stumbled into a Mafioso family and she became a little unsettled. She explained to Patrick about Jack and Mary's lottery winnings and then you could see Patrick's eyes light up. He was in the home of one of the richest families in America and didn't even know it. He apologized to Debbie who told him not to worry. She asked him if it changed anything between them and he said of course not. Little did he know what that really meant.

CHAPTER 20

It was the following Tuesday, December 29th, when Chris Sellers, the Editor of the *Times Union*, the Capital Region's major newspaper, arrived at the Evangeline Career Center with two of his best reporters, Susan Murray and Josh Solomon. Both reporters handle local and national news as well as the political scene at the capitol in Albany. The *Times Union* has a daily circulation of over sixty thousand and a Sunday circulation of over one hundred and twenty-eight thousand subscribers. Many people only buy the Sunday paper for the local supermarket coupons and sale items. Nevertheless, Chris Sellers knew this was a very big story and he received the first interview from Mary Evans and Jack Manning. Of course, the anonymous phone call late last week spurred him on to ask for a meeting. The anonymous call wasn't really anonymous since the call was placed from a local cell number that was easily secured by the newspaper's technology staff. He would hold this news from Mary and Jack. If they asked, he'd tell them that he couldn't divulge this information.

Chris, Susan and Josh were escorted to the boardroom at the Center, where they were met by Karen Steele and Kristen Sanderson. Chris knew both Karen, from her previous position as Assistant Director of the New York

State Labor Department, and Kristen as a mover and shaker attorney from her law firm in Albany. He made introductions to Susan and Josh as well.

"Thank you for inviting us to the Center," said Chris. "We've heard great things about your work here and the resources you've used on behalf of the young people in the City of Troy," he continued.

"Before you get into questions for Mary, perhaps we can give you a little history of this place and what's been accomplished over the last few years," said Karen.

"That would be great," said Chris.

Karen went through the entire timeline of events that led to the creation of the Center and the revitalization of the north central section of the City of Troy. She told the three newspaper visitors about Jack winning the lottery and starting the Evangeline Trust by placing fifty million dollars into the trust to be used over a ten year period for all programs and activities which were further outlined. She emphasized that they pay full property taxes as if they were a for-profit corporation. With that, Karen turned over the meeting to Kristen and she gave Mary Evans' history and background leading up to her winning the national lottery for $480.0 million dollars in Key West, Florida. Then, like clockwork, the questions started coming.

Susan asked Mary her reaction to winning the lottery especially after Jack's good fortune only a few years ago. She asked what the odds were for one person hitting the lottery and the odds for a married couple hitting the lottery separately, years apart, and in completely different locations in the country. The main question was if her winning was on the up and up. This quite frankly upset Mary and she took her time in answering the questions, one at a time.

"The odds of winning the national lottery are two hundred and seventy million to one," she said. "According to a professor of mathematics, the odds of winning the jackpot twice in seven years or less, by the same person, is about four in ten billion. However, we won separately in two different locations, over 1,500 miles apart, so who knows what the odds are for that?" Mary said. "When added together, we believe that we've received the third largest prize in history. Remember, taking the cash incentive now reduces the prize by 40% and any remaining funds, not put into a nonprofit trust fund, is taxed at a New York State and combined federal tax rate of almost 50%. If we moved to Florida, we would save over 9%, which may not mean a lot but it's over twenty million dollars right off the top going to New York State."

"That's amazing," said Chris. "Susan's question about being on the up and up has been brought up by our staff since we received the tip. Can you answer that, Mary?" said Chris.

Mary thought for a minute on how to address this issue. Everyone immediately wanted to read into foul play regardless of the circumstances. She began her answer very slowly so they'd understand the real situation.

"Of course. I bought a ticket at the Quik Mart in Key West, the day before we were leaving to come home. I use the same numbers I always use and it's taken from a published list of the most used numbers for people playing the lottery. I've only used that list to play every week. Jack won his lottery at the Lansingburgh Stewart's store where he worked at the time. He picked his own numbers using birthdays and dates that meant something to him. You can ask him about that," she said. "Furthermore, both the New York State Lottery Commission and the Florida Lottery Commission verified the winning tickets with tons of witnesses including Kristen. So, ask her," she concluded.

Thank you," said Susan. Josh simply nodded his head like he was satisfied.

Kristen added, "Like Mary said, I was there for both

verifications at the Schenectady lottery office and at the Miami Lakes office. Both tickets were authenticated and verified. Any more questions like what've they done or are going to do with the money which seems to be a little more important to the citizens of both areas," said Kristen with a little pissed off voice, not displayed until now.

"I think we got off on the wrong foot here," said Chris. "Can we try again?"

Jack, who'd been sitting there reluctantly, said, "Are you going to ask us what good we accomplished with the money so far or what we're going to do now?"

"Sure," said Chris. "Please tell us your plans."

Mary then reviewed her plans already in place with the fifteen million dollars that Jack had given her from his original winnings. All her activities to date were in programs developed for her hometown of Troy. She explained about the Lansingburgh Academy Charter School and helping the Lansingburgh Boys and Girls Club as well as supporting her fellow ex-nun roommates and her mother. She basically just started moving on her Teresa Trust Fund because of all the time she and Jack had spent developing, funding and working day to day at the Center and renovation efforts in the north central part of Troy.

She mentioned that she'd be gifting $77.5 million dollars to each of two trust funds including the original Teresa Trust Fund set up for her Troy programs and another $77.5 million dollars to be gifted to the Teresa Trust Fund South for south Florida and the Florida Keys. She also mentioned that she and Jack had separate private funds set up and that will eventually be used for long-range goals after this original funding ceases. She mentioned that the original plan was based on a ten-year strategy and then retirement. Now, she said they'd consider moving that up to five years because she knew that their lives would never be the same once this *Times Union* interview was released and picked up by other major media outlets.

The meeting ended with congratulations from Chris, Susan and Josh. As they headed out the door, Chris said that the article outlining their goals and objectives would be positive and he thanked both Jack and Mary for their generosity. He also hoped that their lives would improve greatly after all the fanfare settled down. He asked if he could revisit from time to time and Jack said yes but without Susan. Jack smiled and said, "We don't need negativity anymore than we already have." Chris nodded his head and smiled. He didn't say yes or no but he got it.

After they left, Jack said to Mary that this would be a way of life over the foreseeable future. He then said to Kristen that with all of this going on, they should probably revisit their wills. His will was updated after his winning the lottery but not Mary's, even though Jack gave her fifteen million dollars. Now with her hitting the lottery, and developing an additional trust fund, it might be wise to update her will as well. They each said that they should sit down to discuss it tonight and then have Kristen develop the proper paperwork to make it happen.

Jack knew in his heart that he would wind up giving more money to his children, Debbie and Mark, but how much to give them, he was torn. He didn't want them to have so much that they could sit back and do nothing for the rest of their lives. He saw that Debbie was coming around and would be beneficial as a future board member. He was beginning to trust her after so long doubting her motives. He knew that Mark was just going along for the ride. However, he was well aware of this mother's issues and never took her side. He was stuck because he was just about to graduate and start his job. With that behind him, he did recommend his teacher at the University at Albany, Sam Ryan, for the position at the Evangeline Career Center and that worked out very well. Eventually, he wanted to ensure that Karen was well taken care of but he wanted to incentivize her on a yearly basis and then write her a check when she retired as a surprise gift. Whenever she decided to retire, Jack would ensure that this would happen and set aside money just like he did for his children.

Mary on the other hand had never married before marrying Jack and was an ex-nun. Her mother was alive and needed care which would be handled by Kristen. Her two ex-nun roommates were already set up to receive thirty thousand dollars per year each, tax free for their retirement. Giving them more would be a waste since they wouldn't use it. However, Mary would pick up their medical insurance supplement to Medicare when needed and would pay for any nursing home needs for both. That could amount to a lot of money over the next several years. Mary had enough of her own funds now not to worry about it coming from the trusts.

Originally, when Mary was given fifteen million dollars by Jack, she wanted to keep six million dollars for herself and pay the 50% tax, leaving three million dollars to cover herself, her mother, and her two friends. Now she was covered a hundred times over but had to put it in writing, just in case. Both Jack and Mary agreed, that upon the death of either one of them, all the assets from one would go to the other. It was also set up that the trust funds for both Jack and Mary would have one or the other as the chief executive officer for as long as they wanted to maintain control. The Evangeline Realty Company, Inc. would have the same setup but on a for-profit basis.

Jack and Mary knew where they wanted the money to go to over the next five years for the near future but wanted to protect their assets over the long haul. Jack and Mary both knew what could happen to a non-profit organization that was left in the hands of incompetent people or just plain crooks. It was obvious from dealing with the previous administrators, Herman K. Singer MSW, Executive Director and Marvin Manville, Treasurer, from the Troy Community Council, that they were close to being insolvent because of incompetence and greed.

Jack bailed the organization out as they were heading toward bankruptcy, as long as these two men were fired. To ensure that they'd not come back and sue the organization for letting them go, Jack filed his own lawsuit for a million dollars against each one of them for age discrimination. Jack knew he would never win but with his money, he knew he could keep them tied up for years in court and he wouldn't feel a thing financially. He said if he spent a thousand dollars a day over the next twenty years, he would still have over fifty million left, which was plenty. He laughed and felt relieved at the same time. With this behind them, Jack and Mary could now move forward and not worry if something happened to either of them and they could continue each other's work in each other's memory.

That night, they began to refine their plans. Mary was heading to Miami at the end of January to solidify her newly formed Teresa Trust Fund South to dispense $77.5 million dollars over the next five years, hopefully, and ten years at the latest. Jack and Mary planned to retire with summers in Troy and winters in Key West at their new home. Jack would probably buy a boat with the help of Skip Lennon, their next-door neighbor and friend.

They were a little worried that the house was not really protected from harm since it sat on the street, with the ocean right there. They had installed a state-of-the-art alarm system. They had Jamie Lennon taking care of the house when they were gone. She paid the bills, took care of the SUV and was at their beck and call whenever needed. Mary was also thinking of training her to be a future board member on her trust for south Florida and the Florida Keys. She was very young, very smart and very trainable but she'd have to earn the position. Mary thought she could represent her age group very well and offer valuable suggestions on helping youth to become part of the mainstream of society by graduating from college and being on the cutting edge of technology.

Mary was not only interested in helping The College of the Florida Keys with Jack Traynor as her liaison but she wanted to start a few high-tech businesses that would fully accept these graduates as new employees. Then, they didn't have to leave the Florida Keys because of the high price of housing. They'd have valued jobs where the pay equaled the work and the value equaled the ability to support a family where they grew up mostly in poverty. Mary wanted to change that and break the cycle of poverty for these underserved members of their own community. She would discuss this with Joe Traynor and the president of The College of the Florida Keys when she got back to Florida. They would have a small celebration for New Years' Eve, attend Mass the next day and start figuring out what comes next. They had an inkling that the news coming out of the White House may be a problem down the road. Joe Traynor had heard through the grapevine that there might be a contagious virus heading to the United States from China. There was nothing much to go on but with his various titles in the Coast Guard, FBI and Homeland Security, he was an insider when it came to national security. Unlike an attempted terrorism attack on the United States or cyber-security attack on government or large corporations like SONY in California which was just in its infancy, you could see, feel, touch or hear when it came to viruses. They had stopped previous attempts to poison various government officials but this was not the same. They had no idea and everyone seemed to be downplaying it like it was another form of the flu, which would clear up in warmer weather.

Because of the incident leaving the Fort Lauderdale

Airport, heading home, Jack ordered a private airplane out of the Albany International Airport to transport Mary back to Florida. He was staying for another month in Troy to finish two projects and oversee the beginning steps for the newly created charter school for the north central section of Troy. He would meet her in Key West in late February. He needed to be in Troy to complete all the paperwork and get with the developers to start building the school. Mary's charter school application for the anticipated Lansingburgh Academy Charter School, although looked upon favorable due to the funding already in place, would take a little longer to materialize and start recruiting students for the upcoming fall.

CHAPTER 21

Mary arrived at the Albany International Airport at the private jet terminal gate area at 9:00 a.m., with a flight scheduled for 9:45 a.m. She'd be arriving at the Fort Lauderdale International Airport, hanger 26, early in the afternoon. She was driven to the airport by John Jefferson and followed by Fred Tucker right up to where she checked in. Jack came along and gave her a kiss and a hug and told her to be very careful, after the previous incident in Fort Lauderdale.

Jeff Sheldon, the driver for the law firm, Clyne, Roberts and Lynch, would meet her at the Fort Lauderdale Airport at hanger 26. Sam Mancuso and Pete Williams, her two security team members, would also meet her when she arrived. They both used their leave time with a little help from a call to the Rear Admiral by Joe Traynor. Joe had already mentioned to his Rear Admiral, Jake Barnes, about the $1.2 million dollar donation to The College of the Florida Keys by Mary, which helped keep the place open during a budget crisis. The military paid their own way but couldn't keep the college open by themselves if they went under due to cost restraints. The Rear Admiral was more than happy to help Mary out in the immediate near future but she'd have to select security on her own once she was established down here. Joe mentioned using retirees just like they did using John Jefferson and Fred Tucker, retired Albany FBI agents. Barnes thought it would be worth looking into.

In the meantime, the Rear Admiral had approved six additional Coast Guard enlisted members, three men and three women, all from District 7, under his command to provide security to Mary. Under Mark Silva, from the Miami facility, in addition to Sam Mancuso and Pete Williams, he selected Carlos Garcia and Wilber Morales, both ten-year veterans and fluent in Spanish. Under Joan Talbot's command at the Islamorada facility, with her approval, Rear Admiral Barnes selected Alex Deleon, Mia Santiago, Antonia Andres and Martina Diego. All four were Hispanic and bilingual and closer to Key West at the Islamorada station.

Mary would be staying in Key West most of the time. All six were well trained and Joan Talbot was mentoring young women to enter the Coast Guard. At this point, there are only 321 Hispanic women and 418 women of color in the Coast Guard out of 39,000 members. All six of these chosen to assist Mary were fully trained and would be available over the next few months. Jakes Barnes was well aware of the recruiting effort by Joan Talbot and commended her on her efforts. Allowing these individuals the chance to earn additional money above their pay, only on their time off, would pay off in the long run. Again, their pay ranged in the low $2,000 per month and one week assisting Mary would allow them to increase their personal savings by the same amount.

Mary was unaware that at Joe's request to Rear Admiral Barnes that they had lined up six additional Coast Guard service men and women, for the next several months, who'd alternate and take turns providing security, using their leave time. Most of the new team members spent a great deal of time on their assigned vessels so when they came to port, they were given extensive leaves based on their previous assignments. All of them were keenly aware that they'd be well compensated for their efforts. They were also well prepared and on the cutting edge when crisis arose. Many of them were on various strike teams that would head out to danger in a minute's notice. That wouldn't be an issue while guarding Mary when she was down in the Keys. They also knew they could be pulled immediately if a crisis happened and Mary might be on her own until they were made available once again. Joe Traynor knew this and was prepared to cover her with the help of Skip Lennon and a few retirees living in the Florida Keys if and when necessary. After the appointments, the selected service members thought this might be a cake job and a way to make a few extra dollars. *What could possibly go wrong they asked each other after their selection?*

After landing safely, Mary met with the security team and her driver and headed into downtown Miami where she'd spend the next few days meeting with various people to complete the trust fund team assignments for the newly created Teresa Trust Fund South. She'd make sure that the $77.5 million dollars was fully secured and ready to be available for any projects they deemed appropriate. Once again, she checked into the SLS Brickell Hotel & Residence at 1300 South Miami Avenue, right in the Brickell Plaza, near both the Coast Guard 7th Division headquarters and the law firm.

Mary would have dinner with Sidney Clyne and Jane Swanson at the hotel's restaurant, Fi'lia Brickell, a well-known Italian restaurant at 8:00 p.m. Mary forgot that nightlife in Miami usually started around 10:00 p.m. She laughed to herself and thought that 8:00 p.m. would be considered the early bird special. The next day, she'd be treated to a meeting with the Rear Admiral, Jake Barnes, along with Joe Traynor, who'd be in town for meetings, himself. The meeting was at the Coast Guard 7th Division headquarters, right around the corner from the hotel. She'd them head to the law offices and meet with her attorneys to complete all the paperwork. Joe's wife, Julie, invited Mary to stay with them for a few days at their house in Tavernier so she could meet Tillie, her grandmother, and have Jamie and Linda Lennon over as well. This would be the basis for her Teresa Trust Fund South board and advisory council. Jane could come down as well, stay at a hotel on the beach and enjoy herself. After all, she was a very close friend of Julie's. That's how it all began with the development of the board, with Julie's recommendation.

The next morning, Mary walked over to the Coast Guard headquarters around the corner with Sam Mancuso and Pete Williams. She was cleared through a vast screening process and went to the Rear Admiral's office, followed by Sam and Pete. Mary was met by the Rear Admiral's staff and showed into the Rear Admiral's office where Lieutenant Joe Traynor greeted her, in full military dress.

"Hi Mary. How are you? How was your trip?" he asked.

"Fine, Joe, or should I say Lieutenant Traynor?" as she smiled at him. He smiled back.

"Ms. Evans, I would like you to meet Rear Admiral Jake Barnes, Commander of District 7, headquartered here in Miami. This is the largest presence of the Coast Guard in the United States," he followed up.

"Rear Admiral Barnes, it is my honor to meet you. Thank you for seeing me on such short notice. It's Mary by the way. The Ms. Evans will be changing to Mrs. Mary Manning as soon as I get back. We just haven't had the time," she said.

"My honor as well. Let me introduce you to Lieutenant Mark Silva, from the Fort Lauderdale and Miami offices, and Joan Talbot, Chief Warrant Officer and in command of the Islamorada Coast Guard facility," he said.

"I believe I've met Mark through Joe previously, a while ago when we first met Joe and Julie," she said. "Chief Warrant Officer, it's my pleasure to meet you as well. I know we haven't met but I know that Joe has high regard for both of you," Mary said.

Joan said, "My pleasure. It's nice to meet you, finally. We've heard a lot about both you and your husband from both Joe and Julie. Did you know that when Julie was younger she was our first babysitter for our daughter, Lucy? Lucy runs cross-country with Julie as her coach at Coral Shores High School. It's a small world," she said.

The Rear Admiral led the way to his boardroom attached to his office. There was coffee and Danish set up for the guests. Mary looked around and was immediately impressed by the strength of those at the meeting. They exuded confidence from the top down. As they sat, Jake Barnes mentioned that Joan was a lifer in the Coast Guard and the first female commander of her own facility. This facility was key to all the drug busts throughout the southern state and the Florida Keys. He mentioned that she was Joe's first boss when he came down as an eighteen-year-old, right from his first semester at MIT. After training, Joe showed great aptitude for languages, now speaking Spanish, Russian, Chechen, and learning Chinese. He immediately joined the intelligence ranks and he and Mark Silva had the largest number of arrests in the last ten years. He also mentioned without Joan's supervision and interventions that none of that would have happened. Joe grew from a boy trainee to whom he was today through Joan's leadership, friendship and love. Joe was extremely close to the Talbot family as well as Julie.

The Rear Admiral asked Mary for a little background and for the next half hour, she explained her life from being an ex-nun, to working with youth, to being fired by the Troy

Community Council. She went to tell them about Jack Manning winning the lottery and how their lives changed dramatically. She then explained about their marriage and honeymoon to Key West. She then told them of her winning $480.0 million while on their honeymoon in Key West. This made them the third combined lottery winners in history. She stopped and said, "Is that enough background?" She laughed. There was something about Mary that changed. She was always confident as a teacher in charge of a classroom full of kids but never too sure about herself in adult crowds. She seemed to have changed as much as Jack changed over the last few years.

"Ms. Evans, May I call you Mary?" said Jake.

"Of course," she said.

"Please call me Jake, in this room. I still need to keep up my image outside," he said with a grin. "Joe knows my most inner secrets and he is the only one to call me Jake, when we are alone," he said. "Right, Mark? Right, Joan?" They smiled and nodded.

"Mary, what I was most impressed about you is not the money but Joe told me as soon as he mentioned that the college was in financial trouble, you didn't hesitate. You didn't ask why. You didn't go into a long litany of questions. You simply opened your checkbook and wrote a check for over a one million two hundred thousand dollars, payable to the college. I don't know anyone other than you who would do that," he said.

Mary smiled. "I don't want you to take this the wrong way. Having this much money is a burden. Both Jack and I pledged to spend well over two hundred million dollars in trust funds we set up to help others. We kept a good amount for ourselves but the vast majority is going to others. I couldn't think of a better project to fund than a college with Joe Traynor working for it. If they needed the money they got it."

Joe looked a little sheepishly and embarrassed and tried to lower his head and eyes but the Rear Admiral always admired Joe's strengths and his humbleness. Joan and Mark both smiled at each other knowing how uncomfortable Joe really is at Mary's thoughtful words.

"Mary, I just approved six additional enlisted Coast Guard men and women to serve as your security staff over the next several months. It will be on their own time and you will pay them directly but it is with my approval. Mark and Joan have the list. There are three additional men and three women service members. Four of the six speak Spanish, which is very helpful down here. Also, the three women are stationed at the Islamorada facility under Joan's command. We felt that it might be more comfortable to have women guard you at your home and three of the men are here in Miami and only one at Islamorada. You will still have Sam and Pete to fill in as well. The women are just as effective if not more so than the male members. They are also effective because they will not stand out as security like their male counterparts.

Toward the end of the meeting, Mary asked the Rear Admiral, "Sir, would it be possible to have Joan Talbot serve on my board of advisors as well as Julie Traynor, her grandmother, Linda Lennon and her daughter? The reason I ask is that I am a strong believer in mentoring young women for careers, and down here, the Coast Guard seems to be a natural career, especially for young Hispanic men and women. May I be so bold as to offer the Coast Guard in the Florida Keys, a five million dollar contribution toward training, mentoring educating and recruiting young adults for Coast Guard careers? I am heading to my attorney's office next. I can have a separate fund set up for this purpose by the end of the week," Mary said. "The money is sitting in the account. I am spending $77.5 million dollars for the Teresa Trust Fund South and these funds that I offer to you will come from that trust fund."

Rear Admiral Barnes seemed overwhelmed and that didn't happen very often. He said, "Joe, you said that Mary and Jack were extremely caring and generous but this is so much more than I would have ever imagined. Mary, I have to make a quick call to my superiors in Washington DC but I don't expect a "no", he said. "Thank you. Thank you."

Joan looked at Joe and shook her head. Mark was looking at Joan and both were smiling from ear to ear. None of this was expected. Joan just realized that she would be placed in charge of a five-million-dollar project to increase the number of female recruits into the Coast Guard in the Florida Keys. The excitement finally came through and she said "WOW. JUST WOW." She turned and said, "Was that in my outer voice?"

"Yes, Joan. It was," said Jake Barnes and smiled. He repeated, "WOW, JUST WOW,"

As they were walking out of the Rear Admiral's office, Joe said to Mary, "Mary, I don't know what to say? I know Joan is excited and I am too. I think you gave Jake a heart attack."

"I hope not. But, it was a sincere offer. Joe, you have really good friends and it shows. I'm glad I could help. Sam and Pete will take me down to your house in Tavernier and then I'll wind up at our home in Key West. You're staying here for a few days, I take it?"

"Yes, I have several meetings. As you know, I'm at the college but I'm also doing double duty with a few intelligence breaches here in Miami. I need to translate back and forth between English, Spanish and Russian or Chechen. Not sure. I'll be home after that. Make sure that there's room for Sam and Pete at our house and tell Jamie to set up a bedroom and office for the two ladies who will be providing security in Key West. I want you to meet our president at the college when you have a chance."

"Please thank Jake for the meeting. Joe, thank you for everything. I can see your fingerprints all over this backroom operation of yours. I now understand the sway you have over the others. It is impressive and thank you," Mary said. "I better call Jack before I head to see Jane at the attorney's office."

They parted and Joe went back to a meeting with Jake Barnes. "Impressive woman," said Jake, a man of few words. "I can't believe her decision making skills. Just like that, she handed over five million dollars. How long does it take her to buy a car? Five minutes or so?" he laughed. "Thank you Joe for setting this up. I know Joan is happy. The security team is happy and our bosses will be happy if we get more women in the ranks, especially women of color and Hispanic speaking men and women. I will change the dynamic down here forever. Again, thank you, Joe." Joe simply nodded his head.

CHAPTER 22

Before you head out, I have something that I think you'll need while you're down here," Joe said. "Just in case, and only in case, you get separated from your security team, I have state-of-the-art clip-on GPS chips that can be placed into your shoestrings on your sneakers, or clip on to your regular shoes or clothing. I also want you to keep one in your pocketbook at all times," Joe said.

"You are making me nervous, Joe. Why do I need these devices on me if my security team is always around?" she asked.

"What if they're not always around? What if they get called away for an emergency or there is no one around to protect you in a crowd or at the gas station or in a store? I'm not trying to make you nervous. I'm trying to make you safe. If you don't want the GPS clips then that's fine but I'd strongly suggest you keep them on you at all times. Do you remember being followed going up to the airport in Fort Lauderdale? Anyone can be snatched at any time within seconds," he said.

"Well, I suppose you're right," she said. "Can you show me how to wear the devices without being obvious?"

"Sure. Come over here by the alcove and I will immediately fix your shoes. You can attach the GPS to your clothing where you'll feel comfortable. Have your security team change out the devices every third Saturday morning like clockwork. The devices last for three weeks at a time. Please keep a log going just like you would if you had to take medicine daily at a certain time. I know it's tough but we want to avoid any situation that might be harmful to you. When Jack comes down, we'll supply him with the same items."

"Thanks, Joe for caring. It's appreciated." Mary headed out the door, said goodbye and began walking up the street with Sam and Pete to meet Jane. She felt secure but this kind of rattled her. Boy, was her life changing quickly. At this point, she wondered if she got rid of everything would she be happier? Would anyone believe she gave away everything? Someone would always think she and Jack were rich and might try to take advantage of them or even harm them.

She'd let Jack know that Joe gave her the GPS devices for her clothing, shoes and pocketbook. She was sure that he was right and she was sure that Jack would agree that being cautious was the way to go. Maybe Jack could call Joe and get the devices sent up to him in Troy. He was probably as vulnerable as she was down in Florida. He ran around town attending meeting after meeting. Maybe John and Fred would lose him during the day like they did when he took off while living in the hotel in Albany when he first won the lottery. John sat Jack down and told him what could happen and what had happened to large lottery winners over the past years. Not all of it was pretty. Some winners died. Others lost everything and were taken advantage of on a daily basis. Many thought they were rock stars that no one could touch. They also didn't win enough to afford full-time protection but as John had said if they want to get to you they certainly can at any time or place. They have been cautious over the last few years and now she was down here alone, by herself, and was nervous.

It was a little before noon when Mary left to meet Jane Swanson and Sidney Clyne at their office a few blocks from Coast Guard headquarters and her hotel. They would stay the day and stay at the hotel that night. She originally was going to stay for several days but she now knew the direction that her new trust fund would take her and didn't feel the need to stay. She wanted to head back to Key West as soon as she could after the meeting at Julie and Joe's house. She would head out to Joe and Julie's house down in Tavernier, about eighty miles south of Miami the next day. She would meet with Linda and Jamie Lennon and Julie's grandmother, Tillie. She would let them know that she pledged five million dollars to the Coast Guard for recruitment of young women into the ranks, especially women of color and Hispanic men and women. Being guarded by three Hispanic women when she arrived in Key West would give her greater insight into their specific needs and desires to succeed in a predominately white male field. Joe said he would call the security team that would be guarding her at her house in Key West and let them know to start a log for the GPS devices and change the devices out every three weeks. There would be rotating shifts weekly so the log was instrumental in keeping Mary safe in her own home and around town.

Jane met Mary, Sam and Pete at the elevator to her office. She had lunch set up for everyone in the boardroom. Jane knew that Mary had met with Rear Admiral Barnes and his staff including Joe Traynor but was unaware of what was said or planned. Sidney dropped by the boardroom and waved and said he was available all afternoon if need be and was free for dinner as well. Jane nodded at him as if to say, *"I've got this, Sidney"*. Since all the taxes were being paid as a New York State resident, Jane's task became very clear as to the focus of this meeting. It was to decide how to set up the Teresa Trust Fund South to accommodate any donations that Mary and her proposed team wanted to make. Jane was also well aware of the fact that Mary trusted her and she would always be available no matter the request. The check to cover her husband's medical student loans certainly ensured that. She told Sidney about it to see if there was a conflict or if she needed to share the wealth with the law firm. Sidney said that under the circumstances and taking into account the future benefit of her being here and in charge of the trust for all legal matters far outweighed any present financial benefit to the company. Sidney, in fact, was quite vocal to the other partners that Jane, because of her relationship with Mary and Jack, and especially to Joe and Julie, was going to be a partner by the next year's annual meeting. Not everyone brought in million-dollar fees from a client, who intended to stay as long as the attorney in charge was there. The law firm could acknowledge that fact in an earlier meeting of the partners, unattended by Jane Swanson.

Mary started the meeting by saying, "Jane, let me bring you up to speed about what I've done since I left here to go home and come back and meet with Rear Admiral Barnes just this morning. I now have a full security team, approved by the Rear Admiral that will follow me here and down in Key West. In addition, I need you to set aside five million dollars to recruit, train, educate and meet the needs of women recruits into the Coast Guard in the Florida Keys and Miami."

"Wow, when did this happen?" Jane asked.

"Just this morning. I was highly impressed by Joan Talbot, Joe's close friend and commander at the Islamorada facility. She's been recruiting Hispanic men and women and women of color to the Coast Guard as a side effort. I wanted to formalize that effort in the eyes of the Rear Admiral and his bosses in Washington. Jake said he would make that happen. So, in addition to Julie, and her grandmother, Tillie, and Linda and Jamie Lennon, I want to add Joan Talbot to the mix." She added, "Did you know that Joan was Joe's first boss when he was only eighteen years old when he first joined the Coast Guard? Did you know that Julie was Joan's babysitter for her kids including Lucy who became a cross-country star with Julie as her coach at the high school?"

"Actually, Mary, I did know about Joan and their relationship. I did the closing on their house in Tavernier. I met Joe and Julie through a mutual friend in Albany, who recommended me to them down here. We became very good friends so yes I knew all that," said Jane.

"I forgot that you did. Sorry. I just got so caught up and things are moving fast. Can you meet us down in Tavernier tomorrow and the next day so we can formalize the board and advisory group? I want the groups to be almost the same but separate. I want Jamie to earn her way on to the board because she is so young. I want Joan on the board but more as an experienced advisor because of the Coast Guard connection. Also, the women and one man guarding me down in Key West report directly to Joan."

"Let me check with Nick to see what he has planned. I think it will be fine. I need a room for a day or two. Maybe I can stay with Tillie at her apartment in Key Largo, not that far away. I'll call Julie and ask. I just don't like being in a beachfront hotel, all alone by myself. The Keys are fine but the world is changing and it makes me nervous."

"I understand," said Mary. "No problem. You can drive down by yourself or I can get one of the security team to follow you down as well. I would feel better about it as well now that you brought it up. We need to be careful, Jane. I understand that better today than yesterday. Joe hooked me up with GPS devices for my shoes, clothes and pocketbook. Before he did that, I didn't take it nearly as seriously as I should have."

They met for several hours. They developed a new formal document securing the five million dollars to come from the Teresa Trust Fund South to the Coast Guard. Jane had a staff member take it to Rear Admiral Barnes for his immediate review. He did and forwarded it to Washington. He received an answer back from his Admiral almost immediately. They said that it was a wonderful plan and they would thankfully accept the donation from Mary. Jake told them that Joan Talbot would run the program and all those at the meeting were delighted. Joan was closing in on her retirement within the next few years and this would elevate her status to Lieutenant before she retired. That would bounce her retirement pay up substantially. Little did Joan know that Mary told Jane that she would like to pay for any college expenses for Joan's children, if this worked out. She would give it six months and then fund their education. Jane made a note to follow up and let her know when that date arrived.

Mary, Sam and Pete left around 5:00 p.m. for the hotel. There were no issues walking down the street toward the hotel. Mary bowed out of any more meetings. She would get room service at 7:00 p.m. and then make a call to Jack to let him know what was going on and the decisions she made over the last day or two. She also needed to find out the status of her charter school, The Lansingburgh Academy Charter School, and the progress in securing St. Augustine's school and gymnasium from the Roman Catholic Diocese of Albany. She was a close friend with her pastor at St. Augustine's, who was a close friend of the Bishop. Of course, nothing ever went smoothly in dealing with the Catholic Church. Her becoming an ex-nun seemed to be harder than actually becoming a Sister of St. Joseph in the first place. They were losing so many nuns that they tried to hold on to as many as they could through strong negotiation on the way out. After all, where could the Catholic Church get cheap labor at below minimum wage or no pay at all these days? Nuns and priests were not staying and new nuns and priests were not coming on board. It was a dilemma that was coming to a head. She had more ex-nun friends than nun friends and all those nun friends were now in their seventies and older with limited pensions and nowhere to go.

CHAPTER 23

Mary made it to Julie's house a little after 11:00 a.m. It is about eighty miles south from Brickell Avenue in downtown Miami to Tavernier. It took about an hour and forty-five minutes door to door, heading down the two-lane highway through the Keys. Once again, Sam and Pete took two cars just in case there were any issues or problems with construction, roadways or simply a car being incapacitated. Neither Pete nor Sam saw anything irregular or anyone following them like during the limousine ride to the airport. Perhaps they could rest easy now since that could have been a one-time deal or they were actually just following the car with the reporters. As they were told, it happens a lot. People followed reporters for leads and opportunities to gain access to quick cash or anything of value.

Mary got out of the car and was greeted by Julie, Tillie and Bella. Mary hugged Julie and shook hands with Tillie. She bent down and shook little Bella's hand and said, "It is so nice to meet you, Bella."

Bella said, "Hi. Nice to meet you, too."

Her English was getting better every day. Julie's Spanish lessons were going well but a long way away from being fluent. Joe, on the other hand, was fluent in several languages. When they were alone in the house, he spoke Spanish to both Bella and Julie. Bella was almost seven years old now and in second grade. Her elementary school was close by Tillie's apartment in Key Largo while Julie worked at the Coral Shores High School only a few blocks from their house. Tillie went by the school every day to make sure that Bella got the bus or she stayed with Tillie if Julie had a cross-country meet that day. All in all, it worked out well for everyone. Tillie had always been more of a mother than a grandmother ever since her daughter, Julie's mother, died when Julie was very young. That was a few years before meeting Joe, when Julie was age eleven in 5th grade, when Joe and Joan Talbot showed up for career day at her school. Joan was Joe's boss and he had just arrived on station at eighteen years old. This was the same school that Bella now attended.

Lunch was served on the deck. Linda and Jamie Lennon just arrived from Key West. Joan Talbot showed up as well with her daughter, Lucy. Lucy had a cross-country meet that day and would head out with Julie, who was still the team's coach, still. Lucy was now a senior and had accepted a cross-country scholarship to the University of Miami, a Division 1 university. She was considered one of the best runners to come out of south Florida and the Keys in many years. She was dressed in her uniform and gave everyone a hug and then shook hands with Mary. Joan smiled and thought from babysitter to coach for Julie and baby to full athletic scholarship for Lucy.

As soon as lunch was served and finished, Mary said, "I don't want to keep you ladies but I wanted to let you know my current plans and then pick your brains for what you see as a big need down here in Florida, and particularly in the Keys." She went on to tell everyone, except Joan who already knew about the five million dollar donation to the Coast Guard to recruit young Hispanic women and women of color into the Coast Guard as well as minority men, especially Hispanic men. Mary told those who didn't know, that Joan was the first and only commander and Chief Warrant Officer of a Coast Guard facility in Florida, being in charge of the Islamorada facility. She would make Lieutenant by the time she retired within the next few years. The facility itself was the center for intelligence gathering for drug intervention for the entire region. That's why Joe was so involved with Joan and this facility. Both he and Mark Silva made their names for themselves through massive arrests and confiscation of drugs. The gangs were unaware that Joe spoke English, Spanish, Russian, Chechen and now Chinese and Mark was a Mexican from San Diego and a former gangbanger a long time ago. The things they knew between them, you could neither teach nor learn without the background experiences and knowledge they had. That coupled with a few very well placed close personal friends in the intelligence and espionage arenas didn't hurt, including Jack Forest up in Virginia.

Mary told the group, "Joan, with her permission and with the permission of her boss, Rear Admiral, Jake Barnes, will be in charge of the five-million-dollar project." She added, "If she does retire within the next few years, she will always have a place with the Teresa Trust Fund South to continue her recruitment efforts outside the Coast Guard. I'm sure we can work out something if we continue to fund the program, once it is successful."

Lucy looked at her mother and said, "Wow, Mom. That's great. Dad will be very proud of you. At least it will give you another career once you leave the Coast Guard."

"That's our hope as well, Lucy," said Mary and smiled.

Tillie jumped in and mentioned that seniors in the Florida Keys specifically are having a very difficult time holding on to their homes with increased taxes and utility costs. She also said many of her close friends had to take jobs at local stores for minimum wage just to put food on the table. She told Mary how Julie and Joe had raised over fifty thousand dollars from their wedding for the food bank for their church in Key Largo, St. Justin Martyr. Privately, Tillie would also tell her about the money they found in their attic which they gave to the Coast Guard and made a sizable donation to the same food bank.

Jamie asked if she could speak. Mary said, "Of course, Jamie. I want you to be an advisor to the group on youth initiatives or at least young adult initiatives. I know you're active in your church, The Basilica of St. Mary Star of the Sea.in Key West. I know your mother is as well. Please go on," she said.

Jamie said, "Quite frankly, you have been very kind to my brother and me since we met. In order to survive down here, you have to be rich or start your own business. My brother and I did that and also help my dad with his boat. We both went to the Keys Community College before it became The College of the Florida Keys. They offer tons of courses for businesses attached to marine life and marine activity but there are no jobs that pay more than minimum wage. We also can't afford to buy a house. The average price of a house in Key West is over six hundred thousand dollars and climbing. We don't want to live with our parents forever but something must be done for those who were born here to be able to stay here."

"Hold that thought," said Mary. "We just donated over a million dollars to the college to stay afloat during their economic crisis. They don't have enough students here to really tap the market for careers in jobs on the cutting edge. There are 1,348 students at the college and well over 500 of them are in the military wing. I looked it up for my meeting. The cost per credit hour for a resident of Key West is $128.50 per credit hour and for a non-resident is $592.64 per credit hour. The annual budget is less than five million dollars. I just added more than 20% to the coffers. There are 8,800 students in Monroe County School District, covering all the Florida Keys right up to Coral Shores High School in Tavernier and the elementary schools in Key Largo. We should get a few thousand more to attend if what they offer leads to a good job. What if we go to the college and offer to start business for the courses they teach as long as we can make money to support the business. Funding business to fail is not smart. Up in Troy, we started our own companies to renovate hundreds of houses and supplemented the purchase of the homes with grants."

"Really? You did that where you're from?" said Jamie.

Lucy added, "That's smart. If I didn't get the scholarship to UM then I'd certainly decide to go to The College of the Florida Keys and then join the Coast Guard with a relevant degree that could lead me somewhere. Nobody wants to be poor and no one wants to work for minimum wage. They're just stuck here with no future. Ask all my friends."

Julie said, "As the career counselor for the high school, I can say that Lucy and Jamie are absolutely right."

"Well then, let's build some women-owned businesses that have SBA minority status as women and minorities and get the students certified in careers that pay off. In the Albany area, we work with companies in the high tech field. The Capital Region is known as Tech Valley. However, there are over 2,500 jobs open right now for certified coding employees. All they need is a GED/TASK graduation certificate and from six months to one year of training for a fifty thousand dollar a year starting salary with benefits. We are now training and sending these students to Hudson Valley Community College for an Associates Degree at no cost to them with a guaranteed job at the end. We also subsidize the businesses and take tax credits for employing the long term unemployed."

Mary went on, "I have a lot to think about here but I have

one other opportunity that I would like to discuss. She pulled out an article that she had read the last time she was down here on her honeymoon. "I think the police have a very difficult job to do. There are articles after articles about reforming policing and the blowback from those efforts. As an ex-nun and very strong religious individual, not just Catholic but in general, I think we need to add compassion and a different approach to many issues that could have been resolved with social service and psychologist's intervention before it arises to the death of an unfortunate individual. Not all are minorities who find themselves in these situations, but many are, and it's time to acknowledge we might need something new. She showed them the article. "In a lawsuit that's drawn national attention and statements to the media, an attorney questions the actions of Key West police, teachers and principals in the 2018 arrest of an 8-year-old boy who reportedly punched and threatened a teacher while at school in December 2018. This is a heartbreaking example of how our educational and policing systems train children to be criminals by treating them like criminals. If convicted, the child in this case would have been a convicted felon at eight years old," the attorney said in a prepared statement. "This little boy was failed by everyone who played a part in this horrific incident." The lawsuit does not mention what the Keys Weekly has confirmed through multiple sources that the boy's father had asked for his son to be arrested to teach him a lesson following previous violent outbursts at both Gerald Adams Elementary and a different school he had previously attended. After passing the article around, Mary said that she would like to set up a program specifically for the Monroe County Sheriff's Department and the Key West police department to add several mental health experts to both of their staffs as well as to the schools in this area. "What do you think?" asked Mary to the group. Tillie said,

"I think this would be a wonderful idea but I don't think the lifting on our part will be easy. From what I know of some cops down here, some don't like immigrants or people not like them. Nonetheless, at the last census over 25% of the school student population is Hispanic, mostly Cuban by ethnicity. That's why we are so protective of Bella. As you may not know, Bella was born here after her mother escaped from Cuba and made it to shore. Unfortunately that took a lot out of Bella's mother and she died early when Bella was only five years old. Julie and Joe adopted her after a brief battle with the state of Florida and its bureaucrats but succeeded only because of who they are. They are very well known and Bella will be the beneficiary of that. Not everyone down here gets treated that way. So, good luck. You'll need it," said Tillie. "So, not a good idea?" asked Mary.

"I would wait for a while until we make progress with the college, careers, seniors, food banks and other real daily issues and then tackle that issue once we have made a name for ourselves and have the backing of the community. No offense, Mary but you may be seen as an interloper in the lives of the community," said Linda.

"I'll take your lead, all of your leads," said Mary. She took notes and told everyone that she would develop an outline to move forward. She was going to meet with the president of the college with Jack in a few days and wanted something prepared. She asked everyone if that was okay. They all said yes. Julie told everyone that she was very thankful, as a lifelong "Conch" that Mary would be investing in the people of the community not just investing in things. Her vision was exactly what the community needed especially when backed up with financial assistance.

Jane had gotten there a little late but got most of the gist on how the trust fund would move forward. Jane would be staying at Tillie's apartment as her guest while Mary would stay with Jack, Julie and Bella. They had a spare room all set up that Tillie used whenever she wanted to stay over or babysit Bella so they could go out to dinner. The next day, late in the afternoon, Mary would be picked up by Sam and Pete, who were staying down the road at a local hotel, owned by a friend of Julie's. They didn't need to cover her once Joe arrived home. Once they arrived at their Key West home, the four individuals stationed at Islamorada, under Joan Talbot, would relieve them. She would meet them all at once. She would give them her itinerary. Joe scheduled the college meeting with his boss for Friday at 10:00 a.m.

CHAPTER 24

They arrived at Key West, a little after 5:00 p.m. Traffic was backed up as usual heading down the Keys. They took a few shortcuts but eighty miles down the highway at fifty miles an hour maximum became very monotonous. Sam and Pete introduced the first two members of Mary's security team, Antonia Andres and Martina Diego, the two Coast Guard enlisted personnel under the command of Joan Talbot up in Islamorada. They would stay for a week and then be followed by Alex Deleon and Mia Santiago, the other two under Joan. If Mary stayed in Key West then this switch would take place every week for the next month. If she headed back to Miami, then Sam and Pete would come back as security and be backed up by Carlos Garcia and Wilber Morales, making the security teams complete in both areas. All of the recruits were bilingual with a minimum of ten years of service in the Coast Guard. All were enlisted, non-officers but thoroughly trained and members of various elite groups charged with taking down criminals in the Florida region including the surrounding international waters.

Jamie had already been at the house at 10 Allamanda Terrace and she'd made up the two guest rooms for the first two ladies. She also bought enough provisions for two weeks for both sets of security. Before Mary arrived, Jamie met them at the door and took their identification and immediately called Joan Talbot at the facility in Islamorada. She put Joan on Face Time on her iPhone and she identified both ladies as those under her command. Jamie then showed them all the codes for the home, the internet access, cameras and other technology set up to protect Mary and Jack. She made them lunch and had them walk around the home, gardens, and outside area, up and down the street, pointing out her own home with similar security features.

"It's very nice to meet you, Antonia and Martina," Mary said. "May I call you Antonia and Martina?" she asked.

"Of course," they both said at the same time. Antonia added, "We would prefer that you do. Can we call you Mary?"

"Please do," she said as they walked into the house.

Jamie said, "Hi, Mary. They're all set up in their guest rooms and dinner is on at my house. My mother is having a cookout once again. Nothing fancy but my father picked up fresh lobsters and shrimp from the dock and will be heading home in a few minutes.

Antonia looked at Martina with a smile on her face as to say, *"Not a bad gig, huh? And, we're getting two thousand dollars a week, doubling our take home pay."*

Jamie introduced her brother, Tom, and her parents, Linda and Skip, to Antonia and Martina as they entered their backyard only steps away from Mary's house. During dinner, Mary gave them both the rundown on how she and her husband, Jack, wound up here in Key West. To say they were shocked was an understatement. Mary told them that she'd be giving away $77.5 million dollars in both south Florida and the Keys as one area and the same amount up in the Capital Region of New York State. She told them the plan was to be carried out over five years and no more than ten years and then she and Jack would retire to both places, depending on the season.

Now Antonia and Martina understood the need for security. Sam had lightly touched on the circumstances and mentioned the ride to the airport as a cautionary tale so they wouldn't get complacent. They also knew that Joan wanted them to succeed, make some money for savings, and progress up the same path that she had. Both Antonia and Martina knew the relationship with Joe and Julie Traynor as well as Mark Silva and all they'd accomplished down here. Both thirty years old and single, they knew what it was like to be on your own. They were flabbergasted about Mary being an ex-nun and how both she and Jack had both hit the lottery. They were amazed that they are now in the same house where Jack had previously read off Mary's winning lottery ticket numbers purchased in Key West as the only winner. They vowed to be vigilant.

The next morning, Joe picked up Mary at her house around 9:30 a.m. Antonia and Martina followed them in two cars, just as Sam and Pete had done previously. They knew that Joe was now a Vice President at the college but also a full-time officer in the Coast Guard with credentials from the FBI and Homeland Security. They also knew that as they spoke to each other in Spanish that Joe was fluent and understood every word even though he never let on. They all pulled up in the lot adjacent to the president's office at the college and walked into the building. Antonia and Martina would patiently sit and wait outside the boardroom. Everyone in the president's office was well aware that Joe, Antonia and Martina were fully armed and ready in case of any problem. This was accepted as a daily occurrence since the college had a military education and training side and actually felt more comfortable knowing that security on the campus was maximized by these efforts.

Joe met with Morgan's administrative assistant, Louise Butler, and she was introduced to Mary, Antonia and

Martina. He said, "Antonia and Martina are Coast Guard members and part of the security team for Mary while she's down here. Can they sit outside the boardroom and wait until our meeting is over?"

"Of course, Joe. I'll bring these young ladies out some Danish and coffee from the boardroom before the meeting begins. Is that okay ladies?" she asked.

"That would be great," said Antonia with a nod from Martina.

After they were set up, Joe brought Mary into the boardroom to meet Morgan, his boss and president of The College of the Florida Keys. "Morgan, I'd like you to meet Mary Evans, the individual who so graciously handed us a check to cover our deficit a short while ago," he said.

"Yes, of course," Morgan said. "Thank you on behalf of everyone at the college. We're extremely grateful for your financial assistance. I've heard nothing but good things about you and your husband from Joe," he said.

Mary smiled and sat down. She kind of remembered a few years ago when they got the shocking news that she and Jack and their team had been fired by the Troy Community Council. How sad it was that day and how far they had traveled since that day. Jack became a new man. They were now married and she loved him to death and had since the day they met. The day he hired her straight from the convent was the best day of her life up until she married him.

It had nothing to do with the money and never had. She would be glad when most of it was gone. Not all of it of course. She wasn't that dumb. But now, she had a chance to do some good and help those who needed it the most. She would follow Jack's lead but they did differ in certain areas. She taught math and was very good at it. Business was math. You made money or lost money but it was always based on math. She knew where every dime was and when she got monthly reports from Kristen or Jane or even Jack and the staff at the Career Center, she could hone in and know exactly what was happening from the numbers presented to her. She could do math in her head to six digits with a decimal point. She and Joe were on the same wavelength when it came to math. Joe didn't get into MIT by accident. He left for a reason but it certainly wasn't because he couldn't do the work. He wanted to see the world and make his own way. She now had five years to prove that she could do the same thing but with a lot of money backing her up.

Joe gave Mary's full background to Morgan L. Hennessy, Ph.D. He was rather young at 42, but had the pedigree. He had a Ph.D. in Education from Brown, the same university where Julie got her MFA. Julie had met him on several occasions and Joe felt like a third wheel when they started talking about Brown University, one of the IVY League Universities and the professors they both knew and liked. Morgan even offered Julie a position in the English Department, knowing full well her career at Coral Shores High School and as an outstanding national author, with a growing international reputation for giving young girls and women inspiration and a path to success. He also mentioned that Julie was mentoring Lucy Talbot and all the success she has achieved in such a short time. Morgan was thinking about Mary and how she could fit in to this college and faculty. Mary would change his mind. Morgan gave his background to Mary and she politely listened to every word. He was not a bullshitter as Joe had mentioned he was a straight shooter, which he liked. He appeared to be a good guy, even though he did like his IVY pedigree.

Mary smiled as Morgan summarized his background and where the college currently is and where he and Joe wanted to see it grow. He explained how they went from a community college to a four-year institution offering Bachelor's degrees as well as Associates. They also had a military training and education wing that Joe ran for the services and certification programs that would now include a culinary institute on campus. He alluded to the fact that they wanted to start moving into technology training, certifications, and degrees but it was very expensive to build the infrastructure required to meet the needs of students in technology for the 21st century.

At that point, Mary said, "May I explain the kind of plans I have that may assist you in the areas of technology for the future? All of your degree programs are excellent but do they automatically lead to 100% job placement in jobs starting at fifty thousand dollars and above with benefits?"

"No," said Morgan. "It is impossible for a college to guarantee such a result," he said.

"Not really, would you like me to explain?" she laughed and they picked up on it.

"What?" Joe and Morgan said.

Do you remember the movie, *My Cousin Vinny*, when the prosecutor was badgering Marisa Tomei and wouldn't let her talk when discussing the various automobile models that she apparently didn't know anything about? She said, "Would you like me to explain?" And then tore him apart? Do you remember?" Mary asked.

Both Joe and Morgan broke out laughing. It certainly created a moment with a large grin on her face. "I know how to put technology into your college at no cost to your organization. I know how to start high tech companies. I know how to run and finance those companies and I know how we can do it here in Key West. Might that help?" she asked.

Morgan said with a grin, "Can you explain, please?"

"Of course I can," she said.

She then explained that she was willing to put up twenty million dollars to develop The College of the Florida Keys Technology Park, right on campus. They had more than ample room going to waste because they only had 1,348 students on a campus that could serve over 4,000. She explained how there are over 2,500 coding jobs available within the Capital Region of New York State that are currently left unfilled. She said there was probable five times that in the entire state of Florida. Those jobs paid fifty thousand dollars to start with benefits. You don't need a college degree but you want a degree to move up and make even more money as an administrator. For these jobs you only need a GED based TASC degree, which allows you to enter college for training. The curriculum is well known and includes certification in C++, CSS, HTML, JavaScript, Peri, PHP, Python, Ruby, SQL, and XML. Once trained and certified, students can move from computer programmer to web developer, to front-end developer, back-end developer, full-stack developer, software application developer, computer systems analyst, network systems administrator and finally database Administrator.

"Mary, how do you know all this? We have certified tech staff right here on campus who have never mentioned any of this," Morgan said.

Joe just stared at Mary and was very impressed. He hadn't see the meeting going this way. He thought for sure she might give a few more scholarships or buy equipment but he never thought this would be part of today's conversation.

"I know all this because we are doing this with high school dropouts at the Evangeline Career Center in Troy, started by my husband Jack with several million dollars that he has already given away and proved successful. Money is great but without direction you have nothing but a black hole," she said.

She continued, "Every student who receives a tech certification or a degree who wants a job in technology right here in Key West will be guaranteed a job, no matter what.

I have more than enough money to make it happen. I know you get funded from the state of Florida but I will supplement every dime. I will start several businesses right here on campus and pay you rent for your unused facilities. I will buy all the equipment and allow you to use it for training and certification and I will use it in the businesses created right on campus as a Technology Center. We can get those coding jobs sent here under contract through the Evangeline Career Center, in Troy. Working remotely will be the way of the future, trust me on that. The college and I will be co-owners of the for-profit companies and plow back in every dime needed to ensure that we are on the cutting edge of technology. By the way, I have $155.0 million dollars in two trust funds by myself not even counting Jack's money. We both have an additional $60.0 million dollars each in our own personal accounts, tax-free. I think we can open a few doors here at the college.

What do I want from this? Nothing. I want to get rid of it! Speaking of movies, which I love, do you remember *Brewster's Millions* with Richard Pryor? He had thirty days to get rid of thirty million dollars and instead everything he touched he made money. It was filmed in 1985. Go watch it. I want to spend all the trust funds in five years or have it set up that it works by itself without my intervention or supervision. Maybe, it's your lucky day, guys," she said.

Joe looked at Morgan and then at Mary. He said, "Mary, that's a lot to digest but thank you. You have done your homework. You're right. Just covering the deficit doesn't grow the college and doesn't attract new students. I know from the military side, this may just be the incentive we need to build up our own Coast Guard technology across the board. I'm sure once this gets off the ground, I can bring down the powers that be to see what can be accomplished with a visionary like yourself."

Morgan added, "Where did this come from, Mary? I

know you taught elementary and high school math but where did your vision come from?" he asked.

"It came from having $480.0 million dollars handed to me one afternoon, added to my husband's winning lottery as well. What would we do with that much money? Give it away and watch it wasted or give it to someone with vision who would turn it into an economic engine to support the poor and get them out of poverty. Poverty is killing this country. Having money only in the hands of the rich so they can count it every day is just plain dumb. No one needs that much. As a nun, I took a vow of poverty, chastity and obedience but never of stupidity. I guess currently I am now zero for three, working on avoiding the fourth," she laughed.

"Mary, I have to meet with Joe and the board. I'm sure someone will complicate this plan of yours but I'm sure you are well aware of what happens with bureaucracy. Can we meet again? I'll get papers together about educational programs, training, certifications, rent, contracts and developing new corporations as soon as you walk out the door. I won't let this pass and I mean it. This will put Key West on the map just like your upstate New York Capital Region is known as Tech Valley, we can be "Southernmost Tech" or anything you want it to be. Are you staying around for a while?" he asked.

"Yes, Jack's coming down next week for several weeks and then we're heading back home to Troy. I still have projects up there including a new charter school that is one of my pet projects. It should be official by the time we get back. Thank you Joe for the introduction. Thank you, Morgan, for listening and hopefully fulfilling my dream."

They all shook hands and Joe walked out and met Antonia and Martina and headed for the parking lot. On the way out, she shook hands with Louise.

Joe didn't say anything in front of the two ladies but did

say everything went well and thanks for protecting Mary and Jack. Once home, Joe went out to the backyard with Mary for a private conversation and told her that what she proposed was remarkable and he wanted to personally thank her. Mary told him that it was her pleasure. She needed to talk to Julie, Tillie, Jamie, Linda, Joan and Jane about what just transpired but she said she wanted to move quickly when everyone was in a favorable mood. When left to time, nothing got done. 'Strike while the iron is hot' she said was her motto. *It sure was, thought Joe.*

CHAPTER 25

Jack arrived at the Key West airport late in the afternoon, a little over a week after Mary's meeting with Morgan and Joe. He flew out of the Albany International Airport early in the morning with a direct flight to Tampa. From there he took a puddle jumper to Key West. It was the same flight that they took when he first hit the lottery and Kristen told them to get out of town. She handed him a credit card with a ten thousand dollar credit limit and they used the whole amount. From that original trip, they met Joe and Julie at Sloppy Joe's on Duval Street in Key West one night when they went out for drinks. There were two seats available at the last hi-top table in the bar and Joe and Julie graciously shared it with them. When Jack and Mary told Joe they were from Troy, New York, he said, "No shit, really?" They became good friends. The next day they met the Lennon's through the Traynors and wound up buying a house on the same street as the Lennons. It was a small world.

Jack knew he was taking a chance once he landed in Tampa but at least he had John Jefferson and Fred Tucker drive him to the airport in Albany. He had the GPS chips placed on his clothing, shoes and luggage just in case. John and Fred would be picking them back up at the Albany

International Airport when they flew home in a few weeks. He had to wait an hour in Tampa for the flight into Key West and then was met by Jamie and Skip Lennon. Obviously Skip carried his Coast Guard weapon with him and they were ten minutes from home. As Skip told him originally, he would always be armed after being in the Coast Guard all those years, only retiring a few years ago. The weapon was now part of him.

In the car on the way home, Jack asked Skip and Jamie why their street was named Allamanda Terrace.

Jamie knew the answer to Skip's surprise. She said, "Allamanda refers to a number of tropical shrubs that bear showy flowers, typically yellow or purple," she said. "Being a man, you probably never even noticed the flowers around the block including right in front of your house."

Jack smiled and said, "Thanks for the answer, smartass. Does Mary know this or can I show her my new vast knowledge of our property?"

"Of course Mary knows about Allamanda and what it means. That's the first thing she pointed out that sold her on the house. If you know anything you should know she loves flowers," she said.

"Perhaps, I should pick a bouquet from the front yard and present it to her," Jack said with a smile.

Jamie smiled and shook her head. "Cut those flowers and you're a dead man," she said.

They finally arrived after a ten-minute ride that seemed like an hour. He was glad to be back and missed Mary, terribly. He had good news for her about the approval of her charter school in Lansingburgh and couldn't wait to tell her all about it. He also knew that this vacation might be cut short because the approval package came with a litany of questions and documents to be signed. Mary had to guarantee that the charter school would be fully funded for the first five years and funding had to be set aside into a sinking fund, non-refundable and non-negotiable. Jack knew this would not be an impediment since she already mentally set aside several million dollars for this purpose. Kristen was already working on the paperwork and funding issues. The biggest hurdle would be recruiting staff, teachers and students and opening by fall. It would be a challenge if she was there and a bigger challenge with her down here in Key West. Little did they know that a pandemic would hold back their projects for two years.

Jack walked in to the house and was first met by the security team, Antonia Andres and Martina Diego, who immediately asked him for his identification. Jack smiled and said, "Nice to meet you. I'm Jack Manning, Mary's husband." He handed Antonia his driver's license and passport which he always carried with him.

Mary came into the living room from the kitchen where she was cooking dinner and said to Jack, "Who is this man? I've never seen him before. Did you get his identification?"

Mary could see the confusion on the ladies' faces. "Only kidding Antonia and Martina. This is Jack, my husband. It's been a while since I've seen him so I wasn't sure," she said.

"Thanks," said Jack. "Love you too. Are you going to introduce me to these fully armed young ladies?" He went on, "Hi, I'm her husband, Jack."

"Nice to meet you, Jack. Please don't take it the wrong way. We never met you. Thanks, Mary, for embarrassing us," Martina said and shook her head.

"Sorry, ladies. I guess the joke's on me." Mary went over and gave Jack a big hug and a kiss and said, "Welcome home. I missed you. Dinner will be ready shortly. These two lovely ladies are the Coast Guard's best and will be here for a week, replaced by another two continuously until we leave. However, the Rear Admiral said it is only for a little while and then we need to talk to Joe about getting a few FBI retiree replacements like John and Fred. Maybe they know a few who retired down here and would like the job."

"Sounds like a plan. I'm hungry. Let's eat. I'll put my stuff in our room. It's still our room isn't it?" he asked.

"Of course, but I do have plans for this house so don't get too comfortable," Mary said and laughed.

They all sat down and ate dinner. Mary cooked a turkey breast with mashed potatoes, gravy and stuffing. It was delicious. The ladies weren't used to full course meals with always being on call. They missed half their dinners. After dinner, they all helped clear the dishes and put the pots and pans in the dishwasher. They decided to walk down and greet Linda and Skip. Jamie had a date she told Jack on the way in and Tom was across the road cleaning out the boat and getting it ready for the next excursion the following day. They were being chartered for four days by three couples from Chicago, all celebrating their wedding anniversaries together.

As they knocked on the door, Linda greeted everyone and opened the door. She told them to head back to the deck. She had already planned a short celebration, knowing Jack would be back today. They had drinks and Linda cut a cake she made and served everyone. She asked if anyone wanted to use their pool and no one did so they sat and talked. Mary brought the Lennons up to speed about her meeting with the college and her offer to develop a new hi-tech facility and training, start new businesses and rent space at the college so they would be able to count on income to steady the ship. Jack announced to Mary that both their charter schools in Troy were approved by the New York State Education Department and there was a lot to do within the next month to make sure it happened. Mary was thrilled but now knew she couldn't stay in Key West for long because of the pending paperwork required for the new charter schools.

Right then and there, they decided they would fly back to Troy within the next two weeks to meet their obligations.

Mary was just getting used to the Florida Keys lifestyle. There wasn't a whole lot not to like when you were rich. However, she was well aware of the underlying problems of the have-nots living in Florida, especially in the Keys. She wanted to change that as soon as she could by building infrastructures that would last, backed by real money. That takes time.

On his way home from the college, Joe Traynor stopped by to invite them up to their house in Tavernier over the weekend. Mark Silva and his wife, Louise, and their kids would be there. They were coming down by boat and would dock right around the corner from their house. They would all go out deep-sea fishing and have a picnic on the boat before heading back to Miami.

As Joe parked near the front of the house, Antonia and Martina walked over to his government vehicle and greeted him. It was friendly but they also wanted to prove to Joe that they were very serious about their security obligations to Mary first and by extension to Jack.

Jack said, "Hi Antonia. Hi Martina. Do you need my identification?"

"No, Joe," said Antonia, "but you never know. There could be someone holding a gun on you in the back seat."

"Duly noted," he said. "Nobody's in the backseat. Nobody's in the trunk. Can I come in and see them?"

"Sure," said Martina as they all walked in together.

It was now the last week of February and Mary and Jack originally were going to stay through March but decided to leave two weeks early to get started on the charter school activity if they were to open their doors in the fall.

Joe greeted Jack first and said, "Welcome back." He added, "Mary has been very busy down here. Did she tell you what's going on?"

"She did last night when we were over at the Lennons. I must say, I didn't come close to accomplishing anything like this when I first hit the lottery. I could barely balance my checkbook. It's amazing what a few short years can do to add to your personal education."

"Don't I know it," said Joe. "There's also something I need to tell you on the QT and it might be a very good idea that you're heading back to Troy. Is there someplace we can talk quietly?"

Jack pointed at the sliding glass door leading to the deck and they all walked out and sat down. Antonia stayed in the living room and Martina began her tour of the neighborhood, which she and Antonia did, separately, every two hours, outside of sleeping hours.

Joe said, "Do you remember over the holidays when we spoke that there might be a major health issue hitting the United States? I am privy to a lot of intelligence data. There has been an outbreak of what they are calling coronavirus, or COVID-19, since it started last fall in 2019. It is coming from China but now appears to be coming from Europe as well. They are shutting down all flights from China to the United States but nothing yet from Europe. It is hitting New York City the hardest since this is the hub of international flights from all over the world. It is spreading like wildfire and there is no vaccine or known cure. It appears to be affecting the elderly first and those with various health conditions like diabetes, heart disease and high blood pressure and even those with cancer or who are immune-compromised. So, I would advise you to get your flight back home ASAP. It's not that I want you to leave but I don't think you want to be quarantined here in Florida. They are starting to develop tests to see if anyone has gotten the disease but several people already have died."

"So, Joe, you are telling us to leave Florida and go home because you suspect that this could be a world epidemic?" said Jack. Mary nodded her head in concern.

"If I were you, I would charter the next flight out of here

directly to the Albany International Airport before flights are shut down and that would include private flights."

"Joe, what are you going to do?" said Mary.

"I just told Julie to be very careful at school and to keep an eye on Bella's elementary school. Through my sources, if this continues, schools will be shutting down to stop the spread of the virus and we'll all be working and living at home. I'll have Julie call Tillie and tell her to be ready to stay with us, indefinitely. She is of the age group that we are most concerned with. Julie and I are way too young to be really sick, so they say, but you and Mary may have some concerns being late 40's and early 50's. Your staff up in Troy could also be in jeopardy. Whatever plans we have down here could be put on hold if the college closes or we go directly to Internet classes with no one showing up on campus," said Joe.

"Wow. Thanks, Joe. Without you, we could be stuck here for a very long time. I don't believe being stuck in Florida is a bad thing but our home is still in Troy and Jack's children, Debbie and Mark, are there. My mother is there and so are my ex-nun friends that I lived with for years. Jack, let's book a flight for tomorrow or the next day ASAP. We need to give a heads up to Antonia and Martina or Joe can you do that much better than us. Coming from you, it might carry more weight. I can only imagine if the people down here are stuck at home, can't work, lose their jobs because of it, or can't even get groceries, they are in deep crap. Joe, if you need any money at all, regardless of the amount, as things get worse, if they do, you need to call us for help. We will be there for you," Mary said.

Jack called the Key West airport commercial flight area and booked a direct flight for the Albany International Airport for the next night at 6:00 p.m. They would arrive in Albany before midnight. They were more than pleased to offer a flight to Mary and Jack because they done so before and they became very good customers. At thirty thousand dollars a flight, it was very expensive but wouldn't make a dent in their sizable net worth. What would make a dent would be getting the virus and all that it brought to the community.

Jack called Sam and Pete as well as the Rear Admiral and told them that he recommended that they fly out to Albany ASAP. He sat down Antonia and Martina and told them they would be paid for a full month not just the week so they would have funds on hand in case there were any financial issues coming out of this upcoming potential pandemic. They were very grateful but now very worried. Joe told them to keep this to themselves but to start stocking up on supplies in case of an emergency.

Antonia and Martina brought Mary and Jack to the Key West airport at 5:00 p.m. for their 6:00 p.m. flight. No one at the airport said a word about any potential health issues. CNN, FOX and MSNBC were making inquiries to Congress and the White House to see if there was any news or updates about a pending disaster. Mary told Antonia and Martina that Jamie would drive them back to Islamorada to their Coast Guard facility. Joe had already mentioned to Joan Talbot about a pending crisis and that the two ladies were on their way back. He was heading home and picking up Tillie to at least stay the week until they understood what was happening in the world.

Mary and Jack were met at the Albany International Airport, right before midnight, by John and Fred, in two cars, and they immediately drove back to their home in the Town of Brunswick. Mary had called Kristen to let her know they were coming back immediately and she needed to talk to her the next day and alluded to the fact there may be a pending crisis. She called Karen at the Career Center and told her at length what was going on. Then, Jack called Debbie and told her they were on their way home which surprised her. She said she would stay up to see them when they arrived.

Mary and Jack spoke quietly on the plane. They needed to gather themselves and see what they could do in case this crisis took over the country. They had plenty of money to survive but not enough to cover everyone they knew. Their five to ten year plan to give away all that money may now be spent in only one year to ensure the survival of everything and everyone they know and love. *Let's pray to God this doesn't happen and it all dies out when the warm weather comes just like the flu, Mary thought.*

Chapter 26

Kristen called at 9:00 a.m. the next day. She knew they just got in around midnight and didn't want to wake them too early. Karen had already texted Mary and Jack and said she'd meet them for lunch at their house on Old Plank Road. Jack texted Joe as soon as they landed to let him know they're safe and sound. Jack quickly thanked Joe in a sentence or two and said he would like to talk to him later in the day. Joe texted that he was free after 4:00 p.m. Both Jack's and Mary's heads were spinning from the news, which could be a total disaster for all their plans. That was the least of their worries they said to each other when they got home and had a few quiet moments to themselves.

They needed to be prepared no matter what happens. If they have to scrap their plans, then so be it, they both said. If they need to spend everything sitting in all the trust funds, and in their own personal funds, for that matter, then they both agreed they'd live without it. Neither expected to be rich and at this point neither wanted the burden of wealth, either. Jack was just happy that he married Mary regardless of what happened next. Mary's life had changed so dramatically that she was worried that she was becoming another person entirely and wasn't so sure she was happy with the change. After all, Jack and Mary had nothing before he won the lottery and both were content just being together.

Mary spoke at length with Kristen and told her everything that Joe had said the day before. Kristen said she had watched the news but no one seemed to be that worried and even the president said that it wouldn't really touch the United States and not to panic. Joe told Mary the exact opposite and perhaps the White House was sugar coating the virus and didn't want people to be worried. After all there was an election coming up soon and you don't win elections by giving out really bad news. That's the politician's dilemma. They didn't seem to get brownie points for making everyone safe from a disease that was unknown, nor at a peak, where it was even noticeable at that point in early March. However, there was talk of closing down schools and businesses for a month and that would curtail the virus once and for all. No one knew what to do. People in other countries were getting sick and even dying but not here, not yet. Jack and Mary thought that they had better have some plans just in case. Everyone better have some plans just in case.

Karen showed up for lunch. She thought about inviting Sam Ryan, their controller and vice president of the Career Center, to the meeting. However, she just wanted to get an idea from Jack and Mary what they were thinking. Sam was great with numbers but like a lot of accountants, everything was black or white and everything was going to hell in a handbasket. Karen didn't want that conversation today or even this week, starting with everything going wrong. She needed to feel comfortable with what they could do to survive any pending disaster not just an unknown virus.

Once informed by Jack and Mary, Karen would direct Sam to set up the proper financial procedures with the help of Kristen Sorenson and her fellow tax attorneys at their law firm. You can't move money around like it was still yours. The money is now in a financial trust with rules and, regulations and you had to justify expenditures. Every year there is a full and complete audit from top to bottom and the filing of annual tax records. Virus or not, they had to be on solid ground if they were to deviate from the original plans that were instituted to start the tax-free trusts.

During lunch, Karen had asked them how their trip was and they said short but sweet. Mary then proceeded to tell her what Joe had conveyed to them. After all, he was on top of intelligence for Florida and the Keys and was in constant contact with his Rear Admiral and did other work for the bosses in Washington, D.C. He was only one of a few multi-lingual officers in the Coast Guard, predominately Russian, Chechen and Spanish, now in the process of learning Chinese. His Chinese acumen is what started his interest in what was now coming out of Wuhan, China. He interpreted the intelligence intercepts as best he could for his own team, his Rear Admiral and some in Washington. He knew something was coming soon that could be extremely dangerous to the United States at large. With this knowledge of Joe's background, Mary said to Karen, "Trust whatever Joe tells us. We are fortunate to have a friend like this in high places."

Karen said, "Mary don't get me wrong but it is very confusing on what's coming down the road. What do we do with our current projects? What happens to the charter schools, yours and Jack's? What happens to our students if they can't come to class and get their GED/TASC certificates? What if the shutdown is for longer and there are more restrictions? How do we pay our staff and teachers and all our workers rehabbing all the houses in the neighborhood? What do we do next?" Karen was upset and had no answers. Mary looked to Jack. It was his Center.

Jack turned to Mary and then said to Karen, "Mary has

her own new projects that she'll tell you about but let me address our immediate concerns and your immediate concerns, one question at a time. We have enough money to continue to pay every dime of everyone's salary for at least the next two years. We have enough money to make sure that each student in our Career Center program will receive a stipend as long as they continue to participate and then pass the GED/TASC exam, giving each a high school equivalency diploma so they can head to Hudson Valley Community College. We will supply each student with a computer and an iPad so they can do distance learning from home if that's what happens if we have to shut down. We need online internet teachers or we need to immediately train our staff on how to educate remotely without losing content or students. Set up a meeting with HVCC and get our teachers acclimated with online learning and internet teaching. Call our partners at RPI, Siena and Albany to see what resources they have to help us. Order 100 computers immediately and 100 iPads. Start looking at what we need for personal protection for everyone in our immediate area including families, students, teachers, office and administrative staff. Let's get as prepared as possible."

"That's a big list, Jack but I've never backed down from a challenge," Karen said. "What do I tell Sam about why we're purchasing these items?"

"Tell him that I requested the items and to call me, directly," Jack said.

Mary added, "Karen, even though we have separate trusts, we are willing to join forces until this crisis, if there is one, ends. But, we need to provide strict financial guidelines so that at the end, we don't overstep our legal responsibilities. By the way, your thirty thousand dollar increase in pay for this year will be honored and so will Sam's. You have and will continue to earn it," Mary smiled.

"Thank you," said Karen. She didn't know what else to

say. She was overwhelmed but sincerely wanted to step up and do everything she could to hold things together in light of the pending news.

Mary took another half hour to explain what she was doing down in the Keys and what she would be setting up with The College of the Florida Keys including the new Technology Center, job creation and contracts subbed by the Evangeline Career Center to do online coding for companies in the Capital Region from the college in Key West. That was probably as important to her as anything else. It would keep their relationship strong in the Capital Region and prove that remote jobs are a thing of the future to everyone in south Florida and the Keys. She wanted to keep her promise to Joe, the Rear Admiral and Morgan as well as to her new board and advisory group. No matter what happens in the future she wanted to keep these projects going and make the teams stronger and more resilient if a crisis did hit.

Karen left for the Center and Mary called Kristen back and told her what she told Karen. She also told Kristen that their law firm had better start making plans for self-containment and to keep their firm going strong. Mary said she would continue to support the law firm through fees and would not negotiate prices or fees down if things got worse. If they went longer than a year then all bets were off. She just wanted to see how they could hold on for the immediate future and keep everyone as whole as they could. It became clearer and clearer that they would have to postpone the opening of both charter schools for the fall if those schools already open would have to close. You can't recruit teachers and pay them for a school that couldn't open. You couldn't recruit students for the same reason.

Mary started to feel bad that everything was hanging by a thread. It was better to know than not know and it was better to know exactly how much they needed if everything shut down to keep people safe and secure. She bet that a good chunk of the $77.5 million dollars for each location would be spent just holding everything together if a worldwide crisis hit in the form of a virus pandemic with no testing, no cure, and no vaccine. As an ex-nun, Mary felt that the best thing she could do is start praying along with her friends.

Jack and Mary caught Joe around 4:00 p.m. as expected. They put the call on speakerphone. They told Joe exactly what they had started to plan up in Troy at the Career Center if and when things got worse. Jack mentioned that they started to order one hundred new computers and the same amount of iPads in case they had to teach and train online. Jack also mentioned that he told Karen, his executive director at the Career Center, that he would cover all salaries and student stipends for two years and if it was worse than that then they would have to address the issue. It was clear that the Evangeline Trust Fund that he started with fifty million dollars would have enough to hopefully weather the storm. Jack's conversation made Joe more comfortable that hopefully things would get better and they would be covered for the short term.

At the end of the conversation, Mary asked Joe if he could bring Morgan Hennessey on the line. She wanted to give both Joe and Morgan some assurances about where she stood financially and what she was willing to do for them if there was a crisis. Joe dialed up Morgan, who immediately came on to the phone and said, "Can you all hear me?"

Mary said, "Jack and I can hear you. How about you, Joe?"

"Yes, I called him and we're hooked in together. Morgan, Mary has something to tell you," Joe said.

Mary told Morgan that she would honor everything that they agreed to but if the college shut down and if students couldn't come on campus and if she couldn't rent space for new companies and a Technology Center, they would have to do things differently. She asked Joe and Morgan to get together with their finance staff. She wanted to know if they were to shut down for any length of time, what effect that would have on their budget for this year.

She asked that question because New York State was already having financial difficulty and was asking every department to put together a twenty percent budget cut. That was several billion dollars to the bottom line. She then asked Morgan to estimate how he and Joe could put together a task force to address the new technology innovation that would be part of the new Technology Center on campus. Mary told them that her twenty million dollar offer that she had just proposed could be moved up to cover immediate expenses if it related to keeping the college open and getting new students enrolled. She also mentioned that she had already asked her career center administrators to start conversations on how they could provide remote coding personnel in Key West for Albany-based companies. There were at least ten companies who would immediately contract with the Career Center to hire a minimum of one hundred coders to start upon graduation or if she already had some to start immediately that would be even better. The annual contracts would be enough to cover the salaries, rent, overhead and a small profit for the first year to be shared by Mary and the college.

Morgan said, "Mary, that's quite generous on your part. I don't know what to say but thanks. We will put together a plan immediately with a price tag. It won't be anywhere near twenty million dollars this year but I can't promise that if the crisis comes to fruition. We can only hope for the best and plan for the worst."

"I agree," said Mary. "Please get to us as soon as you can. Joe, we need to speak to Joan Talbot and your Rear Admiral. Can we tie in our Coast Guard bequest to the new college Technology Center and they can share in the technology and training so they can at least stay on top of everything, even if there is a quarantine?"

"Mary, that's a great idea. I'll call Jake and Joan as soon as I'm off the phone," Joe said. With that the conversation ended and Mary wanted to at least call Julie, Joe's wife and Linda Lennon to let them know that no matter what happens their personal trust funds were all set and ready in case they got caught short if a crisis hit. Mary also wanted to switch gears a little and would ask Julie about the status of food banks and schools in Monroe County and how they could be affected. The poorest of the poor in Monroe County, almost 100% covering the entire Keys, worked in the hospitality industry almost 100% without any benefits, living from paycheck to paycheck. What would happen to their families if everything shut down even for a week? She wanted to get an idea of what that would cost if both she and Jack decided to fund different crisis intervention programs. There were 8,800 students in the Monroe County School District from Key Largo to Key West and everywhere in between. Those students had a poverty rate as high as Miami and free and reduced lunch programs provided almost sixty percent of those students with one of their main meals for the day. What would happen if the school closed? What would happen on the weekend when there was no school lunch?

Poverty was a terrible thing. Mary would ask Tillie how she handled that while taking care of Julie as she was growing up. There were some lessons that never changed. Almost sixty percent of families living in Key West lived in substandard apartments because the average home price was six hundred thousand dollars. Mary knew that every dime she released had to be used efficiently or it would be wasted. Just to cover daily lunches for the sixty percent receiving free lunches for one hundred and eighty days a school year at $4.00 a day would cost $3.8 million dollars a year. If every poor student, over 5,000 of them in the Florida Keys, needed an iPad, at $300.00 each minimum, it would cost $1.5 million dollars to purchase those items, not even knowing if they could get the products in on time, train students and teachers, and be up to speed. It was mind-boggling at this point. Mary didn't want to get ahead of herself, but $77.5 million dollars to be used during a crisis would never be enough. Everyone across the country would have the same problems and they would have to deal with them until the crisis ended. Mary was worried that even though the president said there was no crisis, she believed Joe Traynor that something was happening and it would not be good for the country in the very near future. She could only pray.

CHAPTER 27

Starting toward the end of March, it was obvious that something was happening across the country. People were getting sick and seniors living in nursing homes were not only getting very ill but they were dying as well. The state of Washington was the first to see this happen and then New York City became the epicenter for what was now being called a pandemic. Coronavirus or Covid-19 had hit and no one could figure out why. Travel from China had been banned and yet the numbers in New York City and the surrounding areas were being infected the worst in the country. They finally figured out that travel from Europe, and specifically from Italy, which had not been halted, was the main cause. New York City is the destination of many international travelers. It was clear that people from China were heading to Europe because of the ban into the United States, and from there they headed to New York City and out to the rest of the country.

By late spring, thousands of Americans were sick and dying in huge numbers. There was no vaccine and no method of treating the disease. Hospitals were filled to capacity. Ventilators were still in short supply. So many were dying that hospitals had to stack bodies in refrigerated trucks because there was no room left at the mortuaries. It was clear that seniors were the first to be infected. Everyone was waiting for the weather to get warmer. After all, the president said as soon as the weather warmed up, this virus would disappear just like the flu. It didn't happen. Daily briefings by the president and the CDC or Center for Disease Control, did nothing to alleviate American fears.

Late spring, several companies got together to address developing a new vaccine and they were hoping for a breakthrough in record time. Several companies joined together while others went their own way. Many of the companies took funding from the government and several did not. The government-funded projects were listed as government projects and it became a political nightmare. The country was beginning to be divided. Mask mandates and quarantines were put into effect across the country, further dividing friends, family members and the general population. Schools and businesses were closed with no relief in sight. Even the president and his family were diagnosed with Covid-19 and he was rushed to the hospital and received care that no one else had gotten at the time. This made him even more emboldened to say he got over it so everyone else will get the same medicine that he got. It didn't happen. But everyone around him got the same treatment. Eyes were opening and lack of trust from the top started to change the politics of this country.

The death of George Floyd at the hands of the Minneapolis Police was caught on video and released to the public. All hell broke out across the country ending up with a very troublesome event in Washington, where protestors were shot with rubber bullets and brought down by the National Guard on orders from the President, as he walked to the church across the lawn from the White House, holding a bible, upside down. This trial further divided the country, during the middle of the worst pandemic in history as all eyes were glued on the trial that finally convicted the police officer, who's knee was sitting on George Floyd's neck for eight minutes and forty-six seconds on May 25, 2020, killing him in front of the world.

Unemployment went up by the millions and families couldn't pay their rent or even put food on the table. Seniors, thought to be the most affected at the time, were kept inside and they were afraid to even go to the grocery store. Hundreds of thousands were now dead in the United States and the list continue to grow. Holidays were a thing of the past. Thanksgiving came and went. Cars were lined up at food banks and the economy was headed into the tank.

Then, on top of all this, there was a United States presidential election. The president lost by a substantial margin both in the popular vote and in the Electoral College. However, he fought tooth and nail and told everyone that the election was stolen and did everything he could to stay in power. The Supreme Court and other federal courts ruled against him sixty-three times, state by state, but even that didn't stop him. Finally, when the final vote was to be tallied by Congress on January 6, 2021, the President's supporters, after a rally fueled by his words, over ran the Capitol building. The insurrection was finally stopped by the Capitol Police, the National Guard, and the Washington Metropolitan Police. Several people died but the election was certified and a new President was inaugurated on Wednesday, January 20, 2021, at noon, Eastern Standard Time.

While all this was going on for almost a full year, vaccines were being developed and were at the breakthrough stage. Obviously the current President wanted the vaccines to be released before the Tuesday, November 3, 2020 election date. It didn't happen and that brought even more frustration to the President at the time who needed the release desperately because he was so far behind in the polls due to his handling of the virus.

Finally, approval for Pfizer vaccine came first, and then Moderna, second, brought great relief to all Americans. Then came Johnson and Johnson's breakthrough one shot only vaccine. These were released under an emergency use authorization and not fully FDA approved but no one cared if it saved lives. In the summer of that year, under a new President, over two hundred million Americans have received at least one dose of vaccine and hoping for the second. Many were on their way for booster shots for those vaccinated in January and February, with an eight-month waiting period before receiving a booster shot. In the meantime, many Americans have refused to get any vaccination due to their own religious or political beliefs. Many states in the southern United States have such a low vaccination rate that a new Delta variant has been spreading like wildfire, especially among American youth, either under age twelve, who could not be vaccinated or by those over age twelve whose parents would not consent to their vaccination for whatever reason. Infections and deaths have been picking up and unless everyone gets vaccinated there is limited hope that normalization of life will happen. It is clear that Vermont with an over eighty percent vaccination rate and Alabama at under forty percent will have very different economic and health issues down the road.

Jack and Mary's life has also changed dramatically during this time period. They were home on Old Plank Road in Brunswick for almost a year. They started to go out gradually. Regardless of wealth, families still needed to get groceries, go to CVS or pick up a dinner or have it delivered. Churches closed so watching Mass on the computer became the new norm. Debbie stayed with Jack and Mary and actually finished her Master's degree from the University at Albany, online. She also passed her New York State exams for certification and was offered a position by Karen Steele at the Career Center. This pleased her to no end because her father and Mary stayed out of the discussions of employment. Her brother, Mark, had passed his CPA exam and was well entrenched in an Albany-based accounting firm. With Zoom and documentation passed back and forth between accountants and clients through emails and attachments, Mark's life was not interrupted that much. Taxes had to be paid and paperwork could be done anywhere.

Mark announced his engagement to Cara and they were planning for a nice wedding, once the Covid-19 crisis started to clear. Cara's parents were well on board and they decided to wait for a while. Most 21st century couples lived together anyway before getting married so this was not much of a hardship. Mark and Cara visited only occasionally but once all were fully vaccinated, the economy and social life started to open up and normalize, under the new normal.

As more and more people became vaccinated and started to revert back to their normal lives, Jack and Mary had to evaluate where they were and what their promises were to everyone they encountered. They also had to add up all the money they'd spent during this almost fifteen-month period to keep their friends, family, their projects, their promises and what they needed to do to continue back on track.

As soon as the virus hit and lockdowns began, Jack and Mary had assured everyone at the Career Center that their jobs were secure for at least two years. They also had to spend money keeping the Center projects alive through internet access and Zoom. They spent a fortune for cleaning products for all the facilities and for the homes of those in programs. They had to buy computers and iPads for students, both in Troy and in the Keys. They had to close up rehab projects as the winter closed in and they were not allowed to work on anything by New York State law. Construction was closed until further notice. Masks were at a premium and as soon as a few came in, those were gone. They had to work from home and had to order food online delivered at the driveway. If John and Fred were to continue guarding them, then they would be in quarantine with them so they decided that John would stay and Fred would be available for emergencies only. When the vaccine became available, they immediately scheduled appointments. Without the vaccine, they were stuck and continuing to spend money just to stop the dam from leaking. They wanted to regroup and restart just like the economy needed to do. As the pandemic started to ease when the majority in New York State became fully vaccinated, Mary wanted to restart her Florida initiatives but the governor there was sending out messages that didn't match the federal mandates. They knew eventually, hopefully, every state would catch up and life would change for the better.

At first, their students at the Center couldn't receive the vaccine until last, and now all those over age twelve got their shots. Students at the Evangeline Career Center, in Troy, age eighteen and over, couldn't join classes unless everyone in their family, over age twelve, was vaccinated. As far as The College of the Florida Keys went, they had to shut down their facilities and offered remote classes. The military side decided the risk was too great so they cut their student-base by fifty percent at first and now were back in full force with vaccine mandates by the military. Now, the college was back up and running but every day there were mixed messages from the governor of Florida and the federal response. If the college allowed masks, then they wouldn't get any state aid and the staff wouldn't get paid. Politics was the cause. Someone new wants to be President, evidently it was the Florida governor.

The college was now fully opened with minor cases of Covid-19 happening among the non-vaccinated. They had to be admitted by law but these individuals had to be tested weekly until further notice. Anyone enrolled in Mary's special coding classes had to be vaccinated due company policies in New York State, even though they were working remotely because they required all employees to be vaccinated. The training, education, and degrees were all tied to jobs. The companies dictated the jobs, the pay, the benefits, the training and the contract.

During this period during the pandemic, 8,800 students didn't attend classes in person in the Monroe County School District in the Keys. Over fifty percent lived in poverty and in public housing or trailer parks. Many didn't have access to the internet or technology or even owned a computer or an iPad. Food ran short with job loss, store closings, lack of food on the shelves and no transportation, since many couldn't afford gasoline for a car. Jack and Mary donated close to ten million dollars to Florida Keys and Troy, New York food banks, almost one million dollars per month at each region. Most of the money went for food and the rest for salaries of those working at regional food banks, and the cost of transportation. There literally was no free lunch.

All in all, Jack and Mary combined, spent over thirty million dollars in just over a year to keep everything afloat. In many cases, recovery wasn't lack of money but of fear for the future. They thought if they could show their own commitment to as many as they could during this pandemic, then those around them would start to feel more secure and would prove as loyal to them as they did for those most in need. Jack and Mary decided to start up again and tried to put the pandemic behind them. That wouldn't be easy but necessary. Spending thirty million dollars, with half of it as giveaways to help people stay afloat, moved their ten-year timeline closer to Mary's five-year plan. If they ran out of money, Mary thought that might be the best problem they would ever have.

Flights were now available so they decided to see if they

could head back down to Key West. It's been forever since they were there. Thank God that Jamie and Tom, Skip and Linda were there to take care of their place. Mary opened a checking account for Jamie to pay all the bills for the property and to load up on any health related supplies she thought they and her family might need. She paid all the taxes and sewer and water bills along with monthly heat, light and electric. Jamie took the Highlander in for the annual inspection and oil and filter. She hadn't put too many miles on the SUV because they could barely go to the supermarket since nothing else was open. Duval Street, in the heart of Key West, was a ghost town for many months. Their church finally opened with twenty-five percent occupancy, then fifty percent and now was fully opened but masks were still required regardless of what the governor said. Most parishioners at the Catholic Church were older than sixty and didn't want to take a chance.

Jamie said they were ready for their arrival. Masks were still required at all the airports from New York to Florida. Jack didn't want a big bill to fly down to Key West, especially after spending thirty million dollars, fully documented for their accountants and tax records. They would take the same flight down to Tampa and then a puddle jumper to Key West, just like before.

When they arrived, they would be met once again by Martina and Antonia, the two Coast Guard members, who had guarded them previously, when Joe told them to head out because there was a pandemic coming. Once they arrived, they would plan to meet Jane and her legal staff in Miami. Obviously, she would meet with Joe and Morgan at the college. They also wanted to spend a few days on Skip's boat. They missed doing that since forever. Mary needed to bring her board and advisors up to speed since she hasn't been down in a long time. Julie told her to call her and she would arrange to get a babysitter for Bella so Tillie could come with her. Joe would bring them down for the day to Mary's house while he went to the college. He was almost finished with his Ph.D. and wanted to discuss what that meant to them moving forward. As he said, he was being groomed to be the Assistant Superintendent at the Coast Guard Academy up in New London, Connecticut.

CHAPTER 28

When the pandemic first hit, while they were on their flight back from Tampa to Albany, Mary said to Jack, "Can we discuss something that I've been thinking about for a very long time?"

"Sure," he said. "What's on your mind?"

"If there's a pandemic like Joe thinks there will be, then if we're stuck under quarantine for any length of time, I'd like to finally get my Ph.D. in education." She went on to say, "This is probably the first time you've heard it but it's been on my mind for a long time. I got my Masters in teaching at The College of Saint Rose almost twenty years ago. Every teacher in New York State has to have a Master's degree to teach by the end of his or her third year, to become tenured. So, my degree is nothing special compared to every other teacher. It's not that I'm looking for a raise. That's a very good reason since the pay increases by over $3,000.00 a year. But, I would like to go into administration, especially now after what we have accomplished at the Evangeline Career Center. I want to be certified as both a New York State and a Florida School District Administrator, either as a Principal or Assistant Superintendent, or even Superintendent. When I have meetings with educators now discussing education and careers, I'm at a disadvantage when sitting around all the D.'s. They really don't know more, they just think they do and quite frankly, it pisses me off," she said with a sly grin.

"It was also clear when speaking to Morgan that his Ph.D. from Brown University was very impressive and it is but my experience is just as impressive. What I want to do for a thesis is to develop a paper that proves that education without a job is useless for financially poor students. I'm not saying that a liberal arts education is useless but for poor kids, education leading to a job, is the most important tool to break the cycle of poverty and I want to prove it through research and spending millions of my own dollars to prove it. So, I want to get together with Joe and see how he's doing with his Ph.D. program and I would like to follow a similar path. I don't want to go into the military but the lessons learned are the same," she said.

"Well that was a mouthful," said Jack. "As soon as we get back, call Joe and start the ball rolling. From my understanding, they have bent over backward to accommodate him at Barry University in Miami where he's getting his degree. He's doing it through internet classes and mentoring from Barry staff assigned to The College of the Florida Keys facility. Most universities are now bending over backward to be competitive and meet the challenges of people like Joe and older students with real responsibilities. He told me he is well on his way and should be done soon. He needs six credit hours for his thesis, which evidently is education theory for the military with an emphasis on the Coast Guard. He said being very specific gives him a leg up because it has never been done before. Using educational strategies from the Ph.D. in catching criminals is a whole new ballgame. In the past officers didn't have to have a college degree, just years of service. This was the same for law enforcement but they're becoming much smarter and everyone needs a degree to move up."

"Great," she said. "I'll call him tonight."

That night when they got in, Mary called Joe. They'd just finished dinner and he was helping Bella with her math. Everyone knows that Joe does math, six digits with a decimal point, in his head. He said that doesn't help because he doesn't understand the new elementary school math. He laughed and told her if they taught two trains left Chicago at 5:00 p.m., one going sixty miles an hour west and the other going fifty miles an hour east, how far would they be apart after three hours? He said that one he could handle.

"Mary, my Ph.D. program is a snap compared to some poor kid, paying for it himself or herself, taking crap from professors who haven't left the nest in thirty years. My program was tailored for me by Barry University after a call from my Rear Admiral to the president of the university. As you know, I went to MIT, then to Miami-Dade Community College, to the Coast Guard Academy, ending up with my MBA from Rensselaer Polytechnic Institute in Troy. If it wasn't in my own hometown, this world class technology university, I wouldn't even know about it," he said.

Mary said, "Joe, mine is a little different but almost as circular as yours. Like you, I graduated from Catholic Central High School at eighteen years old. I went into the convent with four of my close friends. We joined together and of course none of us remained. I moved to the Sisters of St. Joseph facility in Latham, and from there, they sent me for my teaching degree from The College of Saint Rose. I got my Bachelor's degree and then immediately started teaching at St. Augustine's and got my Master's degree in mathematics. I am a New York State Department of Education certified mathematics teacher, and there are not a lot of us left, especially in the remaining Catholic Schools. I became disenchanted with the religious life and after fifteen years, I left the convent. My first and only job was working for Jack Manning at the Troy Community Council for twelve years. After we got fired, I didn't need much so I went back to both Catholic High as a teacher and to St. Augustine's as a teacher's aid and math specialist. Then, Jack changed my world by hitting the lottery and just handing me fifteen million dollars and brought me in as an equal partner to develop the Career Center and all the other projects. We both already have a Ph.D. in bullshit, coming from these experiences."

"I'm sure you do," said Joe. "What do you want to do for a thesis? Using your money as part of a thesis experiment, fully financed, could be the kicker."

She told Joe exactly what she wanted and that she wanted to receive the same Ph.D. in education that he would be getting but applied to the private sector and public partnership with secondary education and higher education just like The College of the Florida Keys.

Joe told her he would immediately call Jake Barnes, his Rear Admiral, whom she met. He would ask him to once again make the same call on her behalf. He said it might wind up a little different when the pandemic hit and she would have to be flexible. She told him the story of the contortionist who wanted to hire an assistant. He told her that she had to be flexible. She said she couldn't make Tuesdays. Joe roared. "You really are Irish. Aren't you?"

"Barry University offers a Doctor of Philosophy in Leadership and Education Specialization in Higher Education Administration. I needed 54 additional credit hours added to my MBA from RPI and that included the six credits needed for my dissertation. I have less than one year to go and maybe sooner depending on credits for handling a pandemic. I'm not kidding. You probably need less because you're certified in the education field, especially in mathematics, which counts more since there are fewer and fewer mathematics teachers out there. I'll send you the brochure and expect a call from Jake or someone from Barry

University to get the ball rolling."

Mary got off the phone all excited and told Jack everything that Joe told her about his program and how she should expect a call from Jake or the university. She was very happy. Her dreams may just come true. It was several days later when Jake Barnes, Rear Admiral and Joe's boss called Mary directly. He told her he would be honored to speak on her behalf to his good friend at Barry University. He said he would try to get the same deal that he got Joe. He said that she would probably have to pay for it since she was nonmilitary but laughed and said, "I don't think that would be much of a problem, Mary, do you?"

"No," she said and added, "Maybe they'd like a new department chair paid for upon two graduations, Joe and mine, with Ph.D,'s of course," and she laughed.

"You catch on quickly but I hear you really want to prove a point that if there is enough funding, poor kids can compete with the rich when they have a level playing field. Is that about right?"

"Bingo," she said. "I mean, Bingo, sir."

He laughed and said, "Joe said you were a pisser. Are you available on Tuesdays?"

"No, I'm not that flexible."

He told her to expect a call from someone at Barry. He said Joe would send her all the application forms and brochures to get started. Since it was only March and mid-semester, perhaps she could start and do a double session in the summer, both in Florida and here. He told her to get a mentor from either the University at Albany or at The College of Saint Rose. When she was down in Key West, she could probably double up and use Joe's mentor on the same day and time he saw Joe.

The call came from the Dean of the School of Education at Barry University and he told her the application was accepted and she would start this summer, either in person or online depending on the quarantine situation and pandemic overall. She thanked him and he chuckled and said the Rear Admiral said she was loaded and if he treats her right, he might be amazed.

"You never know," she said. She thanked him and was ready to start. She would set up her classroom in her house, She would join Zoom and the college internet, get her documents sent to Barry University and start her thesis. She didn't need the degree to write the paper. She needed the degree to prove that the thesis was well researched, well financed, well thought out and gave precise answers for poverty-based education and breaking the cycle of poverty through education and job creation. She would have a lot to do but she was excited that she was no longer on Jack's coattails even though he never thought that. She now believed that money or no money she could carry her own weight. Of course the money helps she thought and smiled. There is no going back so don't even think about it.

CHAPTER 29

Labor Day came and went. Their charter schools wouldn't open until next year so they had plenty of time to plan. Jack and Mary got their flight to Key West, same as their other trips, and would arrive around 5:30 p.m. after an hour wait at Tampa International Airport. They then took the puddle jumper flight down to Key West. They landed and got their carry-on bags and went to the front of the main building and saw Jamie in the Highlander. Both Martina and Antonia, double-parked with the lights flashing, accompanied her. The rear of the SUV was open and they put in their bags in and closed the door. They hopped into the back seat and Martina moved over. Jamie was driving like it was her own vehicle and for all practical purposes, it was. Antonia sat in the front passenger seat and they all greeted Jack and Mary.

"Long time, no see," said Jamie and smiled.

Martina gave them both a hug and Antonia bumped fists from the front seat. Jamie put on her directional and pulled out into traffic headed home. Like Albany, the Key West Airport was small and very maneuverable. Parking was never a problem. They chatted in the SUV for a while. The three ladies had masks on so Jack and Mary put on theirs as well, even though they were fully vaccinated. Even though the Governor of Florida frowned upon wearing a mask, the military dictated what they would do including mask wearing. Jamie, being one of the last to get vaccinated because of age restrictions, had just gotten her second Moderna vaccination and it would be another two weeks before she was fully vaccinated. Martina and Antonia were vaccinated several months ago under orders from the Coast Guard. There had been worries about breakthrough infections down south but it hadn't caught up in the Keys. As a matter of fact, the Florida Keys had an extremely low rate of infections and deaths compared to the rest of Florida. Everyone spent most of their days outside and masks were still required on Duval Street until further notice. Bars were fully opened however and the workers tended to wear masks in spite of pressure from customers and the state government. When low paid workers got sick, they had no insurance and couldn't work. It was the food bank or nothing so they were very cautious, still.

As they started to enter Allamanda Terrace, Jamie said to Jack, "Jack, why is this called Allamanda? Do you know where that comes from?" She asked with a sly grin.

"Why yes, Jamie, I do know the meaning of the word, "Allamanda". "Allamanda" refers to a number of tropical shrubs that bear showy flowers, typically yellow or purple as you can see from the front of our house all the way down to yours."

"Thank you, Jack," said Jamie.

"How did you know that, Jack?" asked Mary.

"A little bird told me quite a while ago. It's something you don't forget, especially when those are such a beautiful array of plants," Jack said.

"Ladies put on your boots. Evidently it's bullshit season in Key West," said Mary.

Everyone laughed as they pulled up in front of their garage, "Thanks, ladies," said Mary.

"Glad to be back here, once again. I can't believe how long it's been. Almost sixteen months since we headed out at Joe Traynor's request at the start of the pandemic. I just can't believe it's been that long. I can't wait to get started again. By the way ladies, I'm having a few guests over in the next few days so we may have to double up if you don't mind. It should be for a day and no later than two. Julie Traynor and her grandmother and my attorney from Miami, Jane Swanson, will be here around 11:00 a.m. tomorrow for a meeting. Then I'm meeting with Joe and Morgan at the college to see where we stand. Martina and Antonia, I'll need rides wherever I go, as you know. Thanks, though for being here. It is appreciated," said Mary.

Mary had to meet with Joe and Morgan for several reasons. She was following Joe's Barry University Ph.D. curriculum and now had to meet his mentor from Barry University, stationed at The College of the Florida Keys, who would become her mentor as well. Joe would be finishing his degree and thesis by Christmas and no one was sure exactly what his plans were at that point. She wanted him to stay on at The College of The Florida Keys but she knew the Rear Admiral was hoping for Joe to head to the Coast Guard Academy as soon as he got his Ph.D. She would be finished with her degree by late next summer, just in time for their two charter schools to be opened. At that point, she hoped to be certified by New York State as a school district administrator, hopefully as a superintendent. She was also seeking certification as a high school principal and assistant superintendent as well.

The other reason was to see how well their new Technology Center was progressing. During the pandemic, it was almost impossible to buy equipment and train students in coding for jobs already set up with New York State firms located in the Capital Region's Tech Valley. They started with many students who were already proficient in the technology languages required, almost fifty had started and completed the program. Of these, twenty-five started working at the Technology Center in full time jobs. The others were split between continuing to obtain their four-year degree and those ending up in the Coast Guard that had been recruited under Joan Talbot's leadership. Joan had spent almost as much time on the recruitment project as she did running the very important Islamorada Coast Guard facility.

They unpacked their few items since they had a full wardrobe of clothing at the Key West house. It was easier to have clothing appropriate for Key West to stay in Key West rather than drag everything back and forth to New York. After unpacking, they had dinner and watched the news. Jack made a few calls and Mary reviewed all her plans that she wanted to discuss the next day. She always wanted to be as prepared as possible and not waste anyone's valuable time. At 10:00 p.m., Jack and Mary went to bed. Jamie had already left before dinner and Martina and Antonia were cleaning up and putting away the dishes. They would go to their rooms early as well. They needed to report back in by the end of the week for another assignment. They had reports to fill out, time sheets, and pay requests along with background information on their next Coast Guard assignment.

Two new Coast Guard members from Islamorada would replace Martina and Antonia. Alex Deleon and Mia Santiago would be here in the morning. Joan Talbot would come down with them and make introductions. Before the pandemic, they only had Martina and Antonia for protection and it ended rather quickly when they hurried back to New York to avoid any potential quarantine.

The next morning, Joan arrived with Alex and Mia and made the introductions. Martina and Antonia went back to their duties with Joan. Joan told Mary at length about the progress she had made restarting her efforts to recruit minorities and women into the Coast Guard but it was tough under the various restrictions that were in place. Those restrictions were lifted arbitrarily by the Florida government but not by Coast Guard authority so it was getting difficult to maneuver around. They would work on it. Half of the coding graduates, minorities all, decided to join the Coast Guard because of Joan and were now in training in the Technology Center which sorely needed new high-tech recruits.

While Mary was talking to Joan, Jack's phone rang and it was Chris Sellers from the Albany newspaper. Chris asked where he was and he told him they were back in Key West for at least another month, maybe more. Chris asked him if he could do an interview with him over the phone for the Sunday edition. Jack asked him how he got his number and he simply said, "We have our ways but we didn't get it from any of your Evangeline staff, just to let you know."

Jack asked him what he wanted to know and Chris told him that a canary told him that both he and Mary spent around thirty million dollars at food banks and in other areas, not only in the entire Albany Capital District, but also in south Florida and the Keys as well, split pretty much 50/50.

"First, Chris said, "Thank you for all you did. There would be a lot of people going hungry over the last year if it wasn't for you and Mary. I just wanted to ask if this generous contribution cut into your plans for your Career Center here or in Mary's plans for both here and in the Keys?"

"Just let me say, I really don't want our names brought up. If you want to state that the Evangeline Trust Fund and the Teresa Trust Fund donated the money, that's fine. By the way, it was almost two million dollars a month for fifteen months. Some we matched, some we started on our own when there were no programs available. It not only paid for food but also kept these essential workers on the job and paid throughout the pandemic. Overall it covered about five hundred essential workers at each region employed for that time. It also covered all the medical supplies required to keep everyone safe from the virus. That was quite a lot of money in itself." He added, "When the food bank didn't have enough funding, we jumped in. I'm sure you heard through the grapevine where the checks and wire transfers came from. Please don't make a big deal out of it because down the road we're not sure how much longer we can do that without the federal government jumping in. By the way, my share of the thirty million dollars did come out of the bottom line of the Evangeline Trust but Mary is going to spend $77.5 million dollars in this region and will reimburse me in the future if we run short. Do you have any good projects that save lives or at least improve lives in the Capital Region?" he asked Chris.

"I'm sure we can come up with a list," he said.

"By the way, how's my pal, Susan Murray, doing? Does she still think we screwed somebody over to win the lottery?" Jack asked.

"You just won't let it go. Will you, Jack?" as he chuckled. "She said to say hello and thank you for everything you two have done for everyone during the pandemic." She still wants to interview you later on if that's possible?"

"Sure, as long as she does her homework. I want her to produce a list of at least ten million dollars in worthy projects for funding over the next three years for the Capital Region. She'll find out exactly how easy that is to calculate. And, the projects have to be special, meaning that no one else has considered funding it as a worthy cause and she needs to fight for it."

"Point taken, Jack. I'll tell her and thanks for the update.

It will be in Sunday's paper, not about you but about the work coming out of the Evangeline Trust Fund. Can I ask the public for ideas for worthy projects over the next two years that have been left unfunded? Will that help?" asked Chris.

"That would help along with Susan Murray's suggestions," he said.

They said goodbye and would talk in the future. He told Chris to say hello to Susan for him. Chris told him he would send a copy of Sunday's paper to him.

Julie and Tillie arrived right around 11:00 a.m. and soon after, Jane Swanson pulled in. They all had their facemasks on as they knocked on the door.

CHAPTER 30

Mary had greeted Julie and Tillie and then almost immediately, Jane Swanson parked in the driveway as Joan departed and waved to Jane. She got out of her car and looked to see where the front door was. She had never been to Mary's house before. The meetings they'd had were in Miami or at Julie's house in Tavernier. Jack opened the door and welcomed her. Mary came over and gave her a big hug.

Mary said, "Did you find the house okay? Did you use the GPS? It's a little tricky because there are two Allamanda streets. We're the "Terrace" not the "Avenue", It can be confusing."

"No, I found it fine. GPS is a wonderful thing for us directionally challenged people. It practically shouted out, "turn here, stupid," she said and smiled.

Jane greeted Julie and Tillie as well as her new security team. They all went out on the deck and started an early lunch. They were all glad to see each other.

"So, shall I update you on the last wonderful sixteen months?" asked Mary.

"Please do," said Julie. Tillie nodded.

"I just had a quick meeting with Joan Talbot before she left," she said.

Jane said, "I just waved to her as she was leaving and she put her hand up to her ear to call her which I will do as soon as I can. I have to head back to Miami tonight if that's okay. Nick has had a very rough year. Being a doctor at Jackson Memorial Hospital during a pandemic was awful. I don't think I saw him more than an hour or two a week over the last year. He got Covid=19 but soon got over it. It seemed to be a mild case. I was in quarantine for two weeks but then I was able to get my vaccine, double dose, so I'm fine. How's everyone else here?"

"We seem to be fine," said Mary. "We all have been fully vaccinated. Even if we do get the virus, it isn't supposed to be as bad and they say we won't wind up in the hospital or God forbid, die."

"That's great," said Jane. "May I update everyone here on where we stand with contributions in south Florida and the Keys over the last year?"

"Of course, please do," said Mary.

Julie, Tillie, and Jamie, and Linda, who'd just walked in, were all ears. Jane began reading from her notes. "Starting last May, when everything started shutting down and people were losing their jobs left and right, the local food banks started to become overwhelmed. Their donations were down because the companies that donated every day were also shut down. People were missing meals and children went hungry without the in-school breakfast and lunch program. Sixty percent of the students in Monroe County School District are living in poverty and receive aid under the Free and Reduced Food Program. That's 5,800 kids out of 8,800 that were fed by the local food pantries. Mary's Teresa Trust Fund South spent fifteen million dollars over the last year on food purchases for the food banks as well as supplement pay for almost 500 workers throughout the year. There were over fifty food banks that received a million dollars a month in total over the last fifteen months and quite frankly, Mary, I don't know how we can continue this effort, alone," said Jane.

"Wow," said Jamie. "Thank you Mary. I don't know what to say. That's remarkable."

"Well, that's not all she spent here in south Florida and the Keys from south of Miami to Key Largo right down here to Key West. Here are a few of just the Key West food banks that received funding. They include Glad Tidings Assembly of God, Salvation Army, Monroe County Social Services In-Home and Nutrition Services, St. Mary's Soup Kitchen, Star of the Sea Outreach Mission Food Program, Metropolitan Community Church, and the Florida Keys Outreach Coalition for the Homeless, just to name a few. In addition, Joan Talbot spent well over a million dollars in her Coast Guard minority recruitment effort, signing up a minimum of twenty-five fully trained graduates from the coding institute. Mary spent in excess of three million dollars at the college for new state-of-the-art technology equipment and for staff and rent paid to the college. She also set aside trust funds for the Traynors and the Lennons and may I say thanks for helping out Nick with his student loans as well."

Jane added, "Tillie, you're aware that the Teresa Trust Fund South privately donated several hundred thousand dollars for PPE, personal protective equipment, for local senior centers and nursing homes. In all, Mary's trust fund spent fifteen million dollars last year, above and beyond what we planned. It's closer to over twenty million dollars now out of the $77.5 million dollars allocated to this trust fund.

Tillie said, "I was aware that Mary sent PPE to a bunch of senior programs and nursing homes but I had no idea how much that added up to. Thank you Mary. Bless you."

"Enough praise. Thank you. I'm glad we had the money to do what we did. As I mentioned to Jack, his ten-year plan will probably be closer to five years once the pandemic is fully behind us. So, I need ideas, like the Technology Center, education and training for jobs and other programs that benefit families here for the long term. As you know, I'm finishing my Ph.D. as well by next summer and I may have other ideas of what do with that degree, once received. I may stay up in Troy and help run the two charter schools since I will be certified in administration or even head down here and either develop a technology high school or become affiliated with either the college or the school district in Monroe County. I'm not sure yet. Our plans are still in flux but it's worth talking about at least," said Mary.

"As you know," said Julie, "Joe is finishing his thesis and Ph.D. by Christmas. The Rear Admiral wants Joe up at the Coast Guard Academy by spring of next year. Joe loves it here at the college and there are rumors that Dr. Hennessey has been offered another position and the college presidency may be open. Joe will tell you more about it tomorrow. I don't mean to give it away but Joe could be the interim president of The College of the Florida Keys for up to a year while they recruit a new president. If that happens, Joe could stay another year to help develop the Technology Center and set up all the programs for both the military and regular college sides. I think he would love to do that but you never know. Orders are orders. Since Joan Talbot has been working at the college recruiting Coast Guard personnel for technology, she could ease into Joe's job on the military end. This would mean a promotion to Lieutenant, same as Joe got previously. However, when promoted to Captain, the title required for Assistant Superintendent at the Coast Guard Academy, he could be assigned immediately. I've asked Tillie to come with us and that's still up in the air. She loves her life in Key Largo but loves us more. Right, Tillie?" Julie laughed.

"Yes, I love you more. Only because of Bella,

obviously," said Tillie. She laughed too. "I am in a quandary because I have never lived outside of Key Largo in my entire life. Maybe I'll be open to a new adventure. I'll still keep my apartment and come back for the winter though. New London is way too cold for these old bones."

They finished their lunch. Mary asked them about other projects to be funded. She mentioned social workers in the schools and in the sheriff's department and Key West Police Department and they said they would develop a plan that could work emotionally, politically, and be a win-win for everyone. Linda asked Mary if she could visit the Catholic Church and school in town. The Basilica of St. Mary Star of the Sea has been hurting big time throughout the pandemic. Without weekly Mass, donations have slowed considerably. A majority of the parishioners are over sixty years old and it's hard for them to fully support the school as well. Families can't afford the tuition so the kids dropped out and went to public school but never even got to attend in-school class for almost a full year. In the meantime, schools do not have resources to allow students to catch up what they missed academically for an entire year. Repeating the grade is very remote because it would add millions of dollars to the annual budgets of the schools. Sales tax supported the schools but with everything shut down, each school had to take a minimum of a twenty-five percent cut in budgets, adding to the already bad situation. Mary asked Linda to set up a meeting with the pastor and the school principal and to get her as much information as she could. She told Linda not to tell them that she was an ex-nun. She said she would surprise them.

Mary immediately looked up the history and various statistics for The Basilica School of Saint Mary Star of the Sea. They were located on Truman Avenue, one of the main streets in Key West. The church was established in 1868 and the school was founded in 1875, one hundred forty-six years ago. The Sisters of the Holy Name of Jesus started the school. It was honored by Pope Benedict in 2012 as a minor Basilica, thus changing the name to the Basilica School. It has 295 students in elementary grades Pre-K to grade 8. The annual tuition ranged from $6,500.00 for Pre-K to $7,500.00 for grades 6-8. The teacher ratio is nineteen students to one teacher. The annual budget was around $1.5 million dollars and the church subsidy was around a two hundred thousand dollars a year but had been cut back dramatically with low collections during the pandemic. The female base is 41% and the male is 59%. The breakdown by race is 70% White, 23% Hispanic and 7% African American. It is unusual to have more boys than girls but anecdotally boys do better where there is more discipline, like in a Catholic school. There are eleven full-time teachers and seven part-time. Mary knew that eventually, just like up in Troy, she would be roped into helping various Catholic parishes, once they knew her background and that she was now worth a fortune.

Julie and Tillie left and headed home. Jane hung around for a few extra minutes to have Mary sign more documents for the various individual trusts. Mary gave Jane signatory authority to pay the major trust bills just like she let Jamie pay the household bills from a local checking account. Trust but verify has been her motto ever since she heard the phrase many years ago. Mary was once again starting to feel overwhelmed. The new security team of Alex and Mia didn't pay too much attention at first. Alex took the front and Mia was walking around the back and up the neighborhood streets just to familiarize themselves with the area. They were both hesitant to talk to anyone because they haven't been in contact with any of them. They had spoken to Martina and Antonia and got the lowdown as well as speaking to Joan Talbot at length. They were there to guard the house and Mary and Jack.

For the rest of the day, Jack made phone calls and Mary studied up on the college, her program and the Catholic school and church in town. She looked at all her budgets, bank accounts, and balanced her assets to the penny. She helped Jack do the same thing. She still had over fifty million dollars left to do anything she wanted not even counting her own net worth of over sixty million dollars, the same as Jack. Jack was down into the thirty-million-dollar range, especially since he has been working his trust for the past few years. All the earnings from interest more than paid for the attorney fees for handling all the trusts so there was no concern at this point.

CHAPTER 31

Mary got up, ate her breakfast with Jack, and completed reading all her notes for the meeting with Dr. Morgan Hennessey and Joe Traynor at 10:00 a.m. at the college. Mary asked Jack if there was anything he wanted to know since he was not attending the meeting. He didn't think so he told her. This was Mary's show just like it was his responsibility for the Evangeline Career Center in Troy and all the projects coming from that entity. Alex and Mia would bring her to the meeting and serve as her security just as Martina and Antonia had previously.

Jack said he would stay at home as to not cause any blips on the radar since he could be subject to foul play as well. He also knew that Skip Lennon was home for the day and had offered to take him out on the boat if he helped out. Mary knew that was his intention all along and laughed. Skip had a group of Midwestern teachers coming on board for the day and he needed help in addition to Jamie and Tom. Jack loved the fact that he wasn't treated any differently than anyone else along for the ride. Skip told him, since he was interested in eventually buying a good size boat that he would start his lessons when he helped out. Jack thought that was great. They wouldn't be back until after 6:00 p.m. so he told Mary to leave him some dinner or he would get something on the way back. He would call her when they hit the dock.

"Hi Joe. Hi Dr. Hennessey. Thanks for meeting with me today," said Mary.

"Our pleasure," Morgan said. "God, how long has it been since we spoke to each other in person?" said Morgan. "Please call me Morgan by the way. Dr. Hennessey is fine at a board meeting but not worth much other than that."

Joe said, "Hi Mary. How was your meeting with Julie and Tillie and everyone else yesterday? Did you get to accomplish anything? I can't believe it's been over a year since we saw each other. Phone calls back and forth just don't cut it. Joan wanted to be here but it's her busy day up in Islamorada. Evidently, there are several key arrests happening today. It never ends. Pandemic or not, the drugs just keep piling up, day after day. If we get 30% of the drugs coming into the Keys, we're very lucky. However today, it appears to be a multi-million dollar haul. So, Joan can't be here. I kind of miss that activity to tell you the truth."

"That's fine. We talked briefly yesterday. Her recruiting has come along nicely. I hear she got a big chunk of your coding graduates to join the Coast Guard. All are minority and a majority is female. That's exactly what she was hoping for. Jake Barnes, or I should say Rear Admiral Barnes must be very pleased."

"He is very pleased. As a matter of fact, when I get my Ph.D. in December and go to the Coast Guard Academy, she may take my place on the military side at the college. Hell, she spends half her time here now anyway. Since she's already here, she's hoping to get her Master's degree as well so when she retires, she can continue running the Trust for the Coast Guard recruiting effort."

"Master's or not, she will certainly have my vote if she wants to stay," said Mary.

"I'll let her know," said Joe. He then turned to Morgan and started to talk about Mary and his very similar backgrounds to give him a broader understanding of what she has accomplished in life rather than appear to be an empty-headed multi-millionaire.

Morgan turned to Mary and said, "That would be the last thing I would think about you after meeting with you, talking to you, planning strategy and just understanding who you are. I haven't really met Jack yet but I'm sure you are very similar personalities."

"Well, before we discuss our progress over the last year and a half quarantine, let me give you my life's story in the Berlitz version. I have lived in the Lansingburgh section of the City of Troy for my entire life until I married Jack at age 48. I grew up on Sixth Avenue and 120th street, only three blocks from Catholic High. I lived for many years right next to the school with my two closest ex-nun friends. None of us ever made more than $25,000.00 a year, even after we left the convent. That's why we shared an apartment to make it through. Once you leave the convent permanently, it is almost like you never existed. When you take a vow of poverty, chastity and obedience, that's what you get when you leave. You get nothing.

I graduated, just like Joe, from St. Augustine's Elementary School and Catholic High, only blocks away. I entered the convent at eighteen years old and spent fifteen years as a Sister of Saint Joseph. I graduated from The College of St. Rose in Albany with a Bachelor's and Master's in Education and Mathematics and taught in the same schools I'd attended. I am an only child and my father was thrilled that he didn't have to pay for college. He worked the assembly line at Ford Motor Company in Green Island, across the river, making mufflers for forty-five years. My mother was a clerk at the Bon-Ton Dry Cleaners for twenty-five years before it closed. I had never been on an airplane before Jack and I headed to Key West after he hit the lottery. That's where we met Joe and Julie at Sloppy Joes and the rest is history. I had never been more than fifty miles away from Troy in my entire life. Our vacations consisted of camping on Lake George at the New York State Hearthstone Point. Since Jack hit the lottery, he gave me $15.0 million dollars to play with as he said. Then, on our honeymoon down here in Key West, I hit the lottery for $480.0 million dollars on top of Jack's $330.0 million dollars. I guess you would say we are rich but in an unusual way. We are giving most of it away, not all of it, to worthy causes over the next five years. That's the plan and I'm sticking with it. By the way, I copied Joe and I'll be getting my Ph.D. from Barry University next June or July after presenting my dissertation and thesis. It is already written. I've been doing it for ten years now, never knowing if it would happen. It's going to happen and I am very proud of what we have accomplished and where we are headed."

"Thank you, Mary. That's quite inspiring," said Morgan. "I have something to tell you as well. Joe probably knows through the grapevine but hasn't said anything to me or anyone else about it and I'm grateful. I have been offered the position of Provost at Barry University in Miami. I never applied for it but with Barry University faculty teaching here at our college, evidently, they have been made aware of the cutting-edge things we have done thanks to you. The Provost is a member of the president's cabinet and potential replacement when the president of the college retires. As background, the Provost is the chief academic officer of the University and has responsibility for the University's academic and budgetary affairs. The Provost collaborates with the president in setting overall academic priorities for the university and allocates funds to carry these priorities forward. It's a very big job and I would be honored to accept. I haven't told our board yet but I would like for Joe, as soon as he gets his Ph.D. to take over the presidency of this college until a permanent president is chosen. I know he's headed to the Coast Guard Academy but this could help him gain experience for a year and give him more credibility. Also, I would hope that Joan Talbot could take over some of Joe's responsibilities on the military side. She wouldn't be able to fill his shoes academically or his language and intelligence background but she has done a fine job in recruiting minority students to the college and to the Coast Guard."

"Well, that's certainly news to me," said Joe. I don't know if it's possible. I have a time commitment to the Rear Admiral and he is pushing me toward the Coast Guard Academy, big time."

"Joe, it would be quite an honor for you," said Mary. "I couldn't think of anyone more qualified and if I have a vote, even a financial vote based on the funds I have invested here, I couldn't think of a more appropriate solution."

"Thank you, Mary," he said.

"Joe, just so you'll know, I didn't want to say anything to you until I spoke with Rear Admiral Barnes. He said he would take it under consideration. He has a lot riding on you but he also has a lot riding on this college since we are recruiting for the Coast Guard and sending recent graduates to the Technology Center that so sorely lacks youth and new ideas. He said he would get back to me."

"Thanks for telling me. This is quite a shock. I'm glad you told both of us. Mary has placed a lot of faith in us to succeed using her own money. Morgan, did you know that on top of financing the new Technology Center, through her Teresa Trust Fund South, she gave more than $15.0 million dollars to all the food banks in the Keys and south Florida? This is well above what she told us she was planning. I talked to Julie as well and I didn't even know that she spent several hundreds of thousands of dollars on PPE for seniors and nursing homes throughout last year."

"Mary, you are an inspiration. In case you might think about it, I am offering up your name as the next potential president of The College of the Florida Keys. No one has done more in the history of the college to make this a total success than what you have done."

Thank you, I'm honored," said Mary.

The meeting ended and both Mary and Joe walked out to the education building where Mary would meet Joe's mentor from Barry University. Joe would be finishing up within a month and then the mentor would pick up Mary while she was in Florida and then coordinate with Mary's Ph.D. advisor at The College of St. Rose in Albany. She was very pleased with the smooth transition. She would have lunch with Joe, Alex and Mia in the cafeteria and then head over to speak to the pastor of The Basilica of St. Mary Star of the Sea. Being named after Mary, herself made her very aware of Mary, the mother of Jesus, in her life.

Joe said, "Mary, I can't believe that Morgan is placing my name in contention as interim president of the college."

"I can't believe that he was even thinking of me as the future president after you leave. I have no idea what I would do. I'm fifty years old. Jack and we're thinking of retiring after we give away most of our money, probably in the next five years. I was thinking of martinis on a boat, docked in Key West. I wasn't thinking of running a college or even continuing to help at the Career Center in Troy. God, I have a lot to think about. You do too," she said.

After lunch, they said goodbye. Joe wanted to speak to Morgan at greater length. He was overwhelmed at this point, just as Mary was. Alex and Mia drove Mary to the Basilica School. She would get a tour and be met there by Linda Lennon, a very active parishioner. She would meet the principal, Thomas Wright and the pastor, Rev. John Baker, an Assistant Pastor, John Dominique. She was also very interested in meeting with the Sisters of the Holy Spirit, who lived on the church campus. The Sisters of the Holy Name of Jesus were the first to serve many years before.

Mary had forgotten that the recipient of many of the food bank donations went directly to the Mary Star of the Sea Foundation which included their outreach ministry and community kitchen. In the car, she checked how much was donated out of the $15.0 million last year to south Florida and the Keys food banks and she was surprised that it totaled almost a half million dollars in contributions over the fifteen-month period. She was hoping that her name wouldn't be associated with the Teresa Trust Fund but the local papers had started their research and started putting names together and it would only be a short time before they found out who she was and what she had done.

Mary took the tour with Alex and Mia and the principal was quite surprised that she had security. He was really unaware of who or what she has done in such a short time. The school was in decent shape but you could tell that certain repairs had not been done due to low contributions and missed tuition payments over the last year. Of the $1.5 million budget, they would be short almost three hundred thousand dollars this year, two hundred thousand from the parish, and lost tuition payments of over one hundred thousand dollars. The principal was upbeat but not expecting miracles to say the least. After the tour, they went to the rectory and met the two priests. Linda made the introductions and Mary said she would sign up with her husband Jack as parishioners, when they were in Key West. They were regular every Sunday parishioners of St. Augustine's in Troy, New York. That would never change.

Mary asked if she could visit the convent and they walked her over and made introductions. Mary thought it was very sad. The same as when she was a Sister of St.

Joseph. She met twelve nuns residing in the convent, which looked more like an old age home than a robust convent full of lively nuns. The average age, the same as across the country, was near eighty years old. The building was crumbling. It needed a ton of work including hurricane protection. At least the Sisters of St. Joseph in Latham, New York was an upscale viable facility funded by the sale of excess land surrounding the convent. It was in the middle of suburbia, next to Siena College, and considered prime real estate for developers of retirement condos, which were going up daily. Even these sisters had financial problems but not as bad as this convent as Mary looked around. She was very sad. She knew there was a pandemic but not much was done to protect these good sisters, who were the first to die due to age and health conditions. So far, none of the sisters were sick but Mary thought that was a miracle. She needed to do something quickly.

She finally sat down with the priests and told them what she was about. They knew of her because of Linda, obviously, and because of the funding they received for their food bank. She told them that she was an ex-Sister of St. Joseph in the Albany, New York area and she above all wanted to make sure that the nuns living in the convent and the entire staff at the school and at the church were fully vaccinated and had the PPE equipment they needed to be safe. If the priests took that into consideration, Mary told them that the first thing she wanted to do was to upgrade the convent and make it safe and secure and she would pay the entire bill. The sisters would have to move out while the work was complete but she would rent housing trailers to serve as their residence as the work was being completed. Then, she said she wanted to bring the school up to code and rehab it and put in new technology labs and give every student an iPad and a computer for their home use. When those plans were completed, she would make up any deficit over the next two years and bring the school and the church into full financial compliance. However, there would be quarterly reviews and money held if progress wasn't made. The first thing was to address the needs of the retired sisters. The priests were not thrilled with the steps she proposed but they were well aware that there was no free ride. Also, all student late fees would be forgiven and past due tuition payments would be paid. Then, they were on their own. Mary understood all this after converting St. Augustine's School to a New York State Charter School. You didn't keep throwing good money after bad just because your religious leaders said it was so. It was not. Mary said she would meet with everyone at the church site on a weekly basis until all the steps were in place and agreed upon. They shook hands and got up and left.

Walking out, Linda said, "I have never been in such awe as I am right now. Mary that was awesome. There was no lying, no bullshit, no kissing up. On the spot, you told them exactly what you would and would not do. I would never have the balls to do that. I am so proud of you. That's what was needed."

"I learned from the best," said Mary. "Jack was the mildest man you ever met until he hit the lottery and then he changed dramatically. He always had it in him but something clicked. He didn't want to waste his time and said exactly what he would do and he did it. Talk to him and you will see what I learn from him on a daily basis."

CHAPTER 32

"Joe? Please hold for Rear Admiral Barnes," the Rear Admiral's assistant said.

"Hi, Joe. It's Jake here. How are you? It's been a while. I hear good things through the grapevine. What the hell did you do to Joan Talbot? I've never seen her so fired up about anything more than this recruitment effort."

"She's going full speed ahead, sir," said Joe. "She's already got twelve recent coding graduates to join the Coast Guard. All are fully certified and ready to go after initiation and training. They are 100% minority and 75% female from what I know. Not bad, huh?"

"I think Mary Evans, or Mary Evans Manning has stirred up a hornet's nest which is a good thing. I also called a few of her security team members and they seem inspired by her. It's not the money. It's the direct approach, direct answers, either yes or no that seems meaningful to them. She especially enamored Antonia and Martina. Maybe she started out as being timid but she certainly isn't that now. I understand she'll be finishing her Ph.D. in record time and has already written her thesis?"

"Yes, from what I heard. It's just about done. Evidently, she has been thinking about minority education and those living in poverty and how leveling the playing field can help them. It's one thing to give your opinion but she is backing up her opinion with millions of dollars in support to see if her ideas work. The young ladies recruited for the Coast Guard through the coding classes have more than held their own in class and in on-hand activities. They were given every tool they needed to succeed and they did. Of course it comes from Joan but obviously handed down from Mary. I hear she made quite an impact at the Catholic School when she visited. She may peel off a million dollars if they follow her game plan. That's hard to resist whomever it is, including priests and nuns and school principals."

"Wow, Jake. You are in the know. I just heard from Julie who just heard from Linda because it just happened."

"I talked to Joan who told me all about it. She saw Mary yesterday and she told her what she was going to do even before it happened. Joan told me to look out because it could happen to me too," he laughed.

Jake added, "The reason I called is because I spoke to Dr. Hennessey at the college. He told me that he'd be speaking to you about a change in administration. Did he talk to you yet?"

"Yes, he spoke to me yesterday while Mary and I met with him. He told us that he was probably going to take the position at Barry University. It seemed like a good fit and could help us down the road here at the college as well. He told me he spoke to you to ask if he could put my name forward as interim president but I'd have to stay a year to prepare a new president before I could leave for the Coast Guard Academy. He told me that you said you would get back to him. Did you?"

"I just did. I met with my Washington higher-ups and they thought it would be an excellent idea to have you take over as interim president while the board looked for someone permanent. They felt that it could give you leg up at the Academy and the experience alone could be beneficial. It would give you more time to work with Mary to see what else she has planned specifically for the military side, for the recruitment of minorities and for technology training that we so desperately need. What do you think?"

"I haven't had much time to think about it but Julie thinks it would be an easier transition this way and give her and Tillie and Bella more time to adjust to moving. It's especially important to Tillie. Tillie has finally found someone she cares about and it could be difficult in asking her to move. She has been seeing a widower from Pittsburgh for the last two years. Ed Lansing moved down to Key Largo a while ago. He was an engineer for the City of Pittsburgh for many years and retired. He has two married daughters in their late thirties. He is a month younger than Tillie and goes to her church, St. Justin Martyr's in Key Largo. Julie and Tillie haven't been separated since Julie was eight years old. Tillie is her mother, for all practical purposes, not her grandmother."

"I get that, Joe. This could be a Godsend in the timing. She could also travel back and forth when winter comes and stay in Key Largo. We can always arrange transportation by plane or boat. Someone is always coming down here for whatever reason, as you know. Do you want me to call Dr. Hennessey and tell him to move your name forward? What has Mary Evans said about all this," he asked.

"She already said that she was 100% in favor of it. I know Morgan listens to her. He also hinted in so many words that as soon as she got her Ph.D. that she should apply for the position. I think this would ensure that the funding would continue and make him look even better. I'll bet he recruits her as a Barry University graduate for an endowment as well. As you know, she still has a ton of money left to spend over the next five years."

"Money makes the world go round. If Mary wants the job, I'm sure they will consider it or they would be looking at no more funding if they reject her out of hand. I hope their board is smarter than that."

"If I'm there as the interim, I will have their ear and drop the hints that it would be beneficial to consider her. Who knows, maybe she doesn't want to be tied down. We laughed the other day and she said at age 55, now 50, she would like to sit down on a boat and drink martini's watching the sun go down. Maybe she can do both," said Jack.

Alex and Mia drove Mary to the mayor's office, 1300 White Street, in the heart of Key West. She had a 10:00 a.m. meeting with the mayor. Evidently the political scene in Key West has started to reflect the population. The mayor, who won election in 2018 as a Democrat, is the first Lesbian mayor in the history of Florida. Her agenda includes a very strong economic redevelopment for the city and Mary's plans seen to fit right in with her views. Mary could have brought the college officials to the meeting but she was just now starting to feel like she could handle herself in these situations. The Ph.D. curriculum, coupled with the mentoring, seems to spur her on and gave her an inner strength that she didn't know she had.

As she walked to the front door of city hall, the mayor herself met her. The mayor introduced herself and shook Mary's hand and brought her to the boardroom where only she and Mary would meet. Like Mary, the mayor, was born somewhere else and has been a resident of Key West since 2001, She was also a business owner, turning seventy years old this year, born in 1951.

"It's a pleasure to meet you," said Teri Johnson.

"Likewise," said Mary. "Thank you for meeting me today. As you can see I came alone, except for my security team."

"I noticed that," said Teri. "Do you actually need security?"

"I never thought so in a million years but as Joe Traynor pointed out, all it takes is one instance that could change my life. I can certainly afford it and I now believe it's necessary. I also have to wear these tie shoes that have a GPS chip attached to make sure that they know where I am at all times. I hate wearing the chips but I really don't want to upset Joe."

"I met Joe Traynor at the college. He seems like a very put together person."

"He is that and more. My now husband, Jack Manning and I met Joe and his wife, Julie, the first time we came down to Key West after Jack hit the lottery. We were told to get out of town fast. Joe and Julie shared a hi-top table with us one night at Sloppy Joes and the rest is history. Joe, Jack and I are all from Troy, New York, all from the north end of the city, Lansingburgh and Joe and I share an Alma Mater, Catholic Central High School. It's a really small world. He is now Vice President of the college for the military side and a Lieutenant in the Coast Guard. They are grooming him to head to the Coast Guard Academy in New London, Connecticut as soon as he finishes his Ph.D. from Barry University. I'm now in the same program and will receive my Ph.D. early next summer. My thesis is already done. I have a Master's degree in Education and I'm an ex-nun, and a very new wife at age 50." Mary smiled.

Teri said, "That's quite a travel log," and laughed. "My story is similar but different. What did Robert Frost say, "A Road Less Traveled?" She went on, "You said your husband hit the lottery? You did too, right?"

"Yes, I did. Right here in Key West. Jack hit for $330 million back in Troy and I hit for $480.0 million. Together, we have the third highest winnings in history. I have my trust fund and Jack has his. We are each doing our own thing and combining resources where necessary like during the recent pandemic."

"Yes, I am well aware that you and your husband spent over $30.0 million dollars last year, both here and up in New York where you live. Thank you for your very generous food bank donations and pay support for the workers. Thank you as well for the new Technology Center on the campus at The College of the Florida Keys and for starting new business opportunities for coding graduates. That's exactly what I want to do to move forward. I've read up on the Albany, New York Capital District. It's now known as "Tech Valley". I would love to make this the Florida Keys Tech Valley or even Key West Technology Center. Anything will do, I'm all ears as Ross Perot once said."

"We've used that line as well," Mary said smiling.

"What can we do for you and then let me tell you the kinds of help this community needs."

They spoke for over two hours with promises to get together again. Mary told her about the recruitment effort for the Coast Guard minority program, the $20.0 million dollar investment in the college Technology Center, the $1.2 million dollars to cover the college deficit and the funds to fix the status quo at the Catholic Church facilities and school. Mary also dropped hints about social justice and how she really wanted to invest in adding counselors to the police department to address minority issues which were less than stellar due to racial discrimination. She mentioned the child being handcuffed and sent to jail because the father thought it was fine and so didn't the police. She also read up on the growing homeless population in the Florida Keys, with over 500 human beings living unsheltered, including half of them children. She also wanted to address the poverty issue of the 8,800 children in the Monroe County School District with half of them living below or near the poverty line in a community with one of the richest per capita incomes in the country.

Teri asked, "Where did you come from? Did God drop

you off at a bus stop on Duval Street? I can't believe the things you are willing to do to help this community and you don't really even know us. I did my research on you and you are the real deal from everything I heard. I know where you live when you're down here. Can we go to lunch sometime or at least meet frequently to discuss all these topics? I hate to say, as a politician, I need to keep well informed but you, Mary, are the most well informed resident I have ever met."

"Thank you," said Mary. "What you don't know is that my husband, Jack, and I are planning to empty both our trusts within five years by giving to worthy causes. Those causes are not to carry past problems forward. We will only invest in projects that pay off, a dividend if you will that will continue well into the future. However, pandemics are different and food insecurity is as well. We will continue to fund these issues."

She continued. "Through my Ph.D. program and with the help of all my friends, board members and others, they have taught me the meaning of ROI or Return on Investment. I will fund projects that pay for themselves within five years or at a rate of 20% a year. So, by giving the $20.0 million dollars to the college, I expect that it will have an economic impact on this community that will grow 20% a year or double in five years and then it's all gravy. Does that make sense?" Mary asked

Teri said, "Yes, it makes perfect sense. Can you meet with our Economic Development Director and share your plans with him and the staff? Perhaps we can join forces and spend matching funds together so we aren't wasting resources when we should be investing wisely."

"I'll be glad to," said Mary. "Just as a reminder. My plans are my plans and if they meet your goals that's fine but I am still going ahead with what I have envisioned. Please correct me when I'm wrong and I'll be very honest with you when I think it's political bullshit."

Teri laughed out loud and said, "I think we'll get along just fine, Mary. Thanks again for coming in. This has been enlightening."

With that Mary got up, shook Teri's hand, and left the boardroom to meet Alex and Mia for the ride home. She had to be proactive now since the media was starting to hone in on her and wanted a sit down with her. She needed to be very specific with her plans and how she came across on air. Jack could help her with that. She needed both Kristen and Jane to go with her after a well thought out response. She'd call Kristen as soon as she got home. Jane was still nursing her husband back to health but maybe she could come down or at least Zoom a meeting before the media onslaught. She needed at least a week before the sit down.

It was nearly October and then it would be Thanksgiving and Christmas once again. They always wanted to be home for the holidays. They had the annual family dinner at the Career Center and Jack always wanted family over at Thanksgiving, at their own house up on Plank Road. He hadn't seen his children Debbie and Mark in a while. He'd especially grown to like Cara, Mark's future bride. He promised her parents that they would get together and discuss the wedding. Evidently, they thought a late fall wedding would be good.

Mary had to be back down in Miami in early summer to give her thesis presentation and receive her degree from Barry University. Joe had mentioned that he would like to give a party for her when she graduated. As a matter of fact, it's been a few years but Joe, Julie, Bella and Tillie planned on coming up to Troy for Christmas this year, right after Joe graduated. He hasn't seen his father and brother in well over a year and a half since the pandemic started and he missed them. He wanted to show Tillie and Bella where he grew up. Julie had made a number of trips to Troy when she went to Brown University for her undergraduate and Master's degrees. Joe had given her a car to drive around and had to re-register it every year with New York plates so he could pay the insurance. He left the car in his name so she wouldn't have any liability issues. *Boy, that seemed like a lifetime ago he thought.*

CHAPTER 33

Kristen would arrive for the weekend and help prepare Mary for her interview with Michele Richards, the Miami Herald Executive Director, the following Monday at The College of the Florida Keys. Jane Swanson would join Mary and Kristen's planning session by Zoom because of her husband's continued health issues. She would attend the meeting on Monday at 11:00 a.m. and then head back to Miami.

Joe Traynor had already requested the boardroom for lunch for everyone. Joe would introduce the college staff and Dr. Hennessey and then they would take a tour of the new Technology Center, after the presentation and lunch. With Michele Richards would be two members of their editorial board, Luisa Sanchez, an editorial page writer and Amy Donnell, a deputy editorial page editor. The Miami Herald was "the newspaper" for all of south Florida and the Keys. Previous print newspapers have gone strictly to online publications including KcysNct.com and the Key West Citizen. They would pick up the story once printed in the Miami Herald.

Kristen arrived at the Key West airport and was picked up by Jamie, accompanied by Mia Santiago. Alex Deleon, and Mary. Once again, Jack was out on the boat with Skip.

He was becoming quite the sailor, he thought. He volunteered for duty most days that Skip had only day customers so he could get more time learning to sail. When Skip had trips for more than a day, Jack stayed back with Mary. So far, since they had been down here, he's been with Skip over fifteen days. It was enough that he'd started to understand what it took Skip thirty years to figure out. Jack now understood what he didn't know and wanted to improve on those skills before even looking at any specific boats.

As usual, the Highlander was parked right outside the front door of the small airport with its lights flashing like they were waiting for a celebrity. It was very clear that Alex and Mia were armed and standing at attention on either side of Mary. As Kristen came out of the building, Mary waved to her and smiled, "Welcome back my friend. How are you?"

"I'm starting to get the hang of it. Not a bad flight down to Tampa but I tell you, I'll never get used to that mini-car with wings bringing us the rest of the way. I was scared to death getting on. I was scared to death while in the air and especially scared to death while landing. A good size gust of wind hit the plane and I thought I was going to lose my lunch. At least I'm here alive. I liked the private plane better that we got out of Fort Lauderdale," she said and laughed.

"Well, I would take that up with your partners, my dear," Mary said smiling. "Maybe they could figure out how much you're worth to them and then fly you down on a private jet. I'll bet I'm being billed for it anyway," she said and laughed.

"Touché," said Kristen and hugged Mary and was then introduced to Mia and Alex. She said hello to Jamie as well. Once again, the trip to her house was short.

It was Friday night so, Jack, Mary and Kristen headed out to dinner. Alex and Mia would come with them and eat separately so as not to cause a distraction at the restaurant. As usual, Mary picked the restaurant, *La Trattoria*. It was a favorite of Julie Traynor's. It's located in the middle of Duval Street in downtown, Key West, only minutes from their house. However parking is always an issue. The restaurant had been honored numerous times with the People's Choice Award as one of Key West's favorite Italian restaurants and as the best romantic dinner, where the locals eat.

Mary and Kristen started talking shop and Joe raised his index finger to his mouth as to say, "stop, and please enjoy your dinner". They did. Kristen loved the place, the menu and she said they were right, it was a very romantic place. Just like Mary, Kristen had never been anywhere before joining the convent, during her sisterhood years, and up until a few years ago, never on a plane. As she said before, an attorney's office in Florida would be nice. She first thought Miami but now was very enamored by Key West. After dinner, they drove around town for about an hour. It was too crowded to move more than a few miles an hour. They decided to head back home and sit on the deck to watch the sun go down. Key West is known for its sunsets and didn't disappoint anyone. Kristen started to take pictures right next to the dock and she was amazed. She sent the pictures off to her husband and wrote that this is where they are going on vacation next year.

Jane popped in by Zoom and she added quite a bit to the conversation that Kristen didn't know about. When she explained about all that Mary and her trust fund had done over the last fifteen months, she was very impressed. She didn't know about the extent to which the college was funded or how she provided PPR for senior housing and nursing homes or even what she was planning for the local church and school. Kristen only knew about the substantial food bank donations because she and Jack had done the same thing up in Troy.

When the conversation came to what Mary would say or wouldn't say, it became quite animated. Mary didn't want anyone to know where she lived down in Key West but sooner or later she figured out that they would find out and someone would show up at their house. That's why the security teams were so important. However, as Joe said, "If they're after you, they could get you, regardless of the planning you do. You just have to be on your toes at all times." It was a tough way to live but essential to maintain Jack and Mary's own safety. She felt more secure up in Troy, living outside the city limits in the Town of Brunswick, along a very old and narrow country road. She especially felt safe with John Jefferson and Fred Tucker who have been with them from the beginning when Jack first hit the lottery. They have become members of their own family. Hell, they even had their own keys to their house and the Career Center, just in case.

Jane hung up when the Zoom meeting ended. She really felt bad about not being there in person, especially after all Mary has done for her and Nick. Mary told her not to worry about it and to take care of Nick. They had a lot of years left that they could do good things. This was just a blimp on the radar. After all, he worked at Jackson Memorial Hospital in downtown Miami, one of the premier hospitals in the world. He would get better. He seemed to be coming out of the long haul syndrome of Covid-19. He ached all over. He had headaches and lost substantial weight. The headaches seemed to be going away and that allowed him to eat more and regain his strength. After getting the second dose of vaccine, his symptoms seem to be lessening day by day.

Mary and Kristen left for the college around 10:30 a.m. It was only a few minutes away on Stock Island, right down the road. Unfortunately, Jane had to leave around 7:00 a.m. to get there by 11:00 a.m. It was fall and the traffic was starting to pick up with snowbirds from the north with their trailers and campers, going south on a two-way highway for one hundred and fifty miles. Leaving early seemed to help, especially going over the seven-mile bridge heading right in to the Keys. Getting there by 9:00 a.m. meant a good trip. Not getting there by then would ruin your day, on most days. Mary and Kristen waited a few minutes outside for Jane who made it just in time. The staff from the *Miami Herald* was also just getting out of their car, heading to the college president's office and boardroom.

They held the door for each other. Mia went first through the door, followed by Alex at the tail end. Mary, Kristen and Jane followed Michele, Luisa and Amy. Joe Traynor was in the lobby waiting for them and said hello. They followed him up to the stairs where he ushered them into the boardroom. As soon as they walked in, Morgan Hennessey got up from his chair and introduced himself. He pointed out that there was coffee, Danish and bagels but to hold their appetite for a fine lunch provided by their culinary students.

Joe started the ball rolling by introducing Dr. Hennessey, once again, himself and then Mary Evans Manning, Kristen Sorenson and Jane Swanson. Michelle introduced her team which made up the editorial board and writing staff.

The first question to Mary was why the meeting was held at the college. Mary answered that education, training and jobs were at the core of her trust fund projects and she wanted the press to see what the college, not her, has already produced in those areas. The next question was where does she live. She replied that she and her husband, Jack Manning, reside in the Town of Brunswick, outside the city of Troy, New York. She mentioned that when she is down in Key West, she has a place to stay. They then asked her why the name Teresa Trust Fund South and she stated that the "Teresa" is named after Mother Teresa and the south part is separate from the north part, located in Troy. They also wanted to know how it felt being a lottery winner of $480.0 million dollars and how it felt being married to a lottery winner of $330.0 million dollars. She answered that it felt pretty good. She also mentioned that they were keeping a share for themselves, their family and their friends and have paid 100% of the taxes on that money. They also have put aside over $200 million dollars that will be dispersed within a five-year period. Her husband's Evangeline Trust Fund was for $50.0 million and her Mother Teresa Trust was split into $77.5 million dollars for both the north and south Teresa Trust funds. They asked her what they have spent so far, especially during the pandemic. Michele Richards eyes went wide when Jane Swanson read off the dollars spent over the last fifteen months in south Florida and the Keys. Kristen went over what has been spent in the Capital Region area. All three ladies from the Herald were amazed at what was accomplished.

They ate lunch and chatted and it came up about the "Teresa" name again and the Evangeline name as well. Mary laughed and said that Kristen Sorenson, her lifetime friend and attorney, was a former nun, named Sister Evangeline. She said her husband saw it as a sign from God after hitting the lottery so he named his trust fund the Evangeline Trust Fund. She explained that she too was an ex-nun or former nun who always thought well of Mother Teresa. She explained that as a nun for fifteen years, she never had a dime and never thought about money. When she left the convent, the church in its divine wisdom, sent them out the door with nothing but her two degrees from The College of Saint Rose. She continued to teach at local schools and roomed with two other of her best friends, both former nuns. She said her husband, Jack, was and is her best friend. When he hit the lottery, he gave her fifteen million dollars that she didn't know what to do with. Over the last few years, she learned that money opened doors, opened lives and made things better by evening up the playing field and that's what she intended to do. They asked her a few personal questions but both Jane and Kristen stopped her from answering. They didn't need to know where she lived down here.

They all visited the Technology Center. Joan Talbot was there, in her office and was introduced to everyone. She gave a short blurb on the recruitment of minorities for the Coast Guard and technology jobs that were sorely needed. The recent graduates, sitting in the Center, were working hard on projects from the Capital Region of New York, brought in by Mary and Jack through the Evangeline Career Center in Troy. All in all, they believed the meeting went well. Questions were asked and answered-at least most of them. Michele and her staff headed back to Miami, followed by Jane Swanson. Kristen would stay around for the day and would head out the following morning. She was in for a surprise. Mary booked her a private jet home as a birthday present for her upcoming birthday in late October. Mary would be heading back to Troy a week before Thanksgiving so they could participate in the annual feast for students, families, staff and guests. It was the highlight of the year for Jack and Mary.

The Sunday edition of the *Miami Herald* came out the following week. It was a feel-good story, no doubt about it. It explained thoroughly how two people decided to take their winning lottery tickets and turn them into a good deed. The article went through the various trust funds and what they funded so far and what their intentions were over the next five years. They explained that their permanent address was in New York State but they had a place in Key West when they came down for meetings, events and potential proposals. They really pushed the newly created The College of the Florida Keys Technology Center and how it was serving the youth of the community, especially for minorities. They wanted those students to graduate, continue their education and work in the Keys in job that paid well enough that they too could be part of the American dream.

After reading the article in the Sunday *Miami Herald*, the head of the Nationalist Alliance, Ken Meggs, now living in Hialeah, outside Miami, called Kevin Strong, one of his most fervent supporters. Kevin followed the winning lady lottery winner from the lottery office to the Fort Lauderdale International Airport and then lost her. They hadn't heard a thing about her in well over a year. The Nationalist Alliance was very much in debt over the last year because of Covid-19 shutdowns, loss of jobs and loss of donations from its two thousand members. They moved the headquarters from Mississippi to Florida to gain more funding but there are a lot of white supremacist groups in Florida and last count, forty-seven in total.

"Kevin, it's Ken. Did you read the Sunday *Miami Herald* about the lady lottery winner?"

"No, I don't read the paper. Nothing but liberal bullshit in it."

"Get the paper, Kevin. Evidently, she's affiliated with a college down in Key West and lives there somewhere when she's down from New York. We're going broke, Kevin. Have I made myself clear? We need money. Now," he said.

"How the hell am I supposed to find out where she lives? You know, me, Rich and Luther are doing what we can. We're close to broke too. We can't get jobs. We aren't vaccinated and without it, they won't even let us near a business. What the hell are we supposed to do? Rich is living with his mother in Big Pine Key. She's selling her house because they don't have any money. She can't sell it next to a few run-down businesses with a trailer park right next to them. Luther is living with his girlfriend somewhere around here in Hialeah, I think," said Kevin.

"The article mentions the Evangeline Trust Fund and the Teresa Trust Fund South. I'll look into those organizations to see if they own any property in the area. I'll bet the lady didn't put anything in her own name so no one would know where she is. She'd do that if she were smart. I'll get back to you. We need ten million dollars to keep up recruiting. You know they nabbed several of our guys in the January 6th Capitol fiasco. How do you get caught with ten thousand people to look at? It's like getting the only speeding ticket on the highway with fifty cars, all over the speed limit and you get stopped. That's really stupid."

It was a week later and Ken called back Kevin. "Kevin, bingo. I think we might have an address to look at. The Evangeline Trust Fund owns a house at 10 Allamanda Terrace in Key West. It's on Stock Island. You and the boys need to drive by and look around and see what we can do to lure her out so we can snatch her. Does she head to church? Does she have security people and alarms? Does she have any neighbors? Who mows the lawn and does the bushes? Do they bring their garbage out on a certain night? Who does it? We need a woman to walk the street with a puppy to look around. I wish we had a drone to see what's out back but it can't be that complicated. Just because you have money doesn't mean you're that smart."

"Can you send us some money, we're almost broke. Rich has a plain white van. I don't think we should drive the Focus by their house, do you? He's only down in Big Pine Key, only about thirty miles from Stock Island."

"I'll give you some money. Have Luther come by this week since you think he's close by. Don't screw this up, Kevin."

"Rich, it's Kevin. We need to get together with Luther. We have an address for the rich lottery winner down in Key West. Ken wants us to snatch her and get a ransom. We get a big cut of it, which will certainly help us as well as the funds needed to keep the Alliance alive. They're running out of money."

"I'm on it. Call Luther and have him get some money from Ken. Don't get a check. Get cash. We need it. Mom is almost three months behind on the mortgage. I thought it was paid for and it was but she never told me she took out another loan on a house that we can't sell. Just great, huh?" said Rich.

CHAPTER 34

It was early November and Mary and Jack were planning to head back to Troy for Thanksgiving, the last Thursday of the month, the 25th. Jack loved Thanksgiving. It was his favorite holiday. In the planning was great food, football and more football and tons of friends visiting. He and Joe talked about it all the time because Joe felt the same way. The hassles weren't there like at Christmas. They cooked the turkey the day before and only had to heat it up. All the side dishes were ready to go by noon and dinner was between games around 4:00 p.m. When back in Troy, when they were younger, Joe and his brother Pete used to throw the football around with his father. Jack heard the stories, and as an only child, was envious of big families. That's why Jack wanted to surround himself with everyone he knew and loved.

Last year was the first family Thanksgiving at the Evangeline Career Center. Everyone showed up and this year there would be even more but more importantly, there would be take-out meals for shut-ins in the neighborhood as well as seniors in the families they served. Jack and Mary needed to prepare cash gifts for students and staff. Last year before the real pandemic hit, they gave out very substantial gifts. This year, they had to spend a fortune just to keep the place open so they would give gifts to students and staff but no major bonuses and no one actually expected anything. Karen Steele already mentioned to them that it was not necessary because of everything they had already done throughout the year. Millions of dollars to the food bank and keeping staff employed went a long way toward loyalty and it was appreciated.

Since they arrived in Key West after Labor Day, their security team had changed weekly with four different service men and women helping out. Right now, Martina and Antonia were here until they left for the airport. It was getting to be time when they would need to hire some full-time staff as protection since it was wearing on the volunteers from the Islamorada facility. They realized that Joan Talbot went out of her way to make sure they were protected. Of all the staff, Mary's favorites were Martina and Antonia. They just seemed to get along and never complained about any tasks that were required of them.

Alex and Mia were fine but it appeared to be more of a job to them than any perceived friendship. Joe had noticed this as well but he said they weren't there for drinks they were there to protect them. Joe was as right as he was blunt. It was his most amazing trait. He called things the way he saw them, regardless of the consequences. Never ask Joe for a response that you might not like. He will tell you straight out.

Luther had picked up cash from Ken Meggs. Kevin, Luther and Rich split the cash three ways. It was enough to pay for Rich's mother's mortgage and pay some bills. Ken gave them ten thousand dollars in cash and told Luther that he expected to be fully reimbursed as soon as possible. Luther and his girlfriend came down to Key West from Hialeah with her dog. They all went together in Rich's van, after meeting at his mother's house in Big Pine Key. He had GPS on his phone. The van was too old for any new high-tech apps. It was about thirty miles door to door. They drove down the street at dusk and got the house number from the mailbox out front. They went around the corner and left off the girlfriend with the dog and told her to meet them a few blocks away and to act like she lived around there and was out for a nightly stroll.

She walked around the corner with the dog and walked right by Mary and Jack's house. As she walked by, the garage door opened. She saw a couple put their carry-on bags into the back of an SUV. As they were doing that, there were two women standing right by their side, obviously armed and obviously protecting the couple. The girlfriend nodded at them and said hello and kept on walking.

Martina asked, "Have you ever seen her before in this neighborhood?"

All three shook their heads but didn't pay that much attention to the lady with the dog. They also didn't realize that the woman took pictures of all four of them standing by the garage as she walked by. After loading up the SUV, they tool off for the airport. Immediately, the girlfriend texted Luther and said they looked like they were leaving in a Highlander SUV, a newer model, for somewhere and they had armed security. Luther told her to wait for a while and they would come back and meet her at the closest convenience store that they saw coming into town. Luther picked up the Highlander and hung back for a block and then started to follow. It didn't take long to figure out that they were headed to the airport. About fifteen minutes later, Luther parked in the short-term parking area and he and Rich walked over to the entrance and saw Mary and Jack unloading their vehicle and giving hugs to the two ladies with them. As they walked by, they heard Mary say, we'll see you in March. "Have a wonderful Thanksgiving and Christmas. You deserve it," said Mary.

"Well, it looks like we're a day late and a dollar short.

We can't snatch her here. It's the last place we need to be in front of all these security teams and cameras. Let's get out of here. I have to pick up Donna ASAP. She's been texting me like crazy. We need to call Ken and tell him that they left somewhere by plane and we heard them say they won't be back until March. Ken will be pissed but, we have all their pictures and we know exactly where they live. We need to stroll the area and see what people are regularly out on the street and when they pick up the garbage and when cans go out. We need Donna to walk the streets several more times so people think she lives around here. We need an exact plan for when they come back next March."

Ken was not happy at their departure. He was able to find out exactly what flights they were taking and it looked like they were headed back to New York. With 2,000 members in the Nationalist Alliance, he had plenty of computer hackers who got him information whenever he needed it. This was no small operation. They were just running out of money due to the pandemic and lack of employment. That would change drastically with ten million dollars in cash in their hands. He would start checking flight schedules starting in March, from Albany International to Tampa to Key West airports. If Luther, Rich and Donna roamed the area, they might find out exactly when they would be back. Until then, they had to sit tight.

John Jefferson and Fred Tucker were both back in service once again as rules eased around town. They picked them up at the baggage area at the Albany International Airport as soon as they arrived. They both smiled and now understood they were friends of theirs now, more than clients. John and Fred picked up their bags. It was obvious Jack and Mary were tired. They headed back home to Old Plank Road. They would sleep through the morning. It was now the 10th of November, a little over two weeks until Thanksgiving.

Mary had to meet her mentor at The College of Saint Rose on Friday to update him about her scheduled graduation and thesis from Barry University. She wanted to ask him if he would be willing to fly down with her to deliver her thesis and presentation to the Ph.D. committee. Her and Joe's Florida mentor would be there anyway but it would be a nice touch and as she realizes more and more, marketing oneself is everything.

They arrived home very late and were met at the door by Jack's daughter, Debbie, and her "friend" Patrick Valente, who was just leaving. Evidently they have been together since last Christmas. He finished his MBA from Rensselaer Polytechnic Institute and was now working at the university development office. She's still working full-time at the Career Center, so things are going very well thought Jack. He shook Patrick's hand and said Happy Thanksgiving. He told him that he and his parents were more than welcome to come to the Thanksgiving event at the Center and to their house as well on Thanksgiving. Patrick thanked him and turned to Mary and shook her hand and gave a hug to Debbie and said, "I'll call you in the morning. Goodnight everyone. I'm glad you had a safe trip." He headed out and Debbie smiled.

"Things are looking up, hey kiddo?" asked Jack.

"You could say that. With all your globe-trotting, I'm surprised you noticed," she added.

"Oh, he noticed," said Mary as she gave her a big hug and a kiss.

"After you settle in or even in the morning, I need to tell you something about mom. I'm sure you'll want to know," said Debbie.

"Want to know what? Is she okay?" asked Jack

"No, she's not, dad," Debbie said.

"Let's talk about it right now," he added. Mary did too.

"I hadn't heard from her in quite a while. As you

remember when I told her about Mary winning the lottery, she was quite upset. I think she called the *Times Union* and dropped a dime on you. I never got along with Chuck as you know. But, I went to the bank a week ago and saw that mom wasn't there in the manager's office. I thought she was at lunch. I had to cash a check and pay some bills so I asked if she was at lunch. Her assistant manager looked at me with great surprise. She said that Maureen hadn't been to work in some time. Evidently, even though she was vaccinated, she got the new wave, Delta variant, of Covid-19 virus and is very ill. I tried calling her cell phone since she dropped the landline and there was no answer. I went to the house and I saw Chuck. He said she's been in the Samaritan Hospital and then transferred to St. Peter's Hospital, in Albany, last week. She's not on a ventilator and evidently getting better. I went to see her and they wouldn't let me near her. I don't know what to do. Chuck said he can't visit her and he doesn't know what to do either. He got Covid-19 and apparently gave it to my mother. He had no symptoms whatsoever and is back to work. Mom had to go on disability and she can't even collect the higher unemployment benefits because she's sick. Her insurance isn't covering everything and the bills are mounting up. Dad, I know she was really shitty to you and Mark and me, but I don't want her to die, you know?"

Both Jack and Mary hugged her and said that whatever she needed she would get. Jack popped open a beer for all three of them and then said, they would see her come hell or high water the next day. He needed to have Kristen, the Diocesan lawyer, pull strings to get them in to see Maureen. If she needed long-term care, they would contact the Eddy in Troy and make arrangements. He also asked her if she could check on the status of Maureen's bills and mortgage and then give Debbie her power of attorney and make her the health care proxy. He would open new accounts for this purpose and make sure everything was fine until she got better. He had no idea what to do with Chuck Falcone, who helped ruin his marriage originally and been a thorn in Jack's side ever since. He hoped that Chuck's short stay in the county jail after assaulting him a while ago opened his eyes. He wasn't concerned about the house but he didn't think Maureen had a will and if she did he didn't know if she'd added Chuck to the mix. For now, he just wanted Maureen to have the best health coverage she could get. The bank where she worked didn't seem to give a damn one way or the other. He would make a personal visit to the Bank's regional vice president as well and find out her employment status.

CHAPTER 35

By the end of the week, Jack, Mary, Mark and Debbie were able to see Maureen at St. Peter's Hospital. Kristen pulled some strings through the chaplain's office associated with the Roman Catholic Diocese of Albany. One call from the Bishop did the trick. Mary was in a very basic Covid-19 wing. She had a separate room and was sleeping when they arrived. They were told that the visit was for twenty minutes and that was it. As they walked into the room, Maureen turned around and squinted at them.

"Is that you, Jack?" she asked first.

"Yes, it is," he said. "Debbie and Mark are here to see you. Mary's here too. We are only allowed to stay twenty minutes. We would have been here sooner but we didn't know you were in the hospital or were even ill. No one told us. We had to get special permission to come see you."

They all had double facemasks on even though they were fully vaccinated. They knew that Maureen was fully vaccinated too but still got the virus. Thanks to the vaccine, she didn't get worse. She was in the hospital only because of her asthma and weight gain but she didn't need a ventilator, which was the kiss of death. Maureen looked all of her fifty-two years and actually a lot older.

"Once you get out of here, you'll be recuperating at the

Eddy nursing facility attached to Samaritan Hospital," Jack said

The hospital and the Eddy were on 15th street in Troy and not that far from everyone. Chuck could visit her then. He couldn't get permission because he got Covid-19 and they were unsure if he was ever tested or not and they didn't know if he was over it or not. He was at home and he couldn't get unemployment either because of this. He was on disability but he didn't seem to pay any bills anyway.

"Maureen, we just wanted you to know that you don't have to worry about your bills. All of the bills including your mortgage and student loans will be brought up to date and paid regularly. We know Chuck isn't working so we'll also pay all your utilities and hospital bills until you get back on your feet. If you do go back to work, then fine. But, you don't have to worry about that. Just get better for your children," said Jack. Mary took his hand and smiled at him as if to say, *"You're doing a good thing here, Jack, even if it kills you,"* and she smiled.

"Mary, thank you for coming to see me. I'm sorry I'm not in better shape. I'm sorry for a lot of things. Trust me. Debbie and Mark can you stay for a few minutes so I can talk to you?"

Mary and Jack got the hint and said goodbye. Jack took Maureen's hand and gave it a kiss. Mary did the same and they left.

Maureen was getting tired and it was obvious. Debbie said to her mother, "Dad asked me to take care of your health proxy, power of attorney and living will. Kristen Sorenson, Dad's attorney, is drawing up the documents, now. It's so I can pay your bills unless you want everything in Chuck's hands," she said.

"No, I don't want that at all. I know you don't believe me but overall he has been good to me. For how long I don't know. Ask your attorney to draw up a will as well leaving everything to you and Mark. Also, put in the will that Chuck gets fifty thousand dollars out of the proceeds of the sale of the house if needed. I have a retirement from the bank but I don't even know if I have a job when I get back. I do have a small retirement and social security. Is your father serious about helping out with the bills?" she asked.

"Yes, he is. He doesn't hate you mom. I think you truly hurt him to his soul. We're just glad that he found Mary. The money they have is secondary. She loves him, mom. I think she always has. She is a wonderful, caring person. She wanted to come and see you."

"Well, I'm not glad but I did this to myself so I have no one else to blame."

Mark never said a word. He was completely torn. There was his mother possibly dying with Covid-19 and he really couldn't get over his anger about his mother tearing his family apart for what? *For nothing that's what, he thought.*

"Mom, I'm trying to forget and forgive but it's hard. It will take time. If you work on it, I'll work on it. What do you say?" he asked.

"I will," she said and then her eyes closed. She was exhausted. Mark gave her a kiss on her forehead through his mask and nodded to Debbie to do the same. She did and they walked out arm in arm. Maybe, just maybe, there'll be some peace down the road.

They met up with Jack and Mary in the waiting room and they left together for the parking garage. Mark took his own car and headed back to work. Debbie went home with her father and Mary. She took half a day from the Center. She had to keep track just like everyone else if she wanted to keep her job. She did.

It was nearing Thanksgiving week. They usually held the annual Thanksgiving dinner event at the Career Center on the Sunday before the holiday. There were several reasons. The first, it was a weekend day. They also wanted to make sure that all the seniors in the area and those with the students' families had a dinner already for them on Thanksgiving Day. And second, that everyone had plenty of leftover turkey and side dishes including tons of pies to bring home. Giving out frozen turkeys to families was kind of a thing of the past and there was way too much work involved. Just having this catered cost a small fortune. Coming in on the weekend to work together, students, staff, administrators and family members added to the holiday spirit. On Saturday, college football played on the big screen with pizzas filling everyone up. Sunday would have the NFL playing but only outside the dining area. This feature drew the inner-city men and boys with food and football as a preview to the actual Thanksgiving Day events.

Kristen got all the necessary paperwork completed for Maureen's signature. Debbie went to see her and got her signature on the will, health care proxy and power of attorney. Kristen went with her as a witness and to certify the documents. Together, they went over to see Chuck Falcone at Maureen's house in Brunswick. He answered the door after a dozen rings and saw Debbie. He saw Kristen as well and asked them what they wanted. Debbie said she needed to talk to him and this was Maureen's attorney. He started to panic and gulped and then let them in the door. Debbie told him not to worry and told him that she would explain exactly what's going on about Maureen's state of affairs. Debbie wasn't pleased that Maureen would leave Chuck fifty thousand dollars in her will if she died but it wasn't the money. She had totally disliked Chuck from the first day she met him. They argued constantly when Debbie lived there while attending college. That was the reason she moved out and reconciled with her father. At that point, she knew that her father wasn't responsible for any of Maureen's decisions.

Debbie told Chuck that she now had her mother's power

of attorney, health proxy and her will. She said that all Maureen's bills that had to do with the house including the mortgage, taxes, the power company and insurance would be paid for while Maureen was recovering. She said that all the past due bills had been taken care of and brought to a current status. She told him that Maureen's mail would be forwarded to the attorney's office and Debbie would be responsible for paying those bills in a timely manner. She also mentioned that whatever food Chuck bought on a weekly basis would be reimbursed with copies of receipts. She would not pay for his other personal bills or alcohol. Actually, Chuck seemed quite relieved. He knew he could have been dumped on his rear end so he was grateful. He asked what happens when Maureen got better and came home. Debbie said it all depended on the status of her mother's job at the bank. They would deal with it at that time. Debbie also said it would be nice if he visited Maureen when she transferred to the Eddy after he got his Covid-19 clearance. He said he would.

Debbie and Kristen left the house after their conversation and Debbie said, "I think that went quite well. Do you?" she asked Kristen.

"Couldn't have gone better. I think he thought we were throwing him out of the house and he actually looked grateful. I also think you did an excellent job, Debbie. There has been a remarkable change in you over the last year or so. I see it. Everyone sees it. You have confidence in yourself. You now have your Master's degree and a job that you love. It shows. I'm sure your father is very proud of you. I know Mary is and that counts for a lot."

"Actually, I am more pleased about Mary than my father. In time, I always thought he would come around if I did. I was worried about Mary but she's actually great and I can say that to anyone who asks. It wasn't an easy transformation. My brother, Mark, is still going through it, but that's because he has his own life with Cara and doesn't live with us. I was pleased when Mark told mom that he would try if she did."

"I have no idea what's going to happen to your mother but I think this puts her on the right path if she gets better or not. I think she has tons of regrets. That's just my guess but I think I'm right," said Kristen.

"I think you're right too. How about lunch?" said Debbie. With that they headed to downtown Troy, to have lunch and Kristen would drop off Debbie at the Career Center before heading back to Albany.

Because the Thanksgiving dinner event had grown so much, it would be impossible to give gifts on that day to the current students as they did previously. Jack, Mary and Karen decided that during the first week of December, they would hold a Friday night pizza party for the current students only and hand each a $500.00 gift card so they could buy presents for their families. They would do the same for the teachers, and staff but bonuses were out this year since they paid every employee, every week, since the pandemic started. There were no layoffs and it had cost a fortune but it made everyone feel very strongly about their mission and they knew that both Jack and Mary cared about them. They also set up a food bank right at the Career Center so that current and past student family members, who were laid off or unable to work due to quarantine, could count on a weekly food donation.

Most of the employees worked from home online and it seemed to strengthen their understanding of the plan for each student. They communicated by FaceTime and Zoom and some came in to the building, fully masked and vaccinated when they could, to receive hands-on instruction. It worked out and kept the community together. Now that the pandemic was behind them, everyone connected to the Career Center seemed to understand their own personal mission and how it fit into the overall strategy. That allowed Mary and Jack to travel more and gave pretty much full control to Karen Steele. She ran with it and expanded the job creation aspects to now include technology, coding, construction, EMT, as well as continuing to have students complete their education with a GED/TASC degree certified by the New York State Education. Department. As usual, the dinner was a success. Families had more than enough leftovers packed for the real Thanksgiving Day coming up in a few days.

There was a Thanksgiving service at St. Augustine's Church on the eve of the holiday. Mary and Jack always attended the service. This year, Debbie and her boyfriend, Patrick Valente, Mark and Cara, and Mary's two old roommates, Jane and Martha, came with them. They all would be staying at the house this evening into Thanksgiving. John Jefferson and Fred Tucker went with them since there was no one at home. They always cooked the turkey the night before and made pies and the dressing. Jack and Mary, once again, planned on having several guests including Cara's parents and Patrick's parents as well.

Mary's mother wasn't feeling that well either but would come to dinner and leave soon afterward. Louis and Addie Freeman couldn't make it this year because Addie wasn't feeling well. Jack had already dropped off a complete Thanksgiving dinner with all the trimmings to them on the Sunday before, on the way home from the Career Center feast. They spent an hour with them and it was becoming obvious that both Louis and Addie were on the downside and both would need care in the very near future. Since they didn't have children, Jack mentioned to them that both he and Mary would be more than happy to serve as their potential power of attorney and if they wished, they could call on Kristen Sorenson at any time, at no cost to them, to help plan their future.

Everyone at the house seemed to have fun on Thanksgiving Day. The property up on Old Plank Road could have held ten football fields. Jack, Patrick and Mark threw the football around after dinner and between football games. Jack was so tired that he wanted to take a nap but somehow stayed awake until everyone left for the night. John Jefferson left to visit family and Fred Tucker stayed. He would leave in the morning when John came back. They needed a break as well and Jack would talk to both of them and see if they wanted a break and pick a few of their close FBI retiree friends to help out.

Everyone knew that Mary and Jack would be in town until the end of January and that Joe Traynor, Julie, Bella and Tillie would be coming up for Christmas to visit Joe's brother and father and Pete's fiancée, Tanya Fields. With Joe around, John and Fred could take a day or two off since Joe and his family would stay at Jack and Mary's house on Old Plank. It would be a fun time. The Manning's could show Joe and Julie around to see what has been accomplished up here in Troy. Joe would be graduating from Barry University the week before Christmas. They would hop on a plane and get here for the holiday. They would stay through New Year's Eve and Joe would be taking the position as interim president of The College of the Florida Keys, for one year only, and hopefully shorter. He and his family would then head to the Coast Guard Academy as the Assistant Superintendent.

Jack had a surprise for Joe and Julie and called them. He told them not to fly commercial but to be at the private air section of the Key West International Airport on the day they would leave. It was Jack's graduation gift to Joe and a thank you to Julie for being on Mary's Teresa Trust Fund South board. So there would be no question as to if the trip were deductible to any of their trust funds, Jack gifted each to a portion of the trip and paid for it personally. It was his thank you. They could stay as little or as long as they wanted and they would fly home the same way. When they flew back to Key West after the holidays, Jamie would pick them up and take them back to their home in Tavernier. While in Troy, they could get rides from John or Fred or just borrow a car.

They had plenty of room at the house. Jack didn't ask Debbie but suspected that she would be staying with Patrick over the holidays, giving up her room. Fred would give up his as well. They also had an extra room that was only used for an office and Bella could have her own room. By Christmas week, there would be snow on the ground. Jack already ordered lots of stuff from L. L. Bean including a Sonic snow tube, a polar slider, and a snow saucer all for Bella who had never seen snow. He also got her boots. warm gloves, a ski hat and a snow jacket after calling Tillie and getting her measurements. Tillie told him that she had seen snow only once in Florida. She had only been north once to attend Joe's mother's funeral many years ago.

Jack wanted it to be as much a surprise for Joe and Julie as it was for Bella. There was no problem for the adults. Everyone in upstate New York had plenty of winter clothing to keep an army warm. Jack made sure that the snowmobiles were tuned up and ready to go. Mary had surprised him when they first moved in and bought Jack a pair of brand new snowmobiles. *He thought she was kidding when she said they got so much snow up on Bald Mountain that they needed snowmobiles to get around. He smiled and remembered, she wasn't kidding.*

CHAPTER 36

It was the Saturday after Thanksgiving that Jack got the call from St. Peter's Hospital in Albany that they were discharging Maureen to The Eddy Nursing Home in Troy that afternoon. Debbie had some work to do at the Career Center that morning so Jack called her to let her know that as soon as Maureen arrived, he and Mary would head over to make sure that Maureen had everything she needed. He asked Debbie to call Chuck Falcone to let him know. She did but had to leave a message. He wasn't there. Debbie said as soon as her father got the call, she would head up from the Career Center and meet him and Mary at the front door of The Eddy.

It was around 2:00 p.m. when they all arrived at the nursing home. Maureen was in a wheelchair near the front desk and appeared to be fast asleep. It looked like Covid-19 really did a number on her. She appeared at least ten years older. She seemed like she had been in the nursing home for a while. She looked like a long-term resident already. Jack just shook his head and tried to wake her up. Her eyes opened and she saw Jack and said hello. She was trying to keep her dignity but it was not quite on display. Hopefully, after a few weeks, she would be able to go home and perhaps have a visiting nurse check in on her daily. Debbie took responsibility for her care. They certainly hoped that Chuck would help out. If not, his residence would change.

Finally, Chuck Falcone called Debbie and said he was called back to work and couldn't miss or he would lose his job. Evidently, he wasn't as sick as he told everyone and it started to catch up with him. He said he would stop by this evening to see Maureen. What could anyone say? He wasn't married to her. He was a houseguest with benefits, evidently. Jack told Debbie and Mary that he would revisit the arrangement with Chuck if he didn't pull his own weight. Jack's expectations were not high to begin with. After they got Maureen settled and the first month's bill paid, they headed out to get something to eat at the Plum Blossom on Hoosick Street, before heading home. Maureen was in good hands. The Eddy had the highest rating of any nursing facility in the region and at those prices, it should. At least Jack's obligation, if there ever was one, was met and then some.

For the next week, Jack and Mary had purchased over a hundred VISA gift cards to distribute to the students and staff at the Career Center on the planned Friday night pizza party, a few weeks before Christmas. In addition, Mary called Joe at the college and asked him to put together a list of students and staff at the new Technology Center, along with the administrative staff at the college so they too could receive a Christmas VISA card for $500.00 each. Joe was very appreciative of their generosity and thanked them. They also made the arrangements for Joe and his family to fly up to Albany on a private jet and they all would meet them at the airport on Tuesday, December 21st. They would head back to Florida the following Tuesday, December 28th. Joe was graduating on Friday, December 17th at the Barry University campus with a group of fifteen other Ph.D. candidates. The university was having a luncheon in their honor and Rear Admiral Jake Barnes and a few of Joe's closest friends would attend the ceremony along with Jane and Nick, Julie, Bella, Tillie and the Talbots. Joe and Julie had to get back to Tavernier to pack for their trip on the following Tuesday. Jack and Mary will have a surprise dinner for Joe the following day after they arrived for his family up here in Troy.

Mary also wanted to present gifts to the four Coast Guard security team members and to Jamie for all that she has done for them, especially during the pandemic. Mary would overnight a check to each of them and she would call Jamie and thank her personally and let her know to keep an eye out for a UPS truck. Jamie's gift was for $2,500.00 while the others got $500.00 each. She didn't know what to do for Joan Talbot and her family so she would ask Joe what he thought. She was sure that she wasn't able to accept personal gifts, especially after running the special recruitment Trust from the college over the last year. At that point, both Jack and Mary felt they were covered for the holidays. They also had to make sure, for Bella's sake, that Santa Claus came to their house on Old Plank Road, early Christmas morning, after she went to bed. They would leave out cookies and milk for Santa and read the Night before Christmas. They would all attend the 10:30 a.m. Christmas Day Mass at St. Augustine's. It's been a while since Joe had attended his home parish, the parish he grew up in.

Joe's graduation went extremely well. He was very surprised to see Rear Admiral Barnes and his friends at the ceremony. Obviously, Julie, Tillie, and Bella came with the Talbots since they were that close together down in the Keys. The luncheon was first class and Joe accepted his Ph.D. diploma from the Dean of the School of Education. He was surprised to see the president of the college in attendance but then remembered that Jake was a close friend. One call from Jake got him into Barry University and a second call got Mary Evans in as well. Joe and his family stayed overnight at the hotel next to the Coast Guard headquarters. They had dinner and drinks with his friends and headed out the following morning after a quick meeting with Rear Admiral Barnes. It was official. Dr. Joseph Traynor was the new interim president for The College of the Florida Keys for one year or less if they found an acceptable long-term president. He would also be an adjunct at the Coast Guard Academy and participate in various Coast Guard Academy events throughout the year so that when the switch was made, he would be very familiar with all the staff, the teachers, students and the area. For Julie it was almost homecoming since she spent five years at Brown University receiving her Master of Fine Arts where she honed her writing skills and became a well-known national author of books for young women. Brown University was fifty-seven miles away from the Academy and she could make it in less than an hour. She remembers her trips from north of Boston, where she stayed with her best friend, Maddie, during the summer months, while finishing up at Brown. That ride took twice as long and was twice as dangerous driving through Boston almost every day. Since Joe's appointment would be official, Julie started to make inquiries about a teaching position or potential writing position within the Brown University Fine Arts Department. She would have to give up her job at the Coral Shores High School and Tillie would lose her medical insurance since she was on Julie's policy as a dependent. Now, Tillie turned sixty-five and would be entitled to Medicare and she would still need supplemental insurance to cover prescriptions, dental, and vision, along with the other 20% not covered by Medicare. There was a lot to think about but the gift from Mary to the Traynor family for one million dollars would certainly be used for this purpose and to make sure that Tillie was always taken care of when she was unable to take care of herself. Julie vowed that Tillie would be with her every day until the end of her life. That's what she had meant to Julie and to Joe.

Joe, Julie, Tillie and Bella met the private plane at the Key West International Airport. Tillie had flown exactly once in her life and Bella not at all. They were nervous but excited. The pilot and staff couldn't have been nicer. They were familiar with Mary and Jack and thought that these people were just as nice and would be a pleasure to fly them to Albany. They were right. They left around 11:00 a.m. and after being in flight for an hour, they had a special lunch prepared and Bella had a McDonald's Happy Meal all ready for her, served hot with a special prize inside. She was thrilled. Joe, Julie and Tillie had lobster salad sandwiches with champagne and a special graduation cake, made by Julie's favorite baker and delivered just on time to the plane before departure. Everyone was tired so after lunch, they all closed their eyes and took a nap for several hours. Bella woke up and had apple juice and pretzels and played games on her new iPad. It was a non-Santa Clause Christmas gift from Tillie so she was allowed to unwrap it on the plane. Tillie had it fully charged and Julie had loaded it with appropriate age group fun games. Bella was still perfecting her English. As a surprise, so she would never forget her heritage, half her games were in Spanish. Julie was becoming quite proficient and even Tillie got in on the act and was able to carry on short conversations in Spanish. Joe always spoke to Bella in Spanish unless Bella started talking in English and then he would switch.

The plane landed at the Albany International Airport right around 4:00 p.m. They taxied over to the commercial area and unloaded. They were met at the door by Joe's father, John, his brother, Pete, and Tanya Fields, Pete's fiancé. After a few hugs, they walked into the hanger and were met by Mary and Jack and their security team of John Jefferson and Fred Tucker. They would head to Old Plank

Road. It was now Tuesday, December 21st, four days before Christmas. There was snow on the ground and it was around 32 degrees. It looked beautiful. Bella's eyes lit up and so did Tillie's. Bella reached down and grabbed the snow as if it was a dream. The snow was dense so she was able to pack some into her little hands and hurl it at Joe. He laughed and did the same.

"Now children, behave yourself," said Julie. She laughed.

"I didn't remember how beautiful this is for Christmas up here. However it is really, really cold," Tillie said.

They had three vehicles and Joe, Tillie and Bella went with Joe's father. It was only fitting. They had a lot of catching up to do. They would have stayed at John's house in Lansingburgh but there were only two bedrooms, taken up by John and Pete and sometimes guest, Tanya. Having them stay at the beautiful home up on the mountain was very appropriate. John Traynor was responsible for Jack and Mary buying this house. They purchased it after a short lease because they loved it so much. A long-time friend of John's who had retired after his wife died of cancer owned it. John's wife died of breast cancer almost at the same time so they not only were close friends but they had so much more in common.

Bella loved her own little room. The office furniture was pulled out and a single bed placed in the room. Tillie had her own room. It was John Jefferson's and Julie and Joe had Fred Tucker's. Mary brought in professional cleaners to make sure that everything in the house was cleaned and disinfected. There was still a chance of Covid-19, a slim chance, but it was always better to err on the side of safety. They walked in and saw Debbie standing by the most beautiful, real, fresh pine tree all decorated on the top with the bottom completely untouched. Immediately, Bella asked why she didn't finish the tree and Debbie said that she was waiting for Bella to decorate the bottom, all the way up as far as she could reach. Her eyes sparkled and she turned and told her mother in Spanish how happy she was. Debbie answered her in Spanish to everyone's surprise.

"When did you learn Spanish?" asked her dad.

"Since I've been hiding away up here and got my Master's degree, during the pandemic, just like Mary getting her Ph.D., I decided to learn Spanish if I was ever going to head down to Florida for any length of time." She added, "When I heard Bella was coming, I decided to speed up my skills. It's also very helpful at the Career Center. Do you know our Hispanic students have grown leaps and bounds over the last year? When everyone left New York City because of the crisis and no jobs due to Covid-19, a good portion came up here in the Capital Region. The Troy School District has a four-time increase in Hispanic students in one year during the crisis. They couldn't keep up so now, on top of my duties at the Career Center, we have brought in LVA, Literacy Volunteers of America, to help students' parents become proficient in Spanish. You should hang around more, Dad and see what's going on," Debbie said with a smile.

"Me too," said Mary. "I would have never guessed that but should have. Wow are we behind the times."

"Welcome to my world, guys," said Debbie. "By the way, I know Mark and Cara and her family will be here for Christmas dinner but so will Patrick's and all of Joe's family. Let's eat, everyone. I had the grill still out on the deck. Steak and fries for everyone?" she asked.

"Thank you, Debbie," said Jack. "How's your mother today?"

"She's doing okay and Chuck finally made it over to see her. I think it's more of an obligation than a heartfelt decision."

Jack explained, to Joe and everyone, "Maureen got

Covid-19 and was extremely sick. She is getting better and resting at a very fine nursing home for now. We are playing it by ear, day by day."

Everyone in the room knew about Maureen, being Jack's not ex-wife but annulled wife but they were unaware that she was ill. They also saw the kindness of Jack and Mary taking care of Maureen, with Debbie as the main caregiver. This could have gone so much worse if they hadn't let go of their feelings of betrayal. It was working and everyone was glad. They just hoped that Jack and Maureen's son, Mark, would forget and start anew before his and Cara's wedding next fall.

The fire in the fireplace was going strong and everyone was sitting around relaxing. Bella wanted to know how Santa Claus would know that they were here and not at home and how she would get presents. She also wanted to know how Santa Claus could come down a chimney if there was a fire. They explained that the fire would be put out before he would arrive and would be cool enough for him to slide down with all her presents. They also explained that he had plenty of room to land on the house because it was so big. Debbie asked her if she would like to go for a sled ride down the hill in the morning. She would babysit while Joe, Julie and Tillie explored the Career Center. When they came back, her father, Joe, and Jack would take her out on the snowmobiles all around the ten acres surrounding their house.

As Bella's eyes started to close, Mary handed her the biggest Christmas stocking she'd ever seen with her name on it and asked her to tack it to the mantle over the fireplace before she went to bed. Bella was thrilled and immediately fell asleep in Julie's arms.

CHAPTER 37

On Wednesday morning, while Bella was sledding with Debbie, Joe, Julie, and Tillie met with Karen Steele and her staff including Sam Ryan to review all they had done since they opened three years earlier. They would also have a lunch with invited guests including the owners of the high technology companies located within the Capital Region who had started contracts with The College of the Florida Keys. Since Joe was going to be the new Interim President of the college on January 1st, it was appropriate that they shared their plans with the clients and visa-versa. It was also appropriate to have Mary as a guest since she was pumping millions of dollars into the project. Not only did they want contracted jobs, but they wanted their graduates to have the ability to move between regions to learn more, understand regional issues and be part of something even bigger. She wanted her Keys graduates to wind up with RPI degrees and Career Center graduates, who just received their GED/TASC high school degrees, to head down to Florida to be part of The College of the Florida Keys Technology Center. Most of these graduates had never been anywhere outside the region nor had the Key West graduates been anywhere either. It would also be a feather in Joan Talbot's cap if Mary could recruit Career Center graduates, with degrees from Hudson Valley Community College in Troy, to join the Coast Guard down in the Florida Keys. They could get advanced training in coding and technology even before entering the service.

After the meeting, Karen took Joe, Julie and Tillie around to meet the students and then walk the ten-block area that they had been reconstructing for the last three years as the North Central Village with the new charter school being built right in the middle of the village area. All the streets were now paved in brick with turn of the century lamps with solar panels. Almost one hundred homes had been renovated into new units that were for sale at reasonable prices to those currently renting, all supplemented by Jack's program. They saw St. Peter's Church repurposed into a new technology center, manned by RPI student volunteers and a state-of-the-art Career Center with its own Wi-Fi connected to all the colleges locally for online education and training. Joe was amazed at what they had accomplished in the worst section of the city of Troy. Julie wanted to know if this is what Mary had in mind for her Technology Center at The College of the Florida Keys. Mary said it was all tied together but ultimately she wanted to tie this region to Key West, where students, teachers, business people and educators could all move back and forth seamlessly between areas to learn from each other.

Tillie was amazed. She got her high school diploma many years ago but in the past in Florida, women were not treated so well. That's why Tillie wanted Julie to go as far as she could and become a nationally published author. Being attached to Disney as her books turned into movies and television series gave Tillie great pride. Tillie grew up poor and was left to care for Julie by herself as a grandmother with limited resources. She'd brought Julie to her restaurant every night as she worked so Julie could be with her and they could eat dinner together. That's how they survived. As she looked back, drugs had caused major problems in their lives with Annie, Julie's mother succumbing to drugs when Julie was only eight years old. That's why Tillie was so interested in a new program that Mary had mentioned to her when they arrived at Christmas. A new approach was needed for drug addiction, treating it as a family problem no different than literacy or poverty. The problem with one addicted family member became a problem for every member, keeping all of him or her in a downward spiral of poverty.

The article came from Vermont. Mary's good friend, a well-recognized grant writer, helped develop a mentoring program for families at risk, not just children at risk. Having individual mentors for children helped those who had no one in their lives but it didn't help improve the lives of those whose parents had a drug-related problem or were incarcerated. The program started working with the local regional hospital to provide mentoring support to youth affected by opioid addiction. It was apparent that the parents needed as much support as their children because they were the ones addicted, not the children. So, they began an innovative program to match families with an array of mentors for both the parents and the children, to provide a cohesive support team to each family. The project provided an extremely cost-effective solution to increase life skills for the youth and the caregivers. It increased sustainability and goal setting, and decreased high-risk activities and substance abuse for both the children and the parents. The family program was expensive, around twenty thousand dollars per family per year. However, the effective cost savings were ten times higher than the cost per family. Just to keep one person out of jail is a savings of over one hundred thousand dollars per year. The cost of welfare, medical assistance, special education and social services was added on top. Because of the value shown over a three-year period, the Federal government awarded the mentoring program five hundred thousand dollars to serve as a model for replication.

Tillie found that to be amazing. She asked if she could visit the program while they were here for Christmas and Mary was thrilled by her interest. Joe and Jack would meet on other issues concerning the college and the Career Center, and Julie wanted to show Bella around the area including the New York State Museum and the capital. Mary and Tillie left for Vermont two days later to meet with the mentoring staff in Rutland. It was only eighty miles away but a longer trip due to ski season in Vermont. They arrived at noon and had lunch with the director and the staff. He explained all the details and actually had a family show up with a husband and a wife and two small children. The husband was addicted to opioids and had just been released to a drug court, a new concept in Vermont that placed the family with this nonprofit. The husband came from a very poor background and had dabbled in drugs because he didn't have a job. When he got a job, he was fired due to his addiction, making it a vicious cycle. He praised everyone at the meeting for saving his life. He was now clean and attending the Vermont Community College located in Rutland. They couldn't afford daycare so the wife was unable to work outside the home. This also cut into their living conditions making them even worse than before. Arrangements were made by the mentors to place the children in the hospital daycare while the mother got a job cleaning at the hospital while her children received the best care possible. All of this turned their lives around. They also moved away from the block where his family lived, cutting ties with those who aided his addiction. It was quite a story when he finished. Tillie had tears in her eyes and asked him if she could speak to him further. She wanted to see if they could develop a similar program in the Florida Keys. The director told her point blank that it took not just money but a complete commitment to help families like the one presented that day.

Mary was also impressed and found out that the program was reapplying for new investment funds and Mary asked if she could receive a copy of the application to give to both her boards in the Capital Region and Florida. She said, since it was her funding, she could run a pilot project in Rutland for the benefit of those in the other areas. The director was now thought of as the spokesman for mentoring for the state of Vermont and had Bernie Sanders' ear when it came to funding national programs. Mary thought she could fund some of those programs that didn't win or didn't receive enough money to make a difference. As they left Rutland, after many hugs, Mary and Tillie talked all the way home.

Christmas came and went well. Everyone had a great time. Bella didn't want to leave and asked for one more ride down the hill on her sled. She loved her new hat, boots, gloves and coat and asked if she could keep them. Jack said of course. Debbie fell in love with Bella and thought about "What If" with Patrick. Speaking Spanish to Bella was a real treat and gave her more confidence in her own abilities. Joe's family came over several times and they all went to Mass at St. Augustine's together. Santa Claus came and Bella was still looking up the chimney to see how he left all her presents. Thank God, they were flying back on the same private plane or they wouldn't make it. Joe was very pleased that his father and brother had made a name for themselves serving as the primary contractor for Jack on all his projects. Pete asked Joe to be his best man and Tanya asked that Julie serve as her Matron of Honor and Bella as a flower girl. Of course they accepted.

Joe was starting to get nervous. He was to be sworn in on January 1st as the new Interim President of The College of the Florida Keys. He invited Jack and Mary down for his swearing in but they had to stay with work to do on the new charter schools. Joe's father and brother were proud of him but they knew the real job would be coming up as the Assistant Superintendent of the Coast Guard Academy. Both John and Pete had to be at the same meetings as Mary and Jack so they asked if someone could put it up on YouTube so they could watch it.

The weather held out but a New Year's Eve storm was heading their way with a prediction of twelve to eighteen inches of snow. Bella might have liked the pending snowfall but they were sure that Joe was glad to be headed back to Key West and then to their home in Tavernier. They all went to the airport and waved as they flew back home.

CHAPTER 38

Joe, Julie, Tillie and Bella arrived home safely. Mary and Jack went with John and Fred to the airport with the family to make sure they arrived on time and safely. After hugs and kisses, Joe and the family boarded the plane headed back to warmer weather. Bella didn't want to leave but Tillie was still cold from the day she arrived.

After flying into Key West International Airport with a direct flight, they were met by Jamie, Linda and Skip, driving Mary's SUV. Skip would stay with Jamie for the trip north while Linda would drive back home by herself. Linda just wanted to say Merry Christmas and Happy New Year to everyone. As soon as they packed the vehicle, they headed north to Tavernier. Linda waved to them as they pulled out and headed north. They arrived an hour and a half later at their home in Tavernier. Their next-door neighbor knew they were coming home so she turned on the lights as well as the Christmas tree. They each had keys to each other's house in case of problems. Artificial trees are fine down in Florida if you were going to be away for a while. As they headed into the house, Bella's eyes lit up at the tree. Under the tree were presents all addressed to Bella, from Santa. The neighbor hid the packages before they went away and placed all of them under the tree before they arrived home.

"Mommy, look. Santa came here too. Wow. I can't believe it. He left presents in two places to make sure I got something. Come here. You too, Daddy," she said. "Grammy, look what I got!"

Tillie smiled and winked at Joe and Julie. *Good move she thought.*

Bella opened all her presents before they even got the luggage inside. Their neighbor waved to them and blew them a kiss. So did Julie. *What great friends and neighbors, she thought.*

After they settled in, Debbie and Skip said their goodbyes and Happy New Year. Tillie would stay over until after New Year's Day. Her friend, Ed Lansing, would come over for a New Year's Day dinner and take Tillie back to Key Largo that night. After unpacking, they ordered pizza and Joe popped open a few beers. Tillie and Julie shared a bottle of wine. Bella was still sitting on the living room floor, looking at each present intently.

Joe had only a few days left before he took over as Interim President at The College of the Florida Keys. He had to be back at the college on Monday, January 3rd to meet with Dr. Hennessey's staff. They would now be Joe's staff. Dr. Hennessey was already headed up to Barry University. He was fortunate that he was able to get out of his lease in Key West and buy a place in Miami before the holidays. He and his family packed and were gone before the New Year. It wasn't like he moved across the country. He was only a few hours away and Joe would be attending his inauguration as well within a week's time. Joe had to meet the board on the Monday he was returning and give his analysis of where he felt the college was moving over the next year. All the board members were actually grateful to get a reprieve in nominating a new president until the next year. They felt that Dr. Traynor would be a fine substitute in the meantime.

The board was very aware of Joe's connection to the Coast Guard and to Rear Admiral Barnes specifically and his connection to their main benefactor, Mary Evans and her husband, Jack Manning. It was obvious they felt bad when Dr. Hennessey received the job offer from Barry University but they also knew that it wasn't Morgan who balanced the books with the million-dollar deficit. It was Joe Traynor who got a check directly from Mary Evans to cover their deficit for the year. On top of that, it was Joe who got the pledge of twenty million dollars to the college to build a world-class technology center with businesses signing up to hire graduates. As a matter of fact, four of those Albany, New York based technology companies, who had already placed contracts with the Technology Center, would be arriving the following week for a tour of the facility and a meeting to discuss the exact curriculum they required to continue to hire graduates. Those companies would also pay for the education and training components. It was a win-win for everyone with Mary Evans matching contributions dollar for dollar, up to that twenty million dollar bequest. In addition, Rear Admiral Barnes and his bosses in Washington would also attend to open their eyes as to the possibilities of a partnership between colleges, universities, the private sector and the military. This was vastly needed with foreign interests, including Russia, China and Iran hacking various entities throughout the country. The United States needed everyone on board to catch the thieves and fight back to ensure the safety and security of the country. The time was now.

There appeared to be a very smooth transition. After attending Dr. Hennessey's inauguration as the new Provost of Barry University Joe wanted to follow up with his own Dean at the university to see if there were any more requirements attached to his own Ph.D. He also knew that

Barry University also wanted a tie in with the Coast Guard and Joe said he would set up a meeting with a team from the college including Joan Talbot, his technology staff and the Rear Admiral's staff as soon as possible. Joe was on a steep learning curve that he needed to adhere to if he were to make any inroads at the Coast Guard Academy up in New London, Connecticut. Joe had always been proactive and the in the middle of everything but now he need to be directing the charge and developing his own initiatives which matched his experience and training. At first, he thought he might be in way over his head but the last year taught him differently. He was the curve that would make the changes they needed in the Coast Guard and that included the hiring of those who had never been offered the opportunity before. Whomever he trained down here over the next year, he wanted to offer a career path to go the Coast Guard Academy with new innovative technologies and training and strategic planning methodologies based on education and state-of-the-art thinking.

Julie didn't have to be back to Coral Shores High School until January 12th. She was still very active in all her duties at the high school but also had another obligation that could change this high school forever. She sat on Mary Evan's board, along with Tillie, Jane Swanson, Linda and Jamie Lennon and Joan Talbot. Tillie put a bug in her ear about the trip to Vermont to see the value of the family mentoring program. Julie knew how close to her heart this program was because Julie's own mother succumbed to a drug overdose when Julie was only eight years old. Tillie never spoke of it because she didn't want Julie to feel bad but this was different. This was a shining light that with enough funding could change the lives of those growing up poor in the Florida Keys.

Everyone at the high school knew of at least one student whose parent or parents were in prison because of drug issues. The Florida Keys was a hotbed of drug smuggling and utilized the poor to make a quick buck. Julie was always focused on getting kids into college but how could they ever make it when they had no family support system. As Tillie told her, it costs twenty thousand dollars a year to support a family with the infrastructure required to keep everyone safe and away from drugs. Parents needed a GED/TASC and a job and money to support their families. Many only had drug running as an income and sooner or later they would pay the price. The price was always paid to the detriment of the kids. Previously incarcerated individuals had an unemployment rate five times higher than those without a record. The state of Florida spends over $2.5 billion dollars a year supporting the incarcerated population. There are one hundred and forty-five facilities of which only thirteen are for females. There are over ninety-five thousand prisoners in the state of Florida currently. Almost fourteen thousand are imprisoned only for drugs and no other crime. Eighty percent are between the ages of 25 and 49, the average age of a parent of a child in school. It is quite obvious that mentoring these parents is just as important as mentoring the children. If the parents come back into their lives without this program they are potentially doomed to the same fate.

Julie wanted to address this issue and was developing a paper that would do a technology transfer of the Vermont program to the Florida Keys. To address two hundred families in the Coral Shores High School area within the Monroe County School District system would cost close to $4.0 million dollars a year as a pilot program. Once funded by the Teresa Trust Fund South, and proved successful, the school district or even the high school could seek public funding from both the state and Federal sources to continue on. It was worth the challenge. If Julie had to move the following year to New London, she could always count on

Joan Talbot and others to continue to serve in the same capacity. Julie sent her report for Mary's review.

Julie would also sit down with her high school principal and the Superintendent of the Monroe County School District and board to seek approval. She would have Mary invited to speak at the board meeting in February, once they arrived in in Key West. Evidently, they would have all their work completed for the charter schools up in New York and would be staying until early May this year. The school district administration was well aware of what Mary Evans has done for The College of the Florida Keys. Joe had set up meetings with the Superintendent to discuss the recruitment of Hispanic students into the Coast Guard and offered coding classes to juniors and seniors in all the high schools in the Keys. Now it was Julie and Tillie's time to offer a social services solution that would help families out of the cesspool of poverty.

Joe received his appointment as Interim President at the board meeting, Monday, January 3rd. Julie and Tillie showed up along with Joan Talbot and the Lennons. The Rear Admiral would be there next week for a big meeting with the Albany technology firms and college staff. Before the appointment, Joe spent an hour going over the plans for the college for the year. They had already made well over two hundred thousand dollars from their share of the Technology Center, added to the coffers of the college. They were now in a positive cash flow situation due to Mary Evans and things couldn't look brighter. There was a small ceremony after the meeting with a luncheon and everything looked up for the New Year.

Joe headed to Barry University at the end of the week for Morgan Hennessey's inauguration. He met with his former professors and the Dean of his program and asked them to attend the meeting at The College of the Florida Keys the following week. The Rear Admiral popped in at the invitation of the president of Barry University, his close friend. The president was well aware of Joe Traynor and his potential. Evidently, the Rear Admiral told him in great detail of Joe's rise through the ranks and his future position at the Coast Guard Academy. He also told the president to hook on for a ride with Mary Evans because she too was receiving her Ph.D. from the university and was quite capable and had the financial support to do almost anything she wanted. It was clear that there were lots of opportunities floating around a very select group of individuals and organizations and they should jump at the chance to work together.

The following Tuesday, Joe met the plane coming into Key West. Five local Albany, New York technology companies were each represented by their own president. The college had a very nice bus that pulled up and collected the individuals and their luggage. They would be staying at the Southernmost Hotel in downtown Key West at the end of Duval. The college was picking up the tab and received a very nice discount from the hotel. This is where Mary and Jack stayed when they first arrived after Jack hit the lottery. There was nothing to want. As you opened the veranda doors to each room, there was the Atlantic Ocean and only a few feet away were the pool, restaurant, and Duval Street. They checked in and then hopped back on the bus to head to the college. Joe gave them a quick tour. None of the guests had ever been to Key West before. Joe had set up a dinner for them at the hotel from the great menu. The following day, the Rear Admiral, his staff and a few visitors from Washington would arrive as well. The Dean and the president from Barry University would also come. Morgan was not invited, not because he was excluded but he was not the intended target for introduction to the group and they didn't want a distraction.

Julie came down for the dinner and then she and Joe

headed home. She had a big day the next day. She was presenting the Family Opioid Addiction Mentoring Program concept that had been approved by Mary to her high school principal. She was excited and read her notes all the way back. They arrived home a little after 11:00 p.m. Joe had to be back by 8:00 a.m. so he had to leave by 7:00 a.m. in the morning. He would grab a coffee and a few donuts for the road.

Guests started arriving at 9:00 a.m. The Rear Admiral, his staff, and an Admiral from Washington walked in with two of their key technology staff members including one of Joe's best friends from up in Virginia, Jack Forest. Jack started in the Coast Guard with Joe many years ago and was now in charge of intelligence and technology for the entire Atlantic coast region. Joe was thrilled that he was there. They had a lot to catch up on. The Albany business owners arrived and then the president and dean at Barry University walked in. Mary Evans would attend the meeting by Zoom but would only be a silent observer at this point. Joe would point out that she was back in Troy, New York attending to her responsibilities opening two new charter schools.

The meeting went well. Several of the College Board members were there and the exchange between everyone was terrific. The Admiral from Washington was quite impressed and Jack Forest smiled from ear to ear. He had heard that Joe had grown significantly but was more than impressed. He wasn't worried that Joe wasn't ready for the Coast Guard Academy. He was worried that the Coast Guard Academy wasn't ready for him. Joe put on a video that he developed over the year that showed the vulnerability of the technology systems in the United States and how fragile and unsafe these systems are. He brought up speeches from various countries including Russia, Venezuela and China and served as the interpreter for each of the three speakers in their own languages. Everyone was very impressed. They took a tour of the buildings that were converted over the last year into the Technology Center and met some students who were in class in a real learning environment. They went back to lunch and it was clear what they had here was unique. Joe called Mary and asked her what she thought. She was more than pleased and said that she would be glad to offer her opinion over Zoom if he wanted her to do so. He did. Joe explained how they got to this point. He explained Mary Evans and Jack Manning and what their intentions were moving forward. He also explained how they spent an additional thirty million dollars between Troy and Key West to make sure that families never went hungry or unpaid. Everyone there was thoroughly intent on the subject matter at hand. Joe then turned over the meeting to Mary Evans.

She apologized for not being there but said they would be down in late January or early February depending on their work schedule. She told them about her two trust funds and the additional monies she was holding in case she wanted to fund other projects in the future. She announced that she would also be funding Julie and Tillie's Family Opioid Addiction Mentoring Program for Opioid Addiction to the tune of $4.0 million dollars a year to serve up to two hundred families in the Keys to turn their lives around. She asked for their support when talking to the Superintendent and the board for the Monroe County School District. The pilot would start at Julie's high school in the fall. Mary told the president and the dean at Barry University that her thesis and presentation for her doctorate would include the results of the first year of this five-year project. She would fund the first two years herself and then apply for federal and state funding for the last three years. This would be the basis for proving that poor kids could meet the challenges of the 21st century and even up the playing field to rise from poverty. She spoke for twenty minutes and then answered questions for a half hour. Joe was more than pleased. Jake Barnes turned to Joe and nodded his head that this went well for everyone. He closed the meeting and the Albany-based business people would stay for two more days to discuss their individual company needs and the education and curriculum they would require to continue to offer jobs under contract. At that point, it was clear that Joe and Mary were a team and both were on the same page to make all this work for the benefit of the community.

Mary also pointed out that for every student saved from incarceration, the community saved over one hundred thousand dollars a year in taxpayer dollars. She said, "Guys, that's a savings of twenty million dollars a year just for incarceration and not the other problems that go with it. Thank you. Any questions, please call me at any time."

CHAPTER 39

Mary told Jack all about the meeting at the college which she attended by Zoom. She wanted to know if Jack thought she was getting in over her head. After all, only three years ago she was filling in as a substitute teacher at Catholic High and as a teacher's aide and mathematics instructor at St. Augustine's School before it closed. She had confidence in her own abilities as a counselor coming from the Troy Community Council and of course as a teacher for so many years as a Sister of St. Joseph. She had never made more than twenty-five thousand dollars a year but she never needed anything. She lived with her two friends, also both ex-nuns, and they paid the bills on time by sharing what they had. When Jack gave her fifteen million dollars from his winnings, she didn't really know what to do with the money. She knew that closing St. Augustine's School was a real blow to the community and she wanted to make sure the building wasn't left empty like so many other closed Catholic schools in the region.

She had also looked at the Lansingurgh Boys and Girl's Club and saw them struggling to stay open after serving the public for over eight-four years, since 1937. The reason they were struggling was that the grants they used to receive were now going to the school district to perform the same tasks at twice the cost, serving less than half the kids they previously served every day. In fact, the only meal a lot of those kids received came from the Club. Mary wanted to see this continue but the staff was getting on in years and the funding just wasn't there. She wanted to help but not provide 100% of the funding. When Jack first hit the lottery, those were the only two things she came up with other than to help Jack make his dreams come true by starting his own nonprofit right next to the place that fired both of them.

Now, she had so many things on her plate that she didn't even recognize herself in the mirror. How did she get from there to here in such a short period of time? Money, that's what caused this. Lots of money, more than she would need for ten lifetimes. Now, she needed bodyguards, GPS chips attached to her clothing and shoes and in her pocketbook. She didn't want this life but now had to make the most of it. Even if she gave away every nickel she received, no one would believe it. Everyone would always think she was rich beyond belief no matter what she said or did. She could shout about it from the mountaintop and no one would believe her. Jack and Mary had numerous conversations about this. He was getting used to it but she was not. She was afraid to go to church alone just for a few minutes of peace and quiet. She was constantly trained to look around at her surroundings to make sure no one was creeping up on her. She kept wondering why this had happened to either one of them. They didn't have much but after they were fired and Jack's wife left him, then divorced him and left him penniless, Mary and Jack were still the best of friends. When Jack wanted more than that, she was thrilled. When they took trips together to go up to Vermont for the day, she was happy even though it was her car they were driving. She knew that Jack was a wonderful person with a big heart and who was taken advantage of on a daily basis. Now, that doesn't happen.

The new Jack knew exactly what he wants to do with his life and he is making it happen. He has bent over backward for Mary so he could be part of her life forever. They needed to figure out how to divest themselves of money more quickly and with less input once the decision was made. They needed to walk away from what they created so others could step up and be in charge. Mary didn't want to feel ungrateful. That wasn't the problem. She just wanted her life back or at least the part that meant the most to her including her love for Jack, her newfound love for Debbie and even Mark, and a sense of self worth coming from her pending Ph.D. She would focus on a few items and hope for the best.

Jack picked up the phone at home and it was Chris Sellers calling from the *Times Union*. He said he was on speakerphone with Susan Murray and Josh Solomon, who were at the original meeting at the Career Center. Jack was not happy with Susan after almost telling them they were a bunch of crooks that must have had inside information to win the lottery twice. Jack and Mary were both offended and let Chris know that they were not pleased. All the articles were positive but there was still an inkling that they want some dirt on both of them. No one could be that clean or nice or caring or giving, they thought. But the truth was, both Jack and Mary were all of that except Jack had a very bad temper when falsely accused or if someone attacked Mary. Mary knew this and always tried to calm the storm with Jack. He had been doing a good job holding his thoughts and his temper and Mary was proud of him. The way he took care of Maureen showed the kind of grace Jack really had deep down inside.

"Jack, the reason for the call was that you told me to come up with a list of projects for the region that have been left unfunded but were worthy of consideration by the

Evangeline Trust Fund and Mary's Teresa Trust Fund as well. I believe that was our task, correct?" Chris asked.

Jack said, "Yes, Chris, the last time we talked I mentioned that you and your staff and the *Times Union* needed to develop unfunded worthy projects that we could consider over the next three to four years. I still have maybe twenty to twenty-five million unallocated and Mary has in excess of sixty million dollars just for the Capital Region alone. We are also considering funding a project based on a Rutland, Vermont non-profit mentoring program."

"Well, Jack, you were right. It isn't easy coming up with projects to be funded, organized, evaluated and reasoned through to determine if the money will be spent wisely, on unfunded projects that the government won't fund but is drastically needed," he said.

"I told you so," said Jack.

Mary said, "Not easy, Chris, right?"

"No it is not but can I turn this over to Susan first and then Josh?" Chris said.

"Sure, why not," they both said at the same time.

Susan spoke first. "Mary and Jack, thank you for this opportunity to really think about what the community needs to help those most distressed especially coming out of a pandemic. Number one priority should be getting people back to work but not at minimum wages. McDonalds is now paying $12.00 to $15.00 an hour for part-time employment and they can't hire enough help. It's not that people are still collecting an extra $300.00 a week in unemployment which was double their previous paycheck, it's just that employees discovered that if they hold out and don't work for peanuts, their prospects improve. However, this doesn't lead to sustainable long-term jobs with benefits. Mary, we looked at your brochures and now see that there are 2,500 coding jobs still open in the Capital Region. Those jobs require certification only coupled with a GED/TASC high school diploma. The jobs start at $50,000.00 per year minimum with family benefits. We would propose that you allocate $3,500.00 per high school senior for 2,500 seniors in the region to take coding courses and receive certification before they graduate. Then, the companies need to promise jobs to those who receive all their certifications. Also, for those starting college, they can work remotely throughout the year helping to pay for their tuition. We also expect a certain percentage of profits to go back into the Trust to continue its success. What do you think? It will cost under ten million dollars to implement and the payback is over one hundred and twenty five million per year to the Capital Region in salaries alone."

Mary said, "I'll sponsor that and put it in writing and move money into a special fund to pay for it. Are you aware that we are doing exactly this in Key West with the schools and The College of the Florida Keys?"

"No we weren't aware of that. Can we go down and visit and maybe tie the two programs together?" said Josh.

"We are already doing that and five Albany-based technology companies have already gone down for several meetings and are quite impressed and ready to sign contracts to employ students from the college upon graduation," Mary said.

"Boy, you have been busy, Jack and Mary," said Susan.

Anything else?" asked Mary. "So that's ten million out of over sixty million dollars left. Not easy is it guys?" Mary laughed.

"Can I apologize again, Mary and Jack," said Susan. "Pardon my French but I thought this was nothing but bullshit when we first met you. It isn't and I apologize. I couldn't have been more wrong. Please accept my apology."

"I'll do more than that, Susan. Would you like a place on the board of the Teresa Trust Fund? You'll have an equal voice with me, Jack, Karen Steele, Jack's daughter, Debbie, and of course my close friend, Kristen Sorenson," said Mary.

"That's an honor, Mary. Thank you. I don't know if I can accept. I'll have to ask our Editorial Board as you know we can't be on both sides of an issue because it would damage our credibility."

"Chris, you can take the credit for making these suggestions though, right?" asked Mary.

"Yes, and we can play a part by once again asking the public for input while lending a voice for projects underway so everyone who needs help can take advantage," Chris said.

"In addition to this jobs creation project, let me tell you about our Vermont Family Opioid Addiction Mentoring Program. It is a state-of-the-art program developed in Rutland by the director of the mentoring nonprofit. He won five hundred thousand dollars from USDOJ and it has been wildly successful. I am going to match that funding and put forward over four million dollars in the Florida Keys for the same program to be supervised by the Director. I think we need the same program in the Capital Region and I'm willing to place another ten million dollars into a Trust to run with it. What do think?" Mary asked. "By the way, I'm now down twenty million after a half hour phone call," she said and laughed.

"I have one more thought. New York State will revoke prison sentences for those thousands of individuals who are serving jail terms or have served jail terms for marijuana use, which will now be deemed legal. It's great that they'll get out of jail for minor offenses but they still have a record that will not be erased until a lawyer gets it done. That costs money. The State won't do it. On top of that, thousands will be released within the next two years with no job, a record, and no place to go. What are we as a society going to do about that? I'll bet it could eat up the rest of my Teresa Trust Fund and even more. Have you thought about it?" said Mary.

"Mary, thank you for bringing this up. It is obvious that you are burdened by trying to solve previously unsolvable issues.   We need to get together from an editorial standpoint. Will you join us when you're here? When are you leaving for Florida?" asked Chris.

Jack said, "We're leaving in late January, early February and we should be back by the first of May. We have things to finish here and then Mary will be heading back to get her Ph.D. from Barry University. No, Susan. She wasn't given an honorary degree. She earned it and you can see her marks and her thesis if you're interested," he said with a smirk.

"You just can't let it go, can you, Jack," said Chris with a smile.

"He's right. I deserve it," said Susan with a smile. "Friends?"

"Yes, now that we're all on the same page," said Jack. Mary glared at him to say please shut up for once.

Chris said that this might be the most enlightening meeting he's ever attended by phone. He thanked Mary and Jack. Susan and Josh did the same.

"Well that went well. Don't you think," said Jack.

"Sometimes, Jack, you can be quite the asshole, you know?" said Mary with a smirk.

"Yes, it's one of my more endearing traits I've been told."

"Who told you that, Maureen'?" she asked.

"You wound me, honey. That was right to the heart," he said.

"You'll get over it, I'm sure," said Mary with a grin.

Chapter 40

It was mid-January and Jack and Mary were getting ready to head back to Key West. They had several meetings scheduled in Troy but Karen Steele had everything under control. A new class was beginning on February 1st with thirty-six additional students. Thirty-six students had just graduated in December and thirty-two passed their GED/TASC exam with flying colors on the first try. The remaining four needed remedial mathematics and English skills. All four remaining came from the New York City area and had dropped out of high school as soon as they could. They passed the hands-on construction curriculum and would only need in-class assistance to pass the next exam in April. Of the thirty-two, fifteen would go work directly for the Evangeline Construction Company, Inc. which was rehabbing houses within the immediate area. They needed an income to help support their mothers and brothers and sisters, all younger than them and counting on them to help out. Four graduates, all Hispanic, took up an offer from Jack to head to Florida to join the Coast Guard after attending coding classes at The College of the Florida Keys. Jack said he would give them supportive housing and meals and a stipend until they completed their courses and then joined the service. Ten more were headed full time to

Hudson Valley Community College as full-time students with their tuition paid by Jack. Three remaining graduates said they didn't have a clue what they wanted to do so Jack gave them some slack and hired them to work around the Career Center until they decided on a path. Jack told them they had three months. That's when he'd be back from Florida.

Mary talked extensively with Karen and told her about her conversations with the *Times Union* editorial staff. It wasn't so much that she had called their bluff about helping out but once they volunteered a program, she was reluctant not to fund it. So, Mary asked Karen how she could run a program for senior high school students to qualify for 2,500 coding jobs in the region at $3,500.00 each. Karen said she couldn't do it from the new building because it was already filled with the next class of students, starting February 1st. She also said she needed time to get an appropriate coding curriculum based on what these local technology companies needed. Mary asked if ten million dollars over a five-year period would be enough and she said it wasn't the money issue, it was a staffing issue and getting the proper certifications.

Karen said she would set up a meeting with the local BOCES organization for the Capital Region and staff from the various community colleges. Once they were aware that the project was fully funded, she said they would more than likely jump on board. At this point, she couldn't make a promise but saw it as the next step in the evolution of both Mary and Jack's organizations. She promised to meet with Chris Sellers within the next few weeks to discuss their involvement and marketing efforts. That's all that Mary could ask for and thanked her. Karen did mention that they could expand St. Peter's Church and gymnasium for new classroom space to hold up to one hundred students at a time for the six-month curriculum and certification. The space could also be used as a direct link into the high schools themselves and they could hire the school's staff for this program evenings and weekends when the facilities were not in use. The project itself was not cumbersome but to train, educate and certify 2,500 individuals in anything was difficult at best.

In addition, Mary asked Karen how she felt about starting the Vermont Family Opioid Addiction Mentoring Program in their own facilities for the families of those enrolled in their programs and if there was enough space for families of graduates who were still struggling with opioid addiction and needed professional help. Karen jumped all over this after she learned that Mary was going to allocate $4.0 million dollars for 200 families at $20,000.00 per year per family in the Florida Keys, to see if it made a difference. Mary made the same offer to Karen and she was delighted.

"You know this full-time job which I took here to ease my way into retirement is not quite what I expected. I'm not complaining, Mary, but God, can you slow down just a little so we can catch our breath," Karen said with a grin.

"You mean to tell me this is harder than being second in command for the New York State Labor Department?" Mary said with a grin.

"Yes, Mary. It's ten times harder. At the Labor Department I had tons of people I could shove off work to. Here, the shoving off comes from you to me, and then it goes downhill. Don't get me wrong I love it here and everyone else does too. I've never been happier in a job than I am right now. However, I need space to breathe, okay?" said Karen.

"All right. How about a compromise? You don't need to start anything new until we get back from Key West around May. Is that okay?" asked Mary.

"That would be perfect. By then, I can have all the meetings I need and have everything set up to hit the ground running. Thank God you paid everyone's salary for eighteen months while we were quarantined under lockdown. We were Zoomed to death. Everyone here is totally loyal to you and this operation, only because of you and Jack, Mary," said Karen.

"Karen don't sell yourself short. The money was important but you leading the charge here was even more important. They had someone to go to no matter what their issues were from students to employees or just neighbors needing food from our food bank. You were there every waking moment and I love you for that. Jack does too," said Mary.

"Well, thank you. That means a lot more than you know. By the way, I just wanted to tell you that I think Debbie is terrific. I remember the old Debbie when Jack first started this after winning the lottery. Now, she is a grown woman with a Master's degree and an insight into everything happening here. She has thrown her entire being into this place and it shows. She is not Jack's daughter or your step-daughter, she is Debbie Manning, professional social services counselor and I mean that sincerely," said Karen.

"That means a lot to me and I'll tell Jack. I'm sure he'll be very proud of her," said Mary.

They hugged and said goodbye. Jack finished up his meetings as well. He needed to fully review the financial records before he left and to see what funds he needed to transfer into the Career Center's accounts to cover expenses over the next three months while they were away. He called Kristen and gave her the number and the dates when transfers needed to take place. Kristen said she would follow up, after every transfer just to make sure. She also said she was meeting Mary for lunch the next day in Albany and she knew that they would be leaving at the end of the week. Mary and Jack said their goodbyes to everyone in the building and headed home with Fred Tucker waiting for them at the curb. John Jefferson had the day off to go to the dentist. He never complained about anything but you could tell it was really bothering him. He hated root canals but there was no escaping it regardless of his duties to protect Mary and Jack. He would be okay to head to the airport with them at the end of the week.

Mary met Kristen at Jack's Oyster House at the foot of State Street, only a block from Kristen's office. Mary parked in the Maiden Lane lot and met Kristen who was waiting for her at the guardhouse. As they walked through the front door of the restaurant, several people greeted Kristen. Everyone seemed to know Kristen Sorenson. The maître d' welcomed them and showed them to a very nice booth in the back where they could have a quiet conversation.

Mary ordered the signature mignonette oysters on the half shell with spicy cocktail sauce while Kristen ordered baked east coast oysters with mascarpone spinach, cherry wood lardons and allemande parmesan gratin for appetizers. For dinner both ordered diver scallops with smoked butternut, prosciutto, burgundy black truffle with glazed maitake mushrooms. For dessert they split a pistachio gelato. They were full. Kristen picked up the bill on her Visa card and gave a very nice tip. They each had ice teas to drink. This was a special treat for both but they both had stuff to do and after a glass of wine, they would be beat. How do you only drink one glass of wine anyway?

They hardly discussed business at all. They've been friends for almost thirty years and enjoyed each other's company through thick and thin. It wasn't always a bed of roses. Kristen left the convent first and really struggled with her life outside the convent. Thank God she met a wonderful man who became the love of her life, a great friend, then husband and now father of three growing children. He was an ordinary guy, working in an ordinary job, driving a truck for a local food distributor. He graduated from Hudson Valley Community College with a two-year degree but hated school. He went back and got a degree in automotive mechanics and was certified as well. He just loved driving a truck. Kristen attended Albany Law School part-time for five years and graduated with high honors. She passed the bar on her first try and was picked up by her current law firm. No one would have thought that she would be as successful as she was but then again, no one thought an ex-nun could be anything other than a childcare worker or teacher's aide or a teacher at a Catholic school. She was moving quite well up the ladder and then when both Jack and Mary hit the lottery, she skyrocketed into a position as a full partner. She was doing fine but Mary made her career and she was eternally grateful. Her husband never made a lot of money and the gift that Mary gave her to put her children through college meant everything to her.

They finally talked about Mary's next steps and that she and Jack would be leaving for Key West at the end of the week. Kristen would stay on top of the *Times Union* coding project and complete all the funding transfers needed for the new mentoring program as soon as required. Kristen also mentioned that Mary should slow down a little and concentrate on getting her Ph.D. which was her lifelong dream. Mary acknowledged that she was moving maybe a little too fast. She did explain her thoughts that the money had changed her life not so much for the better but she now felt penned in and needed some breathing room. Kristen, being the long-time friend that she was, suggested that with so many changes in her life, maybe she needed a life coach or someone who could help her look at life in a new way and not be so pressured. Kristen knew several individuals that Mary might like and suggested that she take it easy over the next three months while in Key West and when she got back to have a sit-down and re-evaluate where she is now and where she and Jack would like to wind up, after all the donations are made and someone else is running the show. Mary said she would think about it and let her know still having combined over one hundred and thirty million dollars, Between Jack and Mary, tax free, just sitting there after giving away all that money, was still an enormous responsibility, in addition to the trust funds.

It was Friday and their flight for Tampa was leaving at 6:45 a.m. from the Albany International Airport. They didn't want to spend the money for a private flight even though they could certainly afford it. They thought it was a waste to spend thirty thousand dollars for a four or five-hour flight. They thought differently that thirty thousand dollars could provide several families with mentors for an entire year. It made them embarrassed that in fact they had taken private flights but only if they absolutely needed to for safety sake.

They had to change flights in Tampa and take the quick flight down to Key West where they would be met by Martina and Antonia driving Mary's SUV. Jamie was out on the boat with her father and brother for a four-day excursion and wouldn't be back for two days. Everything at their house was set up and ready to go. She had gone grocery shopping and had the refrigerator packed full. The housekeeper came in and sanitized the entire place just to ensure their safety. At their age, Mary and Jack couldn't get the booster and they had no major health issues that required it. Both Martina and Antonia had the booster, which was required by the Coast Guard as soon as it was available for the military. They needed it because they were in and out of all kinds of compromising situations, especially when capturing a cartel boat coming from South America. Who knew what the health was of those captured on the boats. They were criminals or worked for criminals and probably hadn't seen a doctor in their lifetime.

Mary had her agenda for the next few weeks. She was to meet the mayor of Key West again, not just to talk about the homeless but about domestic abuse shelters in the Keys, which were sorely lacking in funding especially after Hurricane Irma in 2017. It was a disaster for these poor women caught between abuse, poverty and homelessness. She also needed to see where Joan Talbot was with her recruitment efforts of minorities for the Coast Guard. The meeting went well with the Albany businesses but she needed to integrate her new program up in Albany to train seniors in high school with the college down here. She had a lot on her mind. She needed dinner and then bed. Tomorrow was a brand new day with lots to do. *What happened to watching the sunset with a martini in her hand on her deck in beautiful Key West, she wondered.*

CHAPTER 41

Mary and Jack had settled in once again hoping to stay for a few months. Everything that needed attention up in Troy was taken care of and funding was put in place to make things happen. They both thought that maybe, just maybe, they could take care of business down here quickly and then do nothing but relax. Skip Lennon promised Jack that he would take him to a few boat dealers in the area so Jack could do a few test-drives and see what he really wanted in the way of amenities. Jack wanted something simple that could take him around Key West and maybe a few miles west and north into the Gulf of Mexico. He wanted a boat that would handle easily and wouldn't need a lot of attention. He also wanted a place to store the boat when they headed back to Troy. While they were in Key West, Jack had his own dock attached to the house, the same as Skip had right down the street, but no storage space. Other than becoming friends, Jack and Mary bought this house from the retiree because of this special docking feature. They also felt that it could offer additional security if they could just hop on a boat a few steps away in case of an emergency.

Mary was meeting with Teri Johnson, the mayor of Key West, in a few days. Previously, they discussed the new businesses to be created through The College of the Florida Keys, right in town but the homeless population seemed to be a major priority as well. Hurricane Irma took a very large toll on everyone in the Florida Keys in 2017, reaching a category 5 on September 5, 2017, from which many had never recovered. There were now more homeless because they actually lost their homes in the hurricane and are now living in shelters or small, donated trailers from FEMA, waiting for housing to open up. Then, the Covid-19 epidemic took place, leaving families even more vulnerable than before, with no place to go. Schools closed and children were stuck in shelters, when they should have been in protective settings with the ability to continue school, like the majority of families throughout the country. They were stuck.

The worst part of the homeless population was those men, women, and children suffering from domestic abuse. Being such a small community, it was hard for the abused to leave home or even find a place to go for help. Along with all these problems, the only domestic abuse shelter lost its certification to operate from the State of Florida Department of Children and Families. Another organization stepped in to help but their financial situation was so bad that many of the employees weren't even paid. A balloon mortgage was due and the organization was flat broke. That's even before the pandemic hit.

The sheriff of Monroe County even explained that the Domestic Abuse Shelter is a critical component of justice in the Florida Keys. This facility is the only one of its kind within a one hundred and twelve mile radius. The State of Florida was so concerned about the financial status that the funding for the shelter went from a grant of over seven hundred thousand dollars a year, paid monthly, to a reimbursement status due to lack of trust by the State. Someone said, "In order to be reimbursed, you had to be burst". They were broke and had no cash flow to carry them and subsequently hundreds of women and children, mostly, were left unprotected, living in poverty, subject to the worse kinds of domestic abuse, with children left unfed and unable to attend school. The situation had not improved since the Florida state budgets had been cut due to the pandemic and its aftermath.

Mary was well armed when she arrived at the mayor's office on Friday. Her security team followed her in the door and took a seat outside the mayor's office. Mary went into the boardroom, adjacent to the office, and was met by Mayor Johnson and a team from the city of Key West. Mary was introduced and the mayor asked her what was on her mind.

Mary said, "Since our last meeting about new businesses, the homeless population right here in Key West and in all the Florida Keys has been on my mind. I did a lot of research. I'm using the research for my thesis for my Ph.D. at Barry University. The main gist is that by leveling up the playing field, children born in poverty, can compete and thrive with those who have the benefits of the middle class. Never did I realize that some children would never have any opportunity at all because they have fallen through the cracks and are unknown to most Americans. I am talking about families living in shelters because of domestic violence. The information I have reviewed has left me in tears. I cannot believe that there are people who have been left this way, unattended with no hope. I want to change this around," she said.

"Mary, how do you plan to do this? We'll be glad to help but you know what our budgets are like here. If you wear a mask you don't get paid. You get fired. You lose your funding. We're in sad shape because of politics, and a growing Covid-19 problem that continues because of lack of resources. What do you suggest?" the mayor asked.

"I haven't completely worked this out but I am willing to provide the following if you are willing to help. I learned a long time ago as a nun that God helps those who help themselves. I will provide immediate funding if you supply the troops needed to be successful. Immediately, I want to reopen the Domestic Abuse Shelter. I'll pay off the mortgage and bring the building up to code, immediately. I'll pay a premium if the work is completed in thirty days. I'll pay double any contract that is reasonable and I know from reasonable, trust me. You had twenty-six beds available. I believe there are at least 200 families living in shelters and FEMA trailers that need immediate help. I want a full-time security staff of a minimum of ten trained individuals to provide protection for these families 24/7. I want a full-time counselor assigned to every ten families. That is the going rate up north and should be easier down here. It's hard to work at twenty below zero but not so bad at sixty degrees. I want to move in prefab housing units onto the property and get a zoning variance if needed. These units are the same that I moved into the convent while we are reconstructing the building. I also want a permanent solution for housing for those suffering domestic abuse and I want the Monroe County Sheriff's Department and the Key West police department to make domestic violence a priority and make these people safe. Also, as a priority, I would especially like your police department to call on our new counselors for ride-a-longs when there is a domestic violence or mental health situation. I am aware of the situation a few years ago when your police arrested a small boy and put him in handcuffs because he was acting up in school. Just because his father thought that was okay, it wasn't as far as I and other professionals in the field are concerned. I hope you take this suggestion into consideration as well. We can address jobs and training and education as soon as we know they are safe. How's that for a start?"

"Mary, do you know how much this will cost?" said the Mayor. "By the way, we are working on mental health issues in regards to arrests and we will address your concerns."

"Yes, I know exactly how much this will cost," she said. "It's not a cost as far as I'm concerned. It's an investment," Mary added.

Mayor Johnson smiled and said, "Would you care to elaborate about the investment?"

"If I have to," Mary said. "I've already done the calculations. You know I'm a certified mathematics teacher, right?"

"No, I didn't know that but I certainly should have expected it," Mayor Johnson said.

"First, the mortgage and the interest should be waived or I'm not doing the deal, which is roughly two hundred thousand dollars. One counselor for every ten families means, twenty counselors over three shifts at forty-five thousand dollars each or nine hundred thousand dollars a year. Ten fully trained security personnel, at forty thousand dollars per year, are four hundred thousand dollars. Since the two hundred families won't all be here at the same time, we'll only need about ten housing units brought to the site and hooked up for sewer and water, heat, light and electricity, and gas for cooking. That's about twenty thousand per month or two hundred and forty thousand dollars. I will pay the entire bill for the first five years but you need to start planning on funding a majority of it as soon as possible. This will not be an entirely free ride. After five years, I will contribute one million dollars per year for as long as I can and as long as the program is well supervised by the Mayor's office and staff. In total it adds up to $1,740,000.00 a year for five years equals $8,700,000.00. This should not solve the problem but put a very large dent into it. Food will come from the food banks we already support. What do you say?"

"Mary within a half hour, you have addressed one of our most difficult issues here in Key West and in all of the Keys. If this works, and I believe it will, we will fight like hell to get funding for year six and we will start after the first year. We will pay for an independent audit and program evaluator from any university you name. The evaluation will cost in excess of fifty thousand dollars for the first year but it will be worth it and used as proof of concept. Does that work for you?"

"Yes, it does. I'll have Jane Swanson, my attorney in Miami, draw up the paperwork, first to secure the building, pay off the mortgage, repair everything and start moving in housing units. We need counselors fast so whatever you can do here, I will reach out to Barry University and our on college down here to get new counselors who have just graduated and need a job. No sense in coddling them. Let them jump into the fire with us," Mary said.

"By the way, do you know of any recent graduates from high school here, who are unemployed and would like a job making fifty thousand dollars a year with benefits after only six months training and certification. The person needs a GED/TASC and we'll get that for them as well. Just call Joe Traynor at the college and he'll set up interviews for anyone you bring forward. I may remind you that this is no joke and don't send us crappy people that you want off your welfare rolls. We found out that's what happens when lazy government workers find a way to ease their jobs. It won't happen here and we will be pissed," said Mary.

"Mary, you shouldn't hold it in. You'll get an ulcer that way," Mayor Johnson laughed. "Just kidding. I hear you loud and clear. You're providing us with resources we never had before and you want us to pony up our time and abilities as a match or it won't work. Right?"

"That's right. I don't have time to waste. Jack and I will give away a majority of our lottery winnings within the next five years to worthy causes that are supported by worthy, caring people. Period. I'm sure I've made myself clear about that everywhere I go," Mary said.

The next day, Mary and Jack took a long awaited trip up to Miami to visit Jane Swanson and her law firm including Sidney Clyne. It's been forever since they've been back for a sit down. Mary wanted to tell Jane all about her new programs for the college and for domestic violence abuse victims. She also wanted her to be fully informed about both their programs at the Career Center in Troy as they moved both organizations closer and closer together. They needed a complete support staff down at the college because Joe Traynor would only be there for a year as the Interim President. After that, he would be up closer to them in Troy, only a few hours away in New London, Connecticut at the Coast Guard Academy.

Mary also wanted to make sure that her studies didn't slide and that her thesis was constantly being updated for her new projects to prove that poverty wasn't a sign of incompetence but a sign of lack of resources. The advisory committee that would be reviewing her thesis for her Ph.D. might just be shocked at how much funding she was allocating of her own money to prove her case. She didn't believe that this had ever been done before. Sure, any businessperson giving a large multi-million-dollar donation to a university could get an honorary doctorate, paid for by the donation. It wasn't unheard of by any means. This might be the first doctorate that spent the money not with a donation to the university but a donation to a philosophy could prove effective that enough money can make changes in people's lives if done the right way, for the right reasons to help others. Only time would tell.

They stayed overnight at the SLS Brickell Hotel &

Residence, only a short walk from the law firm and the Coast Guard headquarters. Mary asked to drop in and see Rear Admiral Jake Barnes and both she and Jack would visit and update him on what they were doing both down in Florida and up in Upstate New York. They also wanted to let him know how valuable Joan Talbot, Joe and Julie and Tillie have been and the progress made. Money helped but competent people ensured that resources were not wasted.

After both meetings with the attorney and the Rear Admiral, they would head over to see her doctoral advisor at Barry University in Miami Shores. From there, they would meet Julie at the Coral Shores High School in Tavernier, only a few blocks from Joe and Julie's house. Mary wanted to surprise Julie by offering her graduating students scholarships not just to The College of the Florida Keys but to other colleges as well. There were about seven hundred fifty students, grades 9-12, so there should be under two hundred students graduating each year. Each student attending college would receive a $5,000.00 gift from the Teresa Trust Fund South. For those attending The College of the Florida Keys, it would amount to a full scholarship for tuition and books. For others it would mean fewer student loans or Parent Plus loans, easing the burden on families. The high school was ranked in the top 1,500 nationally so their students are doing well, they're just poor kids living in Florida, as identified by a significant Free and Reduced Lunch program across the school.

Finally, Mary and Jack, and Alex and Mia, headed back to Key West. Alex and Mia would be replaced once again by Martina and Antonia, whom they would pick up at the Coast Guard facility in Islamorada and drop off Alex and Mia. Joan and her husband, Jeff, and daughter, Lucy, were home at the station and had dinner ready for them when they arrived. Their son was away at college. Mary loved the fresh fish caught in the Keys and Joan did not disappoint. She went to the docks, and being as well known as she was as the head of the Coast Guard in that area, she got first pick of Mahi Mahi, Snapper and Snook and as a real surprise several Islamorada lobsters just caught that day. The eight-month lobster season is always August 6th through March 31st and the regulation and fines are very tight. Mary and Jack, coming at the beginning of February were lucky to get any due to the popularity of the species. Joan added baked potatoes and grilled all the seafood, and added melted butter and garlic as they were pulled off the grill. Mary thought she had died and gone to heaven.

She laughed at Joan and said, "That was delicious. When you come up to visit us in the summertime, you'll have the world's best pizza ever. Maybe it's not lobster but it'll fill the bill."

Joan laughed. She said, "Mary, this is the least we can do for you and Jack. Your generosity is special. By the way, Julie just called me and told me about your offer of scholarships to all the seniors at Coral Shores High School. As you know, Lucy's getting a cross-country scholarship from the University of Miami but it doesn't cover travel, and books, and life in general as we know it. So, again, thank you. We are certainly glad that you and Jack are part of our family now. We wouldn't have it any other way."

"Thank you for that," Mary said. She helped clean up. They had to have dessert. Lucy had baked her first cake and it was delicious. She was quite proud of it and served each a slice with a scoop of ice cream. Mary and Jack could hardly move at that point. Martina and Antonia had supper with them as well and went in and finished packing for the week. They were off for eight days and then would be back hunting cartel ships in and around the Keys, from Key Largo to Key West, where there was another facility. They would meet their ship in Key West, saving a trip back to Islamorada.

It was getting late so as soon as they arrived, everyone unpacked. They had a restful few days and Mary finally enjoyed her martini on the deck watching the sun go down. Jack watched her and saw that finally she seemed content. It wasn't like she was trying just to get rid of every dollar she won but it was with a purpose and each program that she funded took time and study and had to fall into her plans to prove her point. Jack kind of smiled and said to himself that he never tried to prove a point other than sticking it up the rear ends of those who fired him and his team for no reason other than greed. He was well on his way to proving himself and he was certain that Mary was way ahead of him in that category. He was just glad that everything had worked out for them. He was thrilled with Mary as his wife, even more so than as his best friend for all those years. He couldn't be happier. He hoped that she felt the same. He was pretty sure she did.

CHAPTER 42

It was starting to get dark around 8:00 p.m. It was Tuesday, Waste Management garbage can night. Mary would place the cans out by the road tonight for pickup on Wednesday morning around 7:00 a.m. They missed a few pickups before and it was a pain holding trash for an extra full week. This week they had their cans completely filled with garbage and recyclables. It had to go out.

Martina and Antonia were washing the dishes after a late dinner. Jack was on the phone and trying to finish packing so they could head back to Troy. It was late spring but felt like summer down in Key West. Maybe they could get a little relief from the heat going home. Martina and Antonia would drive them to the Key West airport in the SUV and get a ride back to Islamorada from Jamie. Heading back now would give Jack and Mary a few months to get everything set at both school locations. They were both excited because the delay in opening both schools was now closer to two years rather than one because of the pandemic. When it was approved originally, it was at the start of the pandemic and no one could see the future. Both would open this fall, over two years later after the approval. There was no way they could have opened that fall or even for the second fall school year. They were very lucky to open at all this year as the pandemic finally started to ease in upstate New York. It took forever it seemed to upgrade one old building while building the other from the ground up. Hiring administrators and teachers for both had to come with assurances to make them comfortable in coming to both the Lansingburgh Academy Charter School and the North Central Village Charter School. Choosing students was not as big a problem but explaining the lottery system that allowed for an equitable student body was challenging. It was done carefully but not quickly. Both Jack and Mary were actually pleased to be given the extra time to open the schools by the New York State Education Department. They needed every extra day to plan.

They would be back and forth throughout the year but had to be back in Florida in early July so Mary could receive her Ph.D. from Barry University, after her dissertation presentation. They would then head back to Troy for the grand opening of both charter schools in September. They would stay for a week or so in Key West for the graduation and subsequent parties that would be in Mary's honor. While in Key West, she was also going to meet the board at the college since her name had been put forward as a candidate for the presidency of The College of the Florida Keys. The Ph.D. helped. She was interested in the position but the timing wasn't really in the cards with everything else going on. She would decide after her graduation.

They didn't have to be up in Troy for the start of school in September but they were expected and they were both excited. There was no ribbon cutting, grand opening or special event planned. However, at lunchtime on opening day, they decided they would have all the parents arrive and eat lunch with their children on the first day. They thought they could start a new tradition, just like the annual Thanksgiving dinner held at the Career Center for all students, families and even for graduates and their families and of course all the teachers and staff.

Walking down the stairs to the garage, Mary said to no one in particular, "I'm taking out the garbage cans and I may drop over to the Lennons to say goodbye. I won't be long."

Mary opened the garage door and brought out the first can. As she was bringing out the second can, a large van sped down their street and stopped right by Mary's side. The van door opened and two men grabbed her by the arms and threw her into the van. They didn't even wait to close the van door as they took off. Mary was in shock and didn't know what was going on. All of a sudden, she felt a needle stuck into her arm. Within minutes she was out like a light, lying on the floor of the van. The two men in the back told the driver to hurry up because they only had minutes before someone noticed that she wasn't there. The driver headed southeast on Allamanda Terrace toward Allamanda Avenue. He turned left onto Key Haven Road and then left onto US 1 North. It was less than five minutes by the time they got on the main highway going north out of Key West. They drove another twenty-five miles to Tulip Lane in Big Pine Key. They pulled the van into the back of the house so no one would see them. Kevin's Ford Focus was already parked there.

They took Mary out of the van. She was still out and they brought her into the house and put her in the back bedroom with her arms and legs fully secured. They had a lock on the bedroom door from the outside with a padlock so she couldn't get out, not that she was going anywhere in her condition. Kevin Strom turned to Luther Pierce and Richard Butler and said, "Well guys, it looks like we made it. I think the Nationalist Alliance could use about ten million dollars or so this year. What do you think?"

"I think you're right, minus our cut," said Butler. "They'll never find us here," he said.

The plan to kidnap Mary had started well over a year and

a half earlier when they followed her to the Fort Lauderdale Airport in the limousine. Kevin, Luther and Rich had followed the media vehicle that was following the limousine. They lost them on the off-ramp to the airport but were able to pick up the limousine at the ramp back onto I-95 South. They obviously dropped off the lady somewhere, probably at the airport. They followed the limousine right up to the front door at 1395 Brickell Avenue in downtown Miami. Rich jumped out of the Ford Focus and walked into the building. He looked at the plaque for the company locations in the building and saw a law firm on the fifth floor. He also noticed that the elevator stopped on the fifth floor, so it had to be Clyne, Roberts and Lynch. It was the only law firm in the building. They called Ken Meggs and gave him that information.

Ken Meggs the leader of the Nationalist Alliance, said it was difficult but through hacking into the computer systems of Clyne, Roberts and Lynch, they found the incorporation papers for the Teresa Trust Fund South. They also dug up the name of another two corporations, the Evangeline Trust Fund and the Evangeline Realty Company, Inc., both in New York State. They figured they would do more research and see what they could find. It took quite a while to figure out if they had property in Florida under their own names or in a corporate name. Once Meggs read the article in the *Miami Herald*, he thought that she might have a place in Key West, when visiting. He confirmed it when the *Miami Herald* article included the fact she stayed in Key West.

Meggs hackers matched the picture of the winner, Mary Evans, to the pictures taken at the lottery office, over a year ago and just recently in the *Miami Herald* article. Hearing about the Evangeline Trust Fund and the Evangeline Realty Company, Inc. and the Teresa Trust Fund gave Meggs a place to start looking for addresses down in the Keys. After that it was simple. He had his hackers go to the local and state tax rolls and saw that the Evangeline Realty Company, Inc. paid taxes on property in Key West, at 10 Allamanda Terrace, Key West. Bingo. His hackers did a great job in getting him information. This was all he needed.

Before the abduction, after identifying the property, they started their surveillance knowing she would be back in the spring. Driving by and having Donna, Luther's girlfriend, walk her dog they discovered garbage take-out night and Donna simply looked like she was a neighbor, walking her dog. The surveillance paid off when one night they saw Mary Evans bring the garbage cans out around 8:00 p.m. on a Tuesday night. This would be their plan to grab her soon, hopefully, they thought.

The plan worked and they grabbed Mary just like they thought they could. Evidently security was not up to par and she was standing there all alone in front of the garage without a care in the world, so it looked. Before grabbing her, they couldn't believe either how lucky they were or how well they planned. They had never done this before and were very pleased by the results.

It worked and she was now in Rich's mother's back bedroom, knocked out. Luther, Kevin and Rich hoped that it would go smoothly. They would all move after they got the cash and head back to Mississippi with enough to live on with their cut. *So they thought.*

How is she doing back there in the bedroom?" asked Shelby Butler, Richard's mother, who was sitting on the living room couch. "How much am I getting, Richard? I can't sell this house, the only house here with nothing but trailers surrounding it and businesses on a dead-end street, nowhere near the water."

"Mom. You'll live like a queen when we get done. Your job is to make sure she stays in the room. You feed her and get her bathroom needs taken care of. This shouldn't take more than a day or two at most. She's worth a bundle and the Nationalist Alliance will move us somewhere else where they'll never find us. Want a house back in Mississippi on the water, Mom? It's yours if it works out. This is also for our cause. We need to preserve our race. It's gone on too long and we're losing big time. That can't happen. Can it, guys?"

"No it can't and it won't. Shelby if you do your job we'll all be fine. When she wakes up we'll start making calls with our burner phones. I bought ten just in case. We'll get the bag of cash, let her go and we'll head to Tampa first, where no one will be the wiser except for Ken Meggs. We'll head to Mississippi as soon as everything settles down," said Luther.

"We gave her an injection of ketamine which should last about an hour to two hours and could be topped off if needed. She should be coming out of it in a while. She'll be disoriented. We checked and she has nothing on her, no pocketbook, phone or iPad, so we'll have to get the information from her. If not, we'll call the law firm and start the ball rolling. We only want the money, not a murder rap if you know what I mean," he said.

As Jack looked around as he got off the phone, he said, "Where's Mary?"

"She said she was taking out the garbage and might go down to see the Lennons," said Martina.

"I'll go look," said Antonia. They looked at each other like this couldn't be happening. Did they screw up? Did they become complacent and not think that Mary could be in trouble right now? Antonia ran down the stairs and saw the garage door open. The recyclable can was still near the door and not moved next to the regular garbage can that was sitting by the curb. She looked around and ran to the Lennons and knocked loudly on the front door. Linda answered the door and said, "You look flushed, Antonia. What's wrong?"

"Please tell me that Mary's here," she said with watery eyes.

"No she's not. Is she supposed to be here?" said Linda.

Antonia ran back immediately to the house and got on the phone with Joe Traynor. Julie picked up and knew right away that something was wrong. "Joe, it's for you. It's Antonia and I think there's a problem," she said.

Joe grabbed the phone and said, "Speak to me, now."

"Joe, Mary's gone and we don't know where." You could hear the panic in her voice.

"Okay, she's gone. Put your training to work. Check the GPS coordinates. Did she have them on her body?"

"We don't know." Antonia said.

Jack said, "I have her GPS set up on my phone. Hold on a minute." He went to Mary's GPS app and saw that the GPS system was working. He picked up two signals at the same time. He asked Antonia," Did she have her pocketbook, iPad or iPhone with her?"

"No, she went to bring the garbage out. She had her sneakers on and shorts and a blouse. Nothing else."

"So, the activated GPS chips are those attached to her sneakers. I hope whoever took her doesn't look too closely. Now check the video camera in front of the house, now."

Jack was now starting to panic and brought up the video camera. He noticed within the last half hour that a van was moving quickly and stopped in front of the house and took off abruptly within seconds. The van door was open. He turned it back and saw Mary standing by the first garbage can and then she was gone. "She was taken in a van at 8:12 p.m. right in front of the house. It's about a half hour now that she's been missing," said Jack.

Joe watched the GPS coordinates moving up Route 1 North and then the coordinates turned slightly off the highway. He then saw the coordinates slowly stop. The coordinates are (longitude and latitude) 24°41'41.9"N

81°22'18.1"W. Joe immediately put those coordinates into his Google Maps App and found an address of 29108 Tulip Lane, Big Pine Key, Florida.

Joe said to Martina, Antonia and Jack, "I know where she is. It's about 30 miles north of here in Big Pine Key. I put the house number into Google earth and it's a three-bedroom home near a trailer park and a few commercial buildings. One is Bee's Honey Pots on the corner where Tulip Lane meets Route 1. Evidently the house is up for sale. We don't have time to get keys. Martina and Antonia, get suited up, we're going in. Take the Highlander and meet me as fast as you can at Bee's Honey Pots. I'm heading down from Tavernier. It's about the same distance. I'm calling my friend the FBI director, Paul Philips, and letting him know there's a kidnapping in progress and we're going in. He has several agents down here and hopefully they can meet us in a short time."

"Joan. I have an emergency. Mary's been kidnapped in front of her house about a half hour ago. She was putting out the garbage and I need to explain to Antonia and Martina what they are getting paid for at a later time. I need you and several guys suited up and for you to meet me at Bee's Honey Pots on Big Pine Key right off Route 1. It's all the same distance for all of us. We're going in."

"I'm on it," said Joan. "We'll be there."

"Paul, it's Joe. It's an emergency. Mary Evans has been kidnapped and she's being held at Big Pine Keys. I need a few of your guys. I'm using my FBI credentials and my Coast Guard team and we're going in for the rescue. I'll need your guys to clean up. By the way the address is 29108 Tulip Lane, Big Pine Key, Florida. I looked up the owner and it's a Shelby Butler. Can you tell me if Richard Butler has an address?"

"Sure, hold on," he said. Within minutes, he said, "Joe, we lucked out. Richard Butler has the same address."

"Can you tell me if he owns a Ford Econoline van? I have no idea of the year. It's white like every one of them."

Paul came back a few minutes later and said, "Again, we lucked out. He owns a 2005 Ford Econoline van, registered at that address. Why?"

"We have the van on camera in front of the house, not that we need it as evidence but it's nice to know. It looks like the three guys in the Ford Focus who followed Jack and Mary to the Fort Lauderdale airport are involved. Those sons of bitches will be taking a dirt nap by the end of the night."

My guys have been called and are on their way. They're coming from Marathon, not far away. I told them everyone is meeting in the parking lot of Bee's Honey Pot," said Paul.

"Thanks, Paul. You're the best. Let's keep this as low-key as we can. I don't want it going national that a lottery winner has been kidnapped by white supremacists."

"We don't either, Joe. Thanks."

Joe was still busy making calls as he dressed in his tactical gear and unlocked the weapons cabinet in the back bedroom. Julie was worried but knew after listening to the various conversations that Mary was kidnapped and that Joe knew exactly where she was and was going there to rescue her. She knew that was his job and focus and never said a word. He kissed her as was leaving the house and said, "I'll call you when it's over."

He pulled out of the driveway and hit speed dial for Mike Kenny, a detective friend of his from the Monroe County Sheriff's department. Audrey, his wife, picked up, and knew immediately that Joe was in a rush and said, "I'll get him right now."

Audrey, Mike, Joe, and Julie became very close friends when Audrey took care of Tillie when she was in a coma at the Mariner Hospital several years ago after she was run off the road. Once again, when Bella was taken by the state of

Florida after her mother died, and Julie and Joe were in the process of adopting her, both Mike and Audrey stepped in and got the child back into their arms. Neither Joe nor Julie ever forgot their kindness.

"Joe, what's up? Audrey said you were frazzled."

"I am, Mike. Mary Evans, our friend and the lottery winner, has been kidnapped in front of her house in Key West and we have GPS clips on her shoes. Hopefully the kidnappers don't know that. She's in Big Pine Key on Tulip Lane. I have all my team and the FBI lined up to meet there in less than an hour. Can you make it as a member of the Monroe County Sheriff's Department?"

"I'm leaving now. Where are you meeting? Is this a Coast Guard deal or FBI? I know you represent both."

"For this, it's FBI. It's federal and it's kidnapping."

"Got it. See you in a half hour." He said bye to Audrey and told her Joe needed him and he would call her as soon as he could. He told her it was a kidnapping.

Joe arrived at Big Pine Key at 9:45 p.m. in the parking lot at Bee's Honey Pot, the portable toilet company at the corner of Tulip Lane and the main highway. Already there were Martina and Antonia. They begged Jack to stay back home in Key West in case they got a call from the kidnappers on the landline. He wasn't trained for this as he readily admitted. He was very upset that it should never have happened but he was probably as responsible as the two ladies for being too comfortable and not realizing that this could happen in a heartbeat. He was beside himself with guilt and the ladies were as well. They vowed that Mary would be released unharmed and those who did this would pay. *Small consolation, he thought to himself.*

Fifteen minutes later, Mike Kenny arrived in full gear. Two FBI special agents showed up and both spoke to Joe as the lead FBI agent for this operation. Joan Talbot showed up with Alex Deleon and Mia Santiago, the other two members of Mary's security team from the Islamorada facility. In all there was Joe, Joan, Martina, Antonia, Alex and Mia, Mike Kenny and two other FBI agents. They broke up into teams. Joe had downloaded the pictures of the house that was for sale online. Joan brought her drone armed with infrared cameras.

She told the non-Coast Guard team that the Coast Guard uses the Boeing-Insitu ScanEagle, which is a small, low-cost, long-endurance UAV. It carries a stabilized electro-optical and/or infrared camera, on a lightweight inertial stabilized turret system, and an integrated communications system. She put the drone into the air as it flew silently over and around the building, hovering near the windows, snapping infrared pictures and heat sources to determine how many people were inside.

Joe and Joan looked at the iPad and saw there was one warm body in the back bedroom, two in the living room and two in the kitchen. They couldn't tell the sex of the people but they noticed that four of the heat sources were moving around while the fifth was at rest in the back room. They determined that it was Mary. They couldn't afford to make a mistake.

Joe, Martina and Antonia worked their way to the backyard by the back door. Joe noticed both the Ford Econoline van and a Ford Focus parked in the back. He knew this was the right place.

The bedroom was right off the back door entrance so as they entered, they would use smoke bombs and flash-bangs as they entered and Joe would go to the bedroom which he presumed was locked. He had a battering ram with him that weighed a ton but could do the job. Joan stayed with the FBI and Mike was to be a lookout for any Monroe County Sheriff's vehicles, which might arrive once the neighbors woke up, heard the noise, and called 911. Joan would stay by the road with the FBI agents. Alex and Mia would take the front door with the same firepower as Joe had. Mike was backing them up as well, making it three in the front and three in the back to take down four individuals, so they assumed. They had better be right.

Quietly, Joe counted to three, raising his fingers to be seen, and the operation began. He rammed the back door, threw in the smoke bombs, and flash bangs, cleared the path and headed to the back room where he hammered the door. Thank God, Mary was semiconscious on the bed. He grabbed her, threw her over his shoulder and ran out the back door, down the stairs. He brought her to Joan who tried to wake her up. Mary started to realize where she was and began to cry and said, "Thank you. Thank you." Joan, what are you doing here?"

"You're safe, Mary. Your friends are here and thank God that Joe insisted on you wearing the GPS tags on your sneakers all this time. I will never forget that as long as I live. You have great friends, Mary," said Joan.

As soon as they heard the back door breached, Alex and Mia followed by Mike broke down the front door. The three guys and the mother were in shock. Strom and Pierce both pulled their guns as soon as they heard the door breaking but they were unprepared for the onslaught of what was about to happen. Both men were shot dead in seconds. Richard Butler and his mother threw up their hands and said not to shoot. They were told to lie down on the floor, face down, where they were handcuffed and then dragged out. Richard tried to tell them that his mother was not involved. Just being there made her involved. She would never have to worry about paying for a nursing home. The Florida penal system would take care of that. Richard wouldn't have to worry about jail either after Joe was through with him. He would be taken somewhere as a terrorist, lost in the system. Joe didn't want this getting out, especially with what Butler could produce as a lifelong member of the Nationalist

Alliance. His life was over. Joe would make a call to his CIA friend, Mike Hanley, in Miami and work something out.

All the neighborhood lights started turning on. Evidently 911 calls were made and cops started showing up. The two FBI agents and Mike Kenny told them that everything was under control and that it was an FBI terrorist takedown, which would end all police interventions. As everyone emerged from the property, Mary called Jack using Joe's phone and told him she was safe and that they had found her. Jack started asking questions but stopped when Joe got back the phone and told him there was much to discuss later. Joe was taking her to the hospital.

"Mary, you're going to the hospital to see what they drugged you with. We can go to Mariner up by us where we know everyone or down to the Lower Key Medical Center where we don't know anyone. It's your choice. Mike Kenny's wife, Audrey, is one of the head nurses and will meet us at Mariner right on the main highway near our house."

"Let's do that, Joe," she said. They placed her into the Highlander and Martina and Antonia drove her to the emergency room. On the way, they both told he how sorry they were for what happened. They said it shouldn't have happened. Mary asked what happened back at the house in Big Pine Key. They told her two of the kidnappers were killed and two taken into custody. They told her three of them were the men who followed them to the Fort Lauderdale airport. "Thank God for GPS clips tied to my sneakers, huh?" she said.

Joe called Paul at FBI headquarters and told him that Richard Butler and his mother were being taken to the Islamorada Coast Guard facility and locked up. He told him that he made a call to Mike Hanley, his friend in Miami. Mike said he would pick up Richard Butler but leave the mother. Joe asked Paul to pick up Shelby Butler and put her someplace safe and secure for now. They could use her to turn state's evidence against the Nationalist Alliance at a later date. At least she would stay alive. He told Paul that the other two were killed during the operation as they drew their weapons on Mia and Alex, both experienced Coast Guard attack team members. Joe also said that he wanted to be involved in the takedown of the Nationalist Alliance. He was sure he would get information out of Richard Butler and his mother.

Joe was exhausted along with everyone else. It was going on 6:00 a.m. He called Julie who was now getting up and she was greatly relieved. He said he'd be home to change and head to the hospital to check on Mary. Jack thought about taking an Uber up to see Mary but after this incident he didn't want to take a chance. He asked Skip Lennon if he could take him up to the hospital and he said sure. All the Lennons were greatly relieved as well.

Jack thought what could they possibly do to prevent this from happening again without moving from this house that they loved so much? There would be a long thought process on what comes next. Mary could have died. If it wasn't for Joe's insistence on both Jack and Mary wearing GPS tags, Mary could be dead by now. Up until now, domestic terrorists groups were a nonentity and nothing to think about. If they were going to kidnap Mary and get millions to support their cause, he wondered what would happen if they took some of their millions to slow them down. It was something to think about. Jack needed to ask Joe and his people the same questions.

Joe went to the hospital. Mary was released. Audrey was by her side. She thanked everyone and found out the drug used was ketamine, a prescription you could get from your family doctor but a powerful drug just the same. She would be fine.

Julie didn't want to go to the Mariner Hospital. It held very bad memories for her. First, her mother died in her and Tillie's arms of a drug overdose when she was only eight years old, sitting on the ramp to the emergency room where she was pronounced dead. The second included Tillie's brush with death when she was in a coma caused by her car rolling over after being struck by a hit and run driver. The hit and run driver was Julie's father who they had presumed dead from drowning off Big Pine Key. How ironic about Big Pine Key coming up again. She had lost both parents. Her father, at age six, and at age eight, for her mother, Annie. Tillie took over at that point and became her guardian and her only mother ever since. It was a very long day for everyone. Julie couldn't wait for Joe to get back home. It was overwhelming and Joe was fine.

Joe would deliver a completed write-up on exactly what happened so it wouldn't happen again. He also needed to sit down with Martina and Antonia. He knew they felt bad but that wasn't good enough. They got too close to Mary and that didn't help. They lost sight of why they were there. As he said before that Alex and Mia took the job guarding Mary very seriously and that wasn't a bad thing. He needed to talk to his FBI friend in Miami and those up in Albany and explain what needed to be done further. He would check with Mike Hanley and see what information they got from the Butlers. He personally thanked Mike and Audrey Kenny and asked Mike to keep the entire event under wraps for now because they were going after the Nationalist Alliance next.

When Mary and Jack got back to Troy, after this kidnapping attempt, not only would this Key West security team have new instructions but Joe would inform John and Fred on exactly how they were to proceed from now on. He would also advise the Albany FBI Director and friend, Tom Matthews, of exactly what went down in Key West and everything he knew about the Nationalist Alliance.

Joe had to put pressure on Mary and Jack as well. He was their friend but he was more concerned with keeping them safe and alive. Joe knew that one lapse in security or in judgment could lead to very bad consequences. He needed for Mary and Jack to understand that as well. Winning a ton of money is a very good thing but it completely changes your life not just for the better but also for the worse. The only thing that saved Mary's life were the GPS chips tied to her shoes.

CHAPTER 43

Finally, Jack and Mary arrived home. It was late afternoon on Wednesday. They pulled into the driveway with Antonia driving and Martina now paying very close attention.

Mary said, "Damn, looks like we missed the garbage collection again, ladies."

"Mary, that's not funny," said Martina. "We feel bad enough as it is. However, they got the garbage just not the recyclables. Maybe next time."

"Think I'm ever taking the garbage out again?" Mary asked and laughed.

"We'll add that to our duties. It probably should have been on the list anyway," said Antonia.

"Just don't tell Joe Traynor about the garbage joke, please," said Mary.

"I won't. I promise. However you know he wants to speak to you two, don't you?"

"Yes, and we'll face the music. We know Joe is very close to you two but beyond that, he took this as his responsibility and his failure and we are ashamed that he will think of himself that way. He never panics. That's his trademark. Within minutes, he knew exactly where you were and exactly what came next. I remember his best friend, Mark Silva, telling us the story about Joe up in Albany with the take down of one of the Mexican Mafia sons. Mark said Joe knew where the bullets were flying and Luis, that was his name, didn't even know there were any bullets. It was like a premonition with Joe. He just knew. Thank God he did it again," said Antonia. Martina nodded her head in agreement.

"Jack, when is Joe coming here? Is it today?" said Mary.

"He said he had to get to the college for a meeting, on no sleep, and would be here right after that around 6:00 p.m. He wasn't staying. All he wanted to do was make sure you're safe and secure and then he'd head home," said Jack.

On the way to the college, Joe called Mike Hanley to discuss the next steps in dealing with Rich Butler and his mother. He also had to speak with Paul Philips at FBI headquarters in Miami about the Nationalist Alliance and what they planned on doing about it. He was sure that someone would pick up on it very soon and Joe wanted to be ahead of the curve. Right now, he felt obligated to speak directly to Rear Admiral Jake Barnes about the entire incident.

"Hi, it's Joe Traynor. May I speak to Rear Admiral Barnes? It's important," he said.

"Just a minutes, sir. I'll see if he's available," the receptionist said.

"Hi, Joe. I understand there was quite a dustup last night, if I'm not mistaken. A little bird called me today and let me know what happened. I assume you were going to call me but were just a little busy at the moment," Jake said.

"Yes, sir. I was tied up until now and I'm heading down to the college and to see Mary later today. I'm sorry that you were not informed immediately and for that I apologize."

"Don't worry, Joe. I know your intentions and I know you have a one-tract mind when you are in that mode. I'm glad that you saved Mary's life. I also know you're now in cleanup mode with a shovel. Is that correct?" asked Jake.

"Sort of, sir. Mike Hanley is handling one of the kidnappers, the only one left, along with his mother and Paul Philips is getting us together ASAP to do a deep dive into the Nationalist Alliance right here in Hialeah. The guy in charge is Ken Meggs, a long-time white supremacist and founder of the organization. The Butler guy will be taking a boat ride with Mike Hanley and may wind up in places unknown. I'm sure that Meggs will follow his path very shortly. I believe you know that we don't want it out in the public about how easy it is to kidnap multi-millionaires and use them for ransom to further their causes. Am I right?" said Joe.

"You are right but we need to do this as quietly as possible. Is everyone on board?"

"To my knowledge, our security team, the FBI, the CIA, and the Monroe Sheriff's Department are all closed-mouthed about it and it won't go any further. However, there was a killing of two individuals down in Big Pine Key last night and the FBI will be announcing that due to national security issues, there will be no information forthcoming."

"Good," said Barnes. "Let me know what you need. You have all the time you need. Just let Joan know if anything pops up. She was there too, I understand."

"Yes, she was," said Joe. "Our Coast Guard personnel were outstanding. They should be after the way we didn't protect Mary. That's for another day and I screwed up and it's my responsibility first and foremost. They know that and we will correct it, sir," said Joe.

"You can be as hard on yourself as you want Joe but at the end of the day, it was your quick thinking that saved her life. GPS chips on her shoes, huh? Who would have thought?" said the Rear Admiral.

"Thanks, Jake for trying to make me feel better. I don't,

but thanks. I feel like Derek Jeter, sitting next to Joe Torre in the dugout after screwing up. At least Jeter owned up to it and took his medicine. I hope to do the same," said Joe.

"I'll see you in a few days after all this has sunk in and you have all the bad guys responsible. You're a good guy, Joe, and don't forget it," said Jake.

"Thanks, sir. That means a lot," said Joe.

It was getting late and Joe wound up at Mary and Jack's house on Allamanda Terrace right around 6:00 p.m. He sat down and ate an Italian mixed sub from Subway, washed down with a cold Sam Adams. He mentioned that he might just stay here all night after drinking beer. Mary said anytime he wanted. He took Martina and Antonia into the backyard by the deck and spoke to them in a very low voice and explained to them how he screwed up. They felt awful. They knew Joe was taking the blame when he should have taken the accolades for saving Mary's life. They apologized and even offered to leave the service if it would help. He told them that the only thing that would help was to be at their best at all times and not to let their guard down. He also explained that Mary and Jack needed ex-FBI retirees that were still young enough and experienced enough to take over just like John Jefferson and Fred Tucker up in Troy.

Joe left around 7:30 p.m. and headed home. It took a little over an hour. He wanted to be home for Bella before she went to bed and to hug Julie and let her know he was safe and they were too.

The next day, after sleeping until 8:30 a.m., Joe got dressed, showered, ate breakfast and headed out to Miami to meet Paul and Mike, who would meet up outside both their offices. Joe picked the hotel dining room at 11:00 a.m. for the meeting, convenient for both. As Joe walked in, both Paul and Mike were sitting in a back booth. There was no one else around. Joe greeted them and thanked them for the meeting. He sat down and went over everything that happened. Joe felt that they had to intercept Ken Meggs as soon as possible so he wouldn't go missing. On the way up to Miami, Joe had called Jack Forest up in Virginia and asked him to do a thorough investigation of the Nationalist Alliance and Ken Meggs, personally. He also told him, if he could, just like in all the other cases they solved together, to intercept any accounts in any names related to the three kidnappers, Meggs and the Nationalist Alliance. Jack already had an account set up that would receive any and all funds associated with the group. The account would start in the Cayman Islands and be transferred through several international drops before heading back to Jack. The money would be sent directly to Mike Hanley and used to process Meggs and Butler and anyone else they found. It was clear that Butler was already on his way to the ship, outside the international waters of the United States. Through direct intervention and through allowing Butler's mother to go free and he sent far away from harm, he immediately gave up Meggs and the organization.

Meggs was living in Hialeah but unknown to the outside world exactly where he was. Hialeah had good and bad sections like every place else and Meggs was living large on a small estate only a mile from the Florida Lottery Commission office where Mary was presented her oversize check. Joe would be with the FBI crew that would take Meggs into custody and dropped off at the Miami docks onto the same ship that had housed Butler. By the time he was ever released or even brought up on charges, the Nationalist Alliance would be no more and those two killed in Big Pine Key would be long forgotten. Shelby Butler was on her way to the U.S. Virgin Islands until further notice. Both the CIA and the FBI had offices in the region and would continue to check up on her until the Nationalist Alliance and Meggs were no longer in operation. They would house her and take care of her but make no mistake she was in custody of the United States government until further notice.

At 7:00 p.m. the same day, a team from the FBI, Mike Hanley and Joe Traynor broke down the front and back doors of the home of Ken Meggs. He was alone at the time watching ESPN, drinking beer, while eating pizza, without a care in the world. To say he was in shock was an understatement. The crew went through his home like a tornado and took every scrap of paper they could find. Meggs kept protesting that he was an American citizen and had rights and wanted his attorney. Joe looked at him and smiled and told him that he had no identification and they were unable to determine who he was so he would be handed over for deportation, which would take place immediately. He never explained where Meggs was going but the look on Meggs' face said it all. The three who kidnapped Mary screwed up, two were dead, and now Meggs was going to pay the price. By the end of the week, over two million dollars was placed in the hands of Mike Hanley into a secret CIA account established to handle terrorists.

Yes, the United States never defined domestic terrorism but it made little difference to anyone in the room at the time. Meggs was out of business. His two thousand followers wouldn't know what hit them. Jack Forest would follow through the dark web and social media and see what would happen to the group but it was clear, Meggs was the leader and without him, they would fold. One down and forty-six more hate groups to go, just in Florida alone. *It was like throwing a glass of water into the ocean but at least Mary was safe, but for how long?*

It finally hit Mary. She started to shake and began to cry. Jack took her into his arms to try to calm her. Martina and Antonia had tears in their eyes. Mary looked desolate and was starting to come to grips with what happened.

"Mary, hopefully this will pass and never happen again," said Jack.

"How can you know that? I can't let my guard down for one second and this is what happens. I told you I never wanted the money. I wanted to give it all away. I thought by doing good, we could have a nice life and feel good about what we were doing. Now, I just don't know. Do I need a guard to go to the bathroom? I'm not the President of the United States for God's sake," she said.

"Joe said that he'd be back late tomorrow. He had meetings in Miami and told me that I didn't need to know what happens after the fact. He said it would be taken care of and we can move forward and to not worry. I know he's worried so I'm worried as well," said Jack.

Martina said, "If Joe said he would take care of it, he will. We know Joe and his word is his bond. From now on, whatever situation presents itself, this incident will not happen again and we will be fully prepared. I think we took it lightly and Joe was right. Mary paid the price."

Mary looked around the room and started to smile a little. "Well at least it can't get any worse. Can it? From now on we'll be prepared and I'm never taking out the damn garbage ever again!" she said.

The Lennons came over with dinner. Jamie was beside herself. She wasn't around when it happened because she and her brother were helping her father with a cruise that day. She felt so guilty. All this time she has worked for Mary and Jack and not one incident and the fact that Mary bequeathed money to the Lennons on top of paying her a very nice salary, made her feel even worse. Mary told her to stop. It was over and in the past and the future would look very different. She did say that they have to consider moving from this location because it's so close to the road even though they had state-of-the-art security. That security didn't work when they let their guard down.

Mary knew they could sell the place for a nice profit at anytime. However, they were heading back to Troy for the rest of May and June and wouldn't have to worry about it for a while. They would be back to Miami for her graduation from Barry University in July, after attending Joe's brother, Pete's, wedding to Tanya on July 2nd, right on the 4th of July weekend. She would receive her doctorate on July 15th and stay in Key West until the first of August. That would give Jack and Mary one full month to continue to plan their schedules for the new charter schools opening the Wednesday after Labor Day.

Joe didn't want to tell anyone at The College of the Florida Keys what happened to Mary. If it got out, they could downplay it because it happened so quickly and cleaned up even faster. If Mary remained calm, then perhaps this would be in the past. Meggs and Butler were long gone. The Nationalist Alliance was shut down and squeezed of every dime they had. If they ever got back up on their feet, they'd have to start from scratch. They just didn't know if Meggs told anyone else in the organization what they had planned. Jack Forest would continue to monitor every account and every posting on social media.

After the incident and Joe had time to talk to both Mary and Jack, Mary offered to fund any organization that would take down these groups. Of the forty-six left in Florida, there was only a handful that needed immediate attention. Mary told Joe that if any in his inner circle needed any funding to close down any of these groups, they would have it immediately. She didn't place a dollar amount on the offering. She felt her life was saved by these people who cared about her and Jack. She could not put a price tag on it. She immediately asked Jane Swanson to send $2.0 million dollars to Mike Hanley from her own personal accounts and not the trusts. Jane asked her why but she told her it was better if she didn't know.

Mary was torn about telling Kristen about her kidnapping but would do so very quietly when she got back. She didn't want anyone else to know including her friends at the Career Center or her ex-nun friends, or her mother. She and Jack would sit down with John and Fred and explain the entire situation to them. They would ask that they contact both Tom Matthews in Albany and Paul Philips in Miami to see if they could pick up two more ex-FBI retirees that would serve full-time down in Miami when they were in Florida. It was getting obvious that taxing the Coast Guard personnel from Islamorada was placing a heavy burden on both Joe and Joan Talbot.

Later that afternoon, Mike Hanley called Mary and thanked her and he said that her wire transfer had just arrived. He said they had a bead on two white supremacist groups and would work with the FBI in Miami to see how those groups could be disrupted. Joe knew about the transfer from Mary to Mike but would remain passive since he would be out of it within a year, heading to New London, Connecticut for his new job as Assistant Superintendent of the Coast Guard Academy. Joe also knew that he would be receiving a promotion to Captain prior to his moving to New London. You had to be at least a Captain before taking a position of this stature. He might no longer be serving in the trenches as he had in the past, unless it was a very high national security priority. His flexibility to move from agency to agency would be more difficult due to his exposure in his new position.

Joe stopped by the Islamorada Coast Guard facility to see Joan. He said goodbye to Julie and Bella up in Tavernier and would be back that night, but very late. Julie knew things were winding down and she could see it in Joe's demeanor. She was not quite used to it by now but getting there. This was his life and the Coast Guard was counting on him. He walked into Joan's office. She was finishing up paperwork and looked as tired as he did. He gave her a hug and thanked her for everything. He apologized for Mary's incident but she looked at him like she saw him back as an eighteen-year-old just starting in the Coast Guard.

"You have nothing to apologize for, Joe," she said. "Do you know how much money you put into the hands of our people? A ton. That's how much. They have more money saved than they ever had before. It's not your fault that they let their guard down. It was human nature. It will happen again and again but now we fully understand the consequences of that. It won't happen again. Mary said she is getting some full-time ex-FBI retirees to help out down here, which will make me happy as well. I couldn't really keep up with running this place and running the recruitment operation at the college. It's starting to catch up to me. I have about a year left before I retire, Joe. I love doing this but even Mary has to slow down. It's affecting everyone and putting us on pins and needles. It seems like every suggestion gets funded but we don't have any people to run every program. Mary said she would back off for a while and let everyone catch up. Hopefully this incident will be further evidence that we all need to be more guarded in each of our everyday lives," Joan said.

"That's exactly what I wanted to talk about. You hit it on the head. Mary and Jack and I had these conversations and we all agree to take a step back, especially after the kidnapping. Let's not sugarcoat it. It was a kidnapping and Mary could have been killed. We need to recognize that and tighten everything up that she touches," he said.

"Thanks, Joe. I thought I was just getting old and at the end of my time, maybe not. Maybe we all need to settle in a little," said Joan.

"I also wanted to ask you something personal but kept forgetting. Is Lucy really set on going to the University of

Miami in Coral Gables? I know she has been offered a full cross-country scholarship and is All-Florida as the number one female in the State. Hell, she broke all the State of Florida records. I was just wondering because I know the time has passed to apply for the Coast Guard Academy, which was in February. However, she is not only a great athlete but also a gifted student. The Coast Guard Academy is Division 3 not Division 1 but in cross-country it doesn't matter, it depends on your time. She could try out for the Olympics in 2024 as a representative of the Coast Guard Academy. Right now the team is ranked 8th nationally for Division 3. I checked their times and Lucy has beaten every one of them and is near the top already of Division 3. She can only get better. I guess what I'm saying, if she has any doubt at all, to please let me know and Jake will get her in, I'm sure. By this time next week, he'll have every Florida U.S. Senator and House member's letters of support in his hands. Remember, she not only gets a 100% free ride but she gets full stipends for all her incidentals. I'm just annoyed at myself for not thinking of this before now. You Joan, as the recruitment guru of young women and minorities, should also have thought of her. She's perfectly qualified and extremely bright. I would love to have her up there with me and Julie, Bella and Tillie. We can be her family like you were for Julie and me. Remember my weird path to education. I spent one semester at MIT. I quit and joined the Coast Guard at eighteen and met you. I graduated from Miami Dade Community College, then the Coast Guard Academy, then RPI and now a Ph.D. from Barry University. Lucy can skip my journey and head right to the Coast Guard Academy and take up operations research and computer analysis, cyber systems, and national security intelligence. Just a thought," said Joe.

"Can she call you, Joe? Might be nice to head up and be near her old babysitter, Julie," she laughed. "If I'm reading her right, I'm not so sure she's fully onboard going to a Division1 powerhouse like Miami. Hell, Coral Shores High School only has 750 students in total. How many are there at the Coast Guard Academy?" Joan asked.

"There are only 1,250 cadets. It's the same size as The College of the Florida Keys right now. They select about 300 students a year for the freshman class. There are always a few spots open for those who drop out. There are about 2,000 applicants a year but there is a very good application process where Lucy could shine, especially with recommendations from Rear Admiral Barnes and the incoming Assistant Superintendent, namely me. I'll talk to her but let us know quickly. Maybe the University of Miami will redshirt her the first year and she won't run at all. You never know. She should ask that question of her new coaches from the university," Joe said.

Joe headed out to the college. He had his meetings. As Interim President, he was starting to fit in and get organized. The job itself was not hard if they were in the black. Mary Evans saw to that. Running businesses were easy when well funded but not so easy when in a deficit. He kept a tight rein on every program they started. The student body had increased by ten percent this year, strictly because of the coding curriculum leading to a well paying job right in their own hometown of Key West. Joe was thinking about asking Mary if she had any interest in being the new permanent president of the college after receiving her doctorate in July. He knew that being kidnapped put everything in perspective. He hoped that she wouldn't just heads north and stay there, feeling that it would be safer. The people of the Florida Keys needed her, not just her money. Her vision was spot on and backed it with whatever they needed to be successful. That was just the way she was. She kept saying she wanted to give away all her trust fund money in five years but they needed Mary's vision as much as they needed the money. He would give her time to get back to semi-normal. Just like after the Covid-19 pandemic, they called the current time, the new normal. Mary has a new normal. She could carry on like nothing happened or carry on and be fully protected which would gravely interfere with her life on a daily basis. Or, she could simply disappear with Jack to a lovely existence on Martha's Vineyard or some remote island. *Only time would tell, Joe thought.*

Chapter 44

Epilogue

Mary and Jack arrived at the Albany International Airport and were met by John Jefferson, Fred Tucker and Jack's daughter, Debbie. After the kidnapping incident, they figured it would be wise to take a private jet back home instead of going from Key West to Tampa to Albany by Southwest Airlines. Jack thought he might look into buying a private plane rather than a boat after the incident. However, neither could justify spending a million dollars, at a minimum, on a small jet plane and a crew, when that money could go to help those most in need. June was approaching and it was nice and warm in Albany when they landed. Upstate New York went from freezing winter to a very hot, humid, summer overnight. Spring was an illusion with less than a month of beautiful cool days and nights because of global warming.

Debbie gave both her father and Mary a hug when they walked into the private terminal. Debbie was about to be told about the kidnapping by her father on the way home. He could kill two birds with one stone since John and Fred were there as well. No one else needed to know anything about it until Mary felt that the time was right. That included

Jack's son, Mark and Cara, Kristen or Karen Steele. Mary wanted to talk to Kristen first and make sure she was on legal standing if she gave donations to various agencies that were identifying and trying to put out of business white supremacist groups. On the way home, Debbie told them that her mother, Maureen, was recovering nicely at The Eddy in Troy. She said Chuck Falcone had been by to see her every few days and seemed to be concerned. Maureen's bills were being paid but it didn't look like she would be back to her job as the manager of the bank branch in Lansingburgh, anytime soon. She was having some aftereffects including headaches and some nerve pain that they didn't quite know how to treat. She was considered a "long hauler" by the CDC, for those suffering long-term Covid-19 symptoms, or post-Covid-19 syndrome. Everyone suspected that Maureen would retire under Social Security disability in the near future. Banks have merged so many times that employee loyalty was not a priority for upper management. Maureen was a twenty-eight-year employee so she would get disability now, Medicare and a small pension from whatever bank took over when she left. Jack knew this would happen and made arrangements with Kristen Sorenson the day he saw her in the hospital. It was such a shame that a twenty-five-year marriage had to be annulled and have her wind up like this. It was so unpredictable. Jack has come full circle from hatred to pity back to caring. He had Mary now and Maureen had Chuck. It didn't seem like a fair tradeoff.

On the way home, Mary told Debbie, John and Fred exactly what happened down in Key West about the kidnapping. All three were beside themselves and there were tears in Debbie's eyes as she went through the incident. Mary told them that if it wasn't for Joe Traynor, she might be dead by now. She meant it and they knew it. She told them not to mention a word to anyone but everyone around her needed to be on their guard from now on. She said this wasn't the way she wanted her life to turn out but it's exactly what was happening to her in real time and she had to prepare to live with it.

They made it home and John and Fred seemed to be even more cautious than before. It wasn't that Martina and Antonia were not vigilant. It was because they became too close to Mary and Jack and everyone let their guard down, maybe just one time. They never for a minute believed that something like this could happen to either Jack or Mary. Everyone vowed that it wouldn't ever happen again but that was a promise that no one could keep. Mary decided that over the next six weeks, before heading back to Miami to receiver her doctorate from Barry University, that she would sit down and decide what to do with the rest of her money.

Jack had always been clear on his plans. He spent the majority of his lottery winnings on building a state-of-the-art Career Center and would support every student through graduation from this program through college and now was starting a charter school to catch kids even earlier so they wouldn't drop out. Jack started with a fifty million dollar trust fund and still has about half left, unallocated but he knew it would be spent on his current projects for even longer if those projects proved successful and changed lives. He had been doing this for over three almost four years now and was very much on top of everything. Having Karen Steele in charge of the program gave him the assurances he needed that it would continue long after he decided to retire.

Mary, on the other hand, had just started only a short time ago, hitting the lottery on their honeymoon in Key West. Of course, she won a lot more than Jack and had placed $77.5 million dollars in each of two trust funds to serve the New York State Capital Region and south Florida and the Florida Keys, mostly in the Keys. Being the mathematics wiz that she is, the first thing she did was total up all her bequests over the last year and a half or so and see where she stood. From both the Teresa Trust Fund, which served Troy and the Teresa Trust Fund South, she has spent or allocated $72.7 million dollars in both places, mostly spent in Key West. In Key West, she has allocated $51.2 million dollars, leaving $26.3 million dollars unallocated. She didn't even count the $2.0 million dollars she just sent to Mike Hanley to deal with more white supremacists groups in Florida. That came out of her personal cash fund.

In Troy, she hasn't spent nearly that amount. To date, including the charter school, Lansingburgh Boys and Girls Club and the just recently allocated *Times Union* request for coding for 2,500 students for $8.75 million dollars, the total is only $21.5 million dollars allocated or spent, leaving $56.0 million dollars to donate over the next few years. She could also move money back and forth between trust funds depending on need but no one ever said it would be easy getting rid of $155.0 million dollars in five years. Mary shook her head, after all this time and all this money allocated or spent, both Mary and Jack still had, after all the taxes already paid, $68,362,000.00 each, earning interest on tax-free municipal bonds set up by Kristen Sorenson and her very able team of which half of Mary's share was now managed by Jane Swanson down in Miami.

Mary had one more idea but wanted to call the Rear Admiral of the Coast Guard, Jake Barnes, and ask his permission. She wanted to honor the 7th District of Miami with a $10.0 million dollar donation to the Coast Guard Academy in New London, Connecticut in the District's honor. The members of the Coast Guard assigned to that district saved her life. The donation would be anonymous but it would be understood that Joe Traynor would have a say on the funds allocation at the Academy. Again, Mary wanted the same as Joan Talbot. She wanted to recruit minority students and women into the Coast Guard and to eventually serve in high-ranking positions. The $5.0 million spent down in the Keys for recruitment directly into the ranks of the Coast Guard was one thing. This was for education and recruitment, directly into the crown jewel, the Coast Guard Academy. In fact, Joe had mentioned to Mary that he asked Joan if she had ever mentioned the Academy to Lucy and she had not. Joe pushed it even though Lucy had received a scholarship for cross-country at the University of Miami in Coral Gables. As a Division 1 school, it could give or take away a scholarship depending on how the student performed. At the Coast Guard Academy, the performance was based on real life and sports were just a part of that daily activity. It too had a full ride and a career path that couldn't be ignored.

Mary had called Joan and quietly told her about her donation that was approved and asked her to tell Lucy all about it. She didn't want to "recruit" her. She just wanted her to be aware of other potential opportunities if Miami didn't work out. She could always transfer and she would have far-reaching support for her nomination to the Academy.

The month of June was uninspiring according to Jack and he was getting itchy. Having Karen Steele in charge was great but left little for Jack to do by himself all day. He did some hiring for his charter school and picked a principal, one he has known for a long time and respected. He helped Mary do the same but she had already picked people she knew and felt comfortable with. After all, when they closed down St. Augustine's School, the former tenant, it left ten teachers on their own. Mary had worked with these people forever and wanted them back. It didn't matter if it wasn't a Catholic School. An elementary school had to be run efficiently and effectively to meet all the New York State

Education Department standards. All these teachers had years of experience and their new paychecks would probably double their old Catholic school paystubs.

The July 4th weekend was near. Joe's brother, Peter, and Tanya Fields were being married at St. Augustine's Church on Saturday, July 2nd, just like Mary and Jack had done a few years ago. Joe was the best man and Julie and Bella were in the wedding. Bella was the flower girl and totally excited to be back in Troy even though there wasn't any snow. Once again, Joe, Julie, and Bella would stay at Jack and Mary's house, up the hill off Old Plank Road. Tillie stayed home to be with Ed Lansing, her "friend" as she calls him. They have become quite an "item" over the last six months and Julie was wondering if she would even make the trip up to be with them when they moved to the Coast Guard Academy after Christmas. Julie wanted her to come but didn't want to get in her way or hold her back. However, she did have a personal announcement to make to her before they left for Troy and asked her to at least come up for Christmas and maybe through January to help out a little. Tillie was all smiles and said she would be delighted. Julie said there would be room for Ed for the holidays as well but she said he always went back to Pittsburgh to be with his two daughters. He asked her to come this year but she had some explaining to do as to why she couldn't.

The wedding rehearsal went well and they all came back to Jack and Mary's house. Joe's father came. Tanya's parents, sister and brother came by as well. Julie didn't want to interfere with the wedding but asked Tanya quietly if it would be a good time to announce her pregnancy. Tanya was thrilled and said of course. Tanya asked if she could tell everyone to be quiet because Julie had an announcement to make. Everyone's head turned as Julie broke the news that she was pregnant and due Christmas week. Bella was thrilled and asked if they knew what it was and Julie said they didn't want to know. They only wanted a healthy baby regardless of gender. Joe asked Pete to be the godfather and Julie asked Tanya if she would share the honors with Tillie, her grandmother. Tanya had tears in her eyes and thanked her.

Everyone left a little while later. Pete and Tanya wouldn't be flying out until the following day after the wedding to avoid extra stress. Mary turned to Julie and told her what a remarkable young lady she was asking her grandmother to be the godmother along with Tanya. She thought that was awesome and gave her a hug. Joe told her the same thing. Tillie was his mother as well. She was there for him just as if she were his mother too.

The wedding went well and the reception was at the Troy Country Club, off the Brunswick Road. John Traynor, Pete and Joe's father, paid for the entire reception. As he said to Joe, he had never been so flush as he has since he met Mary and Jack. It was an honor to pay for a wedding he never thought would be coming and now had a daughter he loved in Tanya just like he loved Julie and Bella.

The view was wonderful, overlooking the rolling hills and golf course. It was a beautiful setting. There were about one hundred guests. Everyone still had to follow Covid-19 protocols, vaccinations for every guest, but didn't interfere with any wedding plans. Pete and Tanya would be heading to Aruba for their honeymoon and would fly back to Miami and drive down for a week to see Joe and Julie in Tavernier before heading home. Jack and Mary would be heading to Miami for Mary's thesis presentation and doctoral degree on Friday, July 15th. They would fly in early so Mary could practice her speech and presentation to the committee. They would head down to their house in Key West and stay until August 1st and then head back to Troy for the September grand opening of their new schools.

Mary liked the hotel where they always stayed, the SLS

Brickell Hotel & Residence at the Brickell Plaza, near both the Coast Guard 7th Division headquarters and the law firm. She had scheduled meetings with the Rear Admiral unbeknownst to Joe about the donation to the Coast Guard Academy. She needed to be near the law firm so Jane Swanson could put the paperwork together to give to Kristen for the bequest. Both Kristen and Jane wanted to be at her presentation. It was unusual but her graduation with a Ph.D. was very unusual. She did it in record-breaking time and pumped a whole lot of money into the economy doing so. She was going to make a donation to Barry University but wanted it to be much later after graduation so there would be no question that she earned this degree and didn't buy it as so many rich people did. She paid through the nose to prove her point and it worked. Saving the two hundred families from domestic abuse alone saved thousands of dollars in social services budgets. Setting up a minority recruitment program for the Coast Guard placed almost one hundred young adults into the service where they could have long-term careers. Paying to have 2,500 high school seniors have coding certification where they could start earning a decent salary now or head to college with credit hours under their belt, all paid for, made a huge difference. The list goes on and on. Her presentation was for forty-five minutes and then there was an allocation of time for questions by committee members.

The doctoral committee consisted of select Ph. D's from various colleges and universities in the region. There were ten individuals in all. The Dean showed up. Morgan Hennessey was there to answer questions if needed. Jack was there. Joe and the family and the Rear Admiral and his wife were there along with Kristen and Jane. Joan and her husband Jeff and daughter Lucy and Jamie Lennon showed up as well. Mary started to get nervous but began by thanking everyone in attendance. She spoke about her background and her goals and aspirations and her life-long desire to obtain her Ph.D. She then went in and proved her point. The point was that when the playing field was level, people of all ethnic backgrounds, colors, religion and sexual orientations, men and women could compete equally and show remarkable results. In fact, Mary proved that because of poverty, the level of success for those living in poverty and receiving a helping hand did far better than their counterparts that were brought up by affluent families. She proved that desire, coupled with a level playing field made all the difference. Mary was mesmerizing. After a false start, she composed herself and began again. By the end of the allotted forty-five minutes, the committee was in awe of all that she had accomplished.

It was only at the end when someone asked her where she got the money to do this work did she say, "I won it in the lottery. $480.0 million dollars can be very useful in proving your point and making changes to peoples' lives if you so desire." She opened up and smiled and said, "The end."

After the presentation, the committee immediately approved her degree, which would be handed out the following day along with several others who would receive their Ph.D. Each committee member shook her hand and asked her to call, so they could help out in any capacity she chose. She took their business cards and was very gracious. Morgan came over and gave her a hug and said, "Welcome to the club. Of course you can own the club anytime you want." The Dean of Education told her she did a great job, evidently high praise from him. Jake Barnes took her hand and said whenever she wanted to meet and discuss the Coast Guard Academy to let him know. Lucy came over and gave her a hug. So did Jamie. She said her mother was at church. It was a holy day and Mary completely forgot. She said she'd have to make it up. Joe smiled and waved and told her to head back to the hotel where they had a small get together planned. The small get together lasted until 9:00 p.m. By that time everyone was exhausted and said their goodbyes.

Mary would be officially on vacation for one week before heading back home. She'd get her diploma tomorrow with Jack and be guarded by two new ex-retired FBI agents that she had just met today. They would be with her and Jack whenever they came down to Florida. After a short reception, after receiving her degree tomorrow, they would head to Allamanda Terrace in Key West and be met by Martina and Antonia and Joan Talbot who would drive them back to the base at Islamorada. Mary couldn't help but think that she was returning to the scene of the crime. She couldn't get it out of her head. In fact it was the scene of the crime.

Mary had a lot of time to think about the future and how she and Jack could fit in and be happy. She still had a ton of money left and could fund projects well into the future. Should she just fund what she now has and simply extend the time and take care of more people doing the same thing? She didn't want to waste money on private jets or even a trip out into space like some well-heeled gentlemen have just recently done. She paid every dime in taxes that was required. She didn't bend the rules to her benefit. When Amazon pays zero taxes or a billionaire claims to have only made seventy thousand dollars this year and paid less taxes than a school teacher, it is time to re-examine what it means to be a good person. Jack and Mary never wanted or needed eight hundred and ten million dollars even if it got whittled down to a third. Who needed that much money to sit on and do nothing but count it? Monopoly was fun to a point, but then someone always wanted to be the winner and made the game less fun, buying up properties and railroads to block everyone. About halfway through, no matter what age, it became boring as hell.

When they get back home to Troy, both Jack and Mary could welcome new students to a fresh start at a new charter school, one in the north central part of Troy and the other in the north end, Lansingburgh. As an ex-nun, as a teacher, she didn't need anything more than what she had. She had Jack. That's all she needed. She now had a stepdaughter and a stepson. She had meaning to her life. She had a Ph.D. She could be the new college president at The College of the Florida Keys but everyone would say that she bought the position even if she was more qualified than other candidates. She told Joe this when he asked her to take over when he left to head to the Coast Guard Academy. She said she would always want to be affiliated but didn't need the politics or the constant clamoring for extra funding resources. She wanted to fix problems immediately like bringing in ten new portable housing units for those caught up in domestic abuse with no place to go and with no hope. Within months, she turned this around and everyone knew it. That's what she wanted. So, in parting, Mary would ask everyone if you know of a project that needs immediate funding to fix and it's an immediate problem that no one has money to fix, to please let her know. She will take it under consideration. She still had over $80.0 million dollars left in her trust funds and a matching $68,362,000 in tax-free personal funds in her bank account. She still owes Jack $15.0 million dollars he gave her originally when he first hit the lottery, but she didn't think he needed it back, so that's available too. Jack still has half his trust fund left over and a matching $68,362,000 in his personal tax-free account as well. So drop a letter to Mary and maybe, just maybe, it might be your lucky day.

THE END

About the Author

Daniel J. Barrett was born in Rutland, Vermont and has lived his entire life in Troy, New York, ten miles north of Albany. He is a graduate of both Siena College in Loudonville, N.Y. with a BS in Finance, and from Rensselaer Polytechnic Institute in Troy, NY, with an MBA in Management. He has had a varied career, first as a commercial banker, then as the chief accountant and manager of financial and strategic planning for a large division of a major international corporation. He has extensive international experience, traveling worldwide.

Barrett has also served as the first executive director for economic development for a county in New York State, and as the first lay director for a Catholic shrine in Massachusetts. For the last thirty years, he has served as a financial, strategic planning, and educational consultant to corporations, non-profit organizations, colleges and universities, and government agencies.

Barrett continues to live in Troy and has been married to his wife, Sandy, for 53 years this year. They have three children, Sean, Eileen, and Ryan, and four grandchildren, Shannon, Caden, Megan, and Declan. An avid reader, and inspired by numerous authors, Barrett has read almost 3,400 books in the last fifteen years which has helped him craft his two series and eight books.

www.ingramcontent.com/pod-product-compliance
Lightning Source LLC
Chambersburg PA
CBHW061102210726
48294CB00001B/257